Australia

WICKED MISTRESSES

Robyn
GRADY

Trish
MOREY

Jan
COLLEY

Mills & Boon, an imprint of Harlequin (UK) Limited, Eton House, 18-24 Paradise Road, Richmond, Surrey TW9 1SR

AUSTRALIA: WICKED MISTRESSES
© Harlequin Enterprises II B.V./S.à.r.l 2013

Fired Waitress, Hired Mistress © Robyn Grady 2010
His Mistress for a Million © Trish Morey 2009
Friday Night Mistress © Jan Colley 2009

ISBN: 978 0 263 90602 8

010-0413

Harlequin (UK) policy is to use papers that are natural, renewable and recyclable products and made from wood grown in sustainable forests. The logging and manufacturing processes conform to the legal environmental regulations of the country of origin.

Printed and bound in Spain
by Blackprint CPI, Barcelona

FIRED WAITRESS,
HIRED MISTRESS

Robyn
GRADY

THE AUSTRALIA COLLECTION

March 2013

April 2013

May 2013

June 2013

July 2013

August 2013

One Christmas long ago, **Robyn Grady** received a book from her big sister and immediately fell in love with Cinderella. Sprinklings of magic, deepest wishes come true—she was hooked! Picture books with glass slippers later gave way to romance novels and, more recently, the real-life dream of writing for Mills & Boon.

After a fifteen-year career in television, Robyn met her own modern-day hero. They live on Australia's Sunshine Coast with their three little princesses two poodles, and a cat called Tinkie. Robyn loves new shoes, worn jeans, lunches at Moffat Beach and hanging out with her friends on eHarlequin. Learn about her latest releases at www.robyngrady.com, and don't forget to say hi. She'd love to hear from you!

This one's for the mega-talented
'209ers RWA Bootcamp' gals! Thanks Rachel,
Alison and Nikki, for organising a great couple of
days. Onward and upward, ladies!

With thanks, as always,
to my fab editor Kimberley Young
for helping to bring out the best in my work.

CHAPTER ONE

FROM the moment Nina Petrelle opened her eyes, she was painfully aware of three things.

One: she had a pounding great bump on the back of her head. Two: her ankle was stuck in what felt like a soggy, splintered vice. Three: cool, salty water was lapping the length of her prostrate body...was filling her mouth *and* her lungs.

Choking on seawater, Nina came fully to. She sat bolt upright and, an instant later, yelped in hair-raising agony. Gritting her teeth, she clutched at her thigh. When the red-tipped arrows firing up her shin gradually eased, Nina withered back down.

But she wouldn't give in to the tears. *Damned* if she would. Instead Nina thumped both fists hard against the sand.

Little by little over the last two months she'd felt tiny pieces of herself falling away. The sense that she was losing the battle kept rubbing and chipping at her strength until this afternoon, after a gruelling shift, she'd fixed her heart upon escape. But what she'd truly wanted to leave behind—the question she didn't want to face—had followed her.

Lately it had haunted her.

Who am I?

She didn't know any more.

Once life had shone out before her like a glittering golden path. Her father had owned a highly successful engineering firm and, growing up, she'd thought nothing of her family's numerous house staff, nor her expectations of having the best clothes, the best food—the best of *everything*. Of course that had been before her father had died, her manic mother had stripped the family coffers clean and her usually responsible kid sister had got pregnant by a deadbeat who hadn't hung around.

While her mother had gone into a tailspin, Nina had pulled up her sleeves. After completing her university degree, she'd landed a job in publishing—a fast-paced, intense world she adored. Until recently she'd worked as the features editor for an acclaimed teen magazine, *Shimmer.*

Then the blunt axe had fallen.

Along with a number of other staff she'd been retrenched. With a sizeable mortgage, and other commitments, she'd needed a job, but well-paid positions weren't so easy to come by, particularly in her field. With everyone tightening their belts, the shrivelled industry grapevine was as quiet as a church.

One morning, while prioritising her mounting bills, a long-time friend had called. Alice Sully's family owned a travel agency and, if Nina was desperate, her dad could wangle her a stint working on an exclusive holiday retreat; he knew the owner. Waitressing hours there would be long, Alice had warned her, but the money was great.

Slumping with relief, Nina had accepted, and these past six weeks she'd worked her butt off at Diamond Shores, Australia's premier Great Barrier Reef resort.

And not one moment went by when she didn't wish herself back home.

Most of the other staff had let her know they weren't happy that she'd swung a ticket here via the back door. A job at what many considered Australia's holiday Mecca was supposed to be hard-won, and two years helping part-time at the uni cafeteria didn't make muster.

But, needing the work, she'd been determined to do her best. So she held her head high, when most of the time she felt like a big fat pretender. She smiled till her face ached. Even when pampered patrons accused her of getting their orders wrong. Or commanded her to do silly things, like massage their temples for ridiculous amounts of time if they felt a headache coming on. And that was only the beginning. When she crashed, late at night, her dreams were a jumble of spilled cocktails, tumbling plates and an endless parade of growling, super-rich guests.

That was the hardest.

Once *Nina Petrelle* had lounged on the A list. *She'd* sipped chilled Cristal cocktails and worried about little other than her designer tan, acrylic tips, or the lack of room to accommodate her ever-expanding wardrobe. Now, existing on the other side of the glass wall, that kind of over-indulgence near sickened her. She wanted to shake these out-of-touch squillionaires and let them know there were real people out there and they were doing it tough.

But alongside her indignation lived another emotion. A desire that, in the still dead of night, made Nina's cheeks burn with shame.

Envy.

Secretly she craved to cast off her uniform and rest her weary limbs. She wanted to sprawl out on one of those sunwashed deckchairs and beg, borrow or steal the chance to return to the decadence of her previously worry-free life—if just for a day or two.

She hadn't thought she'd miss extravagance. Had never imagined ever wanting to be a society princess again. She had a *new* life, and obscene luxury simply wasn't her any more.

Yet here she was—torn between opposing self-indulgence and desperately wanting it back.

A monster of a wave crashed on the shore and Nina was brought back to the harrowing present. As the sea rushed in, a cry slipped from her throat, but, with water flooding her windpipe, her "Help!" came out a spluttering cough.

Who would hear anyway?

Determined to keep her mind off her troubles, and maybe trim up those saddlebags, this afternoon she'd strolled along the powder-soft sand until she'd reached the island's unpopulated southern tip. Collecting shells and other flux, she'd happened upon a tree fallen across the full width of the beach. Its trunk had looked solid enough, but as she'd leaped over, her foot had broken through a patch of rotting wood. Off balance, she'd tumbled back, and had struck her head on something hard.

Nina touched that stinging lump now, and winced at the same time as another vivid memory flashed to mind.

A heartbeat before passing out she'd seen an angel standing on a nearby cliff…a brilliant vision, arched against the unsettled sky, which had made her heart hammer as well as melt.

She pushed up onto her elbows and angled her throbbing head. Tropical sunshine struggled through darkening clouds to bounce off the jagged ledges, but no angel adorned the cliff's peak.

Pity. The image burned into her brain was of a male

with raven's wing hair, linebacker shoulders and a set of windblown white wings. Given the distance, those few delicious details ought to have been it. And yet a deeper, unshakable impression remained...

Strong, chiselled features. Mesmerising ice-blue eyes. A bare chest bronzed the colour of warm oak. His confident stance had conveyed not only a sense of authority but also...

What was it?

Destiny? Perhaps purpose? And what about the raw sexuality that had rippled off him in blistering waves? Did angels have dibs on that stuff? She'd never seen anything more powerful.

More beautiful.

Before she'd slipped into darkness Nina imagined their eyes had met and a message had passed between them. He'd told her not to worry, that he knew and would protect her.

She looked around, and a slightly hysterical laugh slipped out.

How wild was that? And how fitting. These past months she'd needed a guardian angel and, with another enormous breaker rolling in, never more than now.

The rush of cool water flooded in, higher this time. As the wash ebbed out Nina tried to rotate her trapped ankle, but bit her lip when splinters pierced the skin. She tried sitting up to pry the wood away, but while the area her foot had penetrated was weak, the surrounding timber felt like concrete.

Slumping back, she covered her face with both wet, gritty hands and prayed.

Before her father had died her brother had also passed away, in tragic circumstances. Now her mother, her sister Jill and nephew Codie were the only family

Nina had left. She would give anything—*everything*—to get out of this and get back home to see them all again.

Another wave smashed on the sand. Frothy scallops swirled up, and this time Nina barely held her chin above water. Jill had always said her sister's one big flaw was her reluctance to accept help. Nina only wished Jill were here now. She wouldn't merely accept help, she'd happily beg. That roller about to break looked big enough to drown.

Assessing the dense grey-green foliage behind her, she waited for the cackle of a kookaburra to fade. Then she filled her lungs and, giving it her all, cried out—

"*Heeeelp!* Can anyone hear me? I need help!"

Long before Gabriel Steele heard the distant cry for help, he was hyper-aware of three things.

A: the thousand branches lashing at his flesh as he tore down the slope hurt like a bitch.

B: his new track shoes were worth their weight in gold.

C: he was running out of time.

His heart belting against his ribs, Gabriel kept his eye on each footfall as he rushed to negotiate the rugged decline. Fast was good. Reaching the bottom in one piece was better. He'd be as useful to that woman as a tiger with no teeth if he broke his leg—or his neck.

And why, in high heaven, had she wandered so far from the resort complex anyway?

Standing atop that cliff earlier, contemplating its drop and the danger, he'd seen her advance along the beach—had watched, unconcerned initially, when she'd skipped across that log. As if the wood were paper, her foot had plunged straight through. She'd toppled back, and when her head had hit that rock he'd felt the *thwack* to his bones.

Out cold.

And, because things could always get worse, the tide was pushing in.

He could boast better than twenty-twenty, but a blind man could see the situation looked grim.

Now, with shirt-tails flapping behind him, Gabriel bounced down the same steep track he'd climbed half an hour earlier. So much for stealing time to face a challenge that, for once, had nothing to do with corporate tax law.

In truth, he loathed taking time out from his position as director of Steele Chartered Accountants. During his decade-long rise up the corporate ladder he'd accrued a sizeable fortune, but he still had a way to go before his personal worth equalled that of his more affluent clients. He'd worked too damn hard to slack off now—particularly after breaking a cardinal rule.

Never over-extend.

Four weeks ago he'd taken a huge gamble, investing nearly all his equity in a venture he felt to his bones would pay off. The business's solvency had dropped close to bankruptcy, but if he made every move the right one he knew he could not only turn the entity around, he would also make it the envy of every tycoon in Australasia.

Now was "make or break" time. There was zero room for sentimentality. Less room for weak links.

"Help. *Pleeease*. Help!"

Brought back, Gabriel upped his pace. When a surprise branch whipped his forehead, his roar of a curse rattled the treetops. Once he'd shaken off the stars, he pushed all the harder. He had to reach that woman in time. He'd do the same for anyone.

Wished he *could* have done the same—

He tamped down futile memories to concentrate on his task, on that woman…and on the not unpleasant sensation that had curled in his stomach as he'd watched her from his vantage point earlier.

She seemed somehow familiar, her hair a caramel-gold waterfall pouring down her back, her legs endless, shapely and tanned. Stooping to collect a shell here and there, she'd conveyed a grace that only fine breeding could assure.

And yet her cut-offs were ragged around her firm thighs, and her feet were bare. No Manolo Blahnik flats in sight. Not that those legs needed expensive accessories. He could have watched her toned calves flex all day as she'd sifted through the powder-fine sand and—

A boulder sprang up out of nowhere. Gabriel hurdled and landed safely at the same time as a notion struck.

That was why she seemed so familiar. Watching her in those cut-offs had reminded him of a long-ago childhood vacation by the sea, when he'd gone barefoot twenty-four-seven and his fishing rod hadn't left his hand. Aunt Faith had been a gem, providing her studious nephew with plenty to eat and lashings of love. Despite the tragic circumstances surrounding his mother's disappearance, from the age of four Gabriel had enjoyed a well-rounded, relatively hassle-free upbringing.

Then his best friend had died.

At last Gabriel tore through the last layer of brush and burst into the light. His lungs burning from lack of air, his body lathered in sweat, he spotted the woman twenty metres away. He dug deep to mine what remained of his strength, then sprinted as the spill from a colossal wave consumed her.

His gaze held the circling froth where she'd disappeared until, plunging into the wet cool, he found her and urged her head clear of the torrent. As her arms shot out, and she gasped and coughed, he summed up the dire situation. Her ankle was locked at an ugly angle. No telling if bones had been broken.

One arm supporting her shoulders, he cleaned the filigree of clinging hair from her face as she struggled to take in air. If he'd had time to dwell he'd have said she was beautiful, in a bedraggled, drenched kitten kind of way.

"Can you hear me?" he asked. "Are you all right?"

She grasped the top of her leg and found a grateful smile. "I am now. I'm just a little—" She flinched. "A little in pain."

As the wave sucked back out he laid her down, then manipulated his fingers between her ankle and the wood. It seemed her foot had slipped through a knot; sadly, the surrounding shell felt tough as nails. She wouldn't have been able to budge it even if she'd had the strength to try.

After a couple of tugs, attempting to weaken the wood, he was quietly worried. He inhaled, rallied determination, and gave another, more serious wrench. A small piece broke off, then a bit more. No screams of pain; she gave little more than a thankful shudder as he freed her foot a second before water swept up and their world became a muted, cold-rush blur.

Fully submerged, holding his breath, he relied on his sense of touch to scoop the woman up and heave them both clear of the churning pool. He trudged well out of tide range and, on a sparsely grassed knoll, laid her down. Any minute the steady pump of adrenaline would give way to the burn of muscle fatigue, but for now he'd keep moving.

How bad were her injuries?

As she worked to catch her breath, Gabriel knelt close and collected her ankle. No compound fractures. When he rode two fingers over the arch of her foot, her peach-polished toes flexed up. Cupping her heel with one hand, his other palm resting on her shin, he applied a token amount of pressure to test the ligament. When she didn't complain, he applied a bit more. She cringed, but didn't cry out.

Brave girl.

There were nasty scratches and welts that would ripen to bruises. She'd need an X-ray, and a day or two of rest, but—fingers crossed—in a month or so her ankle would look as good as new.

Searching for other wounds, his gaze travelled the length of her leg, and higher. But at a tug low in his gut—a kick of kindling heat—he averted his eyes and cleared his throat. Inviting as she looked—wet tee-shirt moulding to the swell of her breasts, nipples puckered beneath transparent white interlock—this was *so* not the time.

He swept sand into a slanting step with one hand and then, to help with the swelling, set her foot upon the "pillow." Finally falling back on his rump, he laid one forearm on a raised knee, dragged down a settling breath, then blew it out in a rush. His heart was chugging like a steam train. He hadn't felt this juiced in years—not since torturing himself competing in tri-athlons in his late teens. Great for building stamina. Not so good for fending off ghosts.

He told her, "Nothing appears to be broken." *Thank God.*

Her chest deflated as she wheezed out a breath. "You sure? Coz it really isn't my day."

He grinned at her impish tone, her slight but sexy lisp. "You're scratched up, and—"

"My God—" Her eyes went wide in horror. "So are you."

As if to prove her point, a warm trickle slid past the corner of his eye. He ran his thumb over his temple, inspected the smear of blood, then swiped the red on his soaked chinos.

No headache. No sting. "Nothing serious."

Her unconvinced gaze zigzagged over his scored torso. "That's a whole pile of 'nothing serious,' if you ask me."

Her concern was appreciated, but he'd live. Thankfully so would she.

"There doesn't appear to be any ligament damage."

"Are you a doctor?"

"An accountant."

She looked uneasy. "No offence, but I thought accountants were supposed to wear black-rimmed glasses and look kind of nerdy."

He smiled. "No offence taken."

He'd worn just that type of glasses once—not that she needed to know. They were strangers, thrown together by situation and sheer luck. Of course that didn't mean they couldn't get to know one another. Might be the extraordinary circumstances, the overload of adrenaline, but somehow she seemed…

Different.

Oh, he dated. Hard not to when he was considered one of the country's most eligible bachelors, and friends constantly set him up with "possibilities." And, sure, women were nice. Hell, he wouldn't want to live in a world without them. But he was way too busy to worry about relationships. Too busy for anything other than casual.

As if that thought were a wish, an alternative vision of this woman swam up in his mind. With the tee removed, shortie-shorts too, her tan would be all over, her breasts mouth-wateringly full. The vee at the apex of her thighs shone with a tantalising tuft of caramel-gold—and *why,* dear heaven, was he letting his imagination run away on him like this?

Gabriel scrubbed his bristled jaw and shook his head clear.

Okay. Cold showers—and/or oceans—weren't cutting it any more. It had been way too long. Still, he could control his overloaded testosterone levels. Willpower, in everything, was his speciality.

He squared his shoulders, then moved to check the contusion on her head. After parting the clotted hair, his fingertips circled the injury and she hissed.

"Sorry," he murmured, then, "No cut. But you've got an egg."

"Laid by an emu, feels like."

Cupping her chin, he checked for uneven dilation of the pupils. When her large jewelled eyes blinked up at him, his groin flexed. Clearing his throat, he reminded himself of their circumstances and edged away.

"You were knocked out. Do you remember how it happened? Your name? Is there any ringing in your ears?"

What were the other signs of concussion?

But she didn't appear to be listening. Rather, those sparkling topaz eyes, surrounded by lush damp lashes, were examining him with new, almost innocent wonder.

"You were standing up there, weren't you? On that cliff."

His brows jumped. "You saw me?"

"Only for a moment." Her gaze dropped before catching his again. "This'll sound crazy, but as I blacked out I thought you were… Well, I thought you were an angel."

He chuckled at her almost reverent tone. "Sorry to disappoint you again." Not a doctor. Definitely not an angel.

As a late afternoon breeze rustled through the palm fronds, and seagulls squawked overhead, her eyes glistened and her brow furrowed more.

"Still, you…you seem familiar."

Really?

Maybe it was more than seaside memories that made her seem familiar too. Had they met before? At a dinner? Maybe they lived in the same neighbourhood? Potts Point, Sydney, was pricey, but then anyone vacationing at Diamond Shores had money and plenty of it.

Before he could ask, she held her head and groaned over an apologetic smile.

"I'm all muddled. My head feels like it's packed with cotton wool."

"I'm not surprised."

She needed that knock checked out properly, along with some painkillers and an appropriate bandage for her foot. She needed civilisation, asap.

"Give me a moment," he said, determined to ignore the creak of tightening hamstrings, "and I'll get you to a doctor."

The island enjoyed a full-time physician, as well as a seaplane and an emergency helicopter, both of which, he believed, served French champagne. Luxury at its decadent best.

"That'd be great," she said, tipping up. "You can lend me an arm. Or I could use a branch for a crutch."

He urged her back down. She needed to rest and lie flat. "You're not walking anywhere."

Her doubtful gaze drilled his. "What'll we do, then? Close our eyes and click our heels three times?"

He grinned. Cute.

"I'll carry you."

"All the way to the resort?" She half coughed, half laughed. "Your arms will break off."

He cocked a brow. "I assure you they won't."

Her cheeks pinked up before she gave a conciliatory sigh. "Look, I appreciate everything you've done. You've been two hundred percent chivalrous and I'll be forever grateful. But I'm not exactly a flyweight."

Correct. She was shapely. Voluptuous, really. Precisely how a woman ought to be.

He cut short his discreet assessment at the same time as she pushed back up on her elbows and sent over an all-settled, I'm-used-to-getting-my-own-way smile. "So, we're agreed?"

His hand on her shoulder eased her down again. "Lie flat." She didn't need to risk nausea or dizziness. "I'll do whatever needs to be done."

"That can't include giving yourself a heart attack." Her eyes lit up. "I know. You can go for help and I'll wait here."

"You need medical attention now, not later."

Besides, he wouldn't leave her alone. She might get it into her head that she knew best and try to limp back to the resort.

"You don't understand," she said. "I was big-boned before getting friendly with the food here. If you've tried the desserts, you'll know you can't stop at one."

Her lush lips were soft and parted now, and a delicate pulse beat at the base of her throat. I wonder what that pulse would feel like against my tongue? Gabriel thought.

Wonder what she'd be like in bed?

"Hello?" she cooed. "Are you listening?"

He grunted, drove a hand through his hair. "Sure. Delicious. No control."

She nodded, then winced and touched her head. "You're all fired up, and obviously capable, but I can't have you putting your back out." She pushed up again. "And, seeing I have final say in the matter—"

"Absolutely you have a say." He tipped her back down. "You can say, *Yes, sir.*"

Her mouth dropped open and a mew of outrage escaped.

Doubly determined, she pushed up again. "I didn't realise I'd joined the army."

"I'll count to three," he warned, half hoping she'd defy him.

She didn't disappoint. "I'm more than capable of making my own decisions, thank you very much."

Done with words, he pointed at the ground. When her face hardened with a you-can't-make-me look, his jaw shifted. He admired spunk, but only one person was in charge here and it was time she learned who that was.

In one smooth, purposeful movement, he angled closer, crowding her back as he bent forward until, eyes gone wide, she lay horizontal again. By the time he stopped crowding, his head was slanted over hers and their mouths all but touched.

His gaze licked her lips as he grinned.

"You were saying?"

CHAPTER TWO

STARING into the wicked eyes of a beast, Nina kept still and swallowed hard.

There she'd been, wondering if she could possibly get out of that fix alive, then *pow!* So broad through the chest, so capable and infuriatingly confident, this superhero type showed up out of nowhere.

But she was confused. Where did he fit on her character chart? Was this man exceptionally good, or primarily perfectly bad?

Anyone with half a brain and a pair of scales must see he couldn't carry her all the way back to the resort. Nevertheless, he hadn't merely dismissed her suggestions. He'd gone so far as to pin her body beneath his to get his point across.

She was trapped. She should be fuming!

Instead her nerve-endings simmered with indisputable awareness, and her fuzzy brain kept wondering how well his lips might fit closed over hers.

"You're quiet," he noted, his mouth a hair's breadth from hers.

Wondering if he might manacle her wrists next—and not wholly against the idea—she squirmed. "I'm thinking."

"About behaving, I hope."

His voice was rough, dangerously deep, and the whisper of his breath against her lips felt far less invasive than it ought to.

"Do I need to point out," she said, "that I'm not the one behaving badly?"

"Won't make a difference. If I let you have your way, you could do yourself another injury." Wet dark hair flopped over his brow when he cocked his head. "Or would you rather I ignore the fact you might have concussion?"

"I'd rather you quit with the caveman mentality."

He growled and leaned a smidge closer. "You're only alive because that caveman mentality got me to you before the sharks tucked in for dinner."

She held her breath while her heart thumped high in her chest.

Oh, crap. She hated to admit it, but his brutish logic made sense. He would never convince her he could carry her all the way back to the resort, but her head did feel light. If she stood up now, tried to walk, she might very well fall over. Maybe even knock herself out a second time. Like it or not, in a roughish kind of way, he was still rescuing her—protecting her—this time from herself.

She issued a reluctant nod and, fire fading from his eyes, he curled away.

As he repositioned himself beside her, the sinking sun fell behind his head, bathing his splendid form in a golden-rose halo. Nina squeezed her eyes shut, then looked again. He wasn't an angel. She was certain of that now. And yet his presence, this scene, everything about this time here with him seemed surreal. Make-believe.

Maybe she was still unconscious? Maybe her lungs were filled with water and she'd hallucinated all this while succumbing to the final phase of drowning? Was she experiencing some incredible dream on her way to the hereafter? That wasn't so unlikely. She'd heard stories before.

Was any of this real?

Determined to find out, she reached and touched his pec, an inch above that small flat nipple. Her fingertip sizzled like creamy butter on a hotplate, at the same time as her centre glowed and blood tingled with fresh life. As her fingers fanned over the black, crisp hair, bolts of crackling electricity ripped through her veins. His flesh was so firm, so masculine and—

She stopped.

Inched her gaze up.

He was looking down his aquiline nose at her fingers—which were kneading the warm cushioned steel as if they belonged there.

Tilting his cleft chin, he raised a dark brow and his entrancing eyes met hers.

"Let me know when it's my turn."

She snatched her hand away. Her breathing was all over the place again and her face was flaming. Simply put, she wanted to die.

"I was just…er…just making sure they were—I mean, that *you* were—" Embarrassed beyond words, she spat out the rest. "I was making sure you were real."

"Oh, is *that* what you were doing?"

His lopsided grin drew a crease down one side of that highly kissable mouth. And his eyes…

They were so clear and bright and *laughing*.

Laughing at her.

She understood why. She was acting like a loon. A suspicious, ungrateful, concussed, groping loon.

But then his gaze sharpened and his expression changed.

"Are you cold?" he asked, edging close again.

"I don't think so." But that noise… Were her teeth chattering? Checking out the clouds building to black overhead, she shivered and instinctively hugged herself. "I am kind of shaky."

A line cut between his brows and he cupped her chin, turned her head gently one way then the next. His gaze intensified, and for a giddy moment Nina imagined she'd fallen head-first into those amazing ice-blue eyes. When he checked her pulse against his platinum Omega, she relented and played compliant patient. After six weeks of serving other people's every whim, there was part of her that needed this one-on-one attention, mandatory though the attention might be.

"What's the verdict, Doc?" Did he want her to open her mouth and say *ah?*

Her answer came when he rolled his shoulders back and peeled off his shirt. Her eyes popped out of her head. *Mamma mia.* What a specimen.

"You need to be kept warm," he told her, stripping a sleeve off one dynamite arm and then the other.

"Thanks," she managed to wheeze, "but I don't think a wet shirt will cut it."

"Body heat will."

"Y-you're going to *hold* me?"

He blindly tossed the shirt on a bush, then loomed over her, the chiselled planes of his face unforgivably close. "Any objection?"

Her gaze zeroed in on his mouth, on the dusky pink of his full bottom lip, and her pelvic floor muscles squeezed.

She'd tried to refuse him before and her opposition

had got her nowhere. If anything, being obstinate had made matters worse. An air of entitlement, albeit tempered by *GQ* looks and bad-boy charm, was a quality that stuck in her craw. She'd kow-towed to similar sorts too often these past weeks…people who would once have classed her as their equal.

All that aside, this guy was no idiot. If he said she needed to be held—hell, he was probably right. And if she must be gathered up against some unknown body… heck, it might as well be his.

When she mustered a haughty look and shrugged one shoulder, he scooped an arm beneath her neck.

"Tell me if I hurt you," he said, careful of her bump and her foot as he lay beside her.

He drew her close until her ear rested on the plateau of flesh and muscle below his collarbone. Despite her irritation, she almost sighed when one iron-warm palm splayed over the small of her back, pressing her deftly against his powerhouse length.

His breath brushed her ear. "How's that?"

She could be smarmy, could fib and say she was uncomfortable; she *was* in a way—only because he had, indeed, been right. It seemed those remarkable arms gathering her near were exactly what her traumatised body had needed.

Comfort…a masculine mountain of it.

She buried her nose in his chest and mumbled, "Better."

She imagined his grin. "Good."

He was damp but hot, as if a furnace were blazing away beneath the skin, and when she closed her eyes everything but the impression of security and strength faded from mind. His earthy scent, mixed with a lingering hint of aftershave or soap, burrowed into her pores and played havoc with her rag-taggle reason.

This felt nice. *He* felt nice. Nice and strong and not-so-plain-or-simple sexy.

She inwardly sighed.

Oh, why not admit it? The throb in the base of her belly wasn't a consequence of relief or gratitude, or even exasperation. It was desire—the forbidden, molten lava kind that blocked out other stimuli, heightened each sense and alerted every fibre. It was the kind of intense physical attraction that had her half convinced she needed to dissolve into this man right here, right now, or simply cease to be.

Crazy.

Clearly the knock on her head had bumped the arousal lever in her brain up to high. Every synapse seemed to have direct dial to the pulse ticking merrily away between her thighs. Every nerve-ending was wired to zap the burning tips of her breasts. All of which made her horribly nervous.

And terribly curious.

They were strangers, brought together by near tragedy. She was a level-headed woman who, admittedly, hadn't had a man in a while. A good while. And certainly never one like *this*. But her urge to gaze up, look into those incredible eyes and offer him her lips…

It was wrong. Totally off beam.

Wasn't it?

A moment ago his bedraggled kitten had wanted to know if this was real. Now Gabriel wondered too. He hadn't peeled off his shirt and drawn her close for any reason other than her shaking. She needed to be kept warm.

Sure, he was benefiting too. Lying on this cushiony spread of sandy grass and listening to the rhythmic wash of waves gave him a chance to recuperate. His system needed a break. Only…

He didn't feel all that relaxed.

His body was a simmering mass of anticipation. His heartbeat was a booming bass beat in his ears. Those symptoms weren't a consequence of exertion any more than the ambitious tightening in his groin, or the groan of awareness building like thermal movement deep in his chest.

He was a man who lived well—the finest food and accommodation, state-of-the-art high-powered cars. But holding a beautiful woman was on a shelf all its own. *She* seemed to be on a shelf all her own.

He was no stranger to sex. Slow sex, hot sex—wild sex even better. But, no matter how stimulating the company, he'd never needed to worry about maintaining a certain level of control. He never truly lost himself in the moment. And yet the desire rippling through his veins now was distinct. Unique.

Disturbing.

It had to be the setting, the extraordinary circumstances, but it was all he could do not to tug this woman's supple curves closer, coax her shapely hips nearer, tilt her chin higher and kiss her.

Hard.

Normally he knew when a woman was interested too. A lidded look. An arched brow. A sensual smile when she caught his gaze and held it. That kind of nonverbal communication had been perfected by nature over eons to ensure the survival of the species. *I'm available. Me too.* No genius there.

But, lying beneath this palm tree with Miz Crusoe nestled alongside him, he was stumped. She'd been grateful, stubborn, teasing, and finally accepting. It couldn't be his imagination that she was enjoying this contact as much as he was.

So where did pumped-up high-stakes drama end, and good old-fashioned foreplay with an attractive, might-as-well-be-naked woman begin? If he rolled more towards her, how would she react? With outrage, as she'd done earlier, before he'd flattened her against the ground to make sure she wouldn't hurt herself? Or would her gaze become heavy with an I-feel-it-too glow?

When she gave a violent shiver, the choice was made for him. Before she trembled a second time Gabriel held her more firmly, grazing a warming palm up and down her chilled arm.

After a moment she looked up, and her full lips twitched. "You must think I'm horrible."

He grinned. "Worse than Godzilla and the giant Powder Puff man combined."

Her perfect smile fanned wider before she sobered. "While I can't condone all your tactics, I truly am grateful. For everything. You're right. I'd have been fish food if you hadn't come along when you did."

"I'm glad I was able to help." More than she'd ever know. "How's your foot?"

Her leg moved and she flinched. "Hurts a little."

"We ought to get moving before the pain gets worse."

She hummed out an affirmation, but then only laid her cheek back upon his chest.

He gauged the sun's heavy position in the sky, the storm clouds meshing together overhead, then closed his eyes and concentrated on the feel of her hand on his ribs.

Ah, what the hell? A few more minutes wouldn't hurt.

His palm trailed her arm again, up over the slender shoulder, down to her elbow. Seagulls wheeled and squawked above while time wrapped around them like a promise-filled cocoon. If anyone had happened along they'd have mistaken them for lovers.

"Guess we really should get going," she murmured. "You've probably got someone waiting."

He nailed the quality in her voice: overly blasé. People came to Diamond Shores to fulfil their island fantasy while soaking up every laid-back luxury. Make the rates exorbitant, and it was a licence to print money. It added up that kitten here was looking to be indulged too. But in what way? And to what extent?

Time for a test line.

"There's nobody waiting in the way you're implying," he said.

"What way is that?"

"How many ways are there?"

"Let's see. You could be here on a reckless weekend with a bud."

"Nope."

"Could be showing a client a good time, hoping to tie the bow on a multi-million-dollar deal."

"Good guess, but no banana."

"You're here with your girl?"

"Don't have one."

Two beats of silence, then her breath brushed his chest again. "Maybe you're here to find one?"

"Is that an invitation?"

She gave a humourless laugh, but didn't search out his gaze. "Believe me, I'm not your type."

"What type are you?"

"I should start with clumsy."

"So this kind of incident isn't a one-off?"

"Yesterday I spilled a drink in the lap of an Arab prince."

He cringed. "Bet he offered to buy you another one."

When she groaned, the vibration blew a pleasant tingling rash down one side of his body. "Hardly."

"International model types weren't the Prince's thing?"

She lifted her head to give him a pull-the-other-one look. "Models are super tall and thin."

"So, not a model?" he conjectured. "More athlete, then. You compete in the European show-jump circuit?"

"Horses make me sneeze. And I'm clumsy, remember? I'd break my neck, and the poor horse's too."

"Okay. Your father's one of the country's leading barristers and you're fresh out of law school, ready to fry your first bad guy's butt," he surmised, and she laughed.

"I like your imagination," she said, "but…"

"I'm off track?"

"Way off."

"A hint would be good."

"But not as fun as hearing what you come up with next."

Her eyes were dancing now, and a stream of hair had fallen down the centre of her forehead, criss-crossing her slim straight nose. He scooped the hair behind her ear and his blood heated more.

"Got it." He lowered his hand. "You're a misunderstood heiress running from the press."

"Not this year."

He chuckled, so she did too, but then she winced and touched her head.

His stomach muscles crunched and welts stung for the first time as he sat up. "How's the lump?"

"Only hurts when I laugh."

He mock-frowned. "I can be serious."

"Tell me something I don't know."

"I want to hold you closer."

Her hand drifted away from her bump. "You want to do what?"

"Hold you closer."

Her eyes rounded to saucers.

"That's not a command, by the way," he added. "More a suggestion."

"If I say no?"

"We head off to the resort."

"If I say yes?"

"Then I'll add another wish to my list."

She blinked several times, as if she were having trouble taking it all in, but she didn't try to wriggle away. In fact she leaned nearer. "Tell me."

He craned his neck to graze his lips over the satin and grit of her brow, and the contact made the skin tighten over his flesh. "I'd do this."

He heard her intake of air, felt her slight tremble as he grazed again.

Her hand bunched slowly on his chest, sending positive signals to regions below.

"And then?" she asked.

He cupped her nape, his thumb circling the base of her neck before his hand slid around to her chin. His lips skied down the slope where a moment ago he'd brushed her hair away.

"I'd tip your chin higher." With a knuckle, he angled her mouth towards his. "Like this."

Her lips parted as she inhaled, silent but deep, and her heavy gaze sparkled into his.

"Then what?"

Smiling softly, he moved closer.

"Then this."

CHAPTER THREE

THE touch of his kiss was faint, yet the intensity of sensation was all-consuming. The promise of what was to come gave Nina a heady rush and goosebumps down to her toes. Today she'd nearly lost her life, but this—dear heaven—was almost worth dying for.

With his thumb guiding her jaw, he steered her chin higher and kissed her again, this time with his mouth slanted at a different, more exacting angle.

Nina sighed.

He felt like magic…omnipotent, skilled, sultry. This caress was barely there, yet somehow it lifted her to another plane, where warm hands understood how to stroke and leisurely lips knew how to thrill. If there was an advanced school of kissing, this guy had graduated top of the class.

As his mouth reluctantly drew away, the tip of his nose brushed hers. She opened her eyes, and when he opened his, they were a dark, stormy blue-grey, and filled with a latent hunger Nina's surging blood recognised too.

This man was every woman's dream. Masterful, challenging, sexy to a fault. She'd never met anyone like him. She wanted him to kiss her a second time, and then she wanted him to do it again.

One problem.

Did she tell him before or after she wasn't who or what he thought? Not an heiress fleeing from the paparazzi, not the genius daughter of a world-famous barrister, but a rather average, stressed-out waitress, struggling to get through a difficult time.

Good thing he had track shoes on. He might want to run a mile.

"I have to say," he murmured in a rich, drugging voice that spoke directly to her G spot, "that felt good."

Despite her concerns, she couldn't help but smile back. "I second that."

His absorbed gaze dropped to devour her lips. "I vote we get more inventive."

"Which entails…?"

"For you…simply lie back and enjoy."

"Oh, I have to *enjoy* it?" she teased.

He nipped her bottom lip. "That's the idea."

At the notion of total surrender—arms draped over her head, taking every wonderful delight he had to offer—syrupy warmth condensed at the heart of her. The idea of making love with a thoroughly gorgeous man she barely knew was not only reckless, it was irresistible. Who said she wasn't allowed to forget her problems for an hour or two? Wrapping herself in his silver lining sounded pretty good about now.

With a cooling breeze blowing over her skin, teasing her nipples, she wet her lips.

"What about you? Do you get to enjoy it too?"

He shifted up, so that one side of his impressive chest hovered over hers. His arm curled possessively above her head.

"Ask me a hard question."

He kissed her in earnest then, his warmth flashing

heat-lightning through her blood, his mouth irrevocably claiming hers. But not in a gulping, feverish fashion. More with the finesse of a man who knew what women liked. What *this* woman needed.

His slightly roughened palm trailed down her neck. His thumb rested in the hollow of her beating throat before his touch skimmed down her décolletage, then slid to encircle her upper arm, coaxing her up and in. The suggestion of ownership in the gesture was unmistakable, as well as enthralling—all the more so given the way his mouth worked unhurriedly yet intently with hers.

Her arms coiled around his neck and she pulled herself up, offering more, as delectable desire built and bubbled away—a steaming kettle ready to boil. She was physically, helplessly drawn to him, like a tide to the moon or a bird to blue sky. When his tongue probed deeper Nina whimpered with mind-tingling longing, and a strange sense of belonging seeped through her.

This embrace wasn't merely great, it was fated. In this thin slice of time she wasn't Jill's sister or little Codie's aunt. She wasn't the pampered princess who'd once had everything, or the twenty-year-old who'd slogged her guts out to ace her journalism class. She wasn't a magazine editor who'd found herself at a crossroads.

At this moment she was pure woman, hovering at the pinnacle of creation's best ever kiss. She felt so fired up she could barely breathe—but, unlike during her near drowning moments ago, she didn't want to come up for air. She'd much rather relinquish herself to her mystery man's caress until she expired from exhaustion and sheer joy.

When his thumb brushed the outside of her breast

she groaned. The sensitive peak tightened and her leg instinctively moved in. But the scratches on her ankle rubbed and, wincing, she jerked back an inch. When he pulled back too, the set of his jaw and refocusing eyes said he'd remembered where they were.

Oh, but this couldn't end now. What were a couple of scratches compared to the chance to truly escape and float on cloud nine?

Her arm still around his neck, she tugged. "I'm perfectly fine—honest."

His chin kicked up a notch. "You don't know how much I'd like to believe that."

Her fingers filed up through the back of his hair. "Believe it."

He set his forehead upon hers. "I'm afraid this, my dear, is not the time."

She pouted. "Really?"

"*Really,* really."

Sorry. She couldn't accept it. Her hand snaked down and she drew a suggestive circle around his right nipple, smiling when the disc hardened beneath her touch.

Folding her hand up in his, he pressed his warm lips to the palm. "Doctor first. Advanced introductions later."

"Maybe one more quick hello?"

He laughed, a gorgeous black velvet sound she would never tire of hearing. This guy had it all. Looks, charm, Herculean strength. Sure, he was a little over-confident, but, given the circumstances, after that kiss, she could find it in her heart to forgive him.

"Later," he confirmed, and cocked an enquiring brow. "Maybe over dinner?"

Nina's expression dissolved into a walking-on-air smile.

Fate was so unpredictable. A couple of months ago she'd had the next ten years mapped out—work her way up the magazine industry ladder and ultimately secure a spot on a top international rag overseas. By that time Jill would have met the guy of her dreams and Codie would be a real little man. One day Nina had hoped to find her soul mate—someone who truly understood and respected her.

Then her life had landed in a dumpster.

From heiress to editor to wayward waitress. What came next?

When her Galahad sprang to his feet and dusted himself off, Nina sighed. The most amazing few minutes of her life were over. But there was always dinner tonight.

Or was there?

The clientele here seemed oblivious to everything other than their own over-inflated issues and comfort. They lived to compare carats over a leisurely back rub or two. Was this man cut from that same cloth? How would he react when he found out he'd been making love to the hired help?

And, if that wasn't enough to dampen those dinner plans, there was always the resort's staunchest staff rule. No socialising with guests. *Ever.*

His shadow crept over her a second before his strong arms scooped beneath her shoulders and knees. Jolted back, she pushed against his chest. "What are you doing?"

"We've had this discussion."

"I'm not sure we came to any decision." None that she'd been happy with.

"If memory serves, you called me a caveman, I beat my chest, and the matter was settled. Now, we need to hurry. Rain's on the way."

Folding her arms over her waist, she tried to weigh herself down—not that she wasn't heavy enough. Nevertheless, he swooped her effortlessly up.

His white teeth flashed. "Light as a feather."

Uh-huh? Veins were already popping at his temples. She could sense the strain in his arms. Why-oh-why had she taken that slab of chocolate torte back to her room last night?

"Put your arms around my neck," he ordered.

"So you're intent on doing this?" *Giving yourself a hernia.*

His response was a sexy wry smile.

She held his gaze, then finally exhaled. He was implacable. What choice did she have? She only hoped he didn't keel over from a coronary before he'd finished saving her.

She was securing her arms around his hot neck when a light bulb went off in her head. "Hey, I've had another thought. You could make a tray out of a big banana leaf and pull me along. Like a snow sled, only on sand."

His eyes narrowed even as he smiled. "No bananas growing here."

"Well, you must have a cellphone. You could call for the helicopter to chopper me out. We could make a giant X on the beach with driftwood so they know where to land, and—"

Her words were cut off when his mouth took hers. And just like that the magic was in full swing again, drifting over her like tingling confetti as his kiss worked its spell and he urged her against his granite-like frame.

She dissolved into him. Melted completely. Of its own volition a hand wandered to the centre of his hard chest, fanned over the rock of a pec, then sailed higher, tracking the topography of the bulging cords in his neck, the sandpaper bristle of his firm square jaw. Only when his mouth left hers did the fog partly lift and she realised.

It was sprinkling rain.

Lifting her face, Nina blinked as another drop hit her cheek, then her arm. When he looked up too, as if waving a green flag, the rain came down in earnest.

She let go a shriek. Could her poor body take another beating?

But, while the rain fell in buckets, the water felt soft and revitalising on her skin. Perhaps it was her near brush with death, the lingering effects of that better-than-bliss kiss, or the fact that for the first time in weeks she felt truly free, but a jet of abandon surged up from her centre and a bubble of laughter escaped. Going with impulse, she shut her eyes and tilted back her head. When she opened her mouth wide, sweet rain filled her throat.

She gulped twice, three times, then, through the gauzy mist of rain, searched out his eyes.

Streams were coursing down his ruggedly handsome face, running off the tip of his nose. He studied her, his head slanted, before a crooked smile broke and he rocked back his neck as she had done. Laughing again, she joined him, and as he held her beneath the opened sky, she felt their strength restored.

Some quenching moments later he shook his head, like a dog after a bath, then near shouted over the water clattering through the layers of thirsty foliage behind them.

"We need shelter."

From beneath sodden lashes, she cast a glance around. The sea had darkened and whipped up too, each slate-green crest rising ever higher before smashing on the shore. The evocative scent of fresh rainfall seemed to rise off the earth's every pore. No birds in the sky, no tiny soldier crabs scurrying over the sand...everything seemed hidden away, as if nature had called a time out.

As the rain fell harder still, he took matters into his own hands—but he didn't charge north towards the resort. Rather he headed inland, weaving with precise guerrilla-like movements through a break in the bush.

"Cover your face," he called as he strode through the underbrush.

She did as he asked and protected herself. "Where are we going?"

Was there a cave close by?

But he didn't answer, and she didn't push. Curling into him, making herself small against the branches lashing by, once again she put her faith in this remarkable man.

Finally his gait slowed, and she was jolted when his shoulder crashed against something hard. Then the rain stopped, although she still heard it...

Thrashing on a roof?

Gingerly she uncovered her face and swiped sopping hair from her eyes, in time to see him kick a crude-looking door shut. The noise of the rain outside was cut off and they were alone, dripping puddles at the inside entrance of what looked to be a cabin—boxy, barely furnished, and located in the middle of the island's dense tropical forest.

He crossed to a single wooden chair set beside a small round table. In the shadowy light she saw a coffee cup pushed near the plastered wall. When he lowered her upon the chair her arm unravelled from around his neck, and as his warmth drew away a violent chill racked her body. She hugged herself as he moved to a kitchenette and flicked a switch. Over the din on the tin roof, her ears picked up the hiss of a kettle.

She twined her legs around one another and, hunching her shoulders, rubbed the gooseflesh on her arms. The exposed beam ceiling was low. An old sepia-tone photo hung on the opposite wall. A gnarly wooden coatstand guarded the door. The only other furniture was a double bed to her right. Shivering, Nina clutched herself tighter. That plump blue and yellow patchwork quilt looked mighty inviting.

The photo on the wall drew her eye. A gently smiling woman sat sloped towards her husband. Humour shone in the man's dark eyes, and Nina almost felt his hand lying upon her shoulder, as it did on his wife's in the picture. The hairstyles and garb said mid last-century.

"How did you find this place?" she asked. Had he stumbled upon it during his walk?

The kettle had boiled and he was sliding a coffee bottle over the counter. It was overly large, with a palm tree embossed on one side. It must have been here as long as that picture.

"This isn't what you're used to, I expect."

An unpolished wooden floor, a square-paned window with no curtain to draw against a view of the deluge. The cabin was austere, but also dry and cosy... and, in its intimate isolation, rustically romantic. But foremost it was somebody else's property. Were the people in that photo still alive? Given the circumstances, she supposed the owners wouldn't mind them sheltering here, but she frowned as he poured water from the kettle.

"Do you think we should help ourselves to the pantry?"

He paused, setting the kettle down, but then sent

over a smile. "This place is mine for the week—along with a bungalow back at the resort."

Nina lifted her brows. So this millionaire liked to rough it? And this was about as rough as it got.

He asked about sugar and milk. It seemed they both liked their coffee black, so he added some cold water from the tap and brought the much appreciated drink over.

Taking the warm mug in two hands, she sipped. The bitter but tasty brew filtered heat through her blood and most of the goosebumps faded.

Running an eye over the kitchen—retro orange tiles, super-old stove, modern microwave—she pressed the mug to her cheek, then her breastbone. "How did you know this even existed?" She hadn't heard a murmur about a rental bush cabin from the staff.

He heeled off his shoes near the cold ashes of the fireplace. "The owner built it decades ago." She had her mouth open to ask more, but he changed the subject. "You need to get out of those clothes."

The nerves high in Nina's stomach kicked—firstly at his words, then at the thought of that double bed and its come-hither quilt. But he wasn't suggesting anything other than the obvious. The rain had set in, and sitting here, shivering and sopping, wasn't smart. They both needed to get dry.

Striding past her towards the bed, he threw back a filmy curtain, which was hooked up to a chrome rail. "I'll run a tub and you can get that grit off."

Nina craned her neck. A chipped porcelain clawfoot bathtub. Hardly five-star—she set her mug aside—but if hot water was involved, she was there.

After he had twisted the stiff faucets, unseen pipes shuddered and groaned to life. He tested the water and, with the other hand propping his weight on the tub's rim, sought out her gaze.

"You okay to undress and get in?"

His question came at the same time as she found her feet. Her blood pressure dropped and, suddenly giddy, she closed her eyes and withered back down.

He was concerned she mightn't be able to manage with her ankle, but for her this last half-hour had moved too fast. First the appearance of her angel on the cliff, then the rescue, heightened by that once-in-a-lifetime kiss. Finally she'd been whisked away to this delectable man's secret lair.

On the beach, as his hands had traced over her body and his mouth had covered hers, she'd craved far more than his kiss. Here was her opportunity. Maybe she ought to take up his offer to help her undress.

She felt a familiar heat and opened her eyes. He was hunkered down beside her, dark brows drawn, the bristles on his jaw rough and close enough to touch.

"Hey...you all right?"

Genuine concern shone in his eyes. For so many reasons, it wasn't the time to think beyond what was relevant. Salt had dried on her skin where the rain hadn't reached. Sand, stuck to her shorts and her back, rubbed against the seat. And her scratches should be washed out properly too. Never mind about getting naked. Right now she needed to get clean.

Carefully she pushed to her feet again. "I think a hot bath is exactly what I need."

He loaned her an arm, collected the chair in his free hand, and she hobbled with him over to the tub. He set the chair below a tarnished brass rack and, before drawing the curtain, said, "That's a fresh towel."

Then the curtain whizzed closed and she was alone.

She slipped out of her clothes. When a perfect fan-shaped shell fell from her shorts pocket she set it on a rickety shelf. A few minutes later she slipped into warm liquid heaven.

Her ankle twinged briefly before she slid against the porcelain until she was fully under. Working her fingertips over her skull and through her hair, she shifted the stubborn sand and salt. After coming up for air, she repeated the exercise twice more. Then she closed her eyes and, resting her neck against the rim, simply floated.

When her nostrils blew air into the water, she yanked herself up with a start. She'd drifted close to sleep, and the bath had lost its steamy edge. Past time to dry off.

But as she reached for the towel her attention honed in on the rain, still thumping on the roof, and the wet clothes piled near the chair.

Her throat closed.

She had nothing to wear.

A gust of wind blew the curtain in, and she snatched the towel to her breast. But the wind dropped just as suddenly as it had appeared and the curtain fell straight again.

Wet hair running rivers over her shoulders, Nina first straddled the bath's rim then, careful of her foot, stepped out and secured the towel under her arms. The door had opened and shut; her companion must have left while she'd been submerged, rinsing out her hair. But where had he gone?

Wondering if she should call out, she instead peeked around the curtain's corner—and her legs all but buckled.

CHAPTER FOUR

NINA'S face flamed and her toes dug into the floor. She'd enjoyed the sight of her half-naked angel earlier, but she had only imagined the full, delectable picture standing before her now.

His back to her, he stood in the middle of the room, saturated—including the towel he now unravelled from around his hips. The moving shadows of early evening had deepened on the walls, but nothing could dim the glistening outline of his broad back as he tossed the towel near the unlit fireplace, where it landed with a heavy *slap*.

Bands of sinew roped in his arm when he stretched to retrieve a second towel from the table, and when he tousle-dried his hair—his long legs braced apart—Nina couldn't tear her gaze from his hamstrings…thick and hard and rock-solid scrumptious. His buns were tight too, and beautifully masculine; she lost her breath each time he rubbed himself and one or the other flexed in turn. When he flicked the towel behind his head and gave his back a two-handed rub down, the rippling muscles sang to her like a Ravel composition come to life.

Too soon he knotted that towel around his hips and thrust both hands through his damp dark hair. At the same time he rotated her way. Her mind slotted into gear and Nina ducked back behind the curtain. Heartbeat knocking at her ribs, she watched his shadow's languid gait as he moved towards the bed. She bit her lip and almost whimpered. To think a man like that truly existed and, better yet, was here with her.

"Are you all right back there?"

At the deep enquiring voice Nina's pulse leapt and she squeaked, "Fine. I'm fine."

"I used the outside shower to wash off."

Outside shower? "Oh?"

"A broken drainpipe," he explained, at the same time as an arm materialised behind the curtain. A green chequered shirt was thrust towards her.

"This'll have to do for now," came the voice, so near and rich the vibrations shot a fiery dart directly at her core. "Can't help in the underwear department," he added as she took the shirt and the hand withdrew. "When you're dressed we'll bandage those cuts. I want to know they're clean."

She finished drying, then slipped the oversized laundered shirt over her head. *Bath, shirt, bandages. Do this, do that.* He might have saved her life, but did he ever give over being such a *boss?*

Shirt-tails brushing her knees, she straightened the collar, then drew back the curtain and said, "You love being in charge, don't you?"

He was crouched by a kitchen cupboard. He seemed to deliberate on his answer and then, hitching back one shoulder, pushed to his bare feet. "It's what I do."

Right. Like Alexander had led armies. Only Alexander hadn't been a bean-counter—

And he hadn't worn jeans like *this* man could.

But even as she unconsciously wet her lips at the

heart-pumping sight standing tall before her, another vision sprang to mind and she couldn't smother a laugh.

A wry glint in his eye, he sauntered over. "What's the joke?"

"It's just *commanding* and *accountant* don't seem to go. I can't help picturing a masked crusader, with a big A on his chest and a turbo-blasting calculator cocked in one hand."

Faint lines branching from the corners of his eyes deepened. "Never underestimate the power of a turbo-blasting calculator." His gaze fixed on hers, he moved closer still, the low band of his jeans riding and sliding with each deliberate step.

"What about you?"

"Me?" Her attention shot up from the dark hair trailing down from his navel. "What about me?"

"We're done with the guessing game. Spill." His pale eyes twinkled. "Who are you?"

Very good question.

"I'm...er...in hospitality."

His eyes darkened. "Here to check out the opposition?"

"I'm a hands-on type."

He nodded as if he understood. "How long are you staying?"

"That's up in the air."

Seemingly not surprised, he undid the first aid kit she now realised he held. "I'm here for a wedding on Saturday."

"The Wilson wedding?"

His gaze sharpened. "You're a friend of April's?"

"Not exactly."

"A friend of the groom's, then? I'm Gabriel Steele, by the way. April's boss. Or should I say former boss."

"The bride-to-be resigned?" she asked, and he nodded. "And you're not happy about it."

A muscle in his jaw jumped twice before he crossed to the fireplace. He placed the first aid kit on the mantel and, with kindling prepared, struck a match. "April's a great PA."

"Guess her fiancé thinks she'll make a great wife." And he didn't want to share with macho man here. Understandable. She'd bet Gabriel had a harem of Girl Fridays back at the office, all eager to rip their veils off.

He retrieved a poker and, with one perfectly sculptured arm bracing the mantel, stirred the embers while virgin flames licked around the logs. "These days I didn't think marriage meant a woman had to give up her career." He sniffed. "But good luck to them."

A vote for feminism? Nina thought not. Did he disapprove of his PA's fiancé? Or were his reasons more personal? Perhaps he had a thing for this April himself? Or was it more a classic case of "eligible male against marriage" syndrome? Those guys ought to form a club.

But then her mind scuttled back to his name.

She'd known a Gabriel once. Of course she hadn't seen or heard from him in years. Not since the funeral.

Her stomach double-clutched at the thought of that day and she studied her host's face again, this time in the wavering firelight. The hawkish nose, the cleft in his shadowed chin, the sharp widow's peak dead centre of his forehead as he set the poker aside.

The Gabriel she'd known—Gabe Turner—had been a friend of her brother's, and they'd made an unlikely pair. While Anthony had been sporty, charming, and much sought after by the girls, Geeky Gabe had sat on the chess squad, had worn his hair parted way over on one side, and had owned glasses with super-thick lenses that darkened when hit by the light. Sadder still, Gabe had been poor…or poor by Petrelle standards.

One day she'd let Gabe into their house—more like a three-storey mansion—and when he'd taken off his shoes at the front door, the fourteen-year-old Nina had been appalled. A hole in both sets of toes. She'd whispered across, asking whether they could perhaps buy him a new pair, but Gabe had pressed his lips together and, hands clenched, strode off to Anthony's room.

She'd only been trying to help, but, thinking back, of course she'd hurt his pride. He'd made a point of avoiding her after that, and heaven knew back then she hadn't been used to being ignored. Consequently, whenever she'd had the opportunity, she'd pestered him to get a reaction. *Any* reaction. Give the guy his due, he had never once lashed out.

"You still haven't told me your name."

The rich timbre of his voice swept her back to the present. He'd moved into the kitchen.

"I'm Nina," she said, and as he flicked a faucet to wash his hands she caught the smirk. Her senses sharpened. "Something wrong with my name?"

"Just the last Nina I knew was as thin as two sticks and went around with a perpetual scowl on her face."

An ex? It didn't sound as if they'd blasted too far off the launching pad. Still, a man with his attributes wouldn't have pined for long.

Sauntering back, Gabriel swept the first aid kit off the ledge. Moving past, he took a seat at the foot of the bed and began to sort through bandages and lotions.

"So, Nina, how do you know the groom? You're not an old flame here to cause trouble?" He looked up, almost hopeful. "Are you?"

"We've never met."

The square angle of his jaw shifted. "You're not a friend of the bride or the groom, yet you're attending their wedding?"

She cleared her throat, formed words in her mind to explain her situation, but those words would not leave her mouth. She *wanted* to tell him. She needed to. She certainly couldn't lie about who she was.

He dabbed a cotton ball with antiseptic, and indicated with a tip of his chin that she should sit too.

"I've got it," he said. "You're a wedding planner. One of the experts people hire to make sure everything's perfect on the day."

Smothering a sigh, she shook her head and joined him.

The line between his brows furrowed again. "You really don't want me to dig any more, do you?"

"It's not that exactly…"

"Look, if you're more comfortable sticking with Nina the Mysterious for now, I'll back off. Privacy can be a huge issue, I know."

She opened her mouth to fess up, but something held her back.

The thing was…she wasn't *sure* who she was any more. With each passing day she wondered more. Being here with this delectable man only seemed to confuse the matter. She was a waitress, yet he was treating her like a princess. Once she *had* been a princess, of sorts, but then her family had lost everything and, not long after, she'd lost her position. Much of her identity had been lost with it.

The truth was she *would* rather remain Nina the Mysterious for now. Lately she'd felt so exposed and raw and vulnerable… She wasn't certain she could stand to peel off one more layer—even to the man who'd saved her life.

Not that she was embarrassed that she'd taken a waitressing job. She would rather step up any day than lie around fanning herself and hoping for some miracle to materialise and get her out of this jam. If she was embarrassed about anything it was that her performance here could have been better. If she was going to stay—and for now she had to—the other staff were right: she needed to take it up a gear.

As if agreeing to put an end to the identity discussion, he nodded at her foot. "Let's fix you up."

He first applied antiseptic to the bump on her head, then to her ankle. A large adhesive bandage was fitted, and a crepe one wound around that. When he was done, she ran two fingers over the joint—which didn't feel nearly as sore as it had.

"Don't have much in the way of other provisions." He pushed on his thighs to stand. "Some bread and spread, if you're hungry. And I do have a bottle of quite passable red wine."

Watching firelight flicker behind his silhouette, shifting ever darkening shapes over the roughly hewn walls, she felt she didn't need another thing other than that fire's heat, this blessed mattress, and her host's not unpleasant company. Despite the sexual awareness bubbling away below the surface—or perhaps because of it—she hadn't felt this stress-free in ages. Being stranded with a gorgeous man clearly worked for her. Why not go for broke?

She smiled on a nod. "A glass of wine would be nice."

In the kitchen, he opened the bottle of red and dug out a packet of peanuts and filled a ceramic bowl.

"Here's a not so interesting fact," he said sauntering back. "When I was a kid I wanted to run a macadamia nut farm."

"Well, I think that's *very* interesting." She accepted a glass and he poured. "I wanted to own a ballet school. What happened to your dream?"

He hesitated in pouring. "I'm not sure. Maybe I should put it on my 'to-do' list."

He raised his glass, she raised hers, and they sipped. The wine was mellow, and trailed warmth from her throat to her belly. Repositioning her weight, she leaned back on one elbow and sipped again.

"So," he said, getting comfortable beside her, "you dance?"

She screwed up her nose. "I was awful. I just liked the costumes."

Grinning, he grabbed some peanuts from the bowl which he'd set between them. "What else do you like?"

"You'll laugh."

"All the better."

"I like boxing."

He spluttered, and hit his chest to help clear his throat. "Didn't you see *Million Dollar Baby?*"

"Not competition boxing. Just mucking around." She protected her chin and jabbed the air. "At the gym." She shrugged. "I'm improving."

Her ankle throbbed once, and pain spiked up her shin. Careful of her wine, she manoeuvred back until she lay on her side, her cheek resting in one palm.

Better.

"What about you?" she asked. "Ever put on the gloves?"

"Nope. But I've tried practically every other sport."

"A figures man crossed with an athlete? I'm seeing that turbo-blasting calculator guy again."

"Ballet and boxing. We all have another side."

She took a long sip. *We sure do.*

"How's the ankle?" he asked, shaking some peanuts in his palm and throwing them back into his mouth.

"Much better."

Chewing, he evaluated the weather through the window. "The rain's set in."

She finished his thought. "And we should bunk down here for the night?"

"Don't know that there's an alternative. The resort doctor can check your head and leg tomorrow." His grin was crooked, and criminally sexy. "I think you'll make it past dawn."

"Thanks to you."

When she smiled over her glass at him, a double-knot in Gabriel's chest yanked tight.

More than ever before he was head-down, needing to ensure that the professional gamble he'd taken turned into a goldmine. Nothing at any point in his career had mattered more, and he'd learned that success meant keeping your eye on the ball. Always.

But as he watched his mysterious Nina in the fireglow—shadow and light playing over her heart-shaped face—a distracting something tugged inside of him. Something intense and pleasant and real.

She was beautiful, certainly—although he doubted she was aware of the power of her smile or how expressive and bright her eyes were. Her body was strong, yet wholly feminine. Sensual. She was all woman.

As she looked up from her glass and back towards the crackling fire—her drying hair splayed over her shoulder—more than physical attraction spoke to him. Even as he instinctively hardened in anticipation of enjoying another kiss or three, an added influence whispered in his ear.

He wanted to put a name to it, but the only word that came to mind hardly fitted. Trust was earned over a lifetime. Something he didn't ask for and rarely gave away.

Still, whatever it was that stirred him up about Nina, it felt good. Even if straight-out lust was way less complicated.

He prised his gaze from her lips and found his feet. "More wine?"

She made a purring sound in her throat, and her heavy-lidded gaze met his. She stretched her good leg straight along the mattress and replied, "Half a glass. Any more after that bath and I might go to sleep."

Relieving her of her glass, he skirted the bed and found the bottle. He poured her half, filled his up, then found a handtowel to mop up the few drops spilled on the cedar table.

"There's a creek out the back of here, filled with fish and some platypus. Or is that platypi?" He rounded the bed and, keeping an eye on his over-full glass, sat carefully down. "I was thinking this afternoon when I first saw you that this place reminds me of a spot my aunt took me on vacation once when I was a kid…"

His words trailed off.

Her arm was stretched out over the quilt, one cheek lying on that inside elbow. Her lips were slightly parted. If he spoke loudly enough she would rouse, but her breathing said she was already on her way to dreamtime. An experience like the one she'd endured today would knock it out of anyone. Couple that with a relaxing soak and glass of good wine…

Still, he was disappointed sleep had taken her so quickly.

His gaze slid down her tranquil form and he gnawed

his lower lip. What should he do about those legs? The wolf inside wanted to leave them exposed, but the reluctant gentleman said she might catch a chill.

Setting down the glasses, he eased the quilt over her body, covering her legs and those peach-tipped toes. Then, so as not to disturb her, he placed the chair before the fire, which had grown to a vigorous state. Stretching the cranky muscles in his legs, he threaded fingers behind his head and clicked his thoughts over to its usual fare. To work. To that crucial venture.

To this island.

After investing so much in this project, his efforts to set this place back well on its feet couldn't fail. Anything that didn't work towards the reestablishment of a healthy profit margin would be culled. Nothing that worked against success would be tolerated. His involvement here must have one outcome and one outcome only.

Absolute success.

He filed figures through his mind—advertising budgets, staff payrolls. Where to cut, where to spend…

But his gaze kept wandering to his slumbering kitten, to the gentle rise and fall of her chest beneath that chequered shirt. He had to let her sleep, and yet with every passing moment—with every whisper at his ear—that new tug inside of him kept willing her awake.

CHAPTER FIVE

NINA dreamed of a tidal wave, a colossal giant that made this afternoon's rollers look like dwarfs.

The wave in her dream curled up, throwing its enormous shadow over her, before crashing an inch behind her running heels. Having thought she was clear of danger, she cried out when its cold fingers coiled around her ankles and dragged her back. She screamed, but she knew no matter what she did, however hard she tried, this time she was a goner.

As the wave overcame her she was drawn down into the churning, bubbling wash. The motion jerked and pushed her. She couldn't breathe, couldn't find the surface. Then something gripped her shoulder, trying to lift her out. Needing precious air, she groped above her head, reaching for the wavering reflections dancing on the water's surface and the shadow waiting beyond that.

Nina's eyes popped open at the same time as she sucked down a desperate gulp of oxygen.

She felt pressure on her shoulder, took in her shadowy surrounds, then heard her name murmured in a gravelled voice. The floating pieces of the jigsaw clicked together and, heart thumping, she rolled over.

In the dying firelight, Gabriel sat on the edge of the bed, one knee angled over the sheet, concern lining his handsome face. As his gaze roamed her brow, her cheek, she remembered her scream from the dream and knew she must have cried out.

Emptying her bursting lungs, she touched her forehead and patted the damp away. "I dreamt I was drowning and you saved me."

A sultry grin sparkled in his eyes. "That wasn't a dream. Here—push up." He helped her to straighten higher on the bed, eased the sheet up, then pulled the quilt around her neck. "You're safe now. Go back to sleep."

In her mind Nina relieved the moment he'd dragged her out of the wash and laid her upon that sandy knoll. Thank God he'd been there.

She hugged the quilt tight.

Thank God he was here now. For the first time in weeks she *did* feel safe and certain.

Lighter rain pattered on the roof. She rubbed one eye, then glanced out of the window. Still dark, but no morning bird calls echoed through the bush outside. How long had she slept?

Gabriel had moved to the fireplace to stir the embers. The room smelled of firewood warmth—the kind electric blankets and heaters couldn't compete with.

Over one broad shoulder, his gaze hooked hers. "You're wide awake now, aren't you?"

She nodded and shifted higher.

"Are you hungry?" he asked, replacing the poker. "Thirsty?"

She wasn't hungry in the least, but... "I'd love a glass of water."

He brought a large glass over, and she drank it down without stopping.

"Better?" he asked when she handed the empty glass back.

"Much. Thank you."

She wiggled and got more comfortable. She felt positively toasty. A little sore from her struggles earlier, but also beautifully rested. This unpretentious atmosphere certainly helped.

"Why did you rent this place?" she asked as he slid the glass onto the side table.

She'd already surmised that he must like to rough it, and she was aware of this cabin's charm, but what deeper reason did he have for preferring bare essentials to the luxury available down the way? Had he played Davy Crockett as a boy? Perhaps he longed to be a social hermit, like Howard Hughes? But then why come to this island at all? Australia's isolated Outback might be a better choice.

He shrugged, and in a trick of the fading firelight his chest seemed to grow before her eyes.

"I had the wedding to come to here, and some business to attend to, but in between I wanted to take the opportunity to really get away. I haven't done that since I was a kid." He nodded at the bed. "Mind if I sit down?" He rubbed his butt. "That chair's not meant for catching zeds."

Without a second thought she moved over, and the mattress dipped as he joined her. He stretched one denim-clad leg down over the quilt; the other foot he rested on the floorboards.

"What kind of kid were you?" she asked, snuggling back down into the pillows, hands clasped under her cheek.

"Typical, I guess. Sometimes lonely. What about you?"

Definitely not lonely. She'd had plenty of friends.

Plenty to keep her occupied. Singing and dancing lessons. An interest in art. "You could've probably summed me up as confident." She wouldn't say *cocky*.

His chuckle warmed her more. "I have no trouble imagining that."

She recalled her idyllic past, how she hadn't wanted for a thing, but couldn't settle on the feeling those memories gave her. "It seems so long ago now...like that girl was someone else." Her mouth tugged to one side and she sighed. That Nina *had* been someone else.

"Sounds as if you'd like to go back."

"Yes. And no." She pushed up onto an elbow. "What I'd like to know is who I'm meant to be now. Who I'll be in the future." She relaxed the tension biting between her shoulders, and almost succeeded in keeping the embarrassment from her voice. "Too much information."

"I'm all for honesty."

Nina blinked over, and watched him watching the firelight. He liked the truth? Maybe she should give it to him. There was something about the intimacy of being surrounded by lush, tropical vegetation, that gave her the courage to try.

"Those questions never bothered me until recently," she ventured. "I had a set of goalposts in my mind—" to be a huge success in publishing "—and I was headed straight for the middle."

"Then something knocked the wind out of you?"

"Exactly."

She'd lost her job, but she might as well have been ploughed down and kicked in the gut. She'd never felt insecure before that, even when her mother had blown the Petrelle money. She'd been angry, yes, and disappointed at such waste. But ultimately she'd known she had her own abilities to rely upon.

Then her livelihood had been ripped out from under her and her confidence had been shaken to her core. She'd felt physically winded for days. But she'd forced herself out from beneath the covers, had mailed résumés off and returned to the gym. She'd promised herself things would work out. She *would* get back on her feet and eventually kick a winning goal right through the centre of those posts.

Only those posts seemed so far away now.

"Worse things have happened in my life," she continued, peering into the flames and remembering her brother's and father's deaths. "But I'd always held it together—"

Stinging emotion filled her throat and she had to stop and swallow. She felt his gaze on her.

"Want to tell me about it?"

Her cheeks hot, she shook her head. She'd said enough. If she said any more she might cry, and that wasn't something she liked to do too often.

"It's nothing that a million other people haven't faced."

"Maybe you're trying too hard not to disappoint other people?" he said. "Or trying too hard not to disappoint yourself. Cut yourself a break. Give it time. I see a strength in you I don't see in too many people."

She coughed out a laugh. "You saw that strength *when?* While I was trapped and screaming for help?"

He slid down a little. With his forehead near hers, their noses all but touching, he mock-frowned at her. "Did you hear the part about cutting yourself a break?"

Her gaze lowered to his mouth, and her own lips tingled with want. His scent was so intoxicating…the temptation to taste him again so strong…

But he moved away and, resting against the bedhead,

threaded his fingers behind his head. Man, he had *the* best set of biceps.

"You said yourself," he told her, "most people face a crisis. More than one. But no one knows what their most vulnerable spot is until fate uncovers it. Recovering from a meltdown can take time, but then you shape up even stronger. Whatever it is you're facing—" he winked across at her "—you'll be okay."

It sounded as if he knew what he was talking about, and, despite feeling low a lot of the time here, this experience *had* toughened her up. She'd found new ways to adapt. New qualities to admire—in others as well as herself.

Still, she couldn't help wincing as a prickly knot formed low in her stomach.

You'll be okay.

She sighed. "I wish I could believe that."

She must have sounded pathetically in need of TLC, because next she knew his arm was around her shoulder and he'd urged her cheek to rest against the slope of his hot bare chest. His fingers trailed up and down her arm before he gave her an encouraging squeeze. "I'll believe in you."

She blew out a quiet breath and, happy to surrender, curled in. With him holding her, his warm breath stirring her hair, anything seemed possible.

Now she'd shared so much, would he open up too?

She hesitated then asked, "Can I ask what your crisis was?"

He exhaled slowly. "I lost someone close. Someone who had faith in me when he didn't need to."

With his voice rumbling against her ear, her heart squeezed for him. Was there anything more difficult than saying goodbye for ever to someone you loved?

"For a long time I felt stuck, wanting to go back and change things," he said, and his hand unconsciously tightened on her arm. "I let that person down."

"I can't imagine you ever letting anyone down." Her palm skimmed higher, to rest where his heartbeat boomed. "You should try to remember why that person had faith in you."

"I never quite worked that one out. But I'll never forget it."

His tone was low and painfully earnest. As far as confessions went, that was a doozy. He seemed so capable; someone to rely on. So where had such an admission come from? Had he confessed that to anyone before? Instinct said not.

She pressed her ear to his heartbeat and, closing her eyes, willed her belief in him to soak through.

Then she smiled. "I might have a solution."

"Tell me." His words were patient, amused.

"Let someone have faith in you again." The same way he said he'd believe in her.

But when he stiffened, a shrivelling feeling fell through her middle. He'd opened up, but clearly she'd overstepped the mark. She hadn't meant to imply he was in any way unreliable, if that was how he'd taken it. So many people must count on him every day in his business life, for starters.

But then he breathed again, deeper than before, and when his arm moved higher his fingers brushed hair away from her face.

"What does having faith mean to you?" he asked, as the embers flickered lower and the room darkened more, cocooning them in their own little world.

"Loyalty," she replied, relieved he didn't sound defensive. "Commitment. Trust."

"Trust..."

When his mouth brushed her crown her pulse quickened, and her nipples hardened beneath the stiff fabric of her shirt. His arm urged her closer, and the growth of his day-old beard rasped over her. As her heart galloped high in her chest his mouth touched her hair, and anticipation sucked through her veins like a thousand-degree backdraft.

"I'd like for *you* to trust me," he said, and he turned her slightly in his arms. But she felt so overwhelmed, her pulse was racing so fast, she couldn't meet his eyes.

They'd kissed on the beach, but that had been different; she'd been swept up in the high-risk animation of the moment. But now every cell in her body was acutely aware of what lay beyond this caress. With each word and enticing touch he'd let her know his intentions. He wanted her to trust him. Enough to take this next step.

A thumb strummed an inch below one shoulderblade. When his chin made its way with an agonising lack of speed across her brow down her cheek to her jaw—when the delicious contrast of his lips whispered over hers—Nina felt so light-headed and doused with desire she wondered if she might faint. Then his mouth parted, feathering over hers, and her core caught light.

More than anything she'd ever wanted, she wanted him to kiss her now. Intensely.

Completely.

"I want to make love to you," he said, and that thumb travelled down the dent of her back. He kneaded the dip at the base of her spine as his teeth nipped and tugged her lower lip. "I want to make love to you like I've never wanted to make love to anyone before."

The gravelled timbre of those words pulled a final

trigger. Mouthwatering hunger flooded her centre, and her body reflexively bowed towards his. But the nerves in her throat were convulsing so badly she couldn't trust herself to speak. So she combed her fingers over the sandpaper of his jaw and let her eyes and her trembling want speak for her.

He turned his head slightly to kiss her palm, then, cupping her bottom, scooped her in while his lips slowly circled over hers. When the thick ridge of his erection ground against her belly, creamy warmth dampened her inside thighs.

"I want all of you," he told her, and then his mouth claimed hers and the velvet heat of his tongue pushed deep inside.

He kissed her for heady, blistering moments, breaking off briefly to murmur again, "I want to feel all of you, taste all of you." His fingers curved around the back of her thigh, between her legs. "Every inch and all night."

Turned inside out, she shook with maddening need. If he wanted her—wanted her all night—she wanted him more.

As they slipped further down the bed he systematically released each button of her shirt. When the last was undone, and she was quivering from head to foot, the backs of his fingers brushed up the curls at the apex of her thighs before drifting higher to trace over her belly.

His eyes found hers, and as his gaze glowed across he wound fabric around two fingers and slid one half of her shirt fully open. His head cocked as he examined the swell of her breast in the firelight, then he rolled her on her back and drove down both sides of the shirt, until the sleeves hung halfway down her arms. His gaze burned over her breasts, then ran a deliberate line of fire all the way down. When, as if more than satisfied, he raised his chin, her lips parted to take in more air.

Where would he kiss her next? The sensitive sides of her waist? The smouldering tips of her breasts? Or would his mouth caress the intimate folds that ached for so much of his touch? Every inch of her begged for the caress of his mouth, the skilled flick and curl of his tongue.

His palm traced up her side and found her breast. The pad of his thumb circled the areola before he gently pinched the tip. She writhed against the sheets and her hand automatically reached to hold his. His hand folded hers back at the same time as his mouth came down, tasting and then laving her nipple, as if it were dipped in thick honey.

Her breathing ragged, she held his head and slipped her good leg around the back of his thigh. His teeth clamped her nipple, and as he drew slowly back she arced with him until he released her to move off the bed.

He unzipped, denim fell, and her eyes rounded. She was more than ready for him; her body was a hopscotch of lit firecrackers waiting to explode. But the sight of his heavy rigid shaft dried her mouth. Everything about Gabriel was larger than life.

Joining her, he eased her up slightly in order to peel the fabric completely from her arms. He tossed the shirt, then lay beside her. In the dancing shadows he searched her eyes. A lazy finger trailed down the side of her ribs, over her hip, and drew a leisurely circle around her navel before his hot palm flattened against her belly. She bit her lip and shut her eyes as his touch delved and slipped between her thighs. When his fingers rode back up and stroked her with just the right pressure, to create just the right burn, she focused inward, concentrating on the rising tide.

With her mind filled with bright darting lights, his mouth covered hers—not gently this time; his tongue probed so thoroughly she wondered if he needed more from her than she could give. But to know the unbridled depth of his desire felt intoxicating. Felt wickedly, wonderfully right.

Her fingers combed up the back of his head, flexing through his hair before sculpting down the sides of his face so she could lock his kiss to hers. She wanted to sear these emotions in her mind...the feel of his jaw working with hers...his magnificent chest grazing her breasts.

She was perched on the teetering brink of release when the kiss ended, a second too soon. He took her wrist, kissing the inside before he moved to position himself above her. Holding her eyes with his, he eased in the tip of his erection, and reflexively her muscles clenched to draw more of him inside.

He began to move, filling her, caressing her. Surrendering to sensation, she fanned her palms over his shoulders as her head rocked back, driving into the pillow. The intensity left perspiration on her brow...left her brilliantly, blissfully out of her mind.

Her nails dug in as she craned up to kiss his chest, so steamy and strong, and all hers for the night.

I knew it would be like this, she thought. This was more than two bodies joining...this was so much more than just sex.

He nipped her chin, thrust again, and hit a spot so high and deep the jolt and thrill tore a sob from her chest. The tremors building in the base of her belly quickened as her throat ached and moisture filled the corners of her eyes. The intensity of pleasure was too much to contain.

She held the hair either side of his temples and, teetering on the edge, thought again, *Are you real?*

He answered her by taking her lips, and when the stroke of his kiss melded seamlessly with the rhythm of his hips the ticking time bomb at her centre compressed and shone, supernova bright.

She began to fold in on herself. With all the world fading away his body braced above hers and the muscles in his big shoulders bunched. When his head craned back, and he bared his teeth at the sky, she felt him shudder and empty his energy inside of her.

Her own tremors rose higher…soaring, spiking.

Peaking.

The instant a thousand waves crashed in at once he groaned, and drank his name from her lips.

CHAPTER SIX

ONCE was only the beginning.

They made love again, and a third time, and as the rain eased and the yellow fingers of dawn reached through that single window pane Nina snuggled back into the incomparable warmth of her lover.

Gabriel sat at the head of the bed, his back against the rest, his powerful arms coiled around her waist. She sat between his legs, her head slanted against his chest, her arms wrapped around his. The previous hours had raced by as if they'd only been minutes.

Tomorrow was almost here.

His chin brushed over her crown and she felt him harden against the small of her back. Teasing, she wriggled against him. "Aren't you sick of me yet?"

"Nope." His expert mouth found the sweep of her neck. Goosebumps erupted down her right side as his teeth danced over the still wanting sweep of skin. He whispered at her ear, "Stay with me."

She froze, then blinked several times. Had she heard right?

"What do you mean, stay?"

He hummed at her temple. "Here. With me."

What a crazy, wonderful idea, but… "Gabriel, I can't."

"Sure you can." He urged her face around and kissed her thoroughly. Her lips felt swollen from his all-night attention, but she only melted again now. Kissing, in all its forms, was his absolute forte.

The kiss broke softly. With a growl in his throat, he circled the tip of her nose with his.

"Stay."

She fisted her hand against his chest. Oh, God, how she wanted to. "It's not that easy."

The light in his gaze dimmed, and for the first time she saw something else in his eyes…something hard and close to unforgiving.

His voice dropped enough to make her shiver. "Is there someone else?"

"Of course not," she shot back, and the light in his eyes faded back up.

"In that case…" he edged her around more "…let me convince you."

Holding her chin in the vee of one hand, he tipped her back until she lay flat. The line of kisses he dropped down to her cleavage blew fresh life into embers wanting to flash hot again. And when his mouth tasted one tender nipple, and his tongue wove down to her midriff, her hands stretched towards him and her fingers twined through his hair.

She wanted to stay—so much that it hurt. But the idea was ridiculous. For one, as long as her ankle held up, she had a shift later today. Which led to a far bigger problem. Gabriel had no idea who she was. Or who she *wasn't*. He'd given her the option of remaining Nina the Mysterious, and at the time withholding her identity had seemed the easier, more attractive option. But that had been before they'd slept together.

The last few hours had seemed surreal. She could

almost convince herself she was just another rich guest enjoying a no-consequences holiday fling with a gorgeous playboy. But of course that dream couldn't last. She couldn't stay. Inevitably they would see each other at the resort and her secret would be out.

She pinched the bridge of her nose to stem the sting of emotion.

Okay. She would simply tell him now. Come clean with everything. Then the ball would be back in his court. He'd said, *I'll believe in you.* Not light words. If it hadn't been a line, he deserved the chance to prove he'd meant it. Prove to her that her faith in him wasn't built purely on firelight and fantasy.

Willing her heart to quit crashing against her ribs, she found a rational voice. "Gabriel, there's something I need to tell you."

His tongue twirled languidly around her navel.

She gripped his arms and tried to pull him up. "Are you listening?"

His mouth only dropped lower. "I can multi-task."

She didn't doubt it. "There's more you need to know."

He grazed all the way up, until his eyes twinkled directly into hers. "All I need to know is…" he tasted her chin "…I want to be with you."

He said it so easily. As if this could really mean more than a night or two if she let it. But she had to face facts. Clearly Gabriel was no novice at this kind of encounter. He'd known what he wanted and he'd set out to get it. She'd be crazy to believe this interlude meant anything more to him than a dab of icing on his holiday cake; she'd seen enough of his I'm-kicking-back-on-vacation type to know. Hell, rather than irritated, he might be *pleased* to discover she was a waitress. The thanks-and-sorry-it-didn't-work-out would be easier that way.

She realised he was looking deeply into her eyes.

A fingertip stroked her cheek. "Hey, what's wrong?"

She sighed. *Oh, just everything.*

"Gabriel…" She tried to find the right words to begin. "This day has been unbelievable. You make me feel so good. *Too* good."

A sexy smile tugged the corner of his mouth before he suckled a line up her throat to her lips. "Trust me. There's no such thing as too good."

Nina woke with a start.

Blinking open her eyes, she remembered the rain… the hideaway cabin in the bush. Foremost she remembered waking in the midnight hours, and how Gabriel's soft, skilled mouth and hard, practised body had claimed hers again and again.

Her every fibre lit up and tingled, recalling the bone-melting orgasms he'd given her. The way his tongue and hands had endlessly explored. She'd mindlessly given herself over to every wondrous stroke and squeeze.

Then he'd asked her to stay.

Her stomach somersaulted. She turned over, tried to focus her sleep-deprived brain, and realised she was alone amid the tangle of sheets. Where was Gabriel? She'd got severely sidetracked last night, but they still had a conversation to finish.

She had a confession to make.

Unfortunately talking quietly in romantic firelight was a far cry from coming clean in the cold light of day. She wasn't a wealthy guest at Diamond Shores. She worked at the resort. She'd let Gabriel believe what he'd wanted about her identity, but now she needed to speak up.

He was attracted to her. He wanted this holiday fling to continue. Only he had no idea who the woman he was making love with was. Hell, *she* didn't know who she was any more—or who'd she'd be next week. Next year.

Nina eased out of bed. Bringing a sheet along, she limped to the window. She had to believe he wouldn't be upset by her news. They'd spent a glorious night together. Precious time not every couple got to enjoy.

She stopped by the window. He didn't appear to be outside. When he hadn't returned after a few minutes she removed her bandage and drew a bath. As she slipped into the warm water she fantasised about him sneaking in and surprising her. But when the bath cooled, she dried and dressed again in the shirt Gabriel had stripped from her late last night. She finger-brushed her teeth with some paste she found while her stomach knotted.

She needed to get this off her chest. How much longer would he be?

Through the smudge of glass, and a break in the canopy of palms and vines, a flawless dome of blue smiled down. The leaves looked greener, hanging low and heavy with morning dew. While the air had felt chilly last night, heat was already building inside the cabin. Another tropical day in paradise.

She'd felt so down of late. In limbo. Lost. Feeling alive again last night had felt so real! The light and smell and sound of everything had seemed amplified. Brighter. She wanted to feel that alive again, and now she knew how to make that happen.

Not by continuing this charade with Gabriel; hiding behind a fantasy, no matter how wonderful, wasn't the answer. She had to step up and get her life back on track as quickly as possible. Until that opportunity arose, she'd put one hundred and ten percent into doing the best job she could here. Put her all into winning even a little respect from her co-workers.

Hope. A real belief that she could regain her pride. Her beautiful night here with Gabriel had given her that.

Her stomach growled. She'd eaten nothing but a handful of nuts since a scant salad yesterday at lunch. When a fruit bowl caught her eye, she chose an apple and chomped as she made her way aimlessly around.

She was about to make herself a coffee when a movement outside caught her eye. She tipped closer to the window and peered out.

Three…no, four wallabies!

When she swung open the door, air, fresh and minty, filled her lungs. She breathed deeply, listening to a symphony of birds, their squawks and chirps and whistles echoing off the treetops and jutting cliffs. To her left, the wallabies' ears turned in her direction.

Three were sunning themselves, resting on their sides on a nearby red and black-patched ledge. The fourth had a joey in her pouch; Nina held her breath as two tiny ears and a black nose twitched from the soft furry purse on its mother's tummy. They were similar to, but far smaller than, their marsupial kangaroo cousins. Their petite jaws munched rhythmically, and Nina longed to furrow her fingers through the thick brown fur of the curved backs. Their strong tails, which ended with a white tip, seemed to go on for ever.

Careful not to startle them, she bit off some apple, crept closer, then lobbed the fruit over. The mother used her tail and small front paws to edge away in the opposite direction. The others twitched their ears, but didn't deign to turn their onyx long-lashed gazes towards their visitor. She sat on a nearby boulder, and after a time one wallaby rocked slowly over. It collected the apple in its paws and ignored her while it chewed.

This same scene would have existed fifty years ago. A *hundred* and fifty years ago. How peaceful it would be to live here without television or the internet, Nina thought. No sales pitches or rush-rush schedules. Just the gentle sights and sounds of timeless nature.

She was about to throw more apple when the wallabies straightened, fully alert. Their ears pricked up and then they bounded off, their tails acting as precision springboards. As they disappeared over the rocks and into the bush Nina heard it too—a motor, distant, but coming this way.

She perched upon the wallabies' ledge and waited to greet her arrival. A few moments later Gabriel appeared, wheeling in a motorbike. Nothing large and mean— rather a fun ride, with chunky tyres obviously meant for off-road.

He stopped when he saw her, and his eyes opened in surprise. "You're up."

She eased off the ledge. "You were up earlier."

He performed a flourishing bow. "Your limousine, *madame.*"

She laughed, but with a touch of irony. She hadn't ridden in a limousine for a very long time.

He kicked down the bike's stand, whipped a carrybag off the handlebars and closed the distance separating them in three long strides. Then arms that felt like heaven gathered her in and his mouth dropped over hers. As one hand edged up to cradle and faintly rotate the back of her head, Nina dissolved into their best kiss yet. Her fingers fanned up to knead the muscle beneath his fresh jersey knit shirt.

His lips left hers reluctantly, coming back to sip again before he deftly took her hand and began to lead her inside. Her mind stopped spinning enough for her to pull up. She wouldn't be distracted again. Before he swept her up into the clouds again they needed to talk. He needed to know this was no run-of-the-mill holiday fling. She needed to lay her cards on the table and own up to who she was…or at least who she wasn't.

When she stopped, he stopped too, a frown tugging at his brows. Then he shook his head as if to clear it.

"I'm an idiot." He swooped her up into his arms. "I forgot your ankle. I'll carry you."

Nina fought the impulse to hold onto him. His no-argument brand of chivalry was intoxicating, but… "My ankle's *fine*."

He wasn't listening. Instead he moved with her towards the open cabin door.

He stepped over the threshold, and a sense of *déjà vu* filtered through her. Had so much time passed since that sudden rainstorm yesterday? They were here again, standing in the exact same spot, and he was just as imposing and commanding and delicious as ever.

But he wasn't heading for the bed. He was looking down at her with a mix of desire and depth and…

Trust?

She cleared the lump from her throat and took a breath. Now or never.

"Last night," she began, "you asked if I wanted to stay."

He nodded.

She blew out a breath. "Well, Gabriel—see, it's like this—"

"You want to go back to the resort, don't you?" His jaw tightened. "You're missing the spa tubs and silver service."

"God, *no.* That's not it at all."

His brows snapped together. "You don't like the resort?"

"If you really want to know…" She scrunched her nose and shook her head. *Not a bit.*

A pulse in his cheek started to tick and his jaw shifted to one side. "So what's wrong with it?"

Nina was taken aback. That stony look and tone… Suddenly he seemed so serious. About her dislike of the resort?

He'd said he'd taken this cabin to get away from it all. She'd believed him. But his questions and the intense glint in his eye didn't sit with his carefree "escape into the wilderness" story. Something didn't add up.

He wanted to know what was wrong with the resort? She quizzed him. "Maybe you should tell *me?*"

He blinked several times before his chin tucked in. "Why would I do that?"

"Because I'm getting the feeling you don't like Diamond Shores so much either."

His pupils dilated, swallowing the pale irises until his eyes appeared almost black. "I'm simply interested."

He crossed the room, sat her on the chair, but she stood straight back up.

His ears were pink with irritation, and there was a weird, distant look in his eye. She wasn't mistaken. There was far more to his questions than simple interest. Did he trust her enough to tell her what was wrong?

Maybe if she gave him a chance to thaw out?

She collected the bottle off the counter to make two strong coffees. But when she screwed the lid it wouldn't budge. She clamped the bottle under one arm and twisted hard. Stuck fast.

In the meantime, Gabriel had frowned over. "Are you staying on the island with friends?"

She sighed. *If only.*

She took a hesitant step nearer. He sounded so gruff. "Why do you want to know?"

"Because I need to know what people are saying. What they're *thinking.*"

When he thumped his fist against the wall she jumped. Then he growled under his breath, something about, "…hiding out here…playing Huck Finn… should be back there, making changes…"

With worry choking off her breath, she slowly brought the bottle close to her chest. "Gabriel…what are you talking about?"

Letting out a defeated breath, he sank into the chair.

"I bought this island a week ago," he ground out. "It's on the brink of bankruptcy, and I'm here to make sure everything and everyone who doesn't perform is eliminated." He lifted his chin. "Pronto."

The coffee bottle slipped from her hands, smashed, and shattered to pieces. As the crash ricocheted off the walls, Gabriel shot to his feet. The way Nina's face had paled, the way her hands clutched at her throat, she might have thrown a javelin that had missed his heart by an inch.

She stared blindly at the mess at her feet, then fixed her huge topaz-coloured eyes on his.

"I broke the bottle," she croaked out, and when her lashes blinked he thought he saw her eyes glisten.

This wasn't the reaction he'd expected. He hadn't wanted three cheers, but owning Diamond Shores wasn't chickenfeed. Or it wasn't to him. His announcement was at least worth a sentence or two of recognition. Still, God knew how much Nina's family was worth. Owning an island might well seem inconsequential to many of the guests who stayed here.

He ground his back teeth and ploughed a hand through his hair. It frustrated the hell out of him. Regardless of how far he'd come, there were still times when he felt like someone's poor relation.

Nina was concentrating on the mess on the floor, as if she couldn't get her mind around how to clean it up.

Rubbing the back of his neck, he moved forward. "Don't worry about that." There was more to worry about than an old broken bottle.

But she didn't seem to hear. Instead her hands covered her face. "Oh, God, what a mess."

He took her hands from her cheeks.

"It's okay," he said more gently. "I'll get someone in to clean it up." But she wound out of his hold, stooped and began to pick up the pieces. He hunkered down and eased the glass from her hand. "You don't need to do that." When she collected another piece, he held her wrist. "*Nina,* I'll get a maid in from the resort."

Biting her lip, she stood and spun away, her hands bracing the counter. "We should go. We should go *now.*"

He tugged an earlobe and groaned.

Okay. He had an idea what was wrong.

Stepping closer, he cupped her shoulders. "Don't be embarrassed. Yes, I own the island, but I'm glad you told me how unhappy you are with the resort."

When he'd arrived three days ago he'd introduced

himself to key people but had insisted that his true identity be kept from the rest of the staff. He wanted to experience April's wedding and the resort incognito. He'd also made it clear he needed to be informed of every suggestion for improvements and all complaints.

After he'd jogged to the resort this morning, to bring back some wheels, he'd dropped in to his bungalow and had been greeted by an avalanche of messages. Various managers wanted his ear. One guest had complained he'd been injured—the result of an incompetent ski-boat driver. A celebrity wedding had been cancelled; the bride had heard rumours regarding "off" seafood. The music at the nightclub wasn't exciting enough. The childminders weren't any fun.

And so it went on.

A meeting was scheduled for the day before he flew back to Sydney—Monday. He and the managers would crunch figures and implement a kick-butt game plan. But this morning he hadn't wanted to face the hassle. Face the possibility that this time he might have gone beyond his limits. He'd only wanted to get back to Nina and re-ignite the fires which had raged within these walls last night.

She affected him like a drug, and he wanted to enjoy that all-over high again and again. But he'd been an idiot, a coward, to buy into that distraction. His captivating lover also happened to be a guest at Diamond Shores—a guest who'd admitted in the plainest of terms how dissatisfied she was with the facilities. Talk about a wake-up call.

Every day, every *minute* counted towards getting this resort back on its feet.

He moved to collect the parcel bag he'd brought in. Nina was right. They needed to go.

"I put your clothes in to be laundered. I had one of the boutique managers—"

"Whose name did you use?"

To clean her clothes?

He frowned. "Mine."

Surely she wasn't concerned about a pair of cut-offs? Although second-hand-looking fashion could be sexy.

He retrieved a wrap and a one-piece from the bag.

So, too, was designer fashion.

From the bottom of the bag he handed over a pair of sunglasses. Her eyes rounded and a puff of wind left her lungs; he might have handed her a priceless jewel.

"I've seen these in the window. They're Bulgari." She pointed out the arms. "Those are real diamonds."

As if on autopilot, she slipped them on and moved to the window to check her reflection. He was feeling somewhat redeemed, thinking about how big a bonus to give that astute boutique manager, when Nina's shoulders came down and she lowered the shades.

She turned back with a sombre face. "I can't accept these."

He gave her a sidelong look. "You don't like them?"

"I *love* them."

"Then don't be modest."

Although he did admire that quality. Women he dated were often eager to hear about gifts—the more expensive the better. When they started talking diamond rings, he stopped calling. He'd had no time for that kind of commitment. He had less time now.

"It's not modesty." She joined him and handed the glasses back. "Not really."

His laugh was edgy. "Nina, you're confusing me."

She inhaled deeply, then her gaze lowered.

Why was she acting like this—avoiding eye contact, drawing away from him? It wasn't that she was overwhelmed by the fact he owned this place. The only other logical answer came to mind.

"I'm not trying to fob you off," he assured her. "These aren't payment or a pay-off for last night. I wanted us to spend the day here together."

He'd wanted her in that bed again tonight. And their time together didn't have to be over.

Why couldn't their connection continue back at the resort? He didn't know how long she was staying, but surely he would be able to wangle at least some quality time with her before he left on Monday.

His hands settled on her hips and he urged her close. "I have an idea. Move your things into my bungalow. You haven't been happy with Diamond Shores, but I'll do everything I can to fix that." His forehead tipped against hers and he grinned. "Our own private beach. The staff will treat you like a princess. There'll be hell to pay if they don't—"

"*No.*"

When she pulled away, the muscles in his gut wrenched. It was all he could do not to drag her back. Was it so important *where* they were?

Their kind of chemistry didn't rely on location. Even if important business was calling him away, they could still come together in the evening. After last night—the way she'd given herself so completely—Nina couldn't pretend she hadn't come to this island seeking a little one-on-one companionship. A fling hadn't figured on his agenda, but it had happened. No reason in the world that it couldn't continue a few more days yet.

But now she seemed determined to play hard to get.

"I want to go back." She lifted her eyes to meet his. "And I want to stay in my own room."

Her cool determination hit him in the chest. He bit down and did what he should have done sooner. He found her arm, brought her back, and held her firmly against him.

His gaze roamed her face as he spoke unforgivably near to her lips. "What about last night?"

He'd meant what he'd said. He'd never wanted to make love to anyone the way he'd wanted to make love to her. He hadn't been disappointed. She hadn't been either; he'd made sure of it. After her abandon, why the hard-to-get act now?

He held his breath.

Or had the act been last night?

Had this time away in the bush been nothing more than an adventure for a bored heiress?

She didn't answer his question. Rather the sparkle he loved to see in her eyes seemed to fade and die.

Gabriel's heart began to pound. He'd spoken to this woman about trust. About faith. And now, just like *that,* she wanted out?

She seemed about to say something more—something important. But then the resignation returned to her face and she put out her hand to accept the clothes. "I'll get changed and we can go."

He thought about her in those cut-offs…in his arms…in her prima-donna life away from here. He thought about how easily she was prepared to walk away, and a cold ball settled in the cradle of his stomach.

Setting his jaw, he handed over the clothes and, kicking himself for almost falling for a rich girl's games, stepped aside and let her pass.

CHAPTER SEVEN

NINA moved behind the curtain and changed into the stunning aqua one-piece and matching wrap Gabriel had brought back from the resort.

She ought to feel beautiful. Special. Instead she felt empty. She'd had such high hopes this morning about how this day would evolve, but in these last few minutes everything had soured.

Gabriel had knocked her for six with his admission that he owned this island. *Owned* it. She hadn't known Diamond Shores had changed hands since Alice had helped her get her job. In effect, Gabriel was her supreme boss; as well as the woman he wanted to sleep with, she was also one of the problems he needed to have removed. How on earth was she supposed to tell him that?

A few moments later they were tearing along the beach, the bike's engine roaring, the ocean waves crashing—and Gabriel's broad, obstinate back in her face. She was torn between needing to wean herself off the magnificent feel of him and desperately wanting to hold on tighter.

As they neared the tall blue side gates of the resort Gabriel changed down gears. When he skidded the bike to a stop, he averted his gaze while she alighted. Her feet on solid ground, she straightened the colourful wrap around her legs, and that empty feeling turned to flat-line hopelessness.

Gabriel Steele's mission here was to wipe out any rot. Given the many eyes and ears around Diamond Shores, her position wouldn't be a secret for long. Soon enough he'd hear about Nina Petrelle—her substandard performance, how the other staff disapproved of her breezy ticket in.

She didn't need to purge herself to him now. Tell him how she'd got to this place in her life. How she'd felt so displaced until he'd brought her back to life last night. He'd find out what he needed to know soon enough. Then it would only be a matter of time before she received her marching orders.

"Can you walk?" He dismounted the bike but kept his sunglasses in place. "I'll organise a motorised buggy if you're not sure of your ankle."

A sea breeze peeled through his dark hair, making it dance above the widow's peak, but his expression—or what she could see of it—remained unmoved. She hated his stiffness, that formal air. A few hours ago they'd talked and laughed and made the sweetest, and at other times wildest love. Now she had trouble imagining how the firm line of that mouth had pressed such tender affection upon her. The most beautiful time of her life was over.

"I'm fine to walk," she told him, determined to hold onto what remained of her dignity. "Thank you."

The mirrors of his glasses flashed in the sunlight as his head dipped a margin. "Can I make an appointment for our doctor to check out your leg and that bump on your head?"

"You've done enough."

Bittersweet longing ribboned around her heart. Yes, he'd done more than enough. He'd saved her life. She was standing here only because of this man's action and focus. That debt could never be repaid. If she felt gutted now, if she wished things could be different—that time could somehow rewind—she needed to remember she'd been given a second chance and go from there.

She headed off towards her quarters. Her vision had blurred and her heart was steadily sinking when that rich, deep voice came from behind her.

"Nina. Wait."

Her breath caught. After dashing a tear away, she spun back round. Sunglasses removed, he stood before her in those sexy jeans, his legs braced apart.

"I want you to have dinner with me tonight," he stated.

The unexpected thrill of having him follow her flashed brighter before it fizzled out. Dinner with Gabriel sounded like heaven, but any liaison was out of the question. When he found out who and *what* she was, he'd understand why.

"Gabriel, please—"

"I'm not taking no for an answer." He took both her hands in his, and the smile that made her melt sparkled up in his eyes. "You know it won't do any good to argue." When she squared her shoulders and stood her shaky ground, he shrugged. "I could always sweep you up and carry you off. It's worked before."

A laugh almost escaped.

From churlish to charming—and Gabriel's charming was so very hard to resist. But she had no choice. Now they were back at the resort, and their positions had changed so dramatically they couldn't go back to "last night."

She was working up another refusal when she spotted a woman in staff uniform gaping over at her: Tori Scribbins—Nina's roommate, and one of her few friends here. Tori's hand went theatrically to her heart and she pretended to faint. Nina's smile broke, and Gabriel's face slanted into her line of vision. With a precision movement he angled her, and next Nina knew she was shrieking with surprise, back in the cradle of those indomitable arms.

Her first instinct was to slap his shoulder, insist he let her down, but more powerful was the knowledge that he wasn't giving up on her. He never seemed to give up.

Maybe, just *maybe*...

Was it too stupid to hope again?

But she'd need to explain what was so difficult to put into words—how she'd come to be on this island, why she'd felt so lost—and she couldn't do that here. They needed privacy. She had a shift in the kitchen that ended at nine tonight. If she went to his bungalow after that...

He'd begun to stride off, but she pushed against his chest to pull him up.

"I'm busy till nine," she shot out.

His pace died while his crooked smile grew. "Which restaurant do you prefer?"

"Can we eat in? At your place?"

The sparkle in his eyes heated up. "It's a date."

Out the corner of her eye Nina spied Tori, leaning against the doorjamb of the room she must be cleaning; her jaw had dropped to the floor. She guessed this scene *would* look pretty remarkable...a strong, handsome, determined man whisking Nina the waitress away.

Tori was a true romantic. She'd be hearing wedding bells and planning honeymoons. Nina wouldn't presume to think that far ahead, but perhaps this rollercoaster Cinderella story might have some kind of happy ending after all.

Gabriel was saying, "Now I've got you, I might as well carry you to your room."

Her room was small and bare and in the staff quarters. No reason she couldn't get everything off her chest there—but no guarantee he would take the news well. Right or wrong, weak or strong, she wanted to hold onto hope as long as she could. Besides, she needed to get to her shift and he needed to get to work…

To his elimination plan.

"I don't want to be carried." But she smiled when she added, "And don't bother arguing this one. Put me down and I promise I'll see you after nine."

He studied her eyes, then reluctantly lowered her to her feet. He stole a lingering kiss from her cheek and murmured near her ear, "I'll have the champagne poured."

After she'd watched him stride away around a clump of pygmy date palms, Nina turned back to Tori, who was madly waving her over.

When Nina reached her roommate, Tori swept her into the suite and clapped the door shut.

Tori's coffee-coloured eyes were dancing with excitement. Her large watermelon wedge earrings swung as she clasped her hands under her chin and literally jumped up and down.

"When you didn't come in last night I didn't know what to think. I was going to call the alert if you weren't back by lunch. Now I understand why you went missing. My only question is…why are you back so soon? You should have called in a sickie."

Nine chewed her lip. She shouldn't blab. She didn't want to risk her secret leaking out before seeing Gabriel tonight. But she simply *had* to talk. She was bursting to spill about the first good thing to have happened to her in weeks.

They'd moved into the main room and now sat together on the massive semi-circular couch which faced a breathtaking view. The flutter in Nina's stomach beat faster as she told all about her fantastical evening—up to the point where her cliff-top angel had confessed his true identity as owner of the Diamond Shores Resort.

Tori slumped against the silk brocade cushions and held her cheeks. "Oh. My. Gosh. I'd have passed out. He *owns* the place? Everything?" Nina nodded and Tori tipped closer. "When are you going to see him again?"

"Tonight. After my shift."

"Are you going to tell him who you are before or after?"

"Before or after what?"

"He throws you down and ravages you, of course."

Nina's sucked down a breath. No use denying she wanted that to happen. A few minutes away from him seemed like an hour. An hour would seem like a week. By tonight she would be near ready to throw herself at him.

But she couldn't afford any more delays. The longer she kept her secret from Gabriel, the more chance he had of finding out the truth. It was better the news came from her.

"I'll tell him as soon as I get there."

They would either kiss, and the fun times would be on again, or he would not be amused and would refuse to contribute to delinquent behaviour as far as resort standards and reputation were concerned. Then again he *was* the boss. He could make *new* rules.

Sinking further into the couch, Tori draped her arms over her head and spoke to the rattan fan, circulating air around the vaulted wood beam ceiling. "I bet he kisses like a dream."

Nina recalled the sensation of Gabriel's lips covering hers…the way his mouth had coaxed her into sublime submission. "He kisses *better* than a dream."

He was drop-dead delectable. That body. That face. That creamy, dreamy voice.

"Maybe he has a brother you could introduce me to?" Tori pushed up and, sashaying over to her vacuum cleaner, gave her watermelon earring a sassy flick. "I could handle putting my duster out to pasture."

Nina was watching that earring swing. "You could get in trouble, wearing those." No jewellery was allowed other than studs and a watch. Mr Dorset, the general manager, was a stickler for dress code. Mr Dorset was a stickler for every rule.

Tori struck a pose oozing with attitude. "You're playing 'to the manner born' and *I* might get in trouble?"

The joke was that Nina *was* to the manner born. She hadn't appreciated the privileges she'd enjoyed growing up. She hadn't missed them when she'd had a well-paid job. Her life had seemed full. She'd been good at what she'd done. Her colleagues had respected her and vice versa.

Tori was deep in thought, fingering that earring. "If you ask me, management need to loosen up. *Don't be overly friendly with the guests,*" she sing-songed. *"Don't cough in public or we'll dock your pay."*

"You wouldn't be docked for coughing." Unless it was excessive.

Adjusting the vacuum head, Tori sent her a dry look. "This place needs a darn good shake-up. And you can tell your rich boyfriend that from me."

"He's not my boyfriend."

"Then what are you waiting for?" Tori stepped on the power, the vacuum roared to life, and she swung her hips in a hoola circle. "Work it, baby."

Promising to give Tori an update, either tomorrow or later that night, depending on how things went, Nina headed off to change. But she was preoccupied with hoping things would go well, buoyed by fond thoughts of her previous job back in Sydney. She'd belonged at *Shimmer* magazine in a way she would never belong here. One thing was certain. She needed to feel that sense of belonging again.

While dragging her uniform out from the single-door wardrobe, the phone extension caught Nina's eye. She'd asked the receptionist at *Shimmer* to keep her ear to the ground; sometimes management cut too many corners and people were needed back to fill the gaps. So why not take the initiative and call?

A moment later a voice Nina didn't recognise answered the connection in Sydney, and Nina cleared her throat. "Hello. Would Abbey King be there?"

"Abbey left last week. Can anyone else help?"

Nina's stomach bottomed out. Abbey was gone too? "Uh, I'm not sure who's there any more."

"May I ask who's speaking?"

"Nina Petrelle."

"And you're enquiring about…?"

"I used to work there."

The receptionist's tone changed, became low and flat. "*Shimmer* have no vacancies at this time."

Nina's hand fisted around the receiver as suffocating heat crept up her neck.

I was in charge of Features, she wanted to say. *I used to buy a latte with extra sprinkles every morning before work. I used to sit around the boardroom and discuss*

*upcoming stories and strategies with my colleagues. I
was part of that office, dammit!*

The receptionist's voice infiltrated the red haze.
"Hello? Were you calling about a job?"

Nina set her teeth. "I already *have* a job."

She slammed the receiver down.

Don't cry. Don't you dare cry.

If she started she might not be able to stop, because
that same draining question was whispering again in her
mind...

Who are you? Where will you end up?

She knew she would survive. It was just a matter of
staying strong.

But if Gabriel threw her out tonight she didn't know
what she'd do.

With a spring in his step, Gabriel headed down the
wide slate path, which was lined by a jungle of lush
tropical garden. Unwilling to admit defeat, he'd made
a no-holds-barred play to see Nina again and she'd acquiesced. He wasn't prepared to throw in the towel
without at least writing a closing chapter to their beach-
side affair.

When he'd told her that he owned this island resort
initially he'd thought she was embarrassed. Then he'd
thought she was being a princess, and then he'd surmised
that he'd merely lost his appeal. But when she'd walked
away, resigned yet also somehow brave, he'd known
something more lay behind her change in attitude.

He remembered their conversation the previous
night...the way she'd opened up.

What had knocked the wind out of her? he wondered. She'd said she wanted to know who she was.
He'd blamed her general dislike of the resort on service

and facilities, but after seeing how bereft she'd looked before he'd called her back, he knew it went deeper than that. The obstacle, the crisis bringing her down, was waiting for her here.

Something dug into his hip. He reached and pulled a shell from his pocket. Before leaving this morning he'd found it on the bathroom shelf. Knowing Nina must have left it there, on impulse he'd taken it with him. He focused on the shell's decorative rays and remembered Nina's incredible smile.

He held the shell tighter.

He wouldn't rest until A: he found out all of Nina's story, and B: he fixed whatever was wrong. If she needed an ally, no matter how busy he got here, he'd be it.

"Excuse me, Mr Steele?"

Gabe wheeled around. Horace Dorset, General Manager of Diamond Shores Resort, was striding up the path. Dorset, with a lemon rosebud adorning his lapel, gave him a pleasant, enquiring look. "Everything well with you, sir?"

"I received your message," said Gabe. Dorset wanted to speak with him about standardising staff prerequisites. Good plan, but not now. "I'll get back to you tomorrow."

Dorset nodded, but didn't bow off. "I see you've introduced yourself to some of the staff."

Gabriel cast his mind back. "No. Only the managers."

"The young lady…?"

Young lady? He meant Nina?

Gabriel laughed. "You're mistaken. Nina's a guest." Dorset's brows slanted, then he shook his head. "You're confusing her with someone else,' Gabriel pointed out. Although he wasn't sure how anyone could mistake an air that confirmed an impeccable upbringing…the way she held herself…the way she spoke.

Dorset thought she was staff? Absurd.

And yet Dorset kept looking at him with something like pity pinching his brows.

Gabriel thought more, then waved an impatient arm towards the hotel. "I saw her go into her room, for God's sake."

"Not *her* room, Mr Steele. A housekeeping trolley was outside. Perhaps Nina entered to help another staff member clean."

Gabriel probed Dorset's cool gaze. If Dorset thought this was funny, he wasn't laughing. "What the hell are you talking about?"

"The woman you saw is a waitress. Nina Petrelle started with Diamond Shores six weeks ago." Dorset's shoulders rolled back. "We like to pride ourselves on our standards, and I'm afraid Nina has made one too many errors. I've been patient so far, but this episode, withholding her identity from a guest—from *you*, Mr Steele—is an infringement that cannot be ignored. Measures must be taken."

Gabriel's mind felt frozen. He opened his palm and glared at the shell. Had he heard her name right?

"The staff are well aware of our number one rule," Dorset continued. "No fraternising with guests. I want you to know I'm very strict on that. It can be tempting for a single young woman to covet what others here enjoy—"

Gabriel shot up a hand. He was interested in only one thing. "What did you say her name was?"

"Nina."

"Last name?"

"Petrelle."

Nina Petrelle. Anthony Petrelle's baby sister?

A thousand memories flashed through his mind—playing touch in the Petrelles' enormous manicured backyard...surfing at Bondi that last summer... Anthony's sister, that right little madam, sticking it to him every chance she got. If she wasn't jeering at his favourite shoes, she was niggling about his numerous after-school jobs, or insisting he should do them all a favour and buy a new pair of glasses.

She'd been the kind of over-indulged kid who had a tantrum if no one noticed the new designer ribbon in her silky blonde hair. Nina Petrelle had been *the* poster girl for spoilt rotten. But for the sake of his friendship with Anthony, who'd been as down to earth as the next bloke, he'd kept his mouth shut.

Gabriel shook his brain and came back to the present.

How the tables had turned. When he'd known Nina last his surname had been Turner, his mother's name. But if Nina didn't recognise him, he sure as hell hadn't recognised her. For one, she was twice the size—and in all the right places. Her hair was six shades darker too.

He remembered her body writhing beneath him in the firelight last night and his insides twisted.

He'd made love to Nina Petrelle?

Dorset's voice cut into his thoughts. "Mr Steele, I apologise for her behaviour. Gold-digging will not be tolerated here. I'll go speak with her now."

As Dorset moved off, Gabriel gripped the older man's forearm. His tone was close to dangerous. "I don't want you to say or do a thing with regard to Miss Petrelle."

"I—I beg your pardon—?"

"You heard me." He released Dorset's arm. "I'll handle this."

Dorset opened his mouth to protest, but when Gabriel glowered Dorset nodded, although clearly unhappy with the decision. "As you wish."

Gabriel continued on to his accommodation, the shell tucked inside one clenched hand. He felt as if his chest had been rammed by a tree trunk.

Yes, when she'd told him her name he'd thought twice, but she looked nothing like the squirt who'd hung around and annoyed the crap out of him all those years ago. What was she doing working here? Her family was loaded.

Perhaps they'd had a falling out? She obviously needed money—badly enough to hunt down and snare herself a millionaire. Although her near drowning must have been an accident; no one would risk their life that way. But clearly she'd taken advantage of the situation from there, playing him with a combination of coy and sassy to see which stoked his fires best.

Let someone have faith in you again, she'd said. Hell, he'd really thought she'd cared.

He kicked open his front door.

What a schmuck!

As he stood in the foyer of his bungalow, another thought sprang to mind.

Nina knew he owned this island, but she didn't know who he was—or rather who he'd been: Gabe Turner, her brother's egghead friend, the "pauper" she'd lived to humiliate. The guy who'd kept his lip buttoned while she tried to put him in his place.

Gabriel's smile was more a sneer.

He couldn't wait to see her face when she found out. But a greater challenge awaited her. Not only was

Nina a down-on-her-luck gold-digger, according to Dorset she was no good at her job. How on earth had she got a position here in the first place?

But the bigger question was…

He dropped the shell and ground it beneath his heel. *How soon could he get rid of her?*

CHAPTER EIGHT

AFTER her shift in the kitchen, Nina showered, slipped into a light summer dress, and made her way to Gabriel Steele's ultra-private bungalow. Her throat was tight with nerves and her stomach was riding a rollercoaster by the time she dropped the knocker on the imposing double doors. After several moments, when no one answered, she dared to turn the handle and ease inside.

Towering potted palms, mirror-polished marble counters, exquisitely crafted teak furniture, fresh sprays of exotic flowers... Surrounded by such luxury, in "guest" versus "employee" mode, she felt the dizzy scent of excess fill her head.

Spending last night with Gabriel in that cabin had been like a beautiful elixir, a once-in-a-lifetime experience which would live for ever in her mind and her heart. Being here in this setting, about to be with Gabriel again, was possibly an even headier thrill. After spending hours packing dishwashers, the sight of that cushiony white couch was almost enough to convince her that indulgence—this kind of over-the-top lavish extravagance—wasn't so offensive after all. She would love to lie back on the couch and put her feet up.

Massaging the weary small of her spine, she did

another sweep of the main room. Gabriel wasn't here. Limping slightly, she edged towards the opened concertina doors.

The full moon spilled a shimmering river of gold across an otherwise black sea. The scent of salt and natural floral perfumes filled the warm air, and on the deck Gabriel stood with a phone pressed to his ear. He wore dark tailored trousers and a crisp white Oxford shirt. His sleeves were rolled to below the elbow, leaving tanned corded forearms exposed. His dark hair was freshly showered, wet and stylishly messy.

The overall picture—complete with a vee of wiry hair visible at his throat and broad shoulders adorned in silk weave—was enough for Nina to clutch at her fast-beating heart. She hadn't thought he could be more attractive than when she'd first seen him—muscles pumped and bare chest battle-whipped.

She'd been wrong.

Without trying, he dominated any scene.

Angling around, Gabriel spotted her. He nodded twice into the phone, gave a parting remark, then disconnected and moved towards her.

"Important call?" she asked, when she might easily have said, *The sight of you turns my legs to jelly.*

"My second in charge," he said, sauntering nearer. "Zane Rutley knows as much about my company as I do, but he likes to keep me up to date. Says there's no rest for the wicked."

"You've known him long?"

"Since university. We duxed Management Accounting and Strategy."

"Ooh, bad boys."

He grinned. "I can't speak for Zane."

She didn't know about Zane Rutley either, but

Gabriel Steele could make any woman melt at a hundred paces. His every move was measured, exact, and at the same time effected with inherent masculine grace. Her cheeks heated. Although he hadn't touched her yet, she was already simmering inside.

When he stopped before her, she expected his mouth to break into his trademark sexy-as-sin smile. She expected him to sweep her up and kiss her as he'd kissed her through the magical hours of last night. But his lopsided grin remained fixed, and the gleam in his eye seemed somehow...cool.

She felt a little off balance when his fingers curled around her arm and his freshly shaved cheek rubbed lightly against hers.

His lips brushed her temple. "How was your afternoon?"

"Busy." Her ankle throbbed to punctuate the point.

He drew away and assessed her butter-yellow dress, his gaze deliberately trailing her shape in a vaguely predatory fashion before he ushered her, a hand on her elbow, towards the outdoor setting.

He indicated an ice bucket. "Champagne?"

"You said you'd have it poured," she teased.

"Nothing worse than when bubbles go flat."

He popped the cork, and foam spilled over the rim to darken the timber near his feet. To take her mind off his intoxicating sandalwood scent, she inspected the champagne label.

"My father used to keep a couple of bottles of that for special occasions."

"It's a rare vintage." He handed her a glass. "Is your father here with you on the island?"

The breath went out of her. "He died a few years ago."

His gaze jumped up from his pouring of a second glass. His searching eyes clouded and his voice dropped. "Nina...I'm sorry."

She sighed quietly. Gabriel could be so strong, yet there were times, like now, he could be so sensitive. As if he truly knew her. Knew her like no one else could.

But then he cleared his throat, raised his glass to his lips, and the deeper moment was gone.

"I bumped into someone this afternoon." He sipped, swallowed. "He told me the most fascinating story."

He was watching her over the rim of his glass and the glint in his eyes now seemed almost steely. She'd seen a few sides to Gabriel—uncompromising hero, charmer, believer, lover. When they'd left the cabin this morning he'd been cagey. But the vibes she caught now didn't fit with any of that.

That pointed gleam in his gaze was enough to make her shiver. Who was the "someone" he'd spoken with?

She sipped champagne without tasting it and when he didn't divulge more she asked, "What did this man say?"

A humourless smile tugged one side of his mouth. "I thought you might like to tell me."

Her breath died in her chest. She closed her eyes as her stomach rolled over twice, then sank to her knees. Her throat convulsed and she swallowed.

"You know."

His chin went up. "I know."

She'd been caught out before she'd had the chance to come clean. Someone had let on that she was an employee of the island and, given the hard line of his jaw, Gabriel wasn't pleased.

She managed to keep her voice steady. "Gabriel, let me explain—"

"I will. But first…"

His palm scooped behind her neck and his mouth opened over hers. The lip-to-lip contact sent jets of recognition shooting through her veins. Every cell in her body seemed to tremble, light up and press in. The renewed awareness was so strong, so vital, it was all she could do to remember that…

That this kiss was different.

Rougher.

Dominating.

When their lips parted, her world had slanted and the room seemed to spin. A pulse beat wildly in his cheek, and if he released her there was every possibility she might slide to the floor. As if reading her thoughts, he dragged out a chair. Numbness taking over, she fell into the seat.

"I took the liberty of ordering," he told her, gesturing to the silver domes set on the table while her mind whirled on. He lifted one dome and the aroma of lobster mornay, scalloped potatoes and buttered asparagus filled her lungs.

He folded into the adjacent slat-backed chair.

"Before you tell your story, Nina, I thought you might like to know more about mine." He removed his dome, then his napkin flicked out with a *snap*. "I became aware that Diamond Shores' previous owner was interested in a buy-out when I paid for April's wedding and reception. She has no family. After her dedication to her job these past five years, that gift was the least I could do." He nodded amicably at her plate. "Eat before it gets cold."

Her limbs were fifty-pound weights. Her lips and tongue were rubber.

"I…I'm not very hungry."

He collected his cutlery and continued his thread.

"You know the resort is running at a loss," he said, in a monotone that still managed to send heatwaves shimmering over her skin. "The hand-over was low-key. Making my presence known here only to the managers was a strategic decision. It's difficult to get an accurate idea of performance when fanfares announce your every move. I needed a clear indication of which heads should roll."

His gaze, holding hers, was both ablaze and cold as a snowstorm. An arctic chill chased up her spine. She couldn't bear the stomach knots a moment longer.

"I was features editor for a teen magazine," she got out, clenching the napkin beside her plate. "I was retrenched along with others. I needed a job, but there was nothing available in publishing. It was all I knew."

All she was.

"That was your crisis?" he surmised, and she nodded. His napkin patted one corner of his mouth. "How did you get a job here?"

"A friend's father knew the owner. The former owner." Or so it seemed.

"You had no experience?"

"Next to none."

His short laugh was abrasive. "No wonder the place is sinking."

She set her teeth, but continued, "Alice said the hours would be long but the money was good. I could make my mortgage repayments." Blindly studying her plate, she leaned back. "I didn't want to lose my house."

When she levelled her gaze at him, something almost human flashed across his face. But then he took a mouthful of champagne and placed the glass down heavily.

"And yesterday?"

"Was my first afternoon off in what seemed like for ever," she said. "I was physically and emotionally drained. Most of the staff don't like me, you see. And it's true I have a lot to learn. They have every right to feel undervalued. That doesn't help the way I feel." Lonely. Very nearly hopeless. "Yesterday I wanted to get as far away from the resort as I could. I started walking, collecting shells to send to my baby nephew back in Sydney."

"Nephew?"

"My sister's baby. Codie's six months old. Jill's a single mum. She deferred her Masters in Biology to look after him for the first couple of years and—" She stopped, sighed. "You're really not interested in any of that, are you?"

Gabriel held his impassive face. She was a consummate manipulator, trying to find his vulnerable spot even now. Years had passed, but nothing had changed. Nina was used to getting what she wanted, and it seemed she wanted his sympathy. Wanted him to bail her out.

This afternoon, when he'd uncovered her game, his chest had filled with rage. Having known the princess fourteen-year-old Nina Petrelle had been, he'd easily joined the dots. He had no idea where the Petrelle fortune had gone, but the woman sitting across from him, trying to tug at his heartstrings, needed money badly enough to don an apron. She'd lucked out when he'd come bounding along yesterday to save her. She'd played her cards well and he'd fallen for her.

To a degree.

He didn't like to be deceived. He'd envisaged sacking her on the spot, throwing her out of her lodgings. He'd imagined the crocodile tears, her pleas, those attempts to use her *femme fatale* skills to get her way. In hindsight he believed only one thing she'd said.

She wanted to find herself—aka needed to have, to hold, real money again.

His money.

His lips stretched over his teeth.

Time for Act II.

"You might recall I said I'd known a Nina once." He collected his cutlery again and cut into firm asparagus. "Tell me, have you ever known anyone else called Gabriel?"

His comment pulled Nina up. Her nape prickled with a different kind of awareness as she nodded. "A friend of my brother's. Gabe Turner."

"What else do you remember?"

"He was a stuffed-shirt geek who my brother, for some reason, adored." That horrid gnawing in her gut deepened. She studied the man sitting opposite and instinctively sat back. "Why do you want to know?"

His ice-blue gaze held hers for an endless moment before he announced, "Because that Gabe is this Gabe. Gabriel Turner is me."

Nina wanted to throw back her head and laugh. She'd never heard anything so ridiculous. Instead she paused to consider the statement more deeply.

"No," she groaned, slowly shaking her head. "You said…your name is *Steele*."

But from the start hadn't there been a distant whisper of this? Seeing him standing on that cliff a second before she'd passed out…even then he'd seemed somehow familiar. This man—the man she'd shared a bed with—he couldn't possibly be that stiff, zero taste, no personality dweeb she remembered from all those years ago.

Could he?

"Turner was my mother's name," he said. "My aunt's name. When I made amends with my father in my late teens, I took his name. Steele."

She snapped shut her hanging jaw. "But those ugly sun-sensitive glasses?"

"Laser surgery."

"Your hair?"

"Comb-overs were never in."

"You look...taller."

"I grew."

"You're *rich*."

He grinned. "Yes, I am."

She studied his face again, and every molecule of oxygen seeped from her lungs.

Oh, God. It was true.

Her fingers started to tingle and her heart began to pound. She needed a paper bag before she hyperventilated and passed out.

"Faith, my aunt, passed away five years ago from a stroke," he said, colouring in the rest. "My father died from a coronary not long after we met."

Her vision clouded and tunnelled in. Aunt Faith... yes, she remembered. His story fitted, but her brain was too overloaded to offer condolences.

As a thousand memories rained down in a battering gale, she peered into Gabe's hard gaze and somehow managed to set her priorities straight. Not having seen her for well over a decade, Gabe Turner had shown up out of the blue and saved her life?

It was magical thinking, but she wondered whether her brother had had a hand in his buddy being in the right place at the right time. Anthony had always looked out for her in a cool, big-brother kind of way. She only wished someone had been there to look out for him when he'd needed it.

Her brow tingled.

Last night Gabriel had said he'd lost someone close. Someone who'd had faith in him when he'd had little in himself. Anthony.

An image dawned—a clear snapshot of her brother's face—and despite the situation Nina's mouth twitched. The image zoomed in to show Anthony's confounded expression and a smile twitched again.

Gabriel pushed his plate aside. "You think this is funny?"

"Can you imagine what Anthony would say if he knew? He'd be thinking what a huge joke this was on us both. Gabe Turner hated me, I hated Gabe Turner more, and Anthony...well, he loved us both."

She'd hated the way Gabe Turner had ignored her. Hated those revolting glasses. Hated the fact that his clothes were dull from too many washes and yet he still filled out trousers better than any boy she'd known. Worse, while he'd struggled to afford new socks, he'd always held his head so high. As if he was better than everyone else. Certainly better than her.

Now Gabe Turner was a wealthy man of the world. A gorgeous multimillionaire with whom she'd made love until both were so spent neither could draw another breath.

Her stomach double-flipped.

Her and Geeky Gabe. How totally weird was that?

She must have been staring at him because he pulled in his chin. "What?"

"Don't you want to know?"

"Know what?"

"Why, when my family was so wealthy, I'm wait-ressing now."

His gaze skimmed her lips, his jaw flexed, then he crossed his arms over that big delectable chest. "That question had crossed my mind."

She was happy to answer. There happened to be a question he might be able to answer for her in return.

"Anthony's death really shook my parents up," she told him. "Me and Jill too, but we were young enough not to understand the full weight of the situation. That Anthony really wasn't coming home and our lives would never be the same. He'd been the jewel in the crown of our family. Everyone loved Anthony. For a long time no one could accept he was gone."

Gabriel's arms slowly unravelled. "It was a tragic accident."

"He loved speed and the idea of taking chances, pushing the limits." Anthony had skinned his elbows and knees more than once shooting the bowl on his skateboard. "He said he was either going into the air force or to work for National Security as a secret agent."

A distant smile shone in Gabriel's eyes. "He'd have done it too. He had the smarts as well as the guts."

The question burned on the tip of her tongue. She'd wanted to know for such a long time, only she hadn't thought anyone would know—not even her father, who'd loved Anthony better than anyone. But Gabe and her brother had been so close.

"Anthony must have known he couldn't possibly do it," she murmured. "Not in the dead of night. The fact that the place was cursed would've been enough to keep *me* away." She cast Gabriel—Gabe—an imploring look over the candlelit table. "Did he talk to you about going there?"

Maintaining a thousand-yard stare past her shoulder, he slanted his head and finally nodded.

Nina's attention picked up, but rather than sharing, Gabriel only thinned the line of his mouth.

"We knew it was some kind of a dare," she prodded. "I heard my parents talking about Roger someone."

"Roger Maxwell."

"That's it. He dared Anthony to scale the north face of Mount Spectre near your school. It had something to do with a girl Anthony liked."

"Roger started ribbing Anthony in front of her," said Gabe, in a low, gravelled tone. "Saying he was a wimp, a chicken, which was the most idiotic thing I'd ever heard. When Anthony laughed it off and went to walk away Roger challenged him. It was only because Roger liked this girl too, and Anthony knew it. Anthony laughed again—until the girl asked whether he was afraid of the curse."

Nina remembered. "A jilted lover was supposed to have jumped to his death there a hundred years ago. He became a ghost who guarded the peak and gave anyone who climbed such a fright that they'd rather fall to their death than face him."

"Anthony wanted a trial run up the cliffside first," he said. "Without Roger and the others looking on."

"I can't believe he risked his life to impress a girl."

"He wanted me to come along."

What? She sat forward. "You were there? My parents didn't ever tell me."

His jaw clenched. "I told him the only way I'd go was if I could manage to catch him when he fell. I knew he could be stubborn, but I didn't think he'd try it. I was so angry with him." He blinked and his voice deepened. "Angrier with myself."

She knew how Gabriel felt…somehow responsible… wanting to rework history. She'd wanted to be there for

Anthony too, to convince him not to be so foolish, and all for the sake of a bet. But no amount of wishing or blame would bring her brother back.

"He made the decision to climb that rock," she assured Gabriel now. "No one else."

His eyes burned into space. "I was his best friend. I should've talked him out of it. Or physically held him back."

The way he'd physically held *her* back yesterday, when he'd dragged her out of the surf and she'd refused to listen to sound advice? She'd thought at the time he was being bossy, but he'd only had her best interests at heart when he'd made sure she'd lain still in case of concussion. All those years ago when she'd hated him—or thought she had—she'd recognised that strength in him too.

Natural. Unswerving.

In her mind she saw Gabriel standing on the very edge of that cliff, the wind gusting through his hair and opened shirt, as if he was daring the gods to force him off. Her gaze roamed the lines of his face and understanding crept in. Now she knew who he was, how their pasts were connected, it seemed obvious.

"You were thinking about my brother yesterday, weren't you?"

One dark eyebrow arched and he leant back. "I didn't set out to climb to the island's highest point. Heights and I don't mix well. I'd had a quiet, uneventful bushwalk in mind, to clear my mind before heading back to the cabin." His gaze dropped and he reached for his glass. "Then you happened along."

She fought the urge to reach over and touch his hand. "Anthony would've been so proud if he'd seen you dashing to my rescue."

His eyes snapped up, but then a shadow of a smile

hovered at the corners of his mouth. His gaze held hers, and as the moment wound down the space between them seemed to thrum with a different, deeper meaning.

But then he sucked back a breath and shoved to his feet. Glaring at the dark rolling sea, he drove a hand through his hair, then set his fists low on his hips. "None of that makes any difference."

"Any difference to what?"

He faced her. "Nina, you can't stay."

Air seeped from her lungs. The present and its challenges rose up again and she slumped.

"You're sacking me." Not a question. Rather a flat-line statement.

What had she expected? A reunion with balloons and a rendition of "Auld Lang Syne"? Bottom line: no matter what vow she'd made to improve, she was a less than competent waitress, and those who didn't perform must be eliminated.

Regardless of the way they'd made love last night, this evening it was *Goodbye, Nina.*

Gabriel turned back to face the ocean, wringing his hands on the rail.

He'd had the scenario worked out. Announce that he knew her identity, then slap her with the final slam-dunk details of his own. Nina had deceived him. Dorset must have thought him a fool to fall for her act. No one manipulated him the way she had and got away with it—particularly when *this* Nina was the obnoxious teen who years ago had rattled his cage any chance she'd got.

And yet—

Dropping his chin, Gabriel clenched the rail and let out a quiet groan.

After speaking about Anthony, he could practically hear his best mate demanding he do something to help his little sister, and do it now. No matter how much he might want to, he couldn't and wouldn't ignore it. Anthony had been too good a friend. God knew why he'd befriended him, the geek, but Gabriel would never forget it.

But throwing money at Nina didn't seem right. He'd never taken charity; Anthony wouldn't have wanted hand-outs either. If Nina was hoping for a signed blank cheque—sorry, not happening.

Keeping her on here was out of the question too. Turning this place around depended on sticking to the narrow but profitable road. Not even Anthony's memory could influence him to jeopardise that success.

There was only one solution. For Anthony's sake— for the sake of what he and Nina had shared last night— he would help find her more suitable employment. Somewhere she could shine, find herself again. And if she gave him any cheek about it…

His mind made up, he angled back. "I have contacts in the industry."

She dragged her gaze from her untouched plate. "What industry?"

"Publishing. I'll set up an interview or two in Sydney."

Her eyes widened and she pushed to her feet. Her mouth worked soundlessly before she breathed out, "You'd do that for me?"

She could be near her sister and nephew, earn decent money. Keep her home. All she had to do was take a job which would be created after he pulled a few strings and stay the hell out of his life. His head—his pride— had been messed with enough.

But she was sighing and shaking her head. "I'm sorry. I can't let you do that."

His temper spiked. "Why the hell not?"

"I can't accept a job I haven't won on my own merit."

Well, she'd done it before, to get her job here. And sleeping with a rich stranger to get a leg up apparently wasn't taboo either.

He leaned back against the rail and slid his hands into his trouser pockets. "Off nepotism? That's very noble."

"Not noble. I've learned my lesson. Next time I move on, it'll be to something I've earned."

His eyes narrowed on hers. She was playing him again, and, *damn*, she was good at it.

"Let me put it this way," he said. "You need a job, a job that you know, and I insist on helping you make that happen."

Her lips pressed together. "No."

He withdrew his hands from his pockets. "Not even if it'll get you back home to your family? I thought you wanted to rediscover yourself—you can't do that here."

"You're right. I can't. Not completely. But I have to believe that my reputation and credentials will get me the right job at the right time. I don't know that I'd ever be able to gain the respect of the staff here. I won't make that mistake twice. I won't jump the queue and take on something I don't deserve."

He stopped less than an arm's length away, and instantly the space between them crackled with heat. Despite their disagreeable past, and the battlefield they occupied now, the grooves in his mind slotted back into blistering memories of last night and the undeniable force that clawed at him whenever she was near.

He set his jaw. Got a grip. Slapped that mental wall back up.

"Nina, you can't continue to work here."

Her slim nostrils flared before she slowly nodded. "I understand. I do." She glanced over their cold meals. "If it's all the same with you, I won't stay for dessert."

She turned, and even as his throat and chest burned he noticed her limp as she walked through into the main room.

And don't bother with the lame act to get sympathy either, he wanted to call after her. He wasn't that much of a sucker.

But when the limp seemed to get worse, the further she walked, Gabriel scrubbed his jaw.

Working all afternoon and half the night, she must have been on her feet the whole time. From Mr Dorset's account, Nina would know she didn't have another card up her sleeve; she couldn't call in sick or beg off early. Had the doctor even checked her out? Gabriel would bet not.

He dragged his hand down his face, tried to come up with another way. Then, cursing under his breath, he strode off to catch her up. This woman would drive him *nuts.*

"For God's sake, Nina, come back and sit down."

The way she was going she'd only cause herself more harm.

When she kept walking Anthony's shadow breathed down Gabriel's neck, and the voice in his head—over his shoulder—grew louder.

Stop her. Make her listen. She's hurt. She's my sister and she needs your help!

Gabriel put some steel in his voice. *"Nina."*

"I'm going."

"Going where?"

She angled back. "I'm looking forward to finding out."

She was so stubborn. So annoying, and so...amazingly attractive. As her eyes glistened into his, his heartbeat boomed in his ears and he knew to his soul what had to be done.

The pull—this fierce physical attraction—was too strong to ignore. No matter how many times she walked away, he would have to bring her back because what he'd tried to block from his mind all the long day *would* happen. He knew it as well as he knew his own name. They *would* make love again and she'd better prepare herself.

The way he was feeling, last night had only been practice.

CHAPTER NINE

GABRIEL strode over and drew her body hard against his. As his mouth came crashing down upon hers, Nina braced herself not to weaken.

In a way, she'd expected this. This man's middle name might be "irresistible," but after that discussion she would rather jump from a plane without a parachute than confirm the terrible, wonderful heat his kiss stirred deep inside her.

He wanted her gone. No problem.

She was going.

Go...ing...

After several breathtaking, ultra-persuasive moments, the kiss softly broke and Gabriel's hot-lidded gaze brushed over her face. His fingertips traced hair from her brow and he murmured, "Are you listening now?"

She swallowed, but held her chin high. "No."

He kissed her again, and those defences crumbled more. Her head told her to pull back, to slap his face; who did he think he was, assaulting her like this? Her body, on the other hand, whispered to her heart to press in more.

His kisses only got better.

When his lips left hers a second time, her breathing was tellingly deep. A practised hand skimmed her side before he took a lingering kiss from her temple, her cheek. To stop herself from snaking her arms around his neck, she fisted his shirt in her hands.

Feeling giddy, she groaned, "What do you want from me?"

He cupped her chin. "You have to ask?"

She closed her eyes and prayed. She had to clear her foggy brain. Had to keep smart. Keep strong.

"You're Gabe Turner," she reminded herself. "You *sacked* me." Her eyes opened. "If you think I'll sleep with you again, you've got rocks in your head."

He scooped her up into his arms and began to walk.

She managed to straighten to a board as her stomach pitched. "I'll scream."

His mouth hooked into the sexiest of smiles. "Promise?"

As he carried her into his bedroom, Nina told herself she should struggle and demand he set her down. She had to put this rabid sexual thirst away. Lock the door and throw away the double-edged key. Because, while this might seem a natural extension of their previous smouldering night together, tomorrow she would pay the price.

She'd already lost her job. She didn't want to lose her self-respect too.

But by the time he stopped in the middle of the shadowy bedroom, and she gazed up into those haunting ice-blue eyes, her arguments had wound down to nought. Rather than warnings she heard only a sweet chorus, urging her to go forward. It was as if history were already written. The deed was already done. Right or wrong, she would go through with this. The reason was simple.

There'd never be another Gabriel. One more time with him would be more than a lifetime with anyone else.

As if he read her thoughts, the lines either side of his eyes crinkled with a soft smile. He crossed the room and set her carefully down beside the bed. Then he flicked down the quilt and stood back, running an eye over her dress, as if approving of the design but also analysing the most effective way to remove it.

Stepping close again, he gripped the hem and the dress slid like butter up over her hips, her waist, her head, finally her arms. While she trembled inside from crown to toe, his hot gaze consumed her. She felt every stroke of his appraisal as it sizzled over her strapless bra, lower, to her abdomen then across her red silk briefs.

His gaze jumped and held hers again while he peeled the shirt off his back and dropped it to the timber floor. With the broad expanse of his chest rising and falling, he pulled her up against his hard heat and, after murmuring that he'd wanted her all day, claimed her mouth with his again.

She'd expected his kiss to ignite her as it had last night, to take over her senses and leave her deliciously weak and desperately wanting. She'd expected the same fireworks to leap up, lighting her blood until flames devoured any lingering whim to resist.

She was surprised.

When they'd lain together last night she'd never felt more alive, more grateful for each breath, and for the man who'd made another day possible. Tonight his kiss went beyond that. This heady emotion wasn't about outside influence or circumstance. It was about them... how well they meshed...how amazingly well they fitted. As his head angled more, and he kissed her thoroughly, her soul floated away and joined his, twining and spiralling off into blessed infinity.

Nina coiled her arms around his neck, unable to imagine anyone feeling as much as she felt at that moment. The desire was both an all-consuming necessity and a magnificent release that remade her, as light as the moonbeams slanting in through the open plantation blinds. No one could ever have felt this deeply before this.

Before them.

His mouth gradually broke from hers to trail down the side of her throat. She arched her neck, allowing him better access, and sighed when he snapped open her bra. As the bra dropped between them, his mouth slid along her collarbone and, one palm supporting her weight, he lowered her back upon the sheets.

He unzipped his trousers and not soon enough stood before her naked. She shouldn't stare. She'd seen him *sans* clothes before. The straight stance, lean hips, hard bronzed frame that tapered into a perfect V. This sight proved yet again that he was no ordinary man. He was so much more than that.

He rested one knee on the bed and, with his hands either side of her shoulders, asked, "You okay? Your ankle?"

Relishing the abandon, she dragged him down. "I'm not thinking about my foot."

While she battled to keep her heart behind her ribs, his palm traced down over her waist, her leg, all the way to her bandage and then up again. Above the knee, however, his direction curled in to feather up her inner thigh. When his fingertips skimmed her panties' damp crotch a flash of darkest desire plunged through her, gripping her insides and coating them with warm liquid want.

Biting her lip, she turned her head towards the pillow. "You want to torture me?"

He chuckled. "Not the word I'd have used."

She found his hand and held his palm against the pulse that was both freeing her spirit as well as compressing every thought and feeling gloriously tight. His lips nuzzling hers, he tugged her panties' crotch aside. At the same time as cool air brushed between her thighs, his mouth left hers. A moment later his warm breath was a whisper away from her most intimate, private place.

Gripping the sheet at her sides, she fought the urge to buck her hips, to let him know how dearly she wanted this. Wanted him. When he urged her folds apart, and his tongue dipped to swirl over the sensitive nub, she bit her lip harder to quell the cry.

"You're beautiful," he said.

Then he kissed her again, with his lips, with his tongue, twirling and tasting until he'd drawn out every ounce of vulnerability she'd ever hidden from the world. She felt the roughness of his beard and the pleasure in his smile as he groaned and hummed against her. The vibration filtered through her blood, igniting a glittering roadmap of longing that swept along her veins. And then…

One second she was vaguely aware of her surroundings, of her individual heartbeat and the rhythmic wash of the waves outside. The next the spiral of sensation had smashed through the ceiling. The tingling burn heightened, deepened, widened, until nothing existed but the heat-lightning rushing over her breasts, scorching her nipples and shooting blazing stars through her mind to her core.

From the moment Nina surrendered, Gabriel knew tonight wouldn't be their last. Holding her now, as she cried out his name, he was struck by another revelation. Whatever lay behind their fiery connection, it was real—and she knew it too. She wanted this to continue as much as he did—if not more.

As her contractions eased, and she breathed out a full-bodied sigh, he pulled himself up over her amazing curves. Her eyes were closed and an almost innocent smile graced her swollen lips. He drank in the sight, drawing out the anticipation, and with every passing second his want for her grew.

Dreamy, she blinked open her eyes. She focused, then her smile fanned and her arms went out to him.

Pressing tender kisses to her brow, he entered her, with finite, together-again care. When he was certain she was ready, when he felt her urgency had built again to breaking point, he gripped the top of the bedhead with one hand and cupped her nape with the other. He looked into her eyes and, in one, long slow act, drove in all the way.

Her head went back and she gasped, at the same time as he summoned every ounce of will-power to stop the intense push from getting the best of him. He couldn't remember having experienced this kind of smouldering force before. It was like trying to catch and hold a fleet of flaming arrows in one hand.

He'd reined himself in and was moving again when the worst possible thing happened. Nuzzling up against his ear, she whispered his name.

A wave swept over his body at the same time as she trailed her fingertips up and down his sides. Goosebumps flashed over his skin and that fleet of arrows shot at his groin. He trembled, shuddered, tucked in his chin. But then she cupped his jaw and craned up to steal a tender yet urgent kiss. With her tongue edging lovingly over his, his erection throbbed and hardened to become near unmanageable.

Struggling to smile, he murmured against her mouth, "Did someone mention torture?"

Her laugh was more of a purr. "I can put you out of your misery."

Her velvet walls contracted around him, squeezing and holding while her teeth tugged his bottom lip. His hand dropped from the bedhead to iron up over her ribcage and knead her breast. As their movements blended and synchronised, he understood he'd never enjoyed an experience quite like this. The fire was so formidable that his blood had turned to lava.

It had nothing to do with their bond over her brother. Nothing to do with saving her life. It was physical, sure, but it was beyond that too. Every ion seemed to fuse in all the right places. She fitted him, he fitted her—everywhere.

Every way.

He took her mouth and kissed her hard as his skin steamed and pressure grew. A moment later she quietened beneath him, shrinking into herself and quivering while her breathing ceased altogether. With every tendon and muscle clenched, he withdrew fully, then filled her once more, hitting a place and a moment so high neither one would reach the ground again without jumping off.

Her fingers dug into his biceps as her frame arched high. The sky opened up—fierce, bright—and Gabriel dived into the light.

CHAPTER TEN

REMEMBERING the bliss of the previous passion-filled night, Nina eased into a satisfied smile a moment before blinking open her eyes to greet what she knew would be a fabulous new day.

With post-dawn shadows dancing over the quiet bedroom walls, and waves thundering on the shore, Nina rolled over. Awake only seconds, already her body ached for Gabriel's touch—and much more.

Her lover lay on his stomach, one muscled arm curled around his head, his bristled jaw resting upon the pillow. His thick sooty lashes were still and his highly kissable lips were parted. She listened to his deep breathing, which was almost a snore, as his broad bronzed back expanded and fell.

Her gaze filtered down.

The white sheet lay over his tight buns. The outline of his legs reached past the end of the bed. She remembered how that long, athletic body had pressed upon hers last night and a bright thrill sailed through her. No one made love the way he did. Physically he was supreme. As far as skill went, he was king. Even now his invisible line reeled her in. It had been there from the first, this unseen primal force that spoke to her soul. Chemistry? Yes.

And something more.

Nina watched him for long moments, enjoying that surreal feeling again. For the first time in so long she didn't feel the pressure to get up and "do." She could lie here all day with him if she wanted.

She no longer had a job to run off to.

Last night Gabriel had clobbered her with the news that he was, in fact, her childhood arch enemy number one: Gabe Turner. He'd followed that up by terminating her employ. Offering to set her up with a publishing job in Sydney didn't fix anything; she wouldn't go down that undeserving track again. But after he'd seduced her—after she'd surrendered and they'd made love half the night—neither had broached the subject of her termination again.

So where did she go from here?

A cool breeze blew up the gauzy curtains and Nina shivered. Rubbing her arms, she eased out from beneath the sheet. She tiptoed to the spare bedroom and entered its *en suite* bathroom. After a long shower, trying to figure out what the heck to do with her life from this point, she grabbed a plush robe off its hook and, fluff-drying her hair with a towel, emerged into the main room.

She stopped dead and caught her runaway breath.

Gabriel spun around to greet her while his dignified guest nodded cordially.

"I invited Dr Newman to check your ankle," Gabriel said.

"Mr Steele filled me in on your ordeal." The doctor indicated she should sit at the dinner table. "You're very lucky he came along when he did."

Nina tried to release the tension gripping her body, but what must the doctor think of her—an employee breaking that most sacred rule and spending the night with a guest? And, regardless of Gabriel saving her life, what right did he have calling the doctor without consulting her first? She felt like a child.

Clutching the robe closer to her neck, Nina cleared her throat. "Lucky…yes. But my ankle feels fine now, thank you."

The doctor pushed his bifocals to the bridge of his nose, then released the clip on his bag. "Nevertheless…"

Nina evaluated the situation. Clearly she was in no position to win a stand-off. Two against one, and her ankle was telling her to cop it on the chin and sit down.

Trying to look poised in her towelling robe, she crossed to a chair, and five minutes later the doctor's examination of her injuries was complete. He fished out some tablets, checked the label, and handed the pack over.

"Anti-inflammatories will help with that slight swelling and any pain." He snapped shut his bag and straightened his tie. "Keep the wounds clean, take it easy on your feet, and call me if you have any concerns."

Gabriel thanked the doctor for his time, and the moment the older man had let himself out Nina stood and gave Gabriel a look.

He arched his brows. "What?"

"I'm old enough to make my own appointments."

He gathered her near, stole three or four slow closed-mouth kisses from her lips, and the lines of her defence typically started to slide.

With a crooked grin, he rubbed the tip of his nose with hers. "I was only looking out for you."

His mouth lowered to kiss her again, but, feeling a little odd with Gabe Turner now that the daylight had come, she dodged and wove out of his arms. She knew he wasn't that proud, aloof teenager any more, but still…

She dug her hands into the robe's pockets. "Don't you think this is weird?"

"You mean how good we are together?"

"That we're together at all." She lowered herself into the couch. "I know time's supposed to heal all wounds, but you really didn't like me."

He tugged his ear. "I wouldn't say that."

She grinned. He might not *say* it, but she knew what he was thinking. Once upon a time he'd loathed the sight of her.

She sat back. "My parents never seemed to notice the battle going on between us, though. I remember one morning Dad said he thought Gabe Turner was a decent, hardworking boy. I chewed my cornflakes, scowling, and wished I never had to see you again."

As he folded down beside her, she stole a glance at him from beneath her lashes. Suddenly feeling like that fourteen-year-old again, she admitted, "My cheeks would burn whenever you walked by without so much as a hello. It was all I could do not to kick your shin."

He chuckled. "Why didn't you?"

"My mother said ladies never resort to violence." Her gaze shied away and her voice lowered. "So I tried to hurt you another way."

She'd let him know that while he might *think* he was hot stuff, he wasn't fit to wash her father's car.

She withered into herself and cringed. "I'm sorry, Gabe. I really was awful."

He was searching her eyes, checking to see if she was patronising him, but then his earnest face dissolved. "Ah, you weren't so bad."

He was being nice. She'd been horrid. But now, as an adult, she could acknowledge that annoying burning tension for what it had been…rumblings of sexual curiosity whenever Gabe Turner's impervious, marvellous presence entered a room. At fourteen, she'd been pretty clueless. Even if someone had pointed out that she'd had a crush on her brother's best friend, she doubted she'd have known what to do about it.

Had he felt attracted to her back then—even in a "she's a pain but still cute" kind of way? What would she have done if Geeky Gabe had silenced her snarky barbs with one perfect, penetrating kiss? At that age it wouldn't have been appropriate.

They'd grown up a lot since then.

She glanced over again, smiled, and swallowed a laugh. "You were such a dork."

"Hey, a lot of dorks have the smarts to make it in this world." He threaded his fingers behind his head. "Anthony, on the other hand, was a complete jock. We made an odd pair—" his gaze intensified "—but we understood each other."

She swung more towards him. "How did you two meet?"

A fond grin hitched up a corner of his mouth. "Anthony's bike had a flat, and I stopped on mine to help. The next day he offered to coach me at gym. I kicked butt with those grades that term, and our friendship went from there."

Remembering her carefree schooldays, Nina felt her heart contract. "I still miss him so much."

Gabriel's arms lowered and he took her hand. "After his accident I felt numb. It took me till midway through university, when I hooked up with Zane, before I got through a whole day without thinking about him."

"You liked uni?"

His thumb stroked the back of her hand. "My aunt worked two jobs to pay for my private school education. I owed it to her to do well." He grinned, remembering. "I wanted to buy her a penthouse in the heart of Sydney, and take her shopping at Tiffany's for genuine pearl earrings."

"*Very* nice." Her tone changed when she added, "Your aunt would be proud of you now."

"I have a way to go yet." He fixed her with a serious gaze. "But we're avoiding a very grave matter."

Nina landed back in the here and now.

Gabriel wasn't that adolescent geek any more. He was her boss, and he'd told her last night she was out of a job. She'd stayed with him last night, but was he about to break it to her that, nice as this little interlude had been, it was time to get her unemployed butt off his island? That their holiday fling was over?

"Thing is," he began, and his hand tightened around hers, "I want to know why you slipped out of bed this morning without at least one kiss to start my day."

She let go that breath. "A kiss?"

"At least one."

He closed in to take what he'd missed. At the same time the knocker fell on the front door. Nina reflexively pulled back, but he tugged her close again.

"Whoever it is," he murmured against her lips, "it's not important."

"How do you know?"

"Because nothing's as important as this."

His mouth covered hers, but the knocker sounded again, and again.

Growling, he pushed to his feet and held up an index finger. "Give me one minute."

But as he strode towards the door Nina gathered her whirling thoughts. This last day and a half she'd felt as if she were on a seesaw—one minute down and out, the next riding a rocket-ship-high.

Two things were certain. Gabriel needed to spend time on getting this island in shape. The working day had begun. It was time he got out there. Beyond that…as much as he inflated her tyres—as much as her switched-on body begged for his attention—she wouldn't set foot in that bedroom again until they'd sorted a few things out.

When Gabriel opened the door, his head pulled back. *Not* who he was expecting.

"April?"

What was his PA—make that *ex*-PA—doing here?

A tissue at her cheek, April dragged herself into the centre of the room. Her diminutive shoulders hunched and blonde hair came forward as she blew her nose.

"I'm not going through with it," she mumbled into the tissue.

Dumbfounded, Gabe followed her. "Through with…? You mean the wedding?"

She fixed him with accusing eyes. "I knew you wouldn't understand."

She'd spoken of nothing else for six months. She'd told him she couldn't live without this guy. She'd said how much her gown had cost, and he'd countered with, "That's outrageous!" Now she was in tears. Calling everything off. And people wondered why he wasn't rushing to tie any knots.

April's watery expression changed as her red-rimmed eyes focused on Nina. "Oh…sorry, I didn't realise you had company."

Nina was smiling uncertainly at their guest, while tugging the tie of her robe a little tighter. Gabriel exhaled. He guessed he should introduce them.

"April, this is Nina. Nina, this is April." He realised how this must look—as if he'd picked her up overnight—and while it shouldn't matter what April thought of anyone he saw, he added, "I've known Nina for years."

Preoccupied, April nodded, then spoke to herself more than to either of them.

"I've only known Liam twelve months. One short year." She collapsed into a chair and gazed unseeing at her sandalled pigeon-toed feet. "I felt as if we'd known each other for ever."

Nina's eyes questioned his. Gabriel shrugged, then edged forward. "What happened?"

"He wants me to sign a pre-nup."

"You didn't discuss it before now?"

In a daze, April shook her head. "He says his parents are insisting."

"I didn't think he had any money."

April slid him a dry look. "Compared to someone like you, no one has any money." She blew her nose again and spoke to Nina. "Would *you* sign a pre-nup?"

Nina blinked several times then stammered, "I—I don't think I'm the one to ask."

"You don't marry someone," April expounded, "commit your life and heart and soul, but have a conditional clause 'just in case.'"

Gabe stifled a groan. He couldn't see the problem. There were plenty of women out there ready to grab what they could. "Pre-nups are common practice these days."

"Well, these days suck!" April blew her nose again. "I'd love him no matter what."

He shrugged. "Then sign."

Nina spoke up. "If he trusted her, he wouldn't ask her to sign."

April sat a little straighter, then gave a solid nod.

Gabriel assessed the situation. He felt a lynching coming on, but realities couldn't be ignored. Pre-nups weren't heartless. They were useful tools in this modern-day, litigious, high-rate-of-divorce society. A better option was don't say I do. Don't move in together. Then property and other entitlement issues didn't become a problem.

Keep it simple.

Fun.

Brief.

His gaze skated to Nina before he crossed to the fridge, extracted juice, and very nearly grinned at a selfish thought. He looked across at April. "You can always come back and work for me."

She hadn't heard. "I can't see a way around this. Liam's gotten so testy all of a sudden. He even complained about the service here this morning."

Gabriel's business mind swooped in. "The service?" Nina's ears seemed to have pricked too.

April unfolded to her feet. "Don't worry. The service is great." Her brows pinched. "A little starchy, maybe." She rubbed her arms. "Too serious, or something. And that main restaurant could use a push into the twenty-first century—" She stopped and her shoulders came down. "But I'm not your PA any more." Her eyes began to fill. "I'm a woman who has to cancel her wedding."

A small sob escaped, and Gabriel strode over to give her a brotherly hug.

"It'll be okay. He's just got cold feet." He shivered, just thinking about it, and he was only a guest.

April blinked her big green eyes up at him. "You're sure that's all it is?"

"April, getting married is scary stuff."

When April's eyes flared and her bottom lip wobbled, Nina came forward.

"What Gabriel means is that it's a big step in any person's life." Nina sent him an "enough on the advice" look, and Gabriel sent back a "what did I say?" shrug. "I'm sure your fiancé will come around."

April heaved a sigh then dredged up a smile. "Thanks—" she acknowledged Gabriel "—both of you. I just hope you're right."

She dabbed her eyes a final time and Gabriel let her out.

At the door, he spun back and rubbed his hands. "Now, where were we?"

"We were feeling terrible for April," Nina reminded him as he spanned the distance separating them with "one-track mind" blinking like a neon sign on his forehead.

He threaded her fingers with his, drew two arcs in the air as he lifted her hands, and kissed each one while keeping his lidded gaze on hers. "If that's what they both want, they'll work it out."

"You're right. If he truly loves her, he'll see nothing should stand in their way."

Gabriel didn't object, but he didn't agree either. He merely began to lead her, hand in hand, towards his bedroom.

But she tugged back. "We need to talk."

"And we will." Hands on her waist, he bounced her up, like a human spear, into the air.

Caught between a laugh and a wail, she clutched onto his shoulders as he let her body slide, bit by bit, all the way down against his hard frame until her feet hovered an inch above the ground and their mouths finally met.

His kiss was drugging…so penetrating and involving that the sheer mastery of it—the undercurrent of ownership it conveyed—robbed her of any sense of time or place. Her nerve-endings were live wires by the time she realised he'd moved them into the bedroom… was lowering and tipping her back against the rumpled sheets and the jumble of downy pillows.

With deliberate calm, he set one fingertip to travel east over her collarbone. Her breasts warmed as his gaze followed the movement of his hand, which had skimmed nearer her cleavage. When his outside finger curved under her robe and over the mound of her left breast heat sizzled through her veins, condensing low in her belly before snaking down to stroke between her thighs.

Eyes drifting shut, she imagined him kneading her flesh, nipping and suckling those sensitive peaks again. When his breath brushed her cheek, her lips parted to take in more air. It was eight o'clock in the morning, and already she craved his mouth working over hers, his tongue delving, darting, showing no mercy and no signs of retreat.

His touch slid higher and found the curve of her jaw. The pad of his thumb circled under her chin before curling up over the rise and applying subtle pressure until her lips parted more. Her want simmered and steamed, a hot iron in the base of her belly. When she forced her eyes open his sparkling gaze was close, and she breathed out his name.

The hold on her jaw tightened as he brushed his bottom lip over hers, gently back and forth, up and then down. As if his erection was the South Pole, and her hips were super-charged magnets, she moved towards him, barely able to smother a moan of pure desire.

She was ready to give herself over to absolute passion when April's tear-stained face flickered into her mind's eye. Nina pushed the image aside—she would self-combust if she didn't feel him inside her again soon—but Gabriel's words...*getting married is scary stuff*...kept rolling over in her brain.

Scary was such an odd choice of word. It conjured up pictures of blood-sucking demons, or speeding around a hairpin turn with no brakes. Getting married *was* a serious affair—no argument. There was lots to consider. Precautions to take. But weddings shouldn't be *scary.*

She realised his mouth had lifted from her collarbone. He was peering into her eyes, concern creasing his brow.

"Nina, what's wrong? Your ankle hurting?"

She released the breath she hadn't known she'd been holding. "I can't stop thinking about April."

His nod was sombre. "It's a worry, but it's their business." His mouth nipped her chin. "Right now, I'm only concerned about you and me."

The warmth of his hand trailed up her leg, but a switch had been flicked on and Nina couldn't switch it back.

"You and me?" she repeated, then shimmied away and sat up. "You're right. We need to talk."

Two fingers trailed down her exposed thigh. "We can talk later."

She flipped the robe over her legs. "We should talk now."

His breath seemed to lock in his chest before he exhaled, rolled on one side and propped his weight on an elbow, head resting on his palm. "Okay. Shoot."

"This is where we are. We know each other's true identities, names, circumstances, past and present. I no longer have a job, and I don't want to be handed another one under the table. Finally, I'm being intimate with the man who gave me the axe."

He considered her summary, then nodded once. "That would be true and correct."

"So I'm thinking…" Her wry gaze darted left and right. "What happens now?"

"You heard the doctor. You need to stay off your feet. Since you're no longer entitled to staff quarters, I'm happy to offer you accommodation here until I leave on Monday."

She muttered, "Nothing like taking with one hand and giving with the other."

Was Gabriel friend or foe? Her guardian angel or the devil in disguise?

He exhaled patiently. "Fact is Gabriel Steele can't retain staff who don't measure up—but Gabe Turner can't turn Anthony's sister out on her ear." He covered her hand with his. "And the man who made love to you all night, who wants to make love to you now, can't either. I'll do anything to help you…except put you on another shift."

Nina chewed her lip. She wanted to tell him that if she was being sacked for impropriety she would argue he'd been the one to seduce *her*.

Sure, she'd been a willing participant. But if she'd spoken up sooner would her being a waitress have made any difference? They still would have slept together. She couldn't see that information stopping him at the crucial point.

"If you won't let me help you land a job," he added, "why not use your recuperation time here helping yourself? There must be connections of your own you haven't tried yet. Places you could contact." He squeezed her hand. "Sharpen up your résumé. Get on the phone."

She'd been ready to be difficult—from the moment he'd rescued her he'd always seemed so eager to run her life. But his idea held merit. And the simple truth was, despite the hot-and-cold journey they'd been on together, she wasn't ready to say goodbye to him yet.

And if she stayed here she might be able to convince him that she needed her job back. She wasn't a quitter. She had something to prove—to him, to the staff, and more so to herself. She hadn't earned her position here. She couldn't change that, but she could make up for it by working even harder and in some small way making a difference. If she was on a journey to rediscover herself, surely making that mistake right was part of it?

And, yes, in the meantime she could put her recovery time to good use—put her all into making sure that the next stop on her journey was the right one, however hard that was going to be. She took a deep breath, praying Gabe would accept what she knew she had to say next.

"Okay," she agreed. "You have a deal." He beamed as he craned up to cement the deal with a kiss, but Nina's hand appeared between their mouths. "On one condition."

He curled away. "I don't like conditions."

"Our relationship will be platonic from here on in."

"Are you *mad?* I can't agree to that."

"I'll give you one very good reason why you should."

He arched a brow. "I'll give you a better one why I shouldn't."

When he came nearer she slipped further away.

"You're on this island to implement the changes needed to turn this place around. You have a finite amount of time, till next Monday, to put to maximum use." She cocked her head. "Tell me truthfully. Wouldn't you rather lie in bed all day with me than go out and strategise with Mr Dorset and co?"

His eyes narrowed. "Clearly that's a trick question. We're living in paradise. We're great together." His eyes sparkled over his grin. "Why not enjoy it while it lasts?"

"I'll tell you why. It's after eight now. Your working day should have already begun. You should be out there knuckling down, making sure you do what you've come here to do. Turn this place around. Make changes for the better."

As she planned to do.

"The problems will still be there at nine." He moved in to kiss her, but she pushed him away as best she could.

"While we're in an intimate relationship you'll be distracted. Then you're going to be upset for letting yourself be sidetracked from your work." Committed to the idea, she shrugged. "For your own good, I'm taking that temptation away."

He shifted her robe and feather-kissed her shoulder. "Did I mention I can multi-task?"

She tugged her robe back. This was a gorgeous place, and he was an amazing lover, but… "If you want me to stay here—if you really want to help me—then you're going to have to let me help you too. I won't loll around with you in bed half the day and then watch you explode like you did at the cabin yesterday because you're angry with yourself for slacking off."

"Being here is different—"

"Yes, it's worse. By tomorrow everyone will know I'm shacked up with a guest."

And she'd thought she'd been a target before. It would be worse for her when it was discovered that Gabriel Steele—the guest she'd temporarily moved in with—was everyone's new boss.

She might as well ask.

"When are you going to tell the staff who you are?"

"Not this visit," he stated. "There's enough to look at with the managers and facilities."

"Don't you want to give them a chance to speak out on what *they* think could make a difference? They're the ones who keep this place ticking over."

The bungalow telephone extension pealed and, closing his eyes, Gabriel rested one stacked fist on his brow. "You're going to tell me to get that, aren't you?"

You bet. "No rest for the wicked."

He sprang over, about to decimate her with a take-no-prisoners kiss, but then a shadow chased over his face and he backed away.

"I hate to admit it, but you're right. As much as I want to stay here with you, I have to do what I have to do."

As he left her alone in his bedroom, Nina let out a long breath. There was another reason she'd put forward her ultimatum, and it was as significant as Gabriel's need to focus on his work, rather than on sex. Self-preservation.

They'd been together perhaps thirty-six hours and, remarkable as it might sound, she'd never felt more deeply about any man. Convincing herself she could have more with Gabriel than a holiday fling would be easier than demolishing a piece of Chef Reynolds' chocolate marshmallow tart. She felt so right when they were together—so perfectly, wonderfully right—as though, even if she never belonged anywhere else, it was okay because she *did* belong in his arms.

But she'd known before that his interest in her was casual, and after his admission about getting married being scary she'd be a fool to think he was after anything remotely long-term. At the moment her self-worth was shaky enough. The last thing she needed was to fall in love with someone who couldn't love her back.

CHAPTER ELEVEN

Late Friday morning, Gabriel returned after his third meeting with the Diamond Shores managers.

He stepped into the bungalow's foyer, wringing his tie loose and expecting Nina to come bounding out, like she usually did, to hear any news. He'd taken her advice and introduced himself to the staff. Since Wednesday he'd met with the resort conference people, recreation personnel, wait staff and, at nine this morning, housekeeping.

The exercise had gone well.

He jogged down the two timber steps that linked the foyer to main room and threw a look around the gleaming furniture and potted palms. Dropping his tie over the back of a bar stool, he moved onto the balcony.

The sky was a flawless early-summer blue, the air was fresh with the scent of brine, and in his private pool, stretched out before the beach, Nina was doing laps. Gabriel's testosterone levels swirled to the roof. He was a heartbeat away from kicking off his shoes, shucking off his clothes and diving straight in.

Nina in a bikini was impossible to pass up.

The other morning she'd told him that she wanted to downgrade their relationship to platonic. She didn't want to be a distraction when he had so much to accomplish here. She'd been right. He *would* rather fool around with her than knuckle down to the massive task of returning profitability to this establishment. And so he'd kept his distance—no easy feat.

But at no time had he actually agreed to her terms.

During business hours things were moving in the right direction, but when night fell the tension back at the bungalow was tripwire-tight. Lounging in the living room, or out on the deck, sometimes Gabriel had to bite his inside cheek to stop from swooping over and stashing Nina away in his room. Watching her concentrate on doing a crossword, or chewing her nails over some reality TV show, was akin to passing out in the world's hottest sauna when the most delectable, quenching nectar was waiting an arm's length away.

He wasn't alone in feeling that fire. He'd caught Nina's hidden looks when he passed, noticed the way her breathing deepened whenever they were close.

Now, with her wet, pumped and half-naked in that pool, was the time to revisit that ultimatum of hers. They were leaving the island on Monday. If she felt half as sexually frustrated as he did, she couldn't refuse the idea of one last hold-onto-your-seatbelts romp.

Moving to the edge of the pool, he hunkered down onto the terracotta tiles. He watched her graceful form glide through the water before she came up for air a foot away. She pushed hair from her face, drove down a big breath, then coughed it back up when she saw him.

He chuckled at her surprise and eventual smile before holding out his hand. "I've given myself the rest of the day off."

"Welcome home."

She took his hand, he helped her out, and she

grabbed a towel off a nearby lounger. He hid his disappointment when that delicious red bikini was part-way concealed as she wiped down her hair and tanned arms.

"I heard you were speaking with Tori today," she said.

His gaze skated up from what he could see of her legs.

"News travels fast." He rubbed the back of his neck. "Remind me who Tori is again."

"Tall, blonde. She might've been wearing watermelon wedge earrings."

"Ah, yes. She had quite a bit to say."

"Anything useful?"

"The gist was the same as my previous staff meetings. She'd like to see protocol and activities relaxed. Less formal. More fun. Or at least room for that somewhere on the island."

"Maybe you should wear Bermuda shorts to the next meeting."

He mock frowned. "I'll take that under advisement. I've been looking through stacks of guest comments," he went on, moving to the sun loungers. "A lot mentioned updating too."

"Facilities?"

"Policies, entertainment, staff uniforms."

"Tori and her earrings will be pleased to hear it."

"I have plenty to go on."

Lashing the towel under her arms, sarong-style, she crossed over.

"What about a staff buddy system? If the longer-serving staff members had younger ones under their care and tutelage we'd get a better vibe through the ranks. There's nothing worse than being told to fold the napkins a certain way and having no idea but being too frightened to ask." Her expression wavered. "I suppose I should have known…"

"No, no. Point taken. Everyone needs to get more involved with the next guy—or gal."

"If guests saw a real camaraderie among the staff, I bet they'd relax more too. You could start a new ad campaign, promoting a more laid-back slant."

Interested, he made a mental note.

"I have some other news." He sat on the end of the nearest lounger. "April's wedding is back on. Her fiancé stood up to his parents' demands and is marrying April with or without the pre-nup."

Nina punched the air—*yes!*—then sat down too. "Good for him!"

"I want you to come with me."

Her animated face froze. "To the wedding?"

"I've put in a special request that the desserts must be doubly to die for."

He could imagine the cogs spinning in her mind. *Should she? Shouldn't she?* Did partnering him at a wedding breach the platonic line she'd drawn in the sand? Mere semantics. That snag would be fixed soon enough anyway.

Finally her expression eased and she nodded. "Sure. I'd love to go."

"Done." He stood and pulled her up too. "Now, grab some shorts and a top. We need a change of scenery."

By noon they were aboard a thirty-six-foot sailing yacht, heading out for a leisurely cruise around some of the other Great Barrier Reef islands. After they'd left the bay and were in open waters, Gabriel let Nina steer.

Her hands clutched the wheel so tightly her knuckles turned white. But he was standing close by, enjoying the view of salt air whipping through her hair while seafaring exhilaration built on her face. When they anchored near a coral ledge, they stripped to swimsuits and slipped into the crystal-clear water. With masks and snorkels they floated out together and wove over a world of marine life that darted between fingers of jade, pink, aqua and vermilion coral.

Iridescent blue angel fish, gold and white striped harlequin tuskfish, parrot fish, butterfly fish...so vivid and brilliant and clear. He chuckled to himself at the fresh wide-eyed wonder behind her mask when she pointed out an ancient turtle swimming by, close enough to touch.

After they'd climbed back on board and showered off, taking advantage of the dwindling breeze, Gabriel manoeuvred the yacht into a remote island cove. There was barely a breath of wind left by the time he dropped anchor.

Perfect. The weather report had been spot-on.

He laid out a picnic blanket on the timber deck beneath the shade of the sail, while Nina organised prawns, oysters, pineapple and fresh mango for a late lunch spread. He poured Chardonnay into plastic goblets and she peeled two enormous prawns. Looking up at the mast, then at the palm trees fringing the unpopulated island's white-lined shore, she bit into the flesh. Chewing, and still looking around, she wiped her fingers on a paper towel.

"Everything's so quiet," she said.

"No wind."

Stretching out her legs and resting back on one arm, she accepted a goblet of wine. "Don't sails need wind? How do we get back?"

"I have oars." He raised his glass. "Cheers."

She smiled. "I'm getting an interesting visual. But really…"

While she sipped, he peered up at the vigilant gulls wheeling overhead. Not a cloud in the sky. Plenty of food and good wine. A beautiful, sassy woman, in an amazing flaming red bikini—who wanted to leave?

He shrugged. "We'll have to wait it out." No need for her to know about the inboard motor.

She sat up. "How long do you think?"

"You have something to rush back to?"

"Not a thing."

He wasn't quite sure how to take her tone. Had she done all she could with regard to finding another job—sending out more résumés, contacting industry friends— Or had she resigned herself to packing up and leaving in a couple of days without a job to go to?

She reached for one side of a mango and turned the skin inside out. Juice exploded and streamed down her forearms. Rushing to suck the fruit, she tried to capture what she could, and a fierce coil of awareness lassoed and tugged at his groin. He drove down a breath and blew it quietly out. She was sexy without trying—but was she doing that on purpose?

She continued to suck and lick the soft orange flesh and then, as if she hadn't known how captivating her ingesting fruit could be, she threw a glance across and smiled.

"I'll be sticky after this," she said. "We could go for another swim."

Or we could make love.

She inclined her head. "Did you say something?"

"I said I don't want another swim."

When he downed half his wine, she blinked twice and her cheeks pinked up beneath her wide-brimmed hat. It was becoming harder to hide his autonomic responses. Harder to pretend he wanted to. His jaw was tight, his stomach too. The back of his neck felt on fire.

"You must be starved," she said.

A tiny rapid pulse beat at the side of her throat. He felt the same rhythm hammering away in his blood.

"Here." She handed over a delicacy. "These oysters look delicious."

Keeping his gaze on hers, he lifted a shell and slid the oyster into his mouth. The salty, slippery, exotic taste only teased him more. It was all he could do to keep his gaze from wandering to her cleavage...to her thighs.

Her bikini wasn't *naughty*, exactly; the fabric covered all the necessary bits. But the legs were cut intriguingly high and her womanly hips were so curvy. Her breasts were pulled up and looked so full that the temptation to drag her over was one he could barely contain.

No doubt reading his mind and wanting to cool it, she turned a little away, curled her legs beneath her and selected another oyster. But as her fork lifted the oyster from its shell Gabriel noticed her breathing had changed. Deeper. Quicker. And the blush which had started on her cheeks had radiated down the slim column of her throat. As the burn at his nape flashed like wild fire over the rest of his body, he clenched his hand against the urge to lean over and press his lips to her throat and that heat.

She edged a plate towards him. "Have some mango. They're so juicy."

He groaned. "I noticed."

"We had two huge mango trees in our backyard. Do you remember?"

If she wanted to change the subject that they weren't discussing, it wouldn't work.

"Trees?" He set down his goblet. "I don't recall."

"Sure you do. You and Anthony stuffed yourselves so much that summer Mum thought you'd throw up."

Gabriel's mind flashed back and he had to grin. He remembered Anthony's mouth stained orange, skins all over the backyard. They'd been barely able to move they'd eaten so much.

Gabriel cleared his throat and moved closer to Nina. He didn't want to discuss old times now.

She bit into a slice of pineapple and chewed contemplatively. "You never stayed at our house for dinner. You always went home to eat."

"Faith liked having family meals around the table," he summed up, then held up the bottle. "More wine?"

Nina declined, then dropped her gaze. "Gabe, you don't have to tell me if you don't want to, but...I was wondering what happened to your mother? Who was she before she had you?"

He lowered the bottle. As mood-killers went, that was a ten. He hadn't spoken about that with anyone. But if Nina wanted to know they'd be here for a while. He guessed he *could* share.

"You want the unabridged version?"

"If you want."

He drove his fingers through his hair and held them there while he thought back.

"Faith and my mother Darlene's parents worked on their landlord's dairy farm. The girls had a good mother and father, but the only speck of luxury in their lives came when they went to the cinema. Darlene worshipped Hollywood films and dreamed of marrying the next Robert Redford or Paul Newman. She planned to live in Los Angeles, but fell pregnant before she'd saved enough for a fare. She didn't tell my father. At eighteen, she didn't want to give her baby up, but she didn't want to wind up with a going-nowhere-nobody either. She had her heart set on a famous, dashing, wealthy husband."

Nina spoke gently. "She didn't think your father was good enough?"

"He couldn't give her the fantasy life she wanted. So Darlene shifted in with Faith, who'd moved to the city. Darlene had her baby, then set out to find a real man." He cocked his head. "My words, not hers, but you get my drift."

Nina got his drift, all right. His mother had robbed Gabriel of the chance to get to know his dad and vice versa. On top of that she'd left him with an echo that reached from past to present, from father to son…

Not a real man.

Nina's verbal darts all those years ago, insinuating he didn't measure up, wouldn't have helped. She'd been young and foolish. After that story she could only imagine how deeply her taunts must have cut.

"That search took my mother to all kinds of inter-esting places—including bars." A muscle in his jaw flexed twice. "One night she didn't come home. The police said she'd just run out on her responsibilities. I was four. When I was eight they charged a man with the rape and murder of three women in the district over the preceding four years."

Her breath caught.

So his mother *hadn't* abandoned her little son. Cold comfort, though, given the circumstances.

His palm lay on the deck. She covered it lightly with her own. "And your father found you years later?"

"I found him." His hand flipped over to hold hers. "Gary Steele remained a bachelor and became ex-

tremely successful in advertising. Quite an irony as far
as my mother's ambitions were concerned."

Nina shifted uneasily. Gabriel was almost gloating that
his father had avoided what could have been a messy relationship with Darlene. But his mother had disappeared
from her son's life by the time Gabriel was four. Hadn't
he ever wondered about his father during that time?

"Why didn't your aunt try to find your dad?"

"She sent a letter a while after my mother vanished
but never got a reply. Gary said he'd moved from that
address years before to live in the UK briefly and never
received it. Faith believed, right or wrong, that she'd best
leave good enough alone. I didn't blame her. Not at all.
She sacrificed a lot to make sure I had what I needed."

"Is that why you're so focused on success now?"

His chin tipped up. "Hmm?"

"To prove to the ghost of your mother," she murmured, "that you're a *real man?*"

He gave her a wily look. "Big leap."

"Not really. My father was the same. He worked
like a dog to prove himself to *his* father."

Her grandfather had been a tyrant, with beady eyes, a
bushy beard and not a kind word for anyone other than
his financial advisor and his bridge partner. Whenever the
family had frequented his mausoleum of a house she and
Jill had stayed glued to her father's side. Anthony had said
Grandad was Blackbeard come back to life, only meaner.

"My dad built on an already successful engineering
empire," she went on, "then spent every moment
worried about holding it together."

His thumb rubbed the back of her hand and his head
angled. "What happened to the money?"

"After my father passed away my mother went
through the lot like tap water."

"Hate to speak ill of your mother, but I bet your dad's rolling over in his grave."

"Meredith always had a champagne taste. My father loved her extravagant nature and bought her way too much. Jewellery, cars, holidays at the best resorts around the world. She got used to over-the-top. Difference was, when my father was alive he'd been able to step on the brakes when need be."

"Poor guy. Worked his entire life for nothing."

"If he hadn't worked so hard maybe he'd still be around. Stress is a killer."

His pale eyes darkened as he leaned closer. "I vote no stress today."

Nina's skin flashed hot. The intent in his voice, in his eyes, said only one thing. He wanted to kiss her. Way more than kiss.

But, no matter how the air snapped and crackled whenever they were together, she'd made herself clear the other day. Sex was best kept out of the equation. Firstly, she was a distraction he didn't need right now. Secondly, unfairly or not, he'd dismissed her from her job. Thirdly, if she got any more involved—if she fell any deeper—he'd most likely take her heart too.

She shucked back her shoulders. "I won't play this game. I know what you're thinking."

"Tell me."

He tipped nearer still and, heart beating fast, she tipped back. "I thought we'd put this behind us."

His eyes smouldered. "Guess you thought wrong."

As his gaze flicked over her lush parted lips, he slid a hand around her nape to bring her close. But she pulled back, and the first inkling of suspicion faded up in her eyes. She blinked rapidly, as if her mind was catching up with the evidence at hand.

"You planned this, somehow, didn't you?" She snapped a glance at the sky, the sail. "I mean mooring here, when the breeze was set to run out."

He pressed a sensual kiss to her bare shoulder. "Now, how could I do that?"

"You *knew* I wouldn't be able to escape."

"Do you want to escape?"

She growled in her throat, but this time didn't pull away. "You're twisting things."

He wound her arm around his neck.

"Organising this boat," she said. "Sailing out here… All the time you were planning, saving this up—"

His mouth caressed the sensitive spot below her collarbone. "And I'm about to blow."

She stiffened against him. A tense moment passed before the pressure building between them seemed to ignite, expand and then release. After letting out a long-suffering sigh, she trembled and finally furled her fingers up the back of his hair.

Sighing softly, she grazed her cheek against his. "Oh, Gabe, I'm about to blow too."

He smiled to himself.

Score one for the weather man.

He lovingly nipped her chin. "What happened to putting this behind us?"

"What happened to no escape?"

He was about to kiss her the way he'd dreamed of kissing her these past drought-ridden days when something—or someone—seemed to tap him on the shoulder. When he tried to ignore it, the tap came again.

He swore to himself. What a time to get the guilts.

He held her arm and asked, in all earnestness, "Nina,

I want to know if you have any real concerns about this…"

Her lips feathered over his. "I'll let a real man kiss them away.'

When she pulled him down on top of her, he happily fell.

"Lord above, I've missed this," he murmured, snatching kiss after kiss while her sexual hunger spiked and relapsed into that raw, lethal need. "I missed you so much."

She ground herself up against him while her fingers dug into his biceps, and all thought but for him dropped away.

Drunk with passion, they rolled over on the blanket, one way then the other, their mouths locked as their hands sought out places that ached for attention. Her breasts burned to know the stiff, moist stroke of his tongue. Her sex throbbed to feel him deep inside her. When he ripped her bikini top off, the thrust of her desire for him hit like a nuclear blast.

His mouth on her throat, he dragged off her bikini bottoms. She yanked at his fitting trunks while her other hand fanned the warm rock of his chest. When more of his scent filled her lungs she felt almost too dizzy with longing to breathe.

He found her wet and hypersensitive. With one mighty arcing action he swept the plates of food well aside and then kissed her again, his tongue edging over hers, probing deeper, as if no matter how long or how hard they stayed connected he could never get enough.

She held him close, one knee measuring his side before his mouth left hers and his head lowered. When his lips suctioned around her nipple, drawing her deeply into his mouth, bright fountains of colour were released in her head. Her fingers knotted in his hair and that leg coiled over his back.

As the fever took hold, and her arousal clamoured at the ceiling, she reached, trying to tug again at his trunks. He wrangled out of his wet shorts. A second later his pulsing erection pushed against her hip, then cooler air brushed her body as his heat drew away.

Dizzy with need, she opened her eyes. Craning up onto her elbows, she was ready to cry out—*Don't you dare leave me now.*

But he was kneeling over her, his fists coming down either side of her shoulders. His eyes were stormy and his nostrils flared with the effort to take in enough air. Then he slowly lowered, to tease her, rubbing the head of his erection over her intimate folds, making her bloom and throb all the more. When she moved provocatively beneath him, teasing him back, his control snapped in two. He entered her more roughly than he'd intended, hitting a place that made her jump and rock her head to one side.

Concerned, he grabbed her shoulder. "Nina, are you all right?"

She wet her lips and sighed long and loud. "Do it again."

A hot, lazy smile curved his lips before he filled her once more, and a jet of high-octane sparks showered up, setting every part of her alight. Nina was washed away on the climbing tide. The energy spiralled higher, condensed tighter, until the heart of her cried out for release. But another part of her wanted this ecstasy to last—wanted this fire to rage on and on and out of control.

When he sank into her again, the force of her orgasm

ripped a cry from her lips. Pulsating energy contracted, then tore her apart, spraying sparks of pleasure through her blood. She was vaguely aware of his release too, of his fingers digging into her hip, of his chest rubbing high against hers as he shuddered and let his heat flow.

Curling her arms up over her head, Nina pressed against her lover's hard, slick body, soaking up the peak of their magic. And exhausted moments later, when he lay beside her and pulled a corner of the blanket over them both, she knew she'd never felt more content.

She was never more herself than when Gabriel held her like this.

He was the perfect rogue. A fantastic lover. But anyone could fathom why he wasn't after long-term. Why marriage was *scary*.

Scars from his past. No belief in happily-ever-afters. He'd lived his whole life knowing his mother had put her ambition before her little son's best interests. He'd deserved to know his father. He'd deserved a mother who hadn't roamed around searching for her fantasy meal-ticket at night. No wonder he was cynical.

But Nina hoped he would discover real love one day. She could imagine him standing at the altar, wearing a crisp black suit, his tanned hands clasped before him, his smile serene. She could see the love in his eyes, the boundless commitment on his face and wished…a silly romantic's wish.

Nina wished the bride was her.

CHAPTER TWELVE

NINA enlisted the help of Julie LaFoy, the manager of the island's many well-stocked boutiques, to help her with a dress for April's wedding.

The gown she chose had been drastically discounted—at least that was what an excited Julie had said. The style blended "red carpet" with chic sarong. Coupled with a pair of elegant matching heels, Nina felt like an island princess. But no one outshone April on her big day.

April wore a traditional gown of white satin, with a sweeping fairytale veil. When she walked down the outdoor aisle, the groom's face split into an adoring smile and one hundred guests audibly sighed. The ceremony was brief, but heartfelt, and when the bride threw her bouquet it sailed right towards Nina's head. She ducked, and the woman behind her squealed on snaring the prize.

As the music went into party mode, and canapés were served, Gabriel took Nina's hand and led her to the dance floor, which was set up beneath an open marquee. When Nina spotted Mr Dorset hovering around the fringes, making sure everything was in order, a shudder shot up her spine. But when Gabriel gathered her in his arms and held her eyes with his she forgot everything other than how her heart wouldn't stop thumping. How much she loved being his date.

This time last week she would never have dreamed she'd be dancing with the most attractive man in Australia... Well, he was to her. His scent, his feel, the way his eyes spoke only to her... This might have been *their* wedding day. She might even believe that the intense depth of his look meant he was thinking the same.

If wishes came true...

With other couples joining them on the floor, Gabriel dance-stepped her smoothly around.

"Your gown is something else," he said, in a low, appreciative voice.

A rush of pride made her glow. The gown was of softest tangerine silk, cinched high on the side of the waist with a diamanté clasp before falling in weightless folds to her ankles. "Feminine," Julie had said. "Timeless..."

His hot fingertips skimmed up and down her back. "I like the colour. The cut. It looks exquisite on you."

The warmth of her blush deepened. He'd told her three times already.

They'd danced for several moments, moving as one to the music, before he murmured near her ear, "I haven't held you for hours."

"Two, to be exact."

"Two hours too long." He grazed a seductive kiss over her brow and she quivered when his lips veered south.

She would never tire of his compliments. Not that this affair would last. In fact, as much as she loathed to admit it, the sooner "they" ended, the better. The way he looked at her—with a heart-pumping combination of protectiveness and desire—she was in danger of convincing herself she meant way more to him than she did. That kind of self-delusion could only pave a fast track to emotional suicide. She would *not* fall in love with someone who couldn't commit and love her back.

She needed to accept this relationship for what it was: an abstract version of a holiday fling. Gabriel saw it that way. In his mind, he had his life and she had hers—or would again when she got off this island. When that would be depended on how he answered her question.

She wanted a chance to somehow validate her place here, in the staff's eyes as well as in her own. She wanted her position here back. If she did a good enough job, surely Gabriel would be proud of her too.

Her cheek was resting on his lapel when an almighty crash exploded directly behind them. Heart in her throat, Nina spun around. A young waitress stood by the nearby cake table, hands over her mouth, her eyes wide with shock. At the waitress's feet lay a stack of broken plates. The top tier of the multi-layered wedding cake was splattered over the debris. Nina shuddered. She could just see Mr Dorset's outraged face now.

She rushed over to help, automatically picking up broken crockery. She caught the stunned girl's eye.

"Run and get a dustpan," she said. "A bin and some paper towels."

Nina hadn't seen the girl before. Around eighteen, she must be new. She reminded Nina of herself her first week here. Uncertain. Wanting to do well. Failing before she'd been given half a chance. No doubt this woman had experience, but accidents happened, and Nina wasn't prepared to stand back and let her get bawled out without standing beside her. She knew too well what it felt like to cop it alone.

The waitress rushed off at the same time as Gabriel knelt down. "Nina, you're a guest here tonight." His hand held hers. "Leave that. Cake's getting on your gown."

"It'll be cleaned up twice as fast if I help."

"There's plenty of staff—"

She cut him off with a look. "I can't stand back and watch."

The waitress returned, and she and Nina dropped broken crockery into the mini-bin. Nina caught the waitress's expression: her blue eyes were wet with gratitude. Nina smiled back and they picked up the pace.

April appeared, hands clasped beneath her crestfallen face. "My cake!"

Mr Dorset was behind her, his expression pinched. Knowing this was Gabriel Steele's affair, he would be doubly ready to vent his wrath.

A puffed-up Dorset had opened his mouth, ready to come down on the young waitress, but something fierce inside Nina leapt, and she stepped up to stand between them.

"I'm sorry, Mr Dorset," she said, feeling braver and more vulnerable than she had in her life. "I knocked the table corner when I passed. I'll pay for any damage."

While Mr Dorset eyed her with obvious suspicion, Gabriel stepped forward too. "Everything's fine here, Dorset. Thanks for your concern."

And as he said the words three wait staff bee-lined it over… Maureen, Judy, and usually grave-faced Jim Olsen too.

"We'll take care of this," Maureen told Nina as she

lowered herself down beside the younger waitress, and Jim produced a dust pan and brush from thin air.

Gabriel held April's shoulders. "There's plenty of cake left." His voice was quiet. "I'll make it up to you, hon—I promise."

April looked between them both, then her brows opened up before she sighed on a forgiving smile. "The day has been so perfect. Something little had to go wrong."

But Nina was too choked up to respond. Before she'd begun work here she wouldn't have dreamed of intervening in a scene like this the way she had. But, no matter the consequences, she'd felt compelled to protect that young waitress in a way no one had stepped up to protect her. And yet Maureen, Judy, Jim…they knew what she'd done, and by their actions they were saying they approved. Tonight, in her finery, she should have felt more alienated than ever from the staff, yet for the first time since arriving on this island she didn't feel like an outsider.

Mr Dorset answered April. "The bride's only job today is to look beautiful. We'll take care of this."

Before Mr Dorset moved off, his gaze found Nina's. Imagination, perhaps, but she thought she recognised a thin glimmer of respect in his eyes.

After Nina had freshened up, she and Gabriel danced for several more songs. Later they chatted with the other guests, and shared a piece of delicious vanilla wedding cake. When numbers began to dwindle they said goodbye and good luck to the bride and groom, and headed off.

Nina was floating. Aside from that unfortunate accident with the plates and the cake, it had been a wonderful day—for so many reasons. Firstly because tonight had been the first time she'd felt in any way accepted by other members of the staff. She'd never forget their expressions and willingness to help after she'd stood up to Dorset. She believed more than ever that the staff buddy system she'd recommended to Gabriel had real merit.

Just as importantly, the evening had been wonderful because of the way Gabriel had genuinely enjoyed himself—despite his aversion to weddings. She'd almost wanted to point it out—*See. It wasn't so scary after all.*

But now her adrenaline had been spent, and she was ready to retire to the bungalow, to be alone with Gabriel and soak up what remained of their time together. Only one more day...

But once they were out of the private party area he headed in the opposite direction, away from the bungalow.

Nina glanced over her shoulder. In the far distance she could make out the hazy lights from his deck, the extra-tall palm trees that marked his front door.

"Where are we going?"

He shrugged out of his dinner jacket and draped it across her shoulders. His subtle masculine scent wrapped around her. "You'll see."

They climbed a winding path, leaving the resort's lights and sounds behind. As the shadows grew darker, and the rustle of fronds grew louder, the track sloped up and became littered with fragrant petals. Then fairy-lights appeared on either side of the track, twinkling so brightly they seemed eager to lead them to some secret, hidden place.

What was at the end of the track?

His arm was around her waist. She leaned towards his solid heat. "This is very mysterious."

He held up his free hand and crossed two fingers. "Mystery and I are like that."

At the top of the modest incline Nina stopped and held her throat as her breath hitched and heart flipped over. A cashmere-soft-looking blanket was laid out before a cosy fire that licked orange and blue flames around a fat crackling log. A silver bucket, holding a bottle of champagne, sat backstage. The scene was circled by those same sweet-smelling blooms, a sea of petals surrounding their own private island.

A rush of tears prickled the backs of her eyes. It was simple, inviting, and possibly the most romantic thing a man had ever done for a woman.

Her knees suddenly watery, she held his arm tighter. "Gabe, this is…amazing."

He helped her down onto the blanket, then moved to the ice bucket. While she dashed away a happy tear, he poured two glasses as an ocean of stars watched over them from their black velvet sky.

His dinner shirt a beacon against the shadows, he handed over a glass and lowered himself beside her.

"It was such a lovely day," she sighed.

"I've been to a lot of weddings but, yes, this one was special."

"Because it was April's?"

"Because you were there." While her heartbeat skipped he sipped, then set his glass aside. "I liked that they wrote their own vows."

"Lots of couples do."

He peered off into the distance and smiled absently. "I liked what Liam said about marrying her being his greatest achievement."

She smiled, remembering too. "I think they'll be very happy."

They watched the lights twinkle for several moments, content to sip champagne and listen to the night birds' calls.

"Thanks for not blowing the whistle on me when I helped that poor waitress tonight," Nina finally said. She'd wanted to say it all night, but now seemed appropriate, away from prying eyes and ears.

"I felt sorry for her, poor kid."

"Mr Dorset wouldn't have."

His chin came up. "To be fair, he has a responsibility to keep the level of service high."

"And the best way to do that is by putting the fear of God into the staff?"

He drew her near and she, a little stiffly, rested her cheek on his broad shoulder again. He didn't want to discuss business tonight. Neither did she. She'd much rather drink in the lake of lights flickering below and enjoy the quiet. Enjoy this time alone.

Maybe if things had been different, if they'd met again under different circumstances, where she'd felt more herself...

But she was forgetting. While she might be trying to overcome and make sense of some personal hurdles at the moment, Gabriel was comfortable with who he was, what he wanted, which was to enjoy this "fling in paradise" while it lasted. As much as she might want to dream, her destiny didn't lie with him.

When some time later he poured the last of the wine, she took the empty bottle to examine it.

"If we put a message in this bottle and threw it out to sea, I wonder where it would end up? I wonder who would read it?"

"What would your message say?" he asked, but before she could answer, he piped up, "I know. We could date it, include a phone number, and tell the recipient to ring and pass on the relevant details."

She laughed. "That's the most logical, geekish thing I've ever heard."

He gave in to a smile. "If I ever need to send a message, I promise to give it more thought."

She set the bottle down. "Gabriel, can I ask you to give something else some more thought?"

"Anything."

"I'd like my job back."

His brows knitted. "We've discussed that."

"You're not still angry with me for not finding the right moment to tell you about my situation here, are you?"

"Of course not."

"I can't pretend I want to be a waitress the rest of my life," she went on. "Simple truth is I needed the money to make ends meet. I was desperate when my friend gave me the heads-up, but from the moment I landed I wondered if I'd made a huge mistake. I made myself ill wondering if, rather than helping, accepting that job had thrown me further off course." She rested her hand on his. "I don't expect you to understand—it's so hard to explain—but I need to finish this, Gabe. Particularly after tonight. I need to find out who I am at the end of this road before I can travel down the next."

He searched her eyes for a long moment, then exhaled and nodded deeply. "If that's what you truly want…if that's what you need…consider yourself reinstated."

She sat straighter. She'd convinced him? "You mean it?"

He smiled. "I'll call Dorset tomorrow. See how soon you can get back on the roster."

She flung her arms around him and squeezed. She'd never dreamed being a waitress again would make her so happy.

"This means so much—and I promise," she said, drawing back and crossing her heart, "I won't let you down."

CHAPTER THIRTEEN

LATE the next morning, Gabriel strode into Ziggies, Diamond Shore's most popular café by the beach. The ocean air was fresh and salty, but with a hint of coconut oil wafting in from the nearest pool. Riots of colourful flowers glistened with beads from the automatic sprinklers' earlier run. He was alone, bleary-eyed and testy. He needed his second cup of coffee.

But his irritation had less to do with caffeine deprivation and more to do with the phone call he'd made earlier that morning. Last night Nina had asked for her job back. She'd spoken about mistakes and roads travelled, and she'd seemed so anguished and sincere by the end of it he couldn't refuse. If it was that important to her, he would make it happen.

Dorset's response on the phone this morning hadn't been what Gabriel had expected. The older man had jumped in and announced that Nina could go back to work right away. Gabriel suspected Nina's actions in helping that waitress at the wedding might have had something to do with Dorset's change of heart. He, too, had approved of Nina's courage and willingness to pitch in, even while wearing an evening gown. She certainly wasn't the Nina that Gabe Turner had once known. She wasn't even the woman he'd met a week ago. Every day she seemed to grow.

Now, as he strode into the café grounds, his mind wound back to the previous night, when they'd returned to the bungalow after the wedding. He'd peeled that delicious dress from her shoulders and taken her to his bed. Their every touch had seemed heightened. The scent of her hair, the powder silk of her skin, the words she'd whispered against the distant roar of waves as he'd brought her closer to each climax.

He wished he could promise Nina more—particularly after April's wedding yesterday. The day had stirred feelings inside him he hadn't known existed… and wasn't entirely sure he wanted to acknowledge. The truest part of him didn't want a heavy relationship—moving in, plans for the future, worrying about whether that future would pan out. If putting so much into hauling this island out of the red was a risk, to his mind getting serious with a woman was like putting a blowtorch to a gas leak. "Serious" led to "marriage," which led to children—and kids deserved the best from both parents. He wasn't ready to think about that yet—wasn't ready to take that risk even with someone as special as Nina.

He walked into the café's alfresco area and indicated to the *maître-d'* that he'd seat himself. Halfway to a vacant table near the railing, he recognised a woman in a floral shift.

Mrs Emily Flounders, from Sydney's North Shore, beckoned him over. "Why, Mr Steele, is that you? We met at the children's charity dinner last month."

Gabe smiled, nodded. "Mrs Flounders." Mr Flounders lowered his paper and Gabe leaned across to shake his hand. "Sir."

Mrs Flounders laced glittering fingers under her double chin. "Things going well, I hope?"

"Very. Thank you."

"We brought Linley along. You remember Linley?" She tipped forward. "Our daughter? You spoke with her at the dinner."

He didn't remember—which said a lot. "Of course. Please give Linley my regards."

A moment later he drew in his chair and spotted Nina, breezing out from the café's interior. He hadn't noticed so much on the other staff, but that uniform *could* do with a brush-up in design—not shorter, nor sexier, nor even more stylish. Just…more colour, more shape, more *oomph.*

Nina screeched to a stop when she spotted him. After sending him a curious *what are you up to?* look, she crossed to the Flounders' table.

Gabriel absently perused the menu, glancing across every few seconds, strangely nervous for her, but proud of her too. She could have taken the easy way out, accepted his help in finding her a suitable job back in Sydney that she'd enjoy. Instead she was here, travelling that road of hers to its natural conclusion— wherever that might be.

Nina was taking the Flounders' order, but it didn't seem to be going well. Mrs Flounders' cheeks were ruddy, and Nina kept crossing out what she'd written. Concerned, Gabriel set his menu aside at the same time as Nina hurried off to the kitchen to place the order. Mrs Flounders waved over the *maître-d'*.

Gabriel couldn't hear the exchange, but it was clear the older woman was complaining about Nina. Mrs Flounders was a pretentious show pony who loved atten- tion. Maybe Nina had had trouble deciphering the doyenne's demands, but that hardly deserved a complaint.

When the *maître-d'* strode away, Gabriel scraped back his chair and followed. Through the round window in the swinging door that led to the kitchen he saw him ripping verbal shreds off Nina. His arms were waving. Gabriel made out a few words...stupid...incompetent...but more obvious was the man's scathing tone.

Nina, however, didn't flinch. She merely looked her boss in the eye and shrugged her shoulders back. Gabriel imagined her topaz eyes glistening, her thumping heart jammed in her throat.

Not on his shift.

Gabriel crashed through the door. He was ready to tell the *maître-d'* to take a hike, but pulled back when he heard Nina's level voice.

"I will not apologise," she was saying. "I did nothing wrong. If anyone should say I'm sorry, that woman should say it to me. And she could throw in a dozen more apologies to the other staff she's put through her wringer since she sat down an hour ago."

The *maître-d'* was clearly shocked. "You are not here to argue—"

"I'm not arguing. I'm simply stating that there's a big difference between making sure the guests are happy and insisting that your staff smile while they lick their boots three times a day."

A general positive murmur went up around the interested kitchen staff. The head chef nodded to his assistant. A waitress had stopped in her tracks, her eyes wide with disbelief and admiration.

The *maître-d'* glowered in their general direction, then redirected his spite towards Nina. "You will go back out there and apologise to the Flounders, then you will attempt to take their order and do it *correctly* this time!"

"I took it correctly the first time, the second time *and* the third," Nina insisted. "That woman is nothing but a contrary snob who thinks it's her God-given right to demean people she considers beneath her."

With a condescending air, the *maître-d'* crossed his arms. "You foolish girl. You know *nothing* of how the other half live."

Her chin kicked higher. "I know more than you'd ever believe."

Gabriel remembered how a younger Nina had once treated him—as if he should lick *her* boots. She'd come a long way. All these years and finally he really thought she got it.

But it was time to bring this show to an end. The other staff were beyond agitated. He didn't want a rebellion on his hands, but he couldn't dismiss Nina—although he would have to talk soundly with her later. While the man she slept with applauded her guts, the businessman standing here needed to repair any damage.

He moved forward. Nina's jaw dropped when she saw him.

"You're having the rest of the day off," he told the *maître-d'*, who reddened more.

"B-but the guests?" he jabbered.

Gabriel relieved him of the menus he held. "I'll look after the guests."

Indignant, the *maître-d'* stood on his toes. "Forgive me, sir, but you have no experience in this field."

"Guess I'd better learn."

As the kitchen staff raised their brows and murmured

more, Gabriel nodded towards the door. The *maître-d'* huffed and strode out.

Nina was tugging at his sleeve. "Gabriel, I need to talk to you."

"We'll talk after this shift," he said, dying to snatch a kiss. He loved her when she was determined. Loved it when she spoke her mind.

And rather than comply she headed for a door—a backroom where a store of food was kept. She hooked a finger for him to follow, and Gabriel's pulse-rate ramped up.

Okay. If she was that insistent they be alone, he guessed he could spare a moment…or two.

He put the menus aside and followed her. The murmurs outside increased before he shut the door. Not needing an invitation now they were alone, he brought her snug against him, felt a surge of desire flare and build. Now he had her pressed close it was going to prove beyond difficult to let her go.

He brushed his lips over hers and, closing his eyes, groaned with unbridled pleasure. "You were sensational out there."

"Gabriel—"

He pulled marginally back. "But I can't have you dressing down superiors in front of the staff. It doesn't look right."

"*Gabe,* listen to me. I've found another job."

His thoughts screeched to a stop. Dumbfounded, he examined her open gaze. "You *what?*"

"A lady I worked with at *Shimmer* told me about a new magazine starting up. I e-mailed my résumé a couple of days ago and this morning the editor e-mailed back. We talked on the phone and…" Her shoulders came down. "She wants me to start next week. I'll be features editor and second in charge."

He butted his shoulder against the wall as his mind clicked over.

Right. Okay. He should be happy for her. Should be smiling.

"That's…great. Wonderful." He exhaled, struck a hand through his hair. "Next week, huh?"

"I'm leaving tomorrow."

His mind and body gridlocked. "As soon as that?" He'd decided he was going to stay on for a while. He hadn't decided how long exactly. He'd planned on telling Nina after her shift. He'd imagined she'd be happy.

"When she told me I had the job," Nina went on, "can you believe I was actually torn? I had something to finish here—I wasn't entirely sure what—so I said I'd call back if my answer was yes." She shook her head as she sighed. "Now, after that scene—when I know I'd only done my job well… That's it for me. I'm done. I don't want to be subjected to this kind of pompous elitism ever again."

Gabriel's mind caught up with his emotions and delayed relief trickled through him. She might be leaving the island, but… "We can hook up again in Sydney."

"That sounds wonderful, except…"

He frowned. "Except what?"

Searching his eyes, she eased out a long breath. "I was feeling so lost and alone…it was what I'd been dreaming of before you came along—lapping up luxury for just a day or two. This time with you has brought back so many memories. Safe memories from when I was young and my family were all together." She rested her palm against his chest. "But that time's over. That's not me any more. I've changed. I don't want to try and fit back into that world. The world of pretentious Mrs Flounders. I'd feel more of a fake than I did being a waitress." Her eyes pleaded with him to understand. "You've made so much of yourself. You deserve all this. But that's *you*, not me. Not any more."

He held her hand against his chest and scoffed. She was making this bigger than it needed to be.

"Nina, we're not doing anything drastic." Like making things permanent. "We're just seeing each other." Sleeping together. "You can still have your life and carry on doing that."

Her throat bobbed on a big swallow and her eyes began to fill. "No matter what life throws my way, I know now I'll adapt. I'll survive. I'll *grow*. But that doesn't mean I want to intentionally put myself in harm's way. I care about you, Gabriel. I care so much it frightens me." Her face softened. "I've never been in love before."

His heart stopped beating. He swallowed involuntarily, then, totally taken aback, coughed out a laugh. "We've known each other a *week*."

"*This* time." Her eyes glistened. "If I agree to see you when we get back you'll end up hurting me, and it'll be my fault for not pulling back now while I still can."

Suddenly the room felt smaller. Where it had been cosy when they'd first entered, now the space felt squashed. The scent of spices and sauces made him want to wheeze. Made him want to clear his throat.

He blindly found the doorknob at his back. "We'll discuss this later."

"Will that change anything?"

He'd be frank.

"If you're talking about long-term, about marriage… no, it won't. And you know enough about me not to ask why." With marriage came expectations, came children. He'd rather not be a father at all than risk being a bad or an absent one. Boys needed their father—one hundred percent and every day.

She cupped his cheek with a caring hand. "You're so committed to this project. You have so much riding on its success. You don't need me getting in the way. You don't need nagging when you're too busy for personal."

His hand tightened on her shoulder before it slid down her arm. He leant back against the door. He felt as if he'd been knocked out in the final round. He hated to admit it, but everything she said made sense. The scenario she'd just given had pretty much been the way most of his so-called relationships had turned out in the past. He'd thought Nina was different, but maybe her added allure was because she'd been so proud and so darn hard to keep.

He might not love her, but he did respect her, and he certainly didn't want to hurt her.

He closed his eyes, saw the only logical answer and forced himself to accept it.

Exhaling, he opened his eyes and nodded. "You're right. If you were my sister, I'd be telling you to run."

She frowned. "This isn't about Anthony."

"No, this is about you being you and me being me."

She was moving on and he wasn't ready to make that move with her. He didn't know that he ever would be.

CHAPTER FOURTEEN

LATER that day, after Gabriel had walked a few miles down the beach, he strode back to the bungalow and immersed himself in figures. Piles of columns and statistics and any other numbers that might help to obliterate that God-awful scene in the café with Nina Petrelle.

There'd been a note on the counter. Nina was staying with her mate back at the staff quarters tonight.

He scrunched up the paper, flicked it into the trash. When night fell, he cracked open a beer and reclined in a deckchair out on the balcony. With the Mikano restaurant's piano tinkling in over the warm air, he watched the waves roll endlessly in, then roll just as endlessly out. He slept not a wink. When a peaceful dawn broke, sienna-gold on the quiet horizon, his eyes were gritty and his throat ached.

He believed he could change Nina's mind. He knew what to say, how to touch, where to kiss, so she couldn't say no. But, as much as the beast inside urged him to persuade her to continue their affair after she returned to Sydney, he simply couldn't be that selfish and hurt her that way.

As he'd said—she was right. His past with women was proof. Nina would only end up hurt.

She wanted his respect and he *did* respect her—her courage, her humour and integrity. But respect and love were two different things. If she was frightened about how much she cared for him, he wasn't too comfortable with his emotions either.

He'd told her his life was too busy to accommodate the kind of commitment she was wanted. But through these long, lonely hours he'd admitted that was a lie. The simple truth was he didn't *want* to be tied down. But it went deeper than that. He didn't want to commit because he didn't need to worry about whether he was good enough. Whether he could provide enough—emotionally, financially, physically.

His mother hadn't given his father a chance and young Gabe had been the one to lose out. He'd come to terms with his mother's choices. He'd forgiven her long ago. But he had Faith and her gentle wise ways to thank for that.

Faith had said, no matter what, he could be anything he wanted to be. But in a dark hidden place, he knew why he'd never let himself get close to any woman.

He didn't believe in that kind of love. And until recently he hadn't found that conviction to be a problem.

At 7 a.m. he showered, dressed, and made his way to the jetty. An hour later he stood when Nina approached, wheeling one suitcase behind her. The ferry-cat to the mainland left in twenty minutes. Twenty minutes and then...

Would he ever see her again?

She didn't seem surprised to see him. Her eyes looked as red as his felt, and it was all he could do not to tell her this was crazy. This didn't have to end.

Instead he remembered her pleas, his long, insightful night, and handed over a tiger shell.

"This is for your nephew." He placed the shiny tawny- and brown-dotted shell in her hand. "Put your ear to the opening and you hear the ocean."

She listened, smiled, and then lowered the shell. "Thank you," she said. "Thanks for everything you've done."

He dropped his gaze and then found her eyes again. "Nina, I did some soul-searching last night."

Her gaze sharpened. "And?"

"I want you to be everything you can be."

In a heartbeat her eyes edged with tears and, although she set her mouth, her bottom lip still trembled. It was the hardest thing he'd ever done, holding back from gathering her close, kissing her brow and telling her... what?

He'd already said he cared. He cared more for her than anyone he'd known. More than Faith, more than his father or Anthony. It was a different kind of emotion. A consuming sensation that affected every inch of him...head, but more so heart. And yet he couldn't tell her what she needed to hear.

So what was the use of tormenting himself? Or her? Why had he come?

"Good luck with your work here," she said.

He blinked against the emotion stinging behind his nose. "Good luck with the new job."

A tear fell from the corner of her eye before she bounced onto tiptoe and stole a kiss from his cheek. Then she was gone, striding off down the jetty, boarding the cat and not looking back.

Soon it began to shower. The shower turned into sheets of rain. After an hour, Gabriel walked home.

He knew he could get Diamond Shores back on its feet. He was well on track now, thanks to Nina and the other staff's suggestions. She was right. No one needed to lick anyone's boots—not in his childhood and not now. He'd make the changes that needed to be made. He'd make the fortune he'd always wanted. He'd prove himself. Reach the top.

Yet all he could think about was how lucky some guy in Nina's future would be and how, without her in his life, he might as well be broke.

CHAPTER FIFTEEN

NINA had been back in Sydney two weeks, and had started her new job at *Real Woman's Life* magazine a few days ago.

She'd fallen straight into the work and had hit it off instantly with her fellow staff. Best was the feeling that she finally fitted somewhere again. Her life was definitely on the upswing. Yet there was a hidden part of her that felt more lost than ever.

Sitting alone on a quiet stretch of Manly Beach, with a chorus of kookaburras heralding in a clear new day, Nina pushed to her feet, dusted off her shorts and headed for the water.

Once she'd loved coming here…laughable attempts at beach volleyball with her friends, devouring great summer reads while the sun warmed her skin. Now blue skies, white sand and the mighty tumble of surf only reminded her of Gabriel.

Almost to the water, she stopped as her insides clenched and tears brimmed in her eyes.

She'd tried to shake off the malady…late-night movies, visits with Jill and Codie, reconnecting with mates and former colleagues. Yet every waking moment his smile seemed to live in her mind. Dazzling. Seductive.

Her dreams were even more disturbing. Sometimes she woke up believing his bone-melting embrace was real. The memory of his night kisses teased her until she thought she might go mad.

She had to talk with him, tell him she'd been wrong, that she was willing to take whatever he could give. Last night the ache in her stomach had been so bad she'd picked up the phone, ready to beg him to take her back.

What did she have to lose? The tragedy she'd hoped to avoid had come. Her heart was broken. Cracked in two. Her professional life was soaring, but on a personal, lovesick note, she doubted she could sink any lower.

And it was that sorry realisation that kept her from crumbling completely. From making another gigantic mistake.

If she called Gabriel and pitched herself back into their affair she would only fall *more* in love. She would be even more heartbroken when they said goodbye again. In not so many words, on that last day, Gabriel had told her to run.

He knew who he was...a playboy millionaire who had success and little else on his mind. But he cared for her. When she lay awake in the midnight hours, staring at the ceiling, she told herself he cared for her more than any woman he'd been with.

Still, he'd let her go.

She *couldn't* take back all she'd said to him. Couldn't let him know she was willing to have her heart decimated again. She might not have Gabriel Steele's love, but she could at least keep his respect.

And so, once she'd gone around that circle of logic a thousand times, she stayed her course. She longed for Gabriel's smile, his touch. But she kept her pain to herself.

But then came the next dilemma.

Would she ever feel whole again…the wonderful, glowing, cherished way she'd felt when she'd been with him? When she looked in the mirror each morning and saw the opacity in her eyes she couldn't imagine feeling that vibrant again.

As cool laces of water washed around her bare feet, Nina wondered where and what her life would be ten years from now. She'd always thought she would find Mr Wonderful, her true soul mate, and she *had*. Love had come at the most unlikely time, when every other aspect of her life had been turned upside down and pulled inside out. But finding love wasn't keeping love. One week after meeting Mr Wonderful she'd lost her love for good.

She gazed out at the Pacific Ocean, glittering with dawn's gentle jewels, and hugged herself as a cool sea breeze combed her hair.

The question she'd asked herself lately hadn't been, *Who am I?* It was *Why am I? Why am I here?*

Why do I matter?

She came up with reasons. Good ones. Reasons that counted. And yet without Gabriel to talk with…to laugh with…to love…those reasons never seemed anywhere near important enough.

Ahead, a bottle lay half buried in the sand. An unusual bottle—bright pink, with a spray of flowers painted on one side. Curious, she collected it and rubbed the wet sand from the glass.

She stopped. Looked harder.

Paper was scrolled up inside.

A message in a bottle.

A wistful smile lifted the corners of her mouth.

On the night of April's wedding Gabriel had asked her what she might write on such a note.

Nina closed her eyes, lifted her face to the northern sky and whispered… *'Wish you were here.'*

Remembering her first vision of him on that cliff, she swallowed the tears backed up in her throat, screwed off the cork and shook the paper out. Unravelling the note, she saw the words were handwritten and slightly smudged. Only two words, and they read:

Turn around.

She blinked several times before tendrils of understanding gripped high around her throat and a flash of heat rushed over her skin. Her head was light and every hair on her scalp was standing on end by the time she did what the note asked. Slowly she edged around, and…

Gabriel! He was standing right there before her, as if he'd materialised out of thin air.

Her shaky grasp on the bottle slipped, but he caught it, as well as her hands, before it hit the ground.

He looked ten times more masculine and handsome than she'd remembered. Those ice-blue eyes burned into hers, warming her all the way through. A raspy shadow darkened his prominent jaw. She loved grazing her palm up the rough of his mid-morning beard.

Or rather she *had* loved doing that.

Nina wondered if her face showed even a tenth of her emotions. She wanted to run away, to beg him to stay. Tell him how desperately she wanted him to hold her.

But she didn't need to ask. Gabriel's strong arms wrapped around her and, still in shock, she didn't resist when he drew her near.

"I remember it all," he said against her ear as she

trembled and he stroked her back. "As if every moment were logged in my brain beneath a magnifying glass. How you chew the end of your pencil when you pore over a crossword. How your foot taps when you listen to your favourite song. How you feel beneath me. Feel around me."

Her voice pushed past the nerves knotted in her throat. "Gabriel...what are you doing here?"

He stepped back and found her gaze.

"Since you left I haven't stopped asking myself whether I could truly keep you satisfied. Day and night, it pounded at my brain. I wanted to come to you, wanted you back, but I couldn't stomach the idea of not measuring up."

He inhaled and his gaze focused more. "Years ago, I vowed I would never be responsible for helping to create another broken home. Then, out of the blue, the answer came to me."

Unable to help herself, she filed her fingers through the sides of his clean dark hair, wondering how she'd lived so long without his touch. Raw hope pushed like a fist against her chest, but she didn't want to jump ahead. Didn't want to hope too much.

"You wanted to discover who you were," he went on, his voice intense and deep. "Let me tell you who you are to me. You're the person I can face any battle with. You're headstrong and beyond beautiful. You're like no one I've ever known. Nina, you're the woman I love and will love for ever. And I'm the man who prays you can forgive me for not realising that sooner and love me back." He found her hands and clasped them to his chest, and that beautiful light she adored shone up in his eyes. "I want to help create a *happy* family. *Our* family. Nina, say you'll marry me."

She felt locked to the spot. The ocean and the sky and the kookaburra calls receded, until she was only aware of her throbbing heartbeat and the deep sincerity in his eyes. Over her clogged throat, she choked out what had played over in her mind these past weeks. He wasn't the only one who'd been asking questions.

"Gabe, you said you didn't want to get married."

She didn't want to believe it—didn't want to think he'd be that cruel—but she had to know if this was another seduction game meant to get her back in his bed.

He tipped her chin up and gazed into her soul. "I was waiting for the right woman, and I can't believe I almost let her go." His arms went around her again. "I want to live the rest of my life with you. Have children together and be there for them every day. I want to sit and watch the sunrise with you fifty years from now. Tell me you want that too." His brow lowered to rest upon hers. "Tell me you still feel the same way."

Her chest squeezed until she could barely breathe. Of course she still loved him. Now that she'd fallen, she couldn't imagine *not* loving him. He sounded so passionate, so focused, but there was something else she needed to say. The part of her that was weeping with happiness was telling her to keep quiet. She wanted to accept his proposal—she'd *dreamed* about it since the day they'd said goodbye—but she couldn't simply push aside what she knew to be true.

"What about your life? Gabriel, I don't want to live in a world of black-tie dinners every other night. I can't be a *real housewife.*" She couldn't be a rich kept woman, with too much time and money on her hands. After all she'd been through, that skin simply wouldn't fit.

"Our life doesn't have to be like that. We don't have to have anyone or anything in our life we don't want to have there. That obstacle's not enough to keep us apart. Nothing is." His determined eyes searched hers. "This connection is real. For ever. We'll *make* it work. Believe it, Nina. Believe it the way I do and nothing else will matter."

A flood of emotion bubbled up. She wanted to laugh. To *cry.* She choked out the words. "You really think so?"

"I love you…and I won't let anything stand in our way."

His head slanted over hers, and when their lips met and his masterful heat and confidence infused her she went to jelly and gave up her arguments. With all her heart, with everything she'd ever been and ever would be, she wanted this. Wanted him.

With tears spilling down her cheeks, she twined her arms around his neck and hitched back a happy sob as his lips reluctantly left hers.

There was supposed to be one special person in this world for everyone.

That's why I'm here, she told herself, feeling the full depth of that truth. *I'm here to love you.* Not above and beyond everything else, but to strengthen and enrich everything else she was now and was destined to be.

"We'll go straight to a store and pick out a ring," he murmured, his voice thick with love and pride.

But as his eyes glistened into hers—so full of conviction and faith—she flexed her fingers into his shirt. "I'd rather go straight home and get reacquainted."

"Why wait to get home?"

Without warning, he hoisted her up, a hand either side of her waist, and swung her around in a giddy, exhilarating circle. Alive with hope. Bursting with passion. Nina's heart was so full she wanted all the world to know this kind of happiness.

They were laughing and out of breath by the time he folded down with her onto the wet sand. As a shallow wave washed in and scalloped around them, she lay over his chest and whispered, "I love you so much. I wanted to call you so much."

His gaze roamed her face and he smiled. "I'm here now."

"Do you think we were in love all those years ago?"

A playful frown pinched his brow. "You were only fourteen."

"Juliet was fourteen."

"I'm more interested in writing our own love story."

He cradled her head, and Nina melted when his mouth claimed hers again.

As a rising swell of trust and passion consumed and lifted her up, in her heart Nina knew just three things:

The very best of her life had just begun…

She wished this kiss could last for ever…

And, as much as she loved this man—and she loved him to the infinite depths of her soul—Gabriel Turner Steele loved her more.

HIS MISTRESS FOR
A MILLION

Trish
MOREY

Trish Morey is an Australian who's also spent time living and working in New Zealand and England. Now she's settled with her husband and four young daughters in a special part of South Australia, surrounded by orchards and bushland, and visited by the occasional koala and kangaroo. With a lifelong love of reading, she penned her first book at the age of eleven, after which life, career, and a growing family kept her busy until once again she could indulge her desire to create characters and stories—this time in romance. Having her work published is a dream come true. Visit Trish at her website, www.trishmorey.com.

To the Maytoners,
every one of you warm, generous and wise.
This one's for you, with thanks.

xxx

CHAPTER ONE

REVENGE was sweet.

Andreas Xenides eyed the shabby building that proclaimed itself a hotel, its faded sign swinging violently in the bitter wind that carved its way down the canyon of the narrow London street.

How long had it taken to track down the man he knew to be inside? How many years? He shook his head, oblivious to the cold that had passers-by clutching at their collars or burrowing hands deeper into pockets. It didn't matter how long. Not now that he had found him.

The cell phone in his pocket beeped and he growled in irritation. His lawyer had agreed to call him if there was a problem with his plan proceeding. But one look at the caller ID and Andreas had the phone slipped back in his pocket in a moment. Nothing on Santorini was more important than what was happening here in London today, didn't Petra know that?

The wind grew teeth before he was halfway across the street, another burst of sleet sending pedestrians scampering for cover to escape the gusty onslaught, the street a running watercolour of black and grey.

He mounted the hotel's worn steps and tested the handle. Locked as he'd expected, a buzzer and rudimentary camera mounted at the side to admit only those with keys or reservations, but he was in luck. A couple wearing matching tracksuits and money belts emerged, so disgusted with the weather that they barely looked his way. He was past them and following the handmade sign to the downstairs reception before they'd struggled into their waterproof jackets and slammed the door behind them.

Floorboards squeaked under the shoddy carpet and he had to duck his head as the stairs twisted back on themselves under the low ceiling. There was a radio crackling away somewhere in the distance and his nose twitched at a smell of decay no amount of bleach had been able to mask.

This place was barely habitable. Even if the capricious London weather was beyond his control, he had no doubt the clientele would be much happier in the alternative accommodation he'd arranged for them.

A glazed door stood ajar at the end of a short hallway, another crudely handwritten note taped to the window declaring it the office, and for a moment he was so focused on the door and the culmination of a long-held dream that he barely noticed the bedraggled shape stooping down to pick up a vacuum cleaner, an overflowing rubbish bag in the other hand. A cleaner, he realised as she straightened. For a moment he thought she was about to say something, before she pressed her lips together and flattened herself against a door to let him pass. There were dark shadows under her reddened eyes, her fringe was plastered to her face and her uniform was filthy. He flicked his eyes away again as he passed, his nose twitching at the combined scent of ammonia and stale beer. So that was the hired help. Hardly surprising in a dump like this.

Vaguely he registered the sound of her retreat behind him, her hurried steps, the thud of the machine banging against something and a muffled cry. But he didn't turn. He was on the cusp of fulfilling the promise he'd made to his father on his deathbed.

It wasn't a moment to rush.

It was a moment to savour.

And so he hesitated. Drank in the moment. Wishing his father could be here. Knowing he would be watching from wherever he was now.

Knowing it was time.

He jabbed at the door with two fingers and watched it swing open, letting the squeak of the hinges announce his arrival.

Then he stepped inside.

The man behind the dimly lit desk hadn't looked up. He was too busy scribbling notes on what looked like the turf guide with one hand, holding the phone to his ear with the other, and it was all Andreas could do to bite back on the urge to cross the room and yank the man bodily from his chair. But much as he desired to tear the man to pieces as he deserved, Andreas had a much more twenty-first-century way of getting justice.

'Take a seat,' the man growled, removing the phone from his ear long enough to gesture to a small sofa, still busy writing down his notes. 'I'll be just a moment.'

One more moment when it had taken so many years to track him down? Of course he could wait. But he'd bet money he didn't have to.

'*Kala ime orthios,*' Andreas replied through his teeth, *I'm fine standing*, 'if it's all the same to you.'

The man's head jerked up, the blood draining from his face leaving his red-lined eyes the only patch of colour. He uttered a single word, more like a croak, before the receiver clattered back down onto the cradle, and all the while his gaze didn't leave his visitor, even as he edged his chair back from the desk. But there was nowhere to go in the cramped office and his chair rolled into the wall with a jolt. He stiffened his back and jerked his chin up as if he hadn't just been trying to escape, but he didn't attempt to stand. Andreas wondered if it was because his knees were shaking too much.

'What are you doing here?'

Andreas sauntered across the room, until he was looming over both the desk and the man cowering behind it, lazily picking up a letter opener in his long-fingered hands and testing its length through his fingers while all the time Darius watched nervously. 'It's been a long time, Darius. Or would you rather I called you Demetrius, or maybe even Dominic? I really can't keep up. You seem to go through names like other people go through toilet paper.'

The older man licked his lips, his eyes darting from side to side, and this close Andreas was almost shocked to see how much his father's one-time friend and partner had aged. Little more than fifty years old, and yet Darius's hair had thinned and greyed and his once wiry physique seemed to have caved in on itself, the lines on his face sucked deeper with it. The tatty cardigan he wore draped low on his bony shoulders did nothing to wipe off the years.

So time hadn't treated him well? Tough. Sympathy soon departed as Darius turned his eyes back to him and Andreas saw that familiar feral gleam, the yellow glow that spoke of the festering soul within. And he might be afraid now, taken by surprise by the sudden appearance of his former partner's son, but Andreas knew that any minute he could come out snarling. Not that it would do him any good.

'How did you find me?'

'That's one thing I always liked about you, Darius. You never did waste your time on small talk. No "how are you?" No "have a nice day".'

'I get the impression you didn't come here for small talk.'

'Touché,' Andreas conceded as he circled the room, absently taking inventory, enjoying the exchange much more than he'd expected. 'I have to admit, you weren't easy to find. You were good at covering your tracks in South America. Very good. The last we heard of you was in Mexico before the trail went cold.' Andreas looked up at the high basement window where the sleet was leaving trails of slush down the grimy glass before he turned back. 'And to think you could still be back there enjoying the sunshine. Nobody expected you'd be fool enough to show your face in Europe again.'

A glimmer of resentment flared in Darius' eyes, and his lip curled into a snarl. The hungry dog was out of its kennel. 'Maybe I got sick of beans.'

'The way I hear it, you ran out of money. Lost most of it on bad business deals and flashy women.' Andreas leaned over and picked up the form guide sitting on the desk. 'Gambled away the rest. All that money, Darius. All those millions. And this—' he waved his hand around him '—is what you're reduced to.'

Darius glowered, his eyes making no apology in their assessment of his visitor's cashmere coat and hand stitched shoes, a tinge of green now colouring his features. 'Looks like you've done all right for yourself though.'

No thanks to you!

Andreas' hands clenched and unclenched at his sides while he tried to remember his commitment not to tear the man apart. A deep breath later and he could once again manage a civil tone. 'You've got a problem with that?'

'Is that why you came here, then? To gloat?' He sneered, swinging a hand around the shabby office. 'To see me reduced to this? Okay, you've seen me. Happy now? Isn't that what they say—success is the best revenge?'

'Ah, now that's where they're wrong.' This time Andreas didn't restrain himself, but allowed the smile he'd been headed for ever since he'd set foot in this rat trap. 'Success is nowhere near the best revenge.'

The old man's eyes narrowed warily as he leaned forward in his chair, the fear back once more. 'What's that supposed to mean?'

Andreas pulled the folded sheaf of papers from inside his coat pocket. 'This,' he said, unfolding them so that the other man could see what he was holding. '*This* is the best revenge.'

And Andreas watched the blood drain from the other man's face as he recognised the finance papers he'd signed barely a week ago.

'Did you even read the small print, Darius? Didn't you wonder why someone would offer you money on this dump you call a hotel on such easy terms?'

The older man swallowed, his eyes once more afraid.

'Did you not suspect there would be a catch?'

Darius looked sick, his skin grey.

Andreas smiled again. 'I'm the catch. That finance company is one of mine. I lent you that money, Darius, and I'm calling in the debt. Now.'

'You can't... You can't do that. I don't have that kind of money lying around.'

He flung the pages in Darius' direction. 'I can do it, all right. See for yourself. But if you can't pay me back today, you're in default on the loan. And you know what that means.'

'No! You know there's no way...' But still Darius scrabbled through the pages, his eyes scanning the document for an out, squinting hard when they came across the clause that proved Andreas right, widening as he looked up with the knowledge that he'd been beaten. 'You can't do this to me. It's no better than theft.'

'You'd know all about theft, Darius, but whatever you call it this hotel is now mine. And it's closing. Today.'

The shocked look on Darius' face was his reward. The man looked as if he'd been sucker punched.

Oh, yes, Andreas thought, revenge was sweet, especially when it had been such a long time coming.

CHAPTER TWO

ROCK bottom.

Cleo Taylor was so there.

Her head ached, her bruised shin stung where the vacuum cleaner had banged into it, and three weeks into this job she was exhausted, both mentally and physically. And at barely five o'clock in the afternoon, all she wanted to do was sleep.

She dropped the machine at the foot of her bed and sank down onto the narrow stretcher, the springs that woke her every time she rolled over at night noisily protesting her presence.

Karma. It had to be karma.

How many people had tried to warn her? How many had urged her to be careful and not to rush in? And how many of those people had she suspected of being jealous of her because she'd found love in the unlikeliest of places, in an Internet chat room with a man halfway around the world?

Too many.

Oh, yes, if there was a price to pay for naivety, for blindly charging headlong for a fall, she was well and truly paying it.

And no one would say she didn't deserve everything that was happening to her. She'd been so stupid believing Kurt, stupid to believe the stories he'd spun, stupid to believe that he loved her.

So pathetically naïve to trust him with both her heart and with her nanna's money.

And all she'd achieved was to spectacularly prove the award she'd been given in high school from the girls whose company she'd craved, but who never were and who would never be her friends.

Cleo Taylor, girl most likely to fail.

Wouldn't they just love to see her now?

A barrage of sleet splattered against the tiny louvred window high above the bed and she shivered. So much for spring.

Reluctantly she thought about dragging herself from the rudimentary bed but there was no way she wanted to meet that man in the hallway again. She shuddered, remembering the ice-cold way his eyes dark pits of eyes set in a slate-hard face— had raked over her and then disregarded her in the same instant without even an acknowledgment, as if she was some kind of low-life, before imperiously passing by. She'd shrunk back instinctively, her own greeting dying on her lips.

It wasn't just that he looked so out of place, so wrong for the surroundings, but the look of such a tall, powerful man sweeping through the low-ceilinged space seemed wrong, as if there wasn't enough space and he needed more. He hadn't just occupied the space, he'd consumed it.

And then he'd swept past, all cashmere coat, the smell of rain and the hint of cologne the likes of which she'd never smelt in this place, and she'd never felt more like the low-life he'd taken her to be.

But she had to get up. She couldn't afford to fall asleep yet, even though she'd been up since five to do the breakfasts and it had taken until four to clean the last room. She reeked of stale beer and her uniform was filthy, courtesy of the group of partying students who'd been in residence in the room next door for the last three nights.

She hated cleaning that room! It was damp and dark, the tiny en suite prone to mould and the drains smelling like a swamp, and if she hadn't already known how low she'd sunk that room announced it in spades. The students had left it filthy, with beds looking as if they'd been torn apart, rubbish spilling from bins over the floor, and an entire stack of empty takeaway boxes and beer bottles artfully arranged in one corner all the way from the floor to the low ceiling. 'Leaning Tower of Pizza,' someone had scrawled on the side of one the boxes, and it had leant, so much so that it was a wonder it hadn't already collapsed with the vibrations from the nearby tube.

It had been waiting for her to do that. Bottles and pizza boxes raining down on her, showering her with their dregs. *No wonder he'd looked at her as if she were some kind of scum.* After the day she'd had, she felt like it.

She dragged herself from the bed and plucked her towel off a hook and her bag of toiletries, ready to head to the first-floor bathroom. What did she care what some stranger she'd never see again thought? In ten minutes she'd be showered, tucked up in bed and fast asleep. That was all she cared about at the moment.

The bright side, she told herself, giving thanks to her nanna as she ascended the stairs and saw rain lashing against the glazing of the ground-floor door, was that she had a roof over her head and she didn't have to go out in today's weather.

"There's always a silver lining", her nanna used to tell her, rocking her on her lap when she was just a tiny child and had skinned her knees, or when she'd started school and the other girls had picked on her because her mother had made her school uniform by hand and it had shown. Even though her family was dirt poor and sometimes it had been hard to find, there'd always been something she'd been able to cling to, a bright side somewhere, something she'd been able to give thanks for.

Almost always.

She sighed as the hot water in the shower finally kicked in and warmed her weary bones. A warm shower, a roof over her head and a bed with her name written on it. Things could always be worse.

And come summer and the longer days, she'd have time to see something of the sights of London she'd promised herself before she went home. Not that there was any hurry. At the rate she was paid, after her board was deducted, it would be ages before she could even think about booking a return airfare to Australia. God, she'd been so stupid to trust Kurt with her money!

A sudden pang of homesickness hit her halfway back down the stairs. Barely six weeks ago she'd left the tiny outback town of Kangaroo Crossing with such confidence, and now look at her. If only she could go home. If only she'd never left! She'd give anything to hug her mum and half-brothers again. She'd even find a smile for her stepfather if it came down to it. But when would that be? And how would she be able to face everyone when she did?

She would be going home humiliated. A failure.

The bright side, she urged herself, *look at the bright side*, as she pulled her eye mask down and snuggled under the covers, the cold rain lashing at her tiny window. She was warm and dry and she had at least ten hours' sleep before she had to get up and do it all over again.

'But you can't close the hotel,' Darius protested. 'There are bookings. Guests!'

'Who will be catered for, as will the staff we have on file from your finance application.' Andreas snapped open his phone, made a quick call and slipped the phone back into his pocket. 'I'm sure the guests won't mind being transferred to the four-star hotel we've chosen to accommodate them in and you can be assured the employees will be paid a generous redundancy.'

He cast a disdainful eye around the room. 'I don't foresee any complaints. And now I want you off the premises. I have staff coming in to take over and ensure the changeover is smooth. The hotel will be empty in two hours.'

'And what about me?' Darius demanded. 'What am I supposed to do? You're leaving me with nothing. Nothing!'

Andreas slowly turned back, unable to stop his lips from forming into a sneer. 'What about you? How many millions did you steal from my father? You happily walked away and left my family with nothing. What did you care about anyone else then? So why should I care about what happens to you? Just be grateful you're able to walk out of here with your limbs intact after the way you betrayed my father.'

A buzzer sounded, the security monitor showing a team of people waiting on the front step. 'Let them in, Darius.' The older man's hand hovered over the door-release button.

'I can help you!' he suddenly said instead, pulling his hand away to join the other in supplication. 'You don't need all these people. I know this hotel and I... I'm sorry for what happened all those years ago. It was a mistake... A misunderstanding. Your father and I were once good friends. Partners even. Isn't there any way you might honour that?'

Andreas dragged much-needed air into his lungs. 'I'll honour it in the same way you honoured my father. Get out. You've got ten minutes. And then I never want to see you again.'

Darius knew when he was beaten. Sullenly he gathered his personal possessions, the form guide included, in a cardboard box and slunk away even as the team filed into the office. Andreas took two minutes to go over the arrangements. Someone would email all forward bookings and advise of the change of hotels while the rest of the team would meet guests as they returned to expedite their packing and transfer to the new hotel. New guests would simply be ferried to the alternative premises nearby. There was no reason for the operation not to go like clockwork.

His cell phone beeped again as he dismissed the team to their duties and he reached for it absently, taking just a second to savour what he'd achieved. The look on Darius' face when he'd realised the truth, that he had lost everything and to the son of the man he'd cheated of millions so many years ago, was something he would cherish for ever. Doubly so because his father never could.

He frowned when he looked at the phone. Petra calling again? *Kolisi*, maybe there really was an emergency.

'*Ne?*'

Half a continent away, Petra's voice lit up. 'Andreas!' She sounded so bright he could almost hear the flashbulb.

'What's wrong?'

'Oh, I've been so worried about you. How is it in London? It is all going to plan?'

Andreas felt a stab of irritation. No emergency, then. Merely Petra thinking she had some stake in what was happening here. She was wrong. 'Why are you calling, Petra?'

There was a pause. Then, 'The Bonacelli deal! The papers are here ready to be signed.'

'I expected that. I told you I'll sign them when I get back.'

'And Stavros Markos called,' she continued at rapid pace, as if he hadn't spoken. 'He wants to know if they can book out the entire Caldera Palazzo for their daughter's wedding next June. It's going to be huge. They only want the best and I told them it should be fine, though I have to put off another couple of enquiries—'

'Petra,' he cut in, 'you know they can. You don't have to ring me to confirm. What's bothering you? Is there something else?'

There was silence at the end of the line, and then she laughed, an uncomfortable tinkle. Or at least, it made him feel uncomfortable. 'I'm sorry, Andreas,' she continued. 'It probably sounds silly, but I miss you. When do you think you'll be back?'

Something clenched in his gut, the pattern of her constant phone calls making the kind of sense he didn't want them to make. But there was no other option. She'd been checking up on him, making sure nobody else was occupying his bed or his attentions while he was in London and she was holding the fort back on Santorini.

He murmured something noncommittal before sliding his phone shut. What was wrong with her? He didn't do relationships. Petra, more than anyone, should have understood that. She'd witnessed the parade of women through his life. Hell, she'd been the one to organise the flowers for them when they were on the inner, the trinkets for them when they were on the outer. But he'd made one fatal mistake, broken his own rule never to get involved with the staff.

Drunk on success and the culmination of years of planning, he'd let his guard down when he'd heard the news that Darius had been found and the trap set. He'd been the one to insist Petra go out to dinner with him to celebrate. He'd been the one to order the champagne and he'd been the one to respond when she leaned too close, all but spilling her breasts into his hands. He'd wanted the release and she'd been there.

What a fool! He'd always assumed she was as machine-like and driven as he was. He'd always thought that she'd understood it was always just sex to him. And yet every time Petra called him now, he could almost feel her razor-sharp nails piercing his skin all over again. But why she'd want to be his mistress when she knew which way they invariably went…

Cold fingers crawled down his spine.

Or did she have something else in mind? Something more permanent she thought she was due after working alongside him for so many years?

Sto thiavolo!

What had his mother been telling him in her recent phone calls? That maybe it was time for him to settle down and find a wife?

And who did his mother like to talk to first, calling the office line instead of his cell phone, because 'her own son never bothered to tell her anything'?

Petra.

Had his mother also confided the news with her good friend's daughter that it was time for her only child to settle down? He'd just bet she had.

Damn. He didn't want to have to find a new marketing director. Petra was a good operator. The best at marketing the package of luxurious properties that Xenides Exclusive Property let to the well-heeled looking for a five-star experience in some of the most beautiful places in the world. She'd single-handedly designed the website that made his unique brand of five-star luxury accommodation accessible to every computer on the planet and made it so tempting that just as many booked through the website alone as booked by personal referral.

He didn't want to lose her; together they made a good team. But neither did he want her thinking she was destined to be anything more to him than a valued employee.

He sighed. What would she do when he found someone else, as he inevitably would? Would she leave of her own accord?

Andreas made up his mind on a sigh. It was a risk he would just have to take. Petra's departure from the business, while inconvenient, was preferable to her making wedding plans. All of which meant one thing.

He wouldn't be returning to Santorini without a woman on his arm and in his bed.

She would have to be somebody new, somebody different, someone who could step into the role of his mistress and then step out when he no longer needed her. No strings. No ties.

A contract position. A month should be more than enough.

Now he just had to find her before his flight back to Greece tomorrow.

He looked around the dingy room and sighed, the weight of years of the need for vengeance sloughing from his shoulders. His work here was done, an old score settled and Darius vanquished. There was no need for him to linger; his team knew what to do. He could hear them now knocking on doors and explaining the move, smoothing any objections with the promise of four-star luxury and their bill waived for the inconvenience. They would make the necessary transfers and see to the stripping bare of the furnishings in preparation for the builders and decorators that would turn this place into something worthy of being included in the Xenides luxury hotel portfolio.

Everything was under control.

And that's when he heard the scream.

CHAPTER THREE

THE earth-shattering sound rang through the basement, followed by a torrent of language Andreas had no hope of discerning. He was down the hallway and at the open door in just a few strides. 'What the hell is going on?'

One of his team was busy backing out of the small room, closely followed by a slipper that flew past his head and smacked into the wall behind. 'I had no idea there was anyone here,' he said defensively. 'It was marked on the plans as a closet. And it's barely six o'clock. What's anyone doing in bed at this time of night, least of all here?'

'Get out!' screeched the voice. 'Or I'll call the manager. I'll call the police!'

So much for everything being under control. Andreas ushered his red-faced assistant out of the way. 'I'll handle this.'

He stepped into the tiny room that smelt and looked more like a broom closet, ducking his head where the stairs cut through the headspace and avoiding the single globe dangling on a wire from the ceiling, under whose yellow light he found the source of the commotion. She was sitting up in bed, or on a camp stretcher more like it, with her back rammed tight against the wall, the bedding pulled up tight around her with one hand despite the fact her fleecy pyjamas covered every last square centimetre below her neck. In her other hand she wielded a second furry slipper.

Her eyes were wide and wild-looking under a pink satin eye mask reading 'Princess' that she'd obviously shoved up to her brow when she'd been disturbed. Some kind of joke, he decided. In her dishevelled state, with her mousy-coloured hair curling haphazardly around her face, she looked anything but princess material.

Then his eyes made sense of the smell. In the yellow light he saw the vacuum cleaner tucked at the end of the bed and the drab uniform draped unceremoniously over the radiator, and one question at least was answered. The cleaner, he surmised, the one he'd spotted earlier in the corridor who'd stunk of beer. No doubt she'd been trying to sleep it off when she'd been disturbed.

He tried to keep the sneer from his lips as he addressed her. 'I must apologise for my people startling you,' he began. 'I assure you, nobody means you any harm. We simply didn't realise you were here.'

'Well, I am *obviously* here and your *people* have a bloody nerve going about bursting into other people's rooms. What the hell are you playing at? Who are you? Where's Demetrius?'

He held up his hands to calm her. She was Australian, he guessed from her accent, or maybe a New Zealander, but her words were spilling out too fast to be sure.

'I think perhaps you should calm down and then we can discuss this rationally.'

Her hand lifted the slipper. 'Calm down? Discuss rationally? You and your henchman have no right barging into my room. Now get out before I scream again.'

Gamoto, the way she clung to those bedcovers as if her virtue were at stake! Did she really think he was going to attack her? It would take a braver man than him to tackle those industrial-strength pyjamas she was buried beneath.

'I'll leave,' he conceded, 'but only so you can get dressed. Come out when you're ready to talk. It is impossible to reason with a woman sitting in bed dressed up like a clown.'

Her jaw fell open, snapping shut again on a huff. 'How dare you? You have no right to be here. No right at all.'

'I have every right! I've wasted enough time here as it is. Now get dressed and meet me in the office. I'll speak to you then.'

He spun away, pulling the door closed behind him, but not before the other pink slipper went hurtling over his shoulder like a furry missile.

He'd barely started pacing the office floor, damning Darius for the spitting, snarling legacy he'd left behind, when he heard someone behind him. He turned to find a young woman in jeans and a top standing there, her expression sullen, her feet bare.

He sighed. *What the hell else*, he thought, *has Darius left me to clean up?* 'Can I help you?'

'You tell me. You're the one who demanded my presence.'

His eyes did a double take. This was the cleaner? The banshee ready to scream the house down in the broom closet? He didn't know what to be more impressed by, her speed in complying with his orders—the women he associated with couldn't effect a quick change if their life depended on it—or the radical change in her appearance.

He asked her to shut the door behind her and he leaned back and perched himself on the edge of the desk, watching her as she complied. She'd discarded the fleecy pyjamas and ridiculous eye mask and pulled on faded jeans and a long-sleeved T-shirt, and that brought the second surprise. She wasn't tall, but what she missed out on in height she made up for in curves. He'd never have guessed there was shape under that drab uniform or hidden away under a mound of bed clothes, but her fitted T-shirt and hipster jeans accentuated the swell of breasts and the feminine curve of waist to hip that had been completely disguised before.

Nor would he have guessed she would scrub up so well. Sure, there were still grey shadows under her eyes, but she looked years younger than the haggard wreck he'd seen struggling with the vacuum cleaner in the hallway, and much less frightening than the banshee he'd encountered so recently in the closet-cum-bedroom. With not a hint of make-up and with her damp hair tamed into some kind of loose arrangement behind her head, a few loose tendrils coiled around her face served to soften features that weren't classical in the least.

She would never pass for pretty, he determined, but if she bothered to make an effort she could probably do something with herself.

Although right now it looked as if she'd much prefer to do something with him, preferably involving knives.

He caught the glower as she folded her arms underneath her breasts and wondered if she had any idea that motion just accentuated their fullness. *Or that it drew attention to their peaking nipples.*

So she hadn't bothered to put on a bra? No wonder she'd been so quick to appear. He was surprised to feel his body stir, but then he'd never had a problem with such time-saving measures, or with breasts that looked like an invitation. Despite the inconvenience, he could only be intrigued by the closet-dweller. He was sure he'd seen no mention of her in the reports that had crossed his desk.

Cleo bristled under the relentless gaze. What was his problem? She'd done what he'd demanded—abandoned any hope of sleep to get herself up and dressed and met him in the office and for what? So his eyes could rake over her as if she were some choice cut of meat in a butcher-shop window?

So maybe the look was marginally better than the one he'd given her in the hallway earlier when he'd regarded her as some kind of scum before sweeping imperiously by, but it certainly didn't make her feel any more comfortable.

Quite the reverse. She rubbed her upper arms, not from the chill, but to ward off the prickling sensation his gaze generated under her skin. And if she was lucky the action might just break whatever magnet hold his eyes had on her breasts.

He only had to look at them for her nipples to harden to rocks.

Damn the man! Arrogance shone out of him like a beacon, but the only thing it was lighting up was her temper.

'Are you going to tell me what this is all about or would you prefer to keep ogling me?' She looked around the office. 'Where's Demetrius?'

'The man you know as Demetrius is gone.'

Of course he would speak in riddles. The man was insufferable. 'What are you talking about? Gone where? When will he be back?' She'd never much liked her boss, who'd seemed more concerned with his form guide than with how his hotel was falling down around his ears, but as far as she was concerned, the sooner he was back, the better.

'He won't be back. This hotel now belongs to me.'

His revelation slammed through her like a thunderbolt. Where did that leave her? Her rapidly chilling toes curled into the cracked linoleum while a shudder of apprehension wormed its way into her mind. Whatever had happened must have been sudden. She'd heard Demetrius on the phone to his turf accountant when she'd finished the last room, just before this man had appeared, larger than life. A bloodless coup. And the man in front of her, with his cold eyes and strong jaw, looked just the kind of ruthless man for the job. Ruthless—but also her new boss. She swallowed, horrified at the impression she'd made so far. Hadn't she flung a slipper past his ear? 'What is this, then, some kind of interview? Okay, my name is Cleo Taylor and I've been cleaning here for three weeks, and doing the breakfasts. Demetrius probably told you—'

'Demetrius told me nothing. There was no mention of you in the list of employees we had.'

'Oh? But then, Demetrius paid me in cash. He said it was better for the both of us.'

'He would no doubt think that.' Andreas understood why. So Darius could pay her peanuts and most likely deduct the majority of it in return for the cot she occupied.

She shrugged, looking confused. 'So… You'll still be needing a cleaner, right?'

'Not exactly.'

'Okay, I do more than clean. I get up at five for the breakfasts…'

'I'm not looking for a cleaner. Or a kitchen hand.'

'But the hotel—'

'Is closing.'

The fear that had begun as a shred of concern exploded inside her in a frenzy of panic. It might be the worst job with the worst pay in the world—but it was a job, and it came with a roof over her head. And now she'd have no job. *And, more importantly, nowhere to live.*

Her mouth was drier than a Kangaroo Crossing summer's day. 'You mean I lose my job.'

He gave the briefest of nods. It might as well have been the fall of the guillotine. Once more she'd failed. Once more she'd bombed. She almost wanted to laugh. Almost managed to, except the sound came out all wrong and this was no place or time for such reactions, not with him here, watching her every move like a hawk.

Oh, Nanna, she beseeched, closing her eyes with the

enormity of it all, *where's the silver lining to losing the worst job in the world?* Unless that was it. She hated the job. Now she had no choice but to find something else. And hopefully, something better.

But it was so hard to think positive thoughts about losing her job when it also meant she'd be losing the roof over her head with it. She opened her eyes toward the window, the rain still pelting against the glass. A bright side. There had to be a bright side. But right now she was darned if she could see what it was.

'When?' Her voice was the barest of whispers. 'How much time do I have?' She would have to move fast to secure something. The little money she had wouldn't last long and if she had to use it for any kind of rental bond…

'Tonight. You need to pack your things and be gone in two hours. The guests are all being transferred to other premises. The builders and redecorators move in to gut the place tomorrow.'

'Tonight? You're closing the hotel so soon?' And panic turned to outrage. 'No. No way you can just walk in and do that!'

'No? And why is that? Surely not some misplaced loyalty to your former employer? I see he showed you none.'

'No, damn you. But it took me the best part of the day to clean this dump. Every single room from top to bottom and now you tell me you're closing it and I could have knocked off at ten this morning? Thank you very much. You could have saved me the trouble!' She flung out her arms to make the last point and then put a hand to her brow, pushing back the hair from her face. Although it was what the action did to her breasts that had his attention.

He didn't know what he'd been expecting, but it wasn't the impassioned response she'd given him. Or the swaying floor show. No sag. Her breasts were full and round and pointed high. Would they look as good uncovered? Would they fill his hands as generously as he imagined they would? Would he like to find out? He needed a woman…

He dragged in a breath, trying to cool his rapidly heating groin, and forced his eyes away. *Sto kalo*, she was a cleaner. A cleaner with a drinking problem if how she'd appeared earlier was any indication. Petra must really be getting to him if he was getting hot under the collar over a cleaner. 'You're mad at me,' he said, reluctantly dragging his attention back to her face, 'because you've spent all day cleaning? Isn't that your job?'

She choked back a sob. Yes, she probably sounded irrational, hysterical, but what did he expect—that she would turn around and calmly thank him for his bombshell? 'You try being a cleaner in a dump like this. I've just had the worst day of my life. How would you like it if you were a cleaner and someone booby-trapped their rubbish? How would you like it if you ended up smelling like a brewery and wearing someone else's dried pizza crusts and then somebody else told you that you hadn't had to clean it up at all, that you needn't have bothered?'

His ears pricked up. Maybe not a cleaner with a drinking problem after all. Maybe he wasn't quite so crazy… 'You don't drink beer? I thought you were an Australian.'

'So that makes me a drinker? No, for the record, I don't drink beer. I can't abide the taste of it. And,' she continued, without missing a beat, 'then I get hauled from my bed and told that my job is over and that I have to leave. And that you want to throw me out in that!' She pointed to the window, where the rain distorted the light from the streetlamps and turned it into crazy zigzags. 'What kind of man are you?'

He wanted to growl. This was supposed to be the most successful day of his life, a day he'd dreamed about for what seemed like for ever. And here he was, being challenged by the likes of this scrap of a woman, a mere cleaner. He ground out his answer between his teeth. 'A businessman.'

'Well, bully for you. What kind of business is it that throws innocent women out onto the street in the middle of the storm from hell?'

He'd heard enough. He turned and flicked an imaginary piece of lint from his sleeve. 'You must have somewhere else to go.'

'Yes. And it's twelve thousand miles away. Shall I start walking now, do you think?'

'Then why don't you just buy yourself a ticket home?'

'And you think that if I could afford my fare home, I'd be working in a dump like this?'

'Do you need to be so melodramatic?'

'No. I don't need to. I'm just doing it for laughs.' She dragged in a breath and threw her arms out by her sides. 'Look, why can't I stay here? Just for tonight. I'll go tomorrow morning, first thing. I promise. Maybe it will have stopped raining by then.'

'The hotel is closing,' he reiterated. 'It will be locked down tonight in preparation for the builders and redecorators coming in tomorrow. The deal was the hotel would be delivered empty.'

'Nobody made a deal with me!'

'I'm making it now.'

It didn't sound like much of a deal to her. 'So where are the guests going? Why can't I go there?' She held up her hand to stop his objection. 'Not as a guest. Surely they could do with a cleaner, with this sudden influx of additional guests.'

He uttered something in Greek, something that sounded to her dangerously like a curse. 'I'll call and ask. No guarantees. Meanwhile you get your things together. I assume that won't take long.'

She sniffed. 'And if they don't have a job?'

'Then you're on your own.'

'Just like that?'

'Just like that.'

She put her hands on top of her head and sighed, locking her fingers together, and turning her head up high, as if to think about it.

But Andreas couldn't think about it. He was too busy following the perfect shape of her breasts, her nipples pulled up high, their shape so lovingly recreated by the thin cotton layer that was all that separated him from them. Her waist looked even smaller now. Almost tiny in comparison as she pulled her arms high, the flare of her hips mirroring the curve above. His mouth went dry.

Damn it all! He yanked his eyes away, rubbing them with his fingers. Anyone would think he'd never had a woman. She was a cleaner. It wouldn't work. Clearly the day had taken more out of him than he'd realised.

'And what about my wages?' She was looking at him, her eyes wide, her arms unhooking. 'Demetrius owes me for more than a week! And surely I'm entitled to some kind of severance pay, even if he was paying me cash, seeing you're the one to terminate my job!'

Silently he cursed Darius again, along with his own team that had failed to pick up this stray employee. 'How much are you owed?'

Cleo did some rapid sums in her head. Math had never been her strong point, so the calculations were a bit rough, but an entire week and a half, less board, that was a considerable sum. 'Fifty quid,' she said, rounding it off, hoping he wouldn't balk.

He pulled a money clip from his pocket, withdrew a handful of notes and then added a fistful more before handing the bundle to her.

Her eyes opened wide as she took in the high-denomination notes and the number of them. Her math was still lousy, but it was more than clear he'd given her way too much. 'I can't take this! There's heaps more than that here.'

'Then consider it a bonus for doing what I ask and getting out of here. Call it your redundancy package, if you like, with enough for your accommodation tonight and probably for an entire week if you play your cards right. Now, it's time you started packing.'

She looked as if she'd rather stay and keep arguing, her mouth poised open and ready to deliver another salvo, but she must have thought better of it. She jammed her lips shut and wheeled around, marching purposefully towards the door, shoving the wad of notes into her jeans pocket as she went. Not that it was any distraction. He was already looking there, admiring the way her denim jeans lovingly caressed the cheeks of her behind as she went. But she stopped before the door and turned, and he was forced to raise his eyes to meet hers.

'I'll go and pack,' she said, colour in her cheeks and fire spitting from her eyes, 'and I'd like to say it's been a pleasure meeting you, but I'm afraid that isn't possible. I'll leave my key in the door. Not that you need it, apparently.'

And then she swept out with her head held high like the princess on her eye mask rather than a redundant cleaner.

There was no need for him to stay. But he sat there, leaning against the desk, thinking that he'd been wrong. She wasn't pretty by any measure, she wasn't tall and elegant like his usual choice of woman, but there was something about her, a fire in her eyes as she'd protested his closure of the hotel, something that had almost burned bright in the seedy air between them. Would she be as passionate in the bedroom, or would she go back to being the bedraggled mouse he'd seen lurking in the corridor?

Damn! Trust Darius to leave him to clean up his rubbish. But he should have expected it.

He rubbed the bridge of his nose, hating the way his thoughts were going. The woman had a point. He, more than anyone, knew what it was like to be left with nothing and without even a roof over his head. He wouldn't wish that on anyone.

He slid open his cell phone, found the direct number for the manager of the hotel the guests here were being transferred to and hit 'call'. It answered within a moment. 'It's Andreas. Have you a position for another cleaner or kitchen hand? There is one here who requires a position, preferably live-in.'

There was a moment's hesitation, but no argument, no question as to qualifications or referees from the manager. That Andreas himself had enquired was all the assurance the manager required, the moment's hesitation all the time he needed to make the necessary rearrangements. Of course, they could use the help, came the answer. And there would be a bed the person could use in a shared room.

Andreas breathed deep with relief. When he'd thought of getting even with Darius, he'd thought they'd covered all the bases with everyone on the payroll. He'd not thought about any other fallout, the ones Darius had been paying on the sly. But now that fallout was well and truly taken care of. His father had been avenged and nobody had been inadvertently left homeless in the deal. It was the best of all worlds.

He tried to recapture the joy, the exhilaration of the day's events. After what he'd achieved after a lifetime of wanting, he should feel better than this, surely. But something still didn't sit right with him. Maybe it was just the adrenaline let-down now that he'd achieved his goal?

Or maybe it was because he wasn't sure that he wanted someone else taking care of fallout that came complete with sweet curves and lush breasts?

He sighed. He might as well go give her the good news. His car was waiting and he had work to do.

She was already struggling out of her room with an over-sized pack when he emerged and he wondered how she'd walk if ever she got it onto her back. It looked almost as big as her. He leaned down and took it from her, lifting its weight easily. Their fingers brushed and she pulled her hand away, tucking it under her other arm. 'So you pack as quickly as you get changed?'

She looked up at him, her cheeks flaring with colour again as he looked down at her, surprised by the extent of her reaction. Did she not want to touch him that desperately, or was it something else she was feeling? Resentment perhaps, or even hatred that he'd bowled her out into such a night. But she'd dragged on some kind of all-weather jacket and her breasts' reaction was hidden from him. 'Please, you don't have to take that. Not after—all those things I said about you. It was very ungracious after you were so generous. I'm sorry. It's been a long day.'

'I found you a job.'

Her eyes opened wide. 'You did?' They were blue, he realised for the first time, the kind of blue that came with the first rays of light on a misty Santorini morning showing all the promise of a new day. And then she smiled. 'But that's fantastic. Thank you so much. Is it a cleaner's job at the other hotel? Can I stay there?'

He'd never seen her smile. He got the impression she didn't use it a lot around this place, but it was like switching on a light bulb and for a moment it switched off his thought processes. He coughed, his mind busy rewinding, rethinking. 'The job comes with accommodation, yes.'

'Oh, I can't believe it. I'm so sorry for all those things I said back there. I really am.' She reached into her back pocket and hauled out the stash of notes he'd given her, pressing them into his free hand. 'Here. I can't take this now. I won't be needing your money.'

A woman who wouldn't take money when it had been given her? He didn't know many women who wouldn't be hanging around for more, not handing it back. So she worked as a cleaner—maybe she was better qualified than he'd assumed.

A month.

That was all he'd need. She wouldn't be the kind of woman to expect to hang around. She wouldn't want more than he was prepared to give.

A month would work out just fine.

CHAPTER FOUR

'KEEP it,' Andreas said, pushing her hand back, curling his fingers around it. 'You'll probably need some new clothes in your new job.'

Cleo solemnly regarded the notes still curled in her palm, her hand small and warm in his. 'Oh, you mean a new uniform.'

'Something like that,' he said, turning away quickly. 'Come on, my car's waiting outside, I'll give you a lift.'

He hauled her bag up the stairs as if it were a handbag and not stuffed full with all her worldly possessions and from there someone else took one look and relieved him of it, following in their wake, holding an umbrella over their heads as they emerged into the wet night. *Who is this man,* she wondered, *to have his own people to fetch and carry and clean out an entire hotel at his say-so?* A line of minibuses waited at the kerb outside, their exhaust turning to fog in the cold evening air. She recognised some of last night's guests being bundled with their luggage into one of the vans.

She started walking to the one behind. 'No,' he said. 'This one's ours.'

She looked where he indicated and did a double take. He had to be kidding. The black limousine stretched for what looked an entire frontage if not the whole block! She swallowed. She'd never travelled in such a vehicle in her life. She flashed a look down at her outfit. Worn farm boots, denim jeans and an old Driza-Bone coat. She looked longingly at the line of minibuses. She'd feel much more comfortable in something like that.

But the chauffeur had the door open, waiting. 'Are you sure we'll both fit?' she asked, but her companion didn't crack a smile, just gestured for her to precede him, and she had no choice but to enter the car.

It was like being in another world as the vehicle slipped smoothly into the traffic. It was bigger than her bedroom in the hotel and she wouldn't have been surprised to learn it boasted its own en suite. The plush leather seats were more like sofas with not a squeak of springs to be heard and they felt and smelled divine. A cocktail bar sprawled along one side, boasting spirits of every colour imaginable, a row of crystal-cut glasses held delicately in place, and then, just when she thought it couldn't get more amazing, there were stars, or at least tiny coloured lights twinkling all over the ceiling. And even as she watched they changed from blues and greens to oranges and reds and back to blues again.

And then there was him. He sprawled on the seat opposite, his back to the driver, one arm along the back of the seat, and with one leg bent, the other stretched long into the space between them. He'd undone his coat and the sides had fallen apart. Likewise the suit jacket underneath, exposing an expanse of snow-white cotton across his broad chest, all the whiter against the olive skin of his face and hands.

He was watching her, she realised. Watching her watching him. Her skin prickled. How could he do that with just his eyes? But it wasn't just his eyes, it was the slightly upturned mouth, the sculpted jaw and the attitude. Oh, yes, he had attitude to burn.

She pressed herself back into the seat, trying to look less overwhelmed, more relaxed. 'I guess you've never met anyone who hasn't been in a stretch limousine before. My reaction must have been quite entertaining.'

'On the contrary,' he said, without moving his eyes from hers, 'I found it charming.'

Charming. Nobody had ever used that word around her before. She wouldn't have believed them if they had. He was no doubt being polite. More likely thinking *gauche*. She felt it. Maybe she should steer the conversation, such as it was, to safer territory.

'Is it far to the hotel?'

'Not far.'

'Do you know what kind of job it is?'

'I think you will perform a variety of tasks. I'm sure you will find them to your liking.'

'Oh.' She wished he could be more specific. 'But it's a live-in position?'

Across the vast interior he nodded, his dark eyes glinting in the light of a passing streetlamp, and for some reason she suddenly felt uncomfortable, as if she'd almost glimpsed something in their otherwise shadowed depths.

'There is just one catch.'

'Oh?' There had to be though, she thought. Why should her life suddenly turn around without there being a catch? 'What is it?'

'The position has a fixed contract. This job will last only one month.'

'I see.' She sank back in her seat. Well, a month was better than nothing. And at least she'd have time to sort something else in between now and then.

'But you will be well compensated.'

She blinked up at him. 'Thank you again for your generosity, Mr...' and she was left floundering, speechless. She was in a car heading who knew where with a man who'd promised her a job somewhere and she didn't even know his name. When would she learn? What the hell kind of mess was she heading for now? 'Oh, My God, I can't believe I'm doing this. I don't even know your name.'

He smiled and dipped his head. 'I assure you, you have nothing to fear. Andreas Xenides at your service.'

Her eyes narrowed. She was sure she'd heard the name, maybe even read something in one of the papers back home before she'd left. But that man had been a billionaire. She didn't tend to meet many of them in her line of business. Maybe this man was related. 'I think there's someone called Xenides with a huge hotel up on the Gold Coast in Queensland.'

He nodded. 'The Xenides Mansions Hotel. One of my best performers.'

She swallowed. 'That's your hotel? You own it?'

'Well, one of my companies. But ultimately, yes, I own it.'

She didn't so much sink back into her seat as collapse against it.

He frowned. 'Does that bother you?'

'Bother me? It terrifies me!' She put a hand to her wayward mouth. Oh, my, the man was a billionaire and she'd thrown a slipper at his head, right before she'd bawled him out in the basement and insisted he pay her wages and find her a re-placement job. As a cleaner. And the amazing thing about it was that he had.

Mind you, the way people were running around after him at the hotel ready to do his bidding, he could probably have found her a job as an astronaut if he'd put his mind to it.

What must it be like to wield that much power? She glanced over at him, her eyes once more colliding with his dark driven gaze. So he was a billionaire. That answered a few questions. But it didn't answer all of them.

'There's something I don't understand.'

'Oh.' He tilted his head to one side, as if almost amused. 'What is it?'

'Why would you care about a tiny dump of a hotel three blocks from Victoria Station? Why buy it? There must be plenty of other hotels better suited to a posh outfit like yours.'

And his eyes glistened and seemed to focus somewhere behind her and Cleo got the impression he didn't even see her. 'I had my reasons.'

She shivered at his flat voice as if the temperature had just dropped twenty degrees. Whatever his reasons, Andreas Xenides struck her as a man you wouldn't want to cross.

Cleo looked away, wanting to shake off the chill, and was surprised to see how far they'd come. She'd expected a lift to another small hotel somewhere close by, as he'd intimated, but she could see now that the limousine was making its way towards Mayfair.

His cell phone beeped and she was grateful he had a distraction. She was happy just to watch the busy streetscape, the iconic red double-decker buses, the black taxi cabs all jockeying for the same piece of bitumen and somehow all still moving. 'Petra, I'm glad you called. Yes, I'm finished in London.'

She wasn't trying to listen to his call, but there was no way she couldn't hear every word, especially when he made no attempt to lower his voice, and it was a relief when he dipped into his native language and she could no longer understand his words and she could just let the deep tones of his voice wash over her. When he spoke English his accent gave his words a rich Mediterranean flavour, a hint of the exotic, but when he spoke in Greek his voice took on another quality, on the one hand somehow harsher, more earthy and passionate on the other.

Much like Andreas himself, she imagined, because for all his civilised trappings, the cashmere coat and the chauffeur-driven limousine, she'd seen for herself that he could be harsh and abrupt, that he was used to making the rules and expecting people to play by them. And definitely passionate. Hadn't he set her own body to prickly awareness with just one heated gaze?

It made sense that a man like him would have a Petra or someone else waiting for him. He was bound to have a wife or a girlfriend, maybe even both; didn't the rich and famous have their own rules? She looked around at the car's plush interior, drinking in the buttery leather upholstery with her fingers and wanting to apologise to the pristine carpet for her tired boots. She gazed out of the tinted windows and caught the occupants of passing cars trying to peer in, looks of envy on their faces, and sighed, committing it all to memory. What would it be like to be one of the Petras of this world? To move in such circles and consider this all as normal?

She smiled philosophically. This was not her world. Any minute now he'd drop her at the hotel to take up her new cleaning position and he'd be gone for ever, back to Petra or another, whoever and wherever she was.

'We're flying back tomorrow,' she heard Andreas say, abruptly switching back to English. 'Expect us around five.'

Cleo wondered at the sudden change of language but continued peering out at the scenery outside her limousine's windows, the magnificent park to their left, the lights from buildings and streetlamps making jagged patterns on the wet roads. Even on a dark, wet night the streets of London fascinated her. It was so different from the tiny town of Kangaroo Crossing, where the main street was dusty and almost deserted after six at night. Here it was so vibrant and filled with life at whatever time of the day or night and she would never get sick of craning her neck for a look at the everyday sights here like Buckingham Palace, sights she'd only ever dreamed about one day seeing.

'*Us*, Petra?' Andreas continued. 'Oh, I'm sorry, I should have mentioned. I'm bringing a friend.'

Something about the way he said those last words made Cleo turn her head, some loaded quality that spoke of a message she didn't quite understand. She didn't mean to look right at him, she intended to swing her head around as if merely choosing to look out of the nearside windows, but her eyes jagged on his and held solid. 'That's right,' he said, holding her gaze and her heartbeat, it seemed, in his. 'A friend. Please ensure Maria has my suite prepared.'

He clicked the phone closed and slipped it away, all the while still holding her gaze.

'Is it much further?' she asked with false brightness, wondering what it was she was missing and why she was so suddenly breathless and why he needed to look at her that way, as if she were about to be served up for his next meal.

'No. Not much.'

As if on cue the limousine pulled off Park Lane into a wide driveway and rolled to a gentle stop. She looked up at the hotel towering over the car. 'But this... This is Grosvenor House.'

'So it is.'

The door opened and cold air swept into the warm interior as the concierge pulled open the door. 'But why are we here? I thought... You said...'

'We're here,' he simply said, sliding one long leg out and extending his hand to her. 'If you care to join me.'

'But I can't go in there. Not like this. I look like I've just stepped off the farm.'

'They'll think you're an eccentric Australian.'

'They must have a staff entrance!' But still, she was already moving towards him, inexorably drawn by his assuredness.

'Come,' he said, taking her hand to help her out. 'These people are paid not to take any notice.'

It was no consolation. She felt like someone who should be staying at some backpackers' hotel, not the poshest hotel in Mayfair. She caught sight of her reflection in the glass frontage and grimaced. She looked like a total hick. Why couldn't he have warned her? But Andreas didn't seem to care. The concierge staff swarmed like foot soldiers around him, taking orders, trying to please, while others ferried her backpack onto a trolley as lovingly as if it were the finest Louis Vuitton luggage.

She followed in his wake uncertain, sure someone was about to call Security and send her on her way, but worry soon gave way to wonder.

She stepped from the revolving door into a lobby of white marble and columns the colour of clotted cream and forgot to think. It was amazing. Luxurious. A fantasyland. It took every shred of self-control she possessed not to spin around in a circle to take it all in. Instead she slipped her Driza-Bone from her shoulders and tried to look as if she belonged. Fat chance.

Could it be possible that she'd soon be working here? At Grosvenor House? Andreas left her momentarily while he dealt with Reception, she guessed to inform the housekeeper she was here, and she drank in the luxury and the ambience. Now she would have a reason to call her mother and not feel as if she had nothing but bad news. After the disaster that Kurt had been and her mother worrying about her working long hours in a seedy hotel, she would be thrilled she'd scored a position in one of London's landmark hotels. She wouldn't tell her it was only for a month. If she played her cards right, she'd have a reference from one of London's top hotels and she would be set for another job.

And maybe some time soon she'd be able to save enough money to pay back the money her nanna had given her and she'd lost when she'd entrusted it to Kurt. At least now she had a chance.

Andreas returned and took her arm and steered her past a suite of red velvet chairs on a round signature rug that reeked money.

'Are you taking me to meet the housekeeper? I'm sure I can find her. I've kept you long enough.'

He didn't look at her, simply kept on walking her into a lift. 'I thought you might like to see your room first, see if it's suitable.' He pushed a button and she frowned. 'Did I tell you you'd have to share?'

His question distracted her. 'You think I mind? Just look at this place.' She paused as the elevator smoothly hummed into motion, suddenly making sense of what had niggled at her before. 'Hang on. We're going up. Surely they wouldn't give staff accommodation on a guest floor?'

He held off answering as the lift doors slid open, welcoming them into an elegant elevator lobby decorated in olive and magenta tones, before he directed her to a nearby door and keyed it open. 'It seems you're in luck.'

And the hairs on the back of her neck stood to attention. 'Tell me this is not my room.'

'Strictly speaking, it's not. Like I told you, you'd have to share.'

She swallowed. 'Then tell me whose room it is. Who would even have a room like this in the Grosvenor to start with— Prince Harry?' And even as she asked the question the chilling answer came to her, so unbelievable that she didn't want to give it credence, so insane that she thought she herself must be. 'It's your room, isn't it? There is no cleaning job. And you expect me to share with you?'

His dark eyes simmered with aggravation. 'Come inside and I'll explain.'

'I'm not going in there! I'm not going anywhere except down in that lift unless you tell me right now what's going on. And then I'm probably heading down in that lift anyway.'

'Cleo, I will not discuss this in public.'

She looked around. 'There's nobody else here!'

A bell pinged behind her, followed seconds later by lift doors sliding open. A group emerged, the women chatting and laughing, their arms laden with shopping bags, the men looking as if they could do with a stiff drink.

She looked longingly at the open lift door behind them. Took a step towards it and then realised. She snapped her head around. 'Where is my pack?'

'No doubt still on its way up. Now come in and listen to what I have to say and if you still want to go, you can go. But hear me out first. I do have a job for you.'

'Just not cleaning, right?' Cleo bit her bottom lip. What kind of jobs did Greek billionaires give girls who'd dropped out of high school and made a mess of everything they'd ever attempted? Definitely nothing you needed qualifications for…

But that made less sense than anything else. Her looks were plain, her figure had always erred on the side of full, and she'd never had men lining up for her favours. Cleaning was about all she was suitable for.

'Cleo.'

He made her name sound like a warning, the tone threatening, but maybe he was right. Maybe she should hear him out while she waited for her pack. Besides, if she was going to let fly with a few choice words of her own, maybe privacy was the preferred option.

And then she'd leave.

Spider legs skittered down her spine at the thought of going out into the cold wet night with no place to go. But she'd face that later. She wasn't going to let the weather dictate her morals. She strode past him into the room, cursing herself for choosing that particular moment to breathe in, wishing that, for someone so aggravating, he didn't smell so damn good.

Thankfully the room was large enough that she could put some distance between them. A lot of distance. She'd been expecting a bedroom, a typical hotel room. She found anything but.

The room looked more like a drawing room in a palace than any hotel room she'd ever seen, a dining table and chairs taking up one end of the room, a lounge suite facing a marble mantelpiece at the other with the dozen or so windows dressed in complementary tones of creams and crimsons.

But she wasn't here to appreciate the fine furnishings or the skilful use of colour. She didn't want to be distracted by the luxury she could apparently so easily take advantage of. Would it be easy? She wondered.

She dropped her jacket over a chair and turned, dragging in oxygen for some much-needed support. 'Okay, I'm here. What's going on?'

She almost had the impression he hadn't heard her as he headed for a sideboard, opening a crystal decanter and pouring himself a slug of the amber fluid it contained. 'You?' he offered.

She shook her head. 'Well? You told me I had a cleaning job at some hotel.'

Still he took his sweet time, taking a sip from the glass before turning and leaning against the dresser. 'While it's not exactly what I said, it is what I intimated. That much is true.'

'You lied to me!'

'I did not lie. I found you a job cleaning at another hotel. And then I decided better of it.'

'But why? What for?'

He drained the glass of its contents and placed it on the dresser in the same motion as he pushed himself towards her. 'What if I offered you a better job? More pay. Enough to buy your return ticket to Australia and a whole lot more. Enough to set you up for life.'

She licked her lips. If she could pay back her nanna what she'd borrowed... But what would she be expected to do to get it? 'What kind of job are you talking about?'

He laughed, coming closer. 'You see why I knew you would be perfect? Any other woman would ask how much money first.'

She sidestepped around the dining table, until it was between them. 'That was my next question.'

He stopped and started moving the other way, slowly circling, step by step. 'How much would be enough? One hundred thousand pounds? How much would that be in your currency?'

She swallowed, too distracted to concentrate on keeping her distance. Her maths might be lousy but even she had no trouble working that one out. Double at least. Her mouth almost watered at the prospect. But she'd heard plenty of stories about travellers being offered amazing amounts of money to courier a box or a package. And equally she'd heard of them getting caught by the authorities and much, much worse. She might have done some stupid things in her life, but she was so not going there. 'I don't want any part of drug money. I'm not touching it.'

He was closer than she realised, his dark eyes shining hard. 'Cleo, please, you do not realise how much you insult me. This would be nothing to do with drugs. I hate that filthy trade as much as you. I assure you, your work would be legal and perfectly above board.'

Legal. Above board. And it paid in the hundreds of thousands of dollars? Yeah, sure. There were jobs in the paper like that for high-school dropouts every other day. 'What is it, then?' she asked, circling the other way, pretending to be more interested in an arrangement of flowers set upon a side table. The red blooms were beautiful too, she thought, touching her fingers to the delicate petals, just like everything else in this room. Did he really expect her to share it with him? 'So what's the job?'

He didn't move this time, made no attempt to follow her, and because she was ready for it, expecting it, the fact he stayed put was more unnerving than anything. 'It's really quite simple. I just need you to pretend to be my mistress.'

CHAPTER FIVE

'PRETEND to be your *what*?' Cleo started to laugh. If ever there was a time for hysterical laughter, this moment was tailor-made, but shock won out in the reaction stakes, choking off the sound and rendering her aghast. 'You must be insane!'

'I assure you I'm perfectly serious.'

'But your mistress? Who even uses that word any more?'

'Would you prefer it if I used the word *lover*?

'No!' *Definitely not lover.* And definitely not when it was said in that rich, curling accent. She didn't want to think about being Andreas' lover, pretend or otherwise. 'I don't know where you got the impression that I might say yes to such a crazy proposition, but I'm afraid you have the wrong impression of me, Mr Xenides. I'm sorry, but I'll have to turn down your generous proposal.'

'Call me Andreas, please.'

She looked over her shoulder anxiously, watching the door, before she looked back. 'And why would a man like you even need someone to act as his mistress anyway? It makes no sense.'

He shrugged. 'Maybe I just don't like to be seen as available.'

'Maybe you should just put out a press release.' She looked

longingly at the door again. 'When is my bag supposed to arrive? I want to go.'

'At least think about it, Cleo. It's a lot of money to throw away. Can you afford that?'

'You're crazy. Just look at me.' She held her arms out at her sides, her heart jumping wildly in her chest, her words tumbling over her tongue. 'I'm a cleaner. I muck out bathrooms and rubbish bins and have the split nails and red hands to prove it. I'm short and dumpy and have never once in my life been called so much as pretty, and you're suggesting I could pretend to be your mistress? Who's going to believe that for a start? They'll think you've gone mad and they'd be right.'

He answered her with a raised eyebrow and a half-hearted shrug as he eased closer. 'I think you underestimate your charms.'

Charms? What planet was this man from? 'Why *me*? You could have any woman in the world. You probably already have.'

He turned her implied insult to his advantage. 'Exactly. Which is why I don't want just any woman in the world.' He was close now, so close she could see the individual lashes that framed his dark eyes, close enough to see his pupils flare as he held out his fingers to her cheek. She flinched but he kept coming, tracing the line of her cheek with the backs of his fingers. 'I want you.'

Her heart missed a beat or two. She tried to shake her head but still his fingers remained, his touch feather-light and yet bone-shudderingly deep in effect.

'I don't... I can't...'

And he pulled his hand away, concern muddying his eyes as if something had just occurred to him. 'You're not a virgin?'

The intimacy of the question threw her for a moment. She could feel her cheeks burning up as she fought to find an answer. 'I thought this was about pretending. Why should whether or not I've ever slept with anyone even be an issue?'

He shrugged. 'Because there will be nights we are forced to share a bed to keep up appearances. And it's not beyond the realms of possibility that as a man and a woman, together, we might wish to seek mutual pleasure in each other's bodies.'

Help! 'So you expect sex, then, as part of this deal?'

He frowned and drew away, as if the very idea of her asking offended him. 'Not necessarily. Just that it may well be a by-product of our arrangement.'

Sex as a by-product of our arrangement?

How formal that sounded. How impersonal. It sounded more like a business deal, which she supposed it was. Not that she'd been involved in too many business deals, especially where they included a sex clause.

'I don't want it,' she ventured, not entirely sure if she meant just the contract or the sex or both. Because there was some-thing about Andreas' touch that sent her senses into overdrive, something about his touch that made a secret part of her ache in ways it shouldn't, especially not for a man she'd only just met, a man she knew nothing about.

'It's a good offer,' he continued, as gently and convincingly as a parent trying to get a child to drink its milk. 'It's a fixed-term contract and in one month you go home. All expenses paid. First-class travel naturally.'

He watched her face, searching for the crack in her resolve. 'And no sex, if that's what you want. Though if it did happen, I can guarantee it wouldn't mean anything.'

His words blurred. *"It wouldn't mean anything."* And all she kept hearing was the echo of the words Kurt had said to her when she'd told him she loved him. And he'd just laughed as he'd yanked up his jeans. *"What's your problem? It didn't mean anything. You really are stupid."*

And all she had felt was the bottom falling out of her world as her newly discovered heart had lain shredded. She'd made a pointless journey, thrown what she'd always believed to be special away on a deadbeat who'd taken everything he could get and left her high and dry.

'You have had sex? Can we be clear on that?' Andreas' uncertain voice came from a long way away and still it brought her hackles up. What did he think now, that she was a complete loser?

'Oh, sure, loads of times.' *Once.* But then why should it matter if he thought her a complete loser? It wasn't as if she hadn't thought the same thing herself.

'Then it's all settled.'

Her head snapped up. 'Hang on, what's settled?' She had a feeling she'd missed something somewhere. Had she said yes and somehow forgotten?

'Tomorrow you will fly with me to my home on Santorini.'

She knew the name. Kurt had wooed her with his promises of travel and sunsets, of short breaks they could take to the Mediterranean, to Corfu and Mykonos and Santorini, of crystal-clear waters and lazy summer days. It had sounded so romantic, but of course, it had all been lies designed to convince her that they had a future together in order to lure her to London. She'd all but given up any hope of seeing anything at all of Europe.

But now she had the chance to go there with Andreas. Was it enough of a reason to say yes?

A buzzer sounded and Andreas moved swiftly to the door, pulling it open to the porter at last with her luggage. 'We will leave at twelve. The morning will be busy with appointments so we will have to start early.

'In the bedroom, thank you,' Andreas directed the porter, pressing a note into his hand.

'No!' she called, surprising them both and causing the porter to wheel around. 'I'll take that.' She grabbed one of the shoulder straps.

'Leave it, Cleo.'

'But there's no point. I was just leaving anyway.'

The porter looked nervously from one to the other, Cleo tugging on the pack, knowing it was her hold on reality and on control, and Andreas glowering until finally the porter decided that discretion was the better part of valour and withdrew, uttering a rushed, 'Call me if you need anything more,' before making himself scarce.

Cleo heaved the backpack onto her shoulder.

'I thought we had a deal.'

'You thought wrong. I never agreed to anything. And I'm leaving.'

'But you have no job, nowhere to go.'

'I'll find something. I'll manage.' She retrieved her Driza-Bone from the back of a chair and bundled it in front of her before being game enough to steal one last glance at him.

Impossibly good-looking. That was how she'd remember him. Eyes of midnight-black and hair that waved thick and dark to collar length, an imperious nose and a passionate slash of mouth it was almost a crime for any man to possess. And a face like slate, just like she'd thought in the hotel, until it heated up and the angles took on curves she'd never seen coming.

But so what? She was leaving. It might be a huge amount of money to give up and already she could hear the girls from her high school singing out a familiar chorus of "loser, loser, Cleo's a loser". But she'd been hearing that chorus a long time and she was used to it. She'd been an object of pity ever since her father had walked out on her pregnant mother, never to be seen again.

And besides, she knew she was doing the right thing. For

Andreas' proposal was flawed. She didn't want the chance of 'sex as a by-product' of anything. She'd had sex that didn't mean anything and she'd hated herself in the aftermath. It had made her feel cheap and disposable and had hurt her more than she wanted to admit. She didn't care for the chance of more, no matter how much he might be paying.

'I'll see myself out.'

'I need you,' he said as she turned for the door.

She halted, her fingers around the door handle. 'I get the impression, Mr Xenides, that you don't need anyone.' She twisted and pulled. She didn't belong here. Now she'd made up her mind, she couldn't wait to get away. Had to get away.

The door was open just a few inches when his palm slammed it shut. 'You're wrong!'

She turned to protest but the words sizzled and burned in the heat she saw coming from his eyes. 'How much will it take, then? How much do you want? I thought you didn't care about money, but you're just like the rest, one whiff and you want more. You're just a better actress. Which tells me you're exactly the woman I need.

'So how much, sweet, talented Cleo? How much to secure your services for a month? One hundred thousand clearly isn't enough, so let's say we double it. Two hundred thousand pounds. Four hundred thousand of your dollars. Would that be enough?'

The numbers went whirling around her brain, so big they didn't mean anything, so enormous she couldn't get a grip on them. Four hundred thousand dollars for a month of pretending to be Andreas' companion? Was she nuts to even think about giving that up? She could go home, pay back her nanna, pay for repairs to the farm's leaking roof that her mother always complained about but there was never enough money to repair, and she'd still have enough left over to buy a place of her own.

More than that, she'd be able to go home and hold her head up high. And for once, just once in her life, she didn't have to be a loser.

But could she do it? Could she pretend to be this man's lover and all that entailed and simply walk away in the end?

She shook her head trying to work it all out. She truly didn't know. If she just had some time to think it all out. 'Andreas, I—'

'Five hundred thousand pounds! One million of your dollars. Will that be enough to sway your mind?'

She gasped. 'You have to be kidding. That's an obscene amount of money.'

'Not if it gets me what I want. And I want you, Cleo. Say yes.'

She couldn't think, couldn't breathe, only one note of clarity spearing through the fog of her brain.

One million dollars.

How could she walk away from that? It was unthinkable, unimaginable, like winning the lottery or scooping the pools. And she'd even get to live on Santorini for a whole month, the island she'd longed to visit, the island Kurt had only talked about visiting for a day or two. Wasn't that some kind of justice? She licked her lips, once more feeling her hold on the world slipping, swaying. 'Just for a month, you say?'

The corners of his mouth turned up. 'Maybe even less if you play your cards right.'

'But definitely no sex. Just pretending. Is that right?'

A shadow passed across his eyes and was just as quickly gone. 'If that's the way you want it.'

'That's exactly the way I want it. No sex. And in one month I go home.'

'No questions asked. First class. All expenses paid.'

She swallowed against a throat that felt tight and dry and

against a fear that he might soon discover he was making the mistake of his life and she'd be booted out with the week. 'I don't know if I'm the right person for the job.'

He slipped the pack from her shoulder and dropped it on the ground beside them before she'd noticed, relieving her of the weight on her back, but not even touching the fear in her gut. 'You'll be perfect. Any other questions?'

She shook her head. How could she expect him to make sense of anything going on in her mind when she couldn't un- scramble it herself? 'No. Um, at least… No, I don't think so.'

He smiled then, as he curved one hand around her neck, his fingers warm and gentle on her skin and yet setting her flesh alight. 'Then what say we seal this deal with a kiss?'

She gasped and looked up at him in shock. That message cleared a way through the fog in her brain as if it had been shot from a cannon. 'We could always just shake hands.'

'We could,' he agreed, both hands weaving their magic behind her head, his thumbs tracing the line of her jaw while he studied her face. 'But given we will no doubt have to get used to at least this, we might as well start now.'

And he angled her upturned face and dipped his own until his lips met hers. Fear held her rigid, that and a heart that had taken on a life of its own and threatened to jump out of her chest. But as his lips moved over hers, gentler than she'd imagined possible, gentle but, oh, so sure, she sighed into the kiss, participating, matching him.

One hand scooped down her back, pressing her to him from chest to thigh, her nipples exquisitely sensitive to the chest that met hers, heat pooling low down between her thighs, making her more aware than she'd ever been of her own physical needs. They called to her now, announcing their presence with logic- numbing desperation until her knees, once stiff with shock, threatened to buckle under her. She trembled, reaching for him, needing something to steady herself as his mouth wove some kind of magic upon her own.

It was just a kiss. Tender almost, more gentle than she would ever expect this man to give, but, oh, so thorough in its impact. Her fingers tangled in his shirt, her fingertips drinking in the feel of the firm flesh beneath and she was sure she felt him shudder. Was this how a man felt, rock-hard and solid, as opposed to a boy? Kurt had claimed to be twenty-six and told her he worked out regularly, but his body had been white-bread soft and just as unsatisfying.

But Andreas felt as if he'd been sculpted from marble, firm flesh over muscle and skin that felt like satin and her fingers itched to feel more. Ached to feel more.

Then just as suddenly the kiss was over, his lips departing, and she was left bereft and breathless blinking up at him. He said nothing, just looked down at her, his dark eyes swirling with questions until a bubble of panic rose up inside her.

Had he spotted her lack of experience? Would he change his mind and toss her out, now that she'd finally agreed to his terms?

'I guess we have a deal,' he surprised her by saying, before letting her go. 'You might want to settle in. I have some work to do with the lawyers and I'll arrange for the necessary papers to be drawn up.'

'The papers?' She'd just been kissed senseless and he expected her to suddenly know what he was talking about. 'What papers?'

'The contract. This is a business arrangement. I think we both need the assurance it will stay that way.'

'Oh, of course.' She nodded as if she understood completely. When what she knew about business law would fit through the eye of a needle. Which was what had got her into her mess with Kurt. *A gentlemen's agreement*, he'd told her, and she'd been fool enough to believe he was gentleman enough to honour the terms. So much for trust.

Andreas clearly wasn't into trust or gentlemen's agreements, for which she should be thankful, even if it rubbed that he might not trust her. But if a contract meant she'd get her money and not get ripped off this time, she could live with it.

A wave of exhaustion suddenly washed over her, the adrenaline rush of the last half-hour, the events of the last twenty-four hours, especially the emotional upheaval of the last four when she'd been wrenched from her bed, catching up with her. She needed sleep and she needed it badly. 'Which way to my room?'

He'd already pulled his cell phone from his pocket and made the connection. He looked up and frowned before turning away, a torrent of Greek pouring into the phone.

Okay, so she'd find it by herself. She hauled her pack over her shoulder and aimed for one of the two doors she knew didn't lead to the hallway outside. One of them would be her room for sure.

She found a bedroom off the living room, a massive king-sized bed covered in almost a dozen pillows taking centre stage. She opened one cupboard and found a line of shirts and trousers hanging inside. Andreas' wardrobe, then. She took another door that led into a massive marble bathroom, complete with bath, shower and bidet, and then took another door out, only to find herself back in the living room where Andreas was still on the phone.

He raised one eyebrow when he saw her emerge and she raised her own. 'My room?' she mouthed quietly and he frowned and pointed to the door she'd first entered and her heart leapt into her mouth. Surely he wasn't expecting them to share? Even though he'd hinted that it might be necessary to maintain the illusion, there was no one else here to pretend for now. And hadn't she made it plain enough that she wouldn't sleep with him? She shook her head and her panicked thoughts must have been laid bare in her eyes. He covered the handset with one hand and pointed to a sofa. 'I'm sleeping there,' he growled. 'The bedroom is all yours.'

She retraced her steps to the bedroom and dug through her bag until she found her pyjamas and toilet bag and ducked into the bathroom, feeling embarrassed and stupid and relieved all at the same time. Of course he didn't want to sleep with her! What the hell had she been thinking? Their deal was for her to *pretend* to be his mistress, not be the real thing. One kiss had scrambled her brain completely. One kiss and she was practically expecting him to make love to her.

She adjusted the water temperature and stepped into the cloudburst of a shower. The pounding of the steamy water was like a salve to her weary muscles and tired body, but still she was out in record time, simultaneously pulling on her pyjamas and cleaning her teeth in case Andreas needed the bathroom. Her stomach rumbled and she realised she hadn't eaten since breakfast. But she was used to that. It was the one reason her jeans fitted her now, rather than stretching at the seams like when she'd first arrived in London. At least her mad job had achieved what ten years of New Year's resolutions had failed to deliver. Anyway, she was too tired to eat now. All she wanted to do was collapse into bed.

She pulled the hair tie from her hair, shaking the damp ends free as she surveyed the object in question. Compared to the camp bed she was used to, the bed seemed to stretch an acre in every direction. And it was all for her. But which side was his? Or did his lordship like to occupy the middle? He might be going to sleep on the sofa outside, but just the knowledge that he'd slept here last night and she could be sharing that same place seemed too intimate, too personal. She hovered at the side a while, before exhaustion got the better of her and she climbed into the closest side, finding herself enveloped in cloud-soft luxury, the scent of Andreas on her pillow, the comforter so soft and warm around her it was like a hug from her nanna.

The bright side, she thought dreamily, was that sooner than she'd expected she'd be home and hugging her nanna again. There was always a bright side.

She pulled her mask over her eyes to shut out the ribbon of light seeping under the door, feeling sleep tugging at her so hard that nothing could keep her awake tonight, not the occasional burst of Greek she could hear coming from the room outside, not regret at making the deal she'd done and not even the fear that, despite his assurances, at any moment Andreas Xenides could walk through that door and climb into this bed.

She yawned. She knew she should care. She wanted to. But not right now. In the morning she'd be able to think straight. In the morning they could set any necessary boundaries.

In the morning…

Andreas was still on the phone when Room Service arrived with the meal he'd ordered in between calls to his lawyers and to the concierge to arrange the round of appointments Cleo would need in the morning. He was hungry and he figured she must be too, and until she'd been thoroughly made over there was little point being photographed with her in any of the restaurants or bars. Before and after shots wouldn't help his cause. In any event, there was something to be said for taking a few hours in private to get to know one another. For, as much as he expected she'd be perfect for his purposes, the contracts needn't be signed until he'd made absolutely certain.

He pushed open the door to the bedroom to let her know their meal had arrived and found the room in darkness, lit only with the light spilling in from the room behind. And there she lay, looking tiny in the big wide bed, her flannelette pyjamas buttoned almost all the way up to her neck like a suit of armour with the quilt pulled up almost as high, and that damned Princess mask hiding her eyes.

The blood in his veins heated to boiling point. She was sleeping? He'd just agreed to pay her a million dollars and she was sleeping as if it were no big deal and she could start earning her money tomorrow?

He was just about to rip the damn mask off when she stirred on a sigh and settled back into the mattress, her breathing so slow and regular that he paused, remembering.

She'd been asleep when his staff had woken her hours ago, he recalled, after being awake since the very early hours, the shadows under her eyes underlining her exhaustion. Maybe he should give those shadows a chance to clear and give the makeover experts a fighting chance to turn her into the woman he needed her to be?

Maybe he should just back out of here and let her sleep?

And maybe he should just climb right in there with her and make the most of his money? She'd said she didn't want sex but he'd never known a woman to turn him down. That she'd been so adamant grated.

There was a knock at the door outside. Housekeeping, no doubt, come to make up the sofa bed, and he turned and pulled the door closed behind him.

He had no need to take any woman. He had an entire month. She would come to him; he knew it.

CHAPTER SIX

IT WAS a strange dream, where people faded in and out of focus, the girls from school with their taunts of loser, her half-brothers hugging the father who looked on her as excess baggage, and Kurt laughing at her, his white chest quivering with the vibrations. From somewhere Cleo could hear the sound of her nanna telling her to look for the silver lining. She spun around trying to find the source of her voice, trying to pull her from the shadows and hang onto her message and drown out the chorus behind her, when a different shape emerged from the mist, tall and broad and arrogantly self-assured.

"I'm scared." It was her voice, even though she'd not said a word, and she wanted to run, tempted to turn back to the mocking chorus behind her, back to the world she knew and understood so well, back to the familiar, but her legs were like lead and she couldn't move and he kept right on coming until he stood head and shoulders above her. And he smiled, all dark eyes and gleaming white teeth. 'You should be,' and then he'd dipped his head to kiss her and she heard nothing but the buzzing in her ears and the pounding of her heart, and from somewhere in the shadows, the sound of her nanna's voice.

'Rise and shine.' The words made no sense until the blow

to her rump, cushioned with the thick quilt but enough to bring her to consciousness with a jump. 'You've got a busy morning.'

The alarm on the bedside table alongside snapped off and she drank in the scent of bed-warmed flesh. *His bed-warmed flesh*. So the alarm was the buzzing in her ears? But what was causing the fizzing in her blood?

She sat up and pushed her mask above her eyes, and then, remembering his comment about dressing like a clown, swiped it from her head. A moment later she wished she'd kept it on. He was naked. Unashamedly naked as he strode to the wardrobe and pulled out a robe. Too late she averted her eyes and, *oh, my*. She felt the blush rise like a tide as the truth sank in—he was huge! Only to have the blush deepen with the next wayward thought.

And if he looks that big now?

She swallowed, pulling her legs up like a shield, wondering why she should be suddenly tingling down *there*. How big he could be had nothing to do with her. It wasn't something she was planning on finding out.

'Hungry?' he asked casually, but her brain had ceased to function on that level. 'You missed dinner,' he explained, slipping into a robe and thankfully tying it at his waist. 'I thought you might be hungry. I've taken the liberty of ordering for both of us. You looked like you could have slept until noon.'

She unplastered her tongue from the roof of her mouth. 'I was tired.'

'Apparently. You slept like the dead. Breakfast will be here in a few minutes and then your first appointment is in under an hour.'

'What appointment?'

'Downstairs in the spa salon. You're booked in for the works by which time the stylist will be here with a selection of outfits. You won't have much time to decide. We're flying out at noon.'

Cleo glanced at the clock; it was only just after seven. 'That's hours away.'

'You'll need every bit of it, so eat up and don't wait for me.' His eyes raked over her and her skin prickled under his gaze. 'You're going to need your strength.'

She shivered as he disappeared into the bathroom. Why did she get the impression he wasn't only talking about her upcoming appointments?

He needn't have worried about her not eating. Room Service arrived with the heavily laden trolley a minute or two later, and the aroma threatened to drive her crazy. The porter had hardly finished serving the breakfast up on the dining table in the next room before she practically fell upon the feast. There was yoghurt and jam, pastries and rolls and toast, along with two massive platters of English breakfast. It was a feast. The coffee was smooth and rich with just the right amount of bitterness to wash it all down. She couldn't remember enjoying a meal more.

Andreas emerged from the bathroom while she was still eating, a towel lashed low around his hips and barefoot, moisture still clinging to his chest and beading in the hair that curled into his neck.

'That's what I like to see,' he said, sitting alongside her at the table. 'A woman with a healthy appetite.'

She managed to swallow her mouthful but it was hard to think about food after that. He was so close she could smell his freshly washed skin, the scent of fine soap and clean flesh challenging her appetite, steering it in another direction completely. He uncovered a platter of croissants, still steaming hot from the oven, and offered it to her.

Turning towards him was one mistake. Looking at him rather than the plate of croissants was a bigger one. His olive skin glistened with moisture under the lights and even as she watched a bead of moisture ran down over his sculpted chest, pausing at the bud of one tight nipple only to sit there, poised on the brink.

She could feel that droplet as if it were on her own skin, feel it rolling down her breast and teetering at her nipple, turning it tight and hard against the soft flannelette of her pyjamas.

She should reach out a fingertip and release it from the tension that kept it hovering. She could at least stretch out one hand and capture the doomed droplet in her palm.

She was too late for either. Gravity won and the droplet fell, swallowed up into his towel. 'Would you care for something?'

She blinked and raised her eyes to find his watching hers, amusement creasing their corners. 'A croissant, or perhaps there's something else you might enjoy more?' Now even his lips had turned up. He was laughing at her and she'd brought it on herself. Nothing unusual in that; she was used to making a fool of herself. It was just she wasn't used to making a fool of herself over a naked chest and a single droplet of water.

'N… No, thank you,' she managed, holding her pyjamas together at the neck as if that would defend her against… Against what? Throwing herself bodily at him? 'I should have my shower. Thank you for breakfast.'

'One thing,' he said, grabbing one hand as she made a desperate bid for freedom, his thumb making lazy circles on her palm as he held her. 'You don't have to thank me for anything. We have a deal. You will act like a mistress and take what is offered you, and I will take what is offered to me. Understood?'

Her hand was dwarfed by his, and so much paler now she'd lost her Aussie year-round tan, and the contrast seemed so much like the contrast between them. Andreas was strong and wealthy and darkly dangerous and she was broke and pale and reduced to making deals to survive. But did he really expect her to offer herself to him? He'd slept out here, the sofa bed still unkempt, sheets and blankets littering the floor, but from the moment he'd awakened her this morning, with his unashamed display of his naked body and his thinly veiled comments, she'd had the sense that sex wasn't far from his mind. *With her?* Surely not.

She swallowed. 'I'll do my job in accordance with the terms of our contract. I can't think what else I could possibly have to offer that would interest you.'

'Exactly what I meant,' he said, his words at odds with the look in his eyes as he let her go.

The rest of the morning passed in a whirlwind. She was ferried down to the salon and secreted away in a private room where it seemed a dozen staff were fully employed in transforming her into someone worthy of being seen on Andreas' arm. Nobody seemed to think it odd, or, at least, nobody made her feel that way and she wondered if Andreas had been right, that the staff were paid far too much to sit in judgement or to care about anything but the service they provided.

Before long, their skilful hands had her relaxing so much that she didn't care. How often did she have a treat like this? Never. She was determined to enjoy it.

In no time it seemed her hair was transformed into a thousand tiny tinfoil packages. A manicure and pedicure followed, along with waxing and a treatment over her new colour before she relaxed into a facial. She felt like a new woman even before the hairdresser studied her, reading her newly coloured hair as a sculptor read the stone, before a make-up artist took her attention, leaving the hairdresser to perform his art.

And finally they were finished. The team gathered around her smiling and waiting for her reaction, but she was too staggered to give one. In the mirror her once-mousy hair gleamed back at her in what looked like a dozen shades of copper to blonde to gold, the skilful cut using her natural wave for fullness while the artful layering somehow seemed to add inches to its length.

And that was just her hair. The make-up artist had turned her eyes into those of a seductress, their blue colouring intensified, the shadows beneath banished, and a woman who had never been pretty felt beautiful for the first time in her life. Tears pricked her eyes and she bit down hard on her lip, trying not to cry, not wanting to ruin all their good work. 'I can't believe what you've all done, thank you so much.' And to the make-up artist, she pointed to her eyes and asked, 'Can you show me how to do this?' and the girl nodded, her smile widening.

'I'd love to. You have such extraordinary eyes to work with. You just have to make more of them. They were just lost in your face before.'

Lost in her face? Or just lost? It could have been the story of her life. But a quick lesson later, Cleo was on her way back to the suite, armed with all the products and cosmetics she would need to reproduce the artists' work.

This time as she walked through the lobby towards the bank of lifts she didn't cringe, didn't expect Security to come running. She was still only clad in jeans and a casual top, but she held her head up high and moved with a confidence she'd never known. One or two heads turned as she passed, and it gave her an unfamiliar buzz. She couldn't keep the smile from her face. Likewise she couldn't wait to show Andreas the transformation.

Except he wasn't in the suite. She shoved aside a stab of disappointment. Of course, he was a busy man; he wasn't going to sit around waiting for her. Besides which, the suite had been turned in her absence into some kind of boutique, with racks of casual, resort and evening wear lining the walls and a stylist named Madame Bernadette who clearly took her job very seriously. No wonder he'd made himself scarce.

Mme Bernadette took one look at Cleo over the top of her glasses, and clucked her tongue. 'Hmm, let's get to work. This may take some time.' She snapped her fingers at an attendant, who meekly bowed and handed Cleo a robe. 'Put that on,' Mme Bernadette instructed. 'We have work to do.'

Two hours later, Cleo was exhausted. She'd lost count of how many times she'd changed, how many times the stylist had poked, prodded and pulled various bits of whatever she had on, analysing the fit, whether it was the sheerest lingerie or the most figure-hugging gown. But she obviously knew her craft, because by the end of it the racks had been depleted. Everything not still hanging was going with them. There wasn't a whole lot left hanging.

For someone who'd survived on the contents of one backpack for six weeks and lately just one pair of jeans and a couple of T-shirts, an entire couture wardrobe for one month seemed like overkill, but Andreas was clearly calling the shots as Mme Bernadette would not be swayed by any talk of moderation.

The dilemma of how it was supposed to fit in her luggage was soon taken care of, as another knock on the door heralded a trolley carrying a suite of designer luggage and two maids who curtsied as they entered—actually curtsied her—before getting on with the business of packing, letting her get on with her own preparations.

It was almost twelve. She had no doubt Andreas would expect her ready on the dot and had no doubt he would also expect to see the new collection put to good use. For that reason she'd chosen a creamy silk blend trouser suit with a silk camisole that skimmed her new shape, no doubt ably assisted with a new bra that was as sexy as it was an engineering masterpiece. It gave her both cleavage and support yet it looked sexy as sin and felt as if it were barely there. With the new sling-backs that added four inches to her height and showed off her newly pedicured toes to perfection, and a blue scarf Mme Bernadette had pressed upon her because it accented her eyes, she felt more feminine than she ever had, as if she'd grown up and made the transition from a child into a woman in the space of just a few hours. She couldn't wait to show Andreas the new her.

Twelve noon came and went. Then twelve-thirty and still there was no sign of Andreas, no calls. She sat in a wing-back chair surrounded by packed luggage, swinging one leg and clicking her newly manicured nails, increasingly nervous about what she was doing.

After a whirlwind morning where there'd been no time to wonder at the recklessness of what she was doing, of agreeing to fly off to somewhere in Greece with a total stranger, she wasn't sure she wanted a chance to think.

Nor did she need the time to wonder if Andreas had suddenly changed his mind, and, having totally sucked her into his plans, he'd left without her. She could imagine he'd worked out that nobody was worth one million dollars for one month of acting. She could equally imagine him laughing at her naivety as he soared thousands of feet above the earth back to his world.

Her stomach clenched. It wouldn't be the first time she'd been cast aside the moment she'd made a commitment. Kurt had chosen his moment with impeccable timing, offering to look after her money and taking everything she'd had to give, first her untested body and then her naïve heart, before cruelly rejecting both. She'd been no more than sport to him, a naïve girl lured overseas and out of reach of family and friends so she could be well and truly fleeced. Once he'd scored both her and her money, he'd discarded her to go in search of fresh prey.

Impatient with the direction of her thoughts, she pushed herself up out of the chair she'd specifically chosen because it was the first thing across the room Andreas would see upon entering, giving up any pretence of appearing cool and calm in favour of striding across the room to the windows, gazing down unseeingly across the busy street to the cool green serenity of Hyde Park beyond.

No, Andreas was no Kurt. He might be arrogant and autocratic, but he would never stoop to such a thing. He'd taken so long to convince her to come with him and he'd gone to such expense. Why do that if he wasn't going to go through with it?

Her hand went to the drapes and she rested her head against it. Although he'd shown no mercy yesterday. He'd invaded the hotel like an army general routing the enemy, the guests evacuated, the sleeping turfed from their beds, and Demetrius summarily vanquished. She shivered. How could a haircut and a suitcase full of new clothes make her blind to what had happened at his behest only yesterday? Was she so fickle?

No, Andreas might resemble a Greek god, but she'd be a fool to assume he would be a merciful one.

The buzzer sounded and she jumped, suddenly all pins and needles as she crossed the room and pulled open the door. The porter nodded. 'I'm here to collect the luggage for the airport. Your car is waiting downstairs, miss.'

She took a deep breath, trying to settle her quivering stomach. So she hadn't been abandoned? That was a good thing, surely? She grabbed her jacket and scarf, threw her bag over her shoulder and marched out, doing her best to play the cool, confident person she was supposed to be when inside even her blood was fizzing. My God, she was actually doing this! She was leaving England for a Greek island with a man she barely knew, a billionaire who needed a pretend mistress.

And yes, he might be arrogant and ruthless and used to

getting his own way, and yes, she'd seen enough of him to know she didn't want to cross him, but it was just for one month. And at the end of that month, she'd walk away a millionaire herself.

How hard could it be?

She smiled as she made her way through the elegant lobby, the waves in her newly styled hair bouncing in time with the tapping of her heels on the marble floor. Finally her luck was changing. Finally Cleo Taylor was going to be a success.

A doorman in a top hat touched a hand to his brow as she emerged. 'Miss Taylor,' he said, as if she were some honoured guest he'd been waiting for and not the hick girl who'd walked in wearing cowboy boots less than a day before, and he pulled open the door to a waiting limousine.

She dipped her head and climbed inside, sliding onto the seat behind the driver, opposite where Andreas was sitting totally engrossed in some kind of report perched on his knees.

'I thought you could probably use the extra time,' he said by way of explanation, flipping over a page without looking up.

'You mean you're blaming me for you being late.'

He looked up at that, looked ready to take issue with her words, but whatever he'd been about to say died before it ever got to his lips. He didn't have to say a word, though, not with the way his eyes spoke volumes as they drank her in, slowly and thoroughly, from the tip of her coloured hair to the winking toenails peeking out at him from her sandals, a slow gaze that ignited a slow burn under her skin, the flames licking at her nipples, turning them hard, before changing direction and licking their way south.

'Cleo?'

'You were expecting someone else?'

The report on his lap slid sideways, forgotten. She smiled. 'Well? Do you think you got your money's worth?'

They'd done something with her eyes, he realised. They'd done something with her hair too, so it was no longer mousy and shone in what looked like a hundred different colours, and her clothes were a world apart from her jeans and cowboy boots, but it was her eyes that looked most different. Before they'd been the misty blue of a Santorini morning, but now suddenly it seemed the mists had cleared and they were the perfect blue of a still summer's day.

'Have I had my money's worth?' he mused, finally getting to her question. She was happy with the results, that much was clear, but not half as happy as he was. His hunch had been right. She would be perfect. 'Maybe not yet. But I fully intend to.' She gasped, colour flooding her cheeks almost instantly, and it was his turn to smile. Her reactions were so instantaneous, so honest. He hoped she'd never lose that. At least, not for the next few weeks.

He picked up the abandoned report and returned to his reading. He didn't want to have to work late.

Not tonight.

Tonight he hoped to have better things to do.

The Jet Centre at London City Airport ushered them through with a minimum of fuss, expediting immigration and customs requirements so that they were ready to board less than forty minutes after leaving the hotel.

She recognised the logo she saw on the side of the small jet they were approaching, the same stylised X she'd seen adorning Andreas' luggage. 'Isn't that your logo?'

Andreas nodded. 'You recognised it?'

She shook her head. He was missing the point. 'You own a plane? Your own jet?'

'Not entirely,' he responded, stepping back to let her precede him up the short flight of steps. 'The company leases it. Along with the helicopter we have for short-haul flights within Greece itself. It is a tax-effective arrangement.'

She shook her head. He imagined she was interested in his financing arrangements? For someone who'd only recently made her first ever flight in a commercial airline, and then cramped in cattle class with three hundred other tortured souls, the concept of having one's own plane at one's beck and call was mind-boggling. She'd thought the limousine was the height of luxury and here he was with his own private jet. *And* a helicopter.

'But there must be two dozen airlines flying between London and Greece every day.'

He shrugged. 'I expect so. But not when I want to.'

That was at the heart of it, she guessed, and what Andreas wanted, Andreas got. After all, wasn't that what she was doing here? And if he could afford to throw away a million dollars plus expenses on her, clearly a million dollars didn't mean very much to him. He had money to burn.

A smiling stewardess greeted her, directing her to a seat, showing her where to store her bag and taking her jacket before disappearing again. Cleo settled herself in, looking around the cabin in wonder and doing a rapid rethink.

The interior oozed comfort, a centre aisle flanked by no more than half a dozen ultra-wide armchairs in dove-grey leather that looked more suited to a fireside setting than to any plane travel she'd ever heard of. She thought about the cramped conditions on her flight to London, the lack of space to store her own things let alone the pillows, blankets and toiletry packs they weighed you down with so that you couldn't even sit down when you boarded, of the man in the seat in front who'd jerked his seat back the first chance he'd had and left it there the entire flight and the child two rows back with the spluttering cough. Who wouldn't choose flying like this over queues and delays and airline food if they could afford it? If you had money to burn, there were no doubt worse ways to spend it.

Andreas dropped his briefcase down on a timber table-cum-desk that extended from the other wall, slipping into the seat alongside her as the attendant reappeared, this time bearing a tray with two filled champagne flutes. 'Enjoy your flight,' she said. 'We'll be taking off shortly and I'll be serving lunch as soon as we're level.'

Andreas took both glasses, thanking her and passing one to Cleo as the plane started taxiing from the apron. 'This toast is to you,' he said, raising his glass, 'and to our month together. May it be mutually—satisfying.'

The glass paused on the way to her lips. How did he make just one innocent word sound so sinful? And what was it about him that provoked her thighs to suddenly squeeze down further into the seat? He watched her over the rim of his glass as he took a sip of the sparkling wine, his lips curled, his eyes charged with a heat that was soon washing through her, closely followed by a crashing wave of fear that sucked the air from her lungs.

He could be a panther sitting there, rather than a man, a big dark cat watching its next meal, waiting. She could even imagine the lazy flick of his tail as he pretended there was no rush...

Oh, God, what was she even doing here? She was an imposter, a charlatan. She'd had sex once in her life and it had been lousy. And here she was, contracted to play the role of this man's mistress for an entire month. Never had she been so unqualified for a position. Never so unprepared.

'You don't like the wine?'

Condensation misted the glass between her fingers. 'I'm not very thirsty. Maybe with lunch. How long is the flight?' She grasped onto anything that might steer the conversation, and her thoughts, into safer territory.

'Four hours, give or take. Unfortunately after our late departure we will have missed the sunset, said to be the most beautiful in all of Greece. You haven't been to Greece before?'

There was that sunset thing again. Maybe that was one thing Kurt hadn't lied about, and now she'd have the chance to experience Santorini's sunset for herself. The bright side, she thought as she shook her head in answer to Andreas' question, definitely a bright side.

'Ah. Then you are in for a treat. I promise you will love Santorini.'

His enthusiasm was infectious and she found an answering smile with no hesitation. 'I look forward to it.'

The jet came to a brief halt at the end of the runway before the engines powered up and the plane moved off. Again Cleo was struck by how different this felt from the hulking jumbo jet that had seemed to take for ever to get going, panels vibrating and overhead lockers rattling as it lumbered along the runway before somehow managing to haul itself up into the air. This jet was small and powerful and accelerated as if it had been fired from a gun.

She held onto her stomach but there was none of the lurching motion that had made her feel queasy in the seven four seven. Instead the ground fell sharply away as the plane pierced the air like an arrow, and Cleo watched the rain-washed view in fascination until cloud cover swallowed both it and the plane. A few moments later they had punched their way through and bright sunshine poured through the large portholes, filling the cabin with light.

'I have some work I must attend to,' Andreas told her, retrieving his briefcase. 'But I have a copy of our contract for you to look over and sign. Will you be comfortable?'

Much more comfortable than if you didn't have work to do. The traitorous thought was as sudden as it was true. When he looked at her in that heated way that he did, it was impossible to think straight. And after the intensive morning she'd had, she could do with a few hours of quiet time curled up in a good book, or a good contract for that matter. 'I'll be fine,' she said a little uncertainly, taking the papers he offered.

He watched her a while, trying to search behind her eyes for what she was really thinking, but he found no hint of machination. Instead her clear blue eyes held without shifting or looking away. He nodded then, turning back to his report, before she might read too much into his gaze.

A woman who didn't need constant pandering, who didn't sulk and was content to let him work when he needed to? She was definitely a rarity. A pity about her 'no sex' demands. *If she were any good in bed, she'd be just about perfect.*

CHAPTER SEVEN

THE cloud cover cleared after lunch when they were some-where over the south of France, revealing a coastline that was staggeringly beautiful even from this height, the world below like a rich tapestry of colour and texture of sea and land and mountains complete with their frosting of snow. Cleo watched the colours change below as they sped towards the night, the shadow moving over the earth as night claimed more and more for its own.

The contract had taken no time at all to deal with, the terms reasonably straightforward, even to her unbusinesslike brain. One month of partnering Andreas in exchange for one million Australian dollars and an all-expenses first-class fare home. Simple really, if she didn't let herself think about whom she was contracting with. No sex seemed such a crystal clear notion until she looked at him and felt that increasingly familiar tingle in her flesh, a tingle that felt too much like longing.

So she wouldn't look at him. Instead she pushed back in the wide armchair that felt more like a bed, shucking off her shoes and tucking her legs beneath her. Once in Greece she'd be four hours closer to home, a four-hour head start when she left in a month to return to Kangaroo Crossing. She smiled when she thought about seeing her mum and her nanna again, and her rough-and-tumble half-brothers who were happiest in their own company and probably hadn't even realised she'd gone yet. She'd send them a postcard the first chance she got, let them all know she was a few hours closer to coming home...

The next thing she knew, she was waking up with a start, struggling to sit up with her chair reclining to near horizontal, a weightless but snug mohair rug covering her.

'You're back with us, then,' Andreas said, putting away his laptop. 'We'll be landing soon.'

She put a hand to her hair, and then to her eyes, worried she'd just undone all the good work of the morning. 'I must have drifted off.' She looked outside her window but it was inky blackness outside, clusters of lights visible way down below, but, more importantly, no reflection to assure her she wasn't wearing panda eyes. Or, worse still, just the one.

'You look good.'

She blinked and turned slowly, not sure she'd heard right or that he was even talking to her.

He was stashing his briefcase away in the compartment alongside his knees, and for a moment she thought she must have misheard or been mistaken. Until... 'If that's what you were worried about.' Now he did turn, and once again she was staggered by the intensity of his gaze and the power he had to skewer her with just one glance. 'Stunning, in fact. I don't suppose I told you that before.'

Nobody had ever told her that before. Let alone a man whose five o'clock shadow only served to increase his eye appeal. Along with his white shirtsleeves rolled up and the dark V of skin at his unbuttoned neck, he looked more like a pirate now than a property magnate. She licked her lips. Boy, she could do with a drink. 'Um. Thank you.' She wanted to believe the butterflies in her stomach were all to do with the fact the pilot had chosen that second to commence his descent, but she'd be lying to herself. For the hungry look she'd seen in his eyes when she'd got his attention in the car was back again, and that had been enough to start the fluttering sensation, enough to switch on the slow burn inside her.

Nobody had ever called her anything approximating stunning before. Nobody. Even her own mother had never got beyond cute. Hearing Andreas say it made it all the more real. *And made him all the more dangerous.*

She injected a lightness into her voice that was at odds with the pounding of her heart. Why let him know how much he affected her? That was never part of the deal. 'Well, it's good to know all this morning's work didn't go to waste.'

She unclipped her seat belt and stood, heading for the bathroom, and she was halfway to escape when the ground went from under Cleo's feet, her stomach suddenly in her mouth. With Cleo thrown offbalance, it took only a jerk of Andreas' hand to steer her towards him. She landed in his lap a moment later, appalled that he'd borne the brunt of her weight as she'd collided against him.

'This is no joking matter,' he warned, showing no discomfiture for her sudden landing, indeed, giving every impression that he welcomed it as he nestled her deeper into his lap. 'This is serious.'

She could see it was. She could feel it was. She looked up at his shadowed face, so supremely confident while she lay there breathless and terrified, her heart thudding like a drum as she battled to get her wayward stomach under control. She was no good in turbulence, she knew from experience, the unexpected motion flipping her stomach end to end.

And right now, sitting on Andreas' lap, was no ordinary turbulence. Flames under her skin licked and curled in all the places their bodies met—where his hands touched her and where her legs lay across his before they spilled over the arm rest, where her breast rested heavy and full against his chest and, most of all, where her bottom pressed tight into his lap. Where something growing and rock-hard pressed back.

She squirmed, embarrassed at the intimacy of the contact. He felt huge, so much bigger than he had looked this morning before his shower, so much bigger than Kurt, and she didn't want to know. Didn't need to know. 'Andreas,' she pleaded, not even sure what she was pleading for as she squirmed some more, the urge to escape such intimate contact warring with an inexplicable need to get even closer.

But his eyes were closed, a frown pinching the skin between his brows, the skin drawn tight across his cheekbones. 'You really should stop wriggling...' he said cryptically, and then he opened his eyes and she read desire in their swirling depths and it only served to confuse her more. 'Unless you're planning on rescinding that no sex condition.'

She launched herself from his lap, scrabbling to get herself upright and away from him. 'Don't flatter yourself! It was you who yanked me into your lap, remember?'

He smiled as she headed, chin up, for the bathroom. 'How could I forget? But it wasn't me who was wriggling.'

Clusters of lights clung to the hilltops off to one side, but it was the air Cleo noticed first as they stepped from the plane, so clear and fresh after London's heavy atmosphere, it seemed to have been washed with the very ocean itself. She inhaled deeply and tried to relax. It wasn't working. The plane might have landed but the flock of butterflies in her stomach hadn't come down with it.

'Welcome to Santorini,' Andreas said, drawing her into the circle of his arm and pressing his lips to her hair as they headed towards a waiting car, its headlights lighting their path. She shivered, as much from the cool night air as from his sudden and unexpected touch, and he squeezed her closer so she had to tuck her arm around him. Clearly the pretence had already begun.

It was no hardship to hold him, there was a firmness about his body that made him a pleasure to touch, and the closer she was to him, the more of his delicious masculine scent she could consume, but it was impossible to relax. Her legs felt stiff, her steps forced, her features tense. It was all for show, all to give the appearance they were lovers. And all of it was fake.

'Smile!' he ordered. 'Anyone would think you were about to meet a firing squad.'

Maybe not, but Andreas was paying her a million dollars to pretend to be his mistress and it was a role she had no concept of. A million-dollar mistress who couldn't sell what she knew about being someone's mistress for one dollar.

She should have told him, should have confessed that her experience with the opposite sex was limited to one lousy time instead of claiming to have had sex 'loads of times'. He'd expect her to know what was expected of her and how to act and he'd have every right to be furious when she didn't. She glanced up at him but his profile was set hard, his jaw line rigid as he scowled at the waiting car, and she thought better of it. Whatever he seemed so upset about, now was hardly the time to confess her inexperience.

Whatever was bothering him didn't stop him hauling her closer to him so that they were joined from shoulder to hip, their legs brushing every time they took a step, limb against limb, flesh against fabric until his heat radiated through her. She looked down at her feet and took a deep gulp of the clear night air. Did he feel it too, this delicious friction? Or was he so used to the feel of women that he didn't even notice? She was sure there was no way she would ever get used to the touch of him.

'Cleo?'

She turned her head up towards his. 'Yes?'

And suddenly he was kissing her. No tender kiss, this one; instead his mouth plundered hers with both savagery and skill that left her once-stiff knees jellied and her senses reeling.

She found her fingers in his thick hair, his breath in hers, and all she knew was that she wanted more. How could he do this to her with just one kiss? She could have been back on the plane, feeling the press of his erection hard against her thigh, the same desperate need building inside like a furnace suddenly given oxygen until she was thinking insane, irrational thoughts. Such as she needed to be closer. Horizontal. *Naked.*

He let her go just as abruptly and it was all she could do to stand. 'Wha…? What are you doing?' She clung to him, breathless, her lips swollen and aching as he scowled again even as he smoothed her hair where his fingers had tangled in it.

'Come on,' he said impatiently. 'There's someone I want you to meet.'

It was a contest which one was the most sleek. The Alpha Romeo had smooth fast lines and sexy red duco. The blonde leaning against the door with the amused look on her face was even sleeker. Skinny blue jeans, a white top and a gold belt all atop a pair of killer sandals had never looked less casual. Despite the new clothes, Cleo immediately felt lumpy and inferior and completely ill at ease.

'Cleo,' Andreas said, 'I'd like you to meet Petra Demitriou, my right-hand man, or, as it turns out, my right-hand woman.'

Petra laughed and shook her golden head, showing off her effortlessly sophisticated up-do and, courtesy of the same movement, the long smooth sweep of her neck. 'Oh, Andreas, and I thought you'd never noticed.' She elegantly unwrapped her long arms from over her ample chest and extended a hand to the visitor, while her razor-sharp eyes gave her the once-over. Cleo got the feeling she missed nothing. The way Petra blinked as her smile widened told Cleo she'd been found wanting.

It was hardly her fault. She was still battling to regain her land legs after that kiss. It hadn't been an air pocket she'd hit this time, it had been an Andreas pocket that had sucked the oxygen from the air and knocked her off her feet.

'Hello, Cleo, it's always nice to welcome another of Andreas' guests.'

The woman had an accent that sounded as smooth as honey and yet came with a chilli bite. So Petra wasn't impressed with Andreas' passing parade of women? But then, who could blame her? No doubt she'd be equally unimpressed if their roles were reversed. So instead of reading anything into the critical once-over and the clearly unwelcoming welcome, she thanked her and took the woman's hand.

Petra's fingers were long and slender and cool to touch and clearly weren't aiming to linger. In the next movement they'd been withdrawn and the other hand was holding out a car key to Andreas. 'I thought you might like to drive the new Alfa Romeo. It just came in today. Cleo and I can sit in the back.' Cleo caught something distinctly unfriendly in her expression the moment before her mouth turned into a smile. 'We could get to know one another while Andreas test-drives his new toy.'

Cleo did a rapid reassessment. Maybe she'd only imagined that sneer? She shrugged, confused by it all, confused by what was expected of her and not wanting to offend anyone. 'Lovely. Thanks.' Anything right now to escape the confusion the man alongside her could wreak with a single kiss.

'I wondered why you decided to meet us, rather than send Nick.' Andreas sounded annoyed, his words clipped.

Petra laughed his comment off as she offered the keys up at eye level like a temptation, her lips pouting seductively behind them. He remembered the pose. It was the same one she'd given when they'd been at that restaurant in Oia and she'd said she'd had too much to drink and asked if he could drive them both home, her hand on his thigh the entire way...

'I know how much you were looking forward to a ride. I thought you might appreciate the key.'

Breath hissed through his teeth. He hadn't had too much to drink tonight and the only ride Andreas was looking forward to right now was apparently off limits. But that Petra could be so obvious when it was clear he had found someone else to spend his nights with only served to confirm he had been right to bring someone home with him.

Thank God he hadn't turned up tonight alone. *Sto thiavolo*, he should have chosen someone who could be a bit more convincing! Cleo was as rigid and stiff in his arms as a store dummy. Even his kiss, designed to show Petra that they were completely and sexually into each other, had backfired. Your mistress wasn't supposed to ask what you were doing when you kissed her, as if you'd taken some liberty. No, it would take some doing to make Cleo more comfortable, and more convincing in her role, but if sex was off the agenda he didn't know what would do it.

He hadn't needed Petra turning up at the airport. Had she imagined that one look at her and his desire would be rekindled, the new lover forgotten? Or had she hoped he'd been bluffing, and that there was no woman? Why else would she dress so provocatively, in clothes that clung to her body like a second skin? He was suddenly beginning to get a new appreciation of his right-hand woman. She'd always been a good operator but he'd never realised just how cunning she was.

'Would you mind if I asked you to drive, Petra? Cleo and I have had such a long day. Haven't we, sweetheart?' The implication hung on his words that he'd had a long night and was expecting another to follow. The endearment was meant to convince Petra. Meanwhile a wide-eyed Cleo looked up at him like a rabbit caught in the headlights. He pulled open a rear door and ushered her in, wishing that just once she might act like the mistress he was paying her to pretend to be.

Petra, left with no other choice but to comply, smiled meekly and slid into the driver's seat.

'Have you eaten?' she asked a moment later as the car's powerful engine turned over. 'I've made you a booking at Poseidon.'

Andreas couldn't fault her logic. It was what he normally did if he arrived with a woman in the late afternoon or evening. Sometimes they'd be in time to catch the sunset, sometimes they'd miss it, but a platter of fresh seafood and a Greek salad filled with olives, feta and fresh tomatoes bursting with Greek sunshine ensured that they would be fuelled for the night ahead.

But not tonight. Not when his so-called mistress was as jumpy as a kitten. Maybe she might relax at the house.

'No, take us straight to the house. We had a late lunch. We will eat later.'

There was silence from the driver and yet Andreas could almost hear her mind ticking over, wondering just what was so important that they would rush back to the house and pouncing on the answer in the very next thought. He wondered how far Petra could be pushed. Would she leave if she could see her position was hopeless? He hadn't wanted to lose her expertise but maybe that would be for the best. No one was indispensable. And he couldn't have her thinking she had claims on him.

Likewise he couldn't have the woman alongside him thinking that she could just sit there, as far away from him as she could get and gaping out of her window like some tourist on a coach tour. Damn it, she was supposed to be interested in him!

He leaned across and wrapped an arm around her, cursing when her startled response earned raised eyebrows from their driver in the rear-vision mirror.

'It's not far to Fira,' he told Cleo as the car powered up the road from the airport.

It was as he said. Within a few minutes the car had climbed its way past small picturesque villages and scattered white-washed hotels to a road along the very edge of the island where it became more built up. On one side the land sloped down gently to where they'd just come, the lights of the airstrip bright in the dark night. On the other side, the land fell away steeply, to a dark flat sea. A scattering of lights shone across the waters while in front there seemed a sweeping curve of lights into the distance that curved in tiers down a hillside before being swallowed up by the darkness.

'It is hard to appreciate in the dark,' Andreas told her, the stroke of his thumb on her upper arm doing all kinds of crazy things to her breathing, 'but Santorini is actually a collection of small islands, the remnants of an ancient eruption. Fira, the capital, is built on the lip of the crater. The lights you see further on belong to the town of Oia. Like Fira, it is a very beautiful town, full of narrow cobbled streets and beautifully restored buildings, centuries of years old. Some say the sunset in Oia is the best in the world. I will take you there if you like.'

She suspected he was merely acting his part, she knew she should be, but still the very picture of sharing a sunset with this man worked its way into her soul so much that she almost wanted it to be real. Her voice, when she found it, was breathless and short, and it was no trouble for her to inject into it the necessary enthusiasm. 'I would like that, very much.'

There was a strangled sound from the front seat, followed

by a cough and a murmured apology. 'Andreas is right, Cleo,' Petra said, steering the car through a succession of narrower and narrower streets, past ornate iron gateways and walls of polished white set off with colourful bougainvilleas that caught Cleo's eye. 'It is only a small island, but there is much to see on Santorini. Will you be staying long?'

Cleo shot a look at Andreas, who was scowling again, and she wondered if it was because she'd made such a hash of things that he was already regretting their deal and the time he'd said they'd have together. 'Maybe a few weeks,' she offered nervously, 'maybe less…'

In the rear-view mirror she saw their driver's eyebrows shoot up as she pulled up before a private garage alongside a red-brick building that wouldn't have looked out of place in Venice and waited for the automatic door to roll up. 'That long? How lovely for you. It will be like a wonderful holiday.'

'Of course,' Andreas added with a growl as Petra steered the car into the garage and pulled to a stop. 'There's every chance she may stay longer.'

'Why did you say that?' Petra had bid them goodnight and left them in the lobby, retiring to her own suite, and meanwhile Cleo had been playing and replaying the words over in her head, so much so that she'd barely taken in the details of the house, other than just a handful of impressions. Grand proportions, furnishings that were both elegant and exquisite, it was more a palace than any humble home she'd ever seen.

'Say what?' Andreas sounded almost bored as he instructed the hired help to take care of the luggage and led the way to his suite of rooms, and yet there was too much coiled tension in his every step, his every movement, for her to believe that. Even his words were brimming with tension. The sound of her heels clicking on the terrazzo floor only served to ratchet it up.

'Why did you say I might stay longer?'

'Because you made it sound like you weren't planning on staying at all.'

'I wasn't sure you'd want me to.'

'And I thought we had a deal.'

Maybe so, but she knew he wasn't happy with her, knew she'd failed to impress him with her acting skills. But what did he expect when she'd never been a mistress, didn't know how a mistress was supposed to act? It wasn't as if she'd blown it in front of his business partners. It had only been his driver—his right-hand woman. *An exceptionally beautiful right-hand woman.*

Could the act all be for her benefit?

'Petra is very beautiful.'

He shrugged, but gave every impression of knowing who he was talking about. 'Is she? She's good at what she does.'

'And she lives here with you, in this—' she looked around her, at the exquisite wall hangings and period furniture '—this *house*?'

'The offices of Xenides Properties are here. I'm often away and Petra works long hours. It's an arrangement that works well for both of us.'

There was no hint of any attachment in his words or the tone of his voice. In fact he could have been talking about any employee. Maybe her hunch had been wrong. Maybe he was just aware of Petra's obvious resentment for his lifestyle and his constant change of companions? Or maybe he was just angry with her own hopeless acting skills. She could hardly blame him if he was.

'Here we are.' A pair of carved timber doors stood at the end of a passageway. He pushed them both open and her eyes opened wide. 'The sitting room,' he said, still moving.

She stayed where she was and let herself gape. By now she

should have been used to the luxury—luxury suites in London hotels, a personal private jet with wrap-around leather and champagne on tap—but still the sheer opulence of his everyday lifestyle made her jaw drop. For this was no rented accommodation or flying office, this was his home. And this one room was large enough to house her entire family back home.

'How much money do you have?'

And he turned and looked at her, a cold expression charging his eyes. 'Does it matter?'

'Well, no. It's just…'

'Do not fear, I have more than enough to pay for you.'

His words shouldn't have stung but somehow they did. The notion he was paying to have her here, to stroke her hand with his thumb and kiss her when he needed to look as if he had someone to kiss.

It wasn't as if he were paying her for sex. She was merely acting. Pretending. And yet there was no pretence about the impact his touch and his kisses had on her. It made no sense. She'd been the one to insist on no sex, so why was it that his touch made her think of nothing else? Why did his kisses make her hunger for that which she had refused to entertain? Did he really not feel it too, this ribbon of desire that seemed to tug her ever closer to his side?

No! Andreas was right. This was a commercial arrangement, not some fairy-tale Cinderella story. In a month's time, or however long it took, she'd leave Santorini and go back to her home in Kangaroo Crossing, albeit a million dollars richer than when she'd arrived. For a girl with her background and her chances in life, surely that was fairy tale enough. And yes, clearly there was no question he couldn't afford it.

'Come on, then,' he said gruffly as he tugged off his tie, pointing towards a door on the far side of the room at the same time. 'Let's get this over with.'

CHAPTER EIGHT

'WHA...? What do you mean?'

Andreas sighed. What the hell had he been thinking to contract this woman to act as his mistress? As an actress Cleo was as stiff and unyielding as a block of cement. As a mistress, she'd been a total failure. And she would continue to be, until she got over this problem she had with being with him. He tossed the car keys Petra had given him onto a dresser where they slid straight off and fell with a clatter to the tiled floor. Behind him she did the startled thing again, jumping as if he'd just thrown the keys at her. And the quicker she got over it, the better. 'What do you think I mean?' He tugged off his already loosened tie and shrugged off his jacket.

Pointless!

She stood there in the doorway to the bedroom, knowing only that he was furious. Meanwhile Andreas had kicked off his shoes and peeled off his socks, tossing them into a corner. The shirt was next, exposing once again that muscled chest to her gaze. She wanted to look away, but she couldn't. She was transfixed.

'Couldn't you have even pretended to be my lover? Why do you have to jump like a startled rabbit every time I touch you?'

'Because you do startle me. I can't help it!'

He swore under his breath. 'We should have slept together last night. Instead we wasted a perfect opportunity to get comfortable with one another.'

His trousers hit the ground and he kicked them carelessly aside. She wanted to resent him for his arrogance, for his knowing that the hired help would pick them up, for his wealth that allowed him to be that way, and most of all for assuming that she would abandon the one condition she'd set on this arrangement. But he made it so hard, too hard, when, instead of mustering a defence, she was busy admiring his lean powerful legs and the way his muscles played under his olive skin with the action.

Her mouth was dry, her blood thick and thumping slow. 'I don't understand. I told you I wasn't prepared to sleep with you.'

He looked up at her then. 'No, you didn't. You said no sex. I told you there would be times where we would have to share a bed and you made no protest.' He looked up at her, her feet still stuck to the floor in the doorway. 'Go on, then, get undressed.'

Her mouth went dry. *Get undressed*. She could be in a doctor's surgery, awaiting an examination, but then the order would be a request and it would be gently and considerately done, with a curtain provided for her modesty and discretion. Here, she was somehow expected to take off her clothes and climb into bed with Andreas glowering at her, dissatisfied and unrepentant. 'Andreas, I…'

But he was already leaving the room, striding barefoot through a door to a room she could see brimming with marble and gilt. Seconds later he returned, stopping dead when he saw her still there, rooted to the spot. 'You're planning on going to bed fully clothed? At least I won't have to put up with that flannelette armour.' The black silk pouch that was his final barrier hit the floor next, leaving him gloriously naked before her. He was beautiful clothed, carrying himself with an authority and presence that turned heads, but naked he was magnificent, broad shoulders that tapered down to a tightly packed waist and lean hips. He was so beautiful, just the sight of him caused her blood to sizzle. She closed her eyes and swallowed hard against a throat filled with cotton wool as he flipped down the covers and slid into the bed.

'Last night,' she began. 'Last night I had my own bed. Why can't I now?'

'Last night we were in London. I told you we might have to sleep together, to keep up appearances. Given there is only one bedroom in this suite and the fact my offices are here, it wouldn't look good if word got out that my latest mistress was sleeping on the sofa, because I certainly don't intend to. Don't worry, I'm sure I can resist you.'

She didn't doubt it. But sharing the same bed as him, lying alongside his naked body when she already knew how his touch turned her flesh alight, she only wished she could be so sure she could resist him.

He pushed himself up on one hand. 'I'm losing patience, Cleo. Are you going to take your clothes off,' he growled, with more than a hint of menace in his voice, 'or am I going to have to come over there and do it for you?'

She shook her head, fear congealing like a ball in her gut. God no, the last thing she wanted was Andreas undressing her. She'd claimed she was experienced. She could do this. But she wasn't about to do it in front of him. She bolted for the bathroom, taking several minutes to calm herself, cooling her burning cheeks with water from the tap. Her luggage had not yet been delivered or if it had, Andreas wasn't telling, so she stripped herself down to the camisole, bra and knickers and wrapped herself in a voluminous robe she found hanging on the back of the door. It would have to do. This wasn't about sex, or so he'd claimed. So what she wore to bed shouldn't matter.

She emerged from the bathroom a good ten minutes or more after she'd entered to find the lights dimmed and Andreas facing away, his eyes closed as if asleep.

Please God he was!

She padded silently to the bed, stood there a second watching him breathe and decided this was it. She'd practically told him she was a woman of the world, claiming she'd had sex loads of times, so just sleeping with a man in the same bed should hardly throw her. She unlaced the tie at her waist and let the robe slip from her shoulders. Andreas didn't stir and she gained confidence. He wouldn't even know she was here. She turned off the light and slipped between the covers, hovering so close to the edge there could be no way he would feel her presence, and he gave no sign that he did, his breathing slow and regular, a pattern that calmed her own frantically beating heart.

On tenterhooks she lay there listening to his breathing, feeling foolish and naïve, even as the curtains of sleep descended one by one, closing around her and pulling her into their embrace, until she was surrounded by them, warm and comforting and reassuring.

And if those curtains felt as if they'd grown arms and legs and were fashioned of silken flesh rather than velvet, and breathed as if the mild night air moved through them, the brush of them on her shoulder like the warm brush of a lover's lips, she could feel no less comforted.

Cleo woke alone in the wide bed to the spill of sunshine through tall narrow windows and a feeling of disbelief suffusing her veins. She was here. She was really here, lying in bed in a centuries-old mansion on a Greek island and last night—last night she'd slept with a real Greek billionaire, a Greek billionaire who'd honoured her condition that sex was no part of this deal!

A shiver ran down her spine. Four weeks, the contract had stipulated. Four weeks she could be here, sharing Andreas' bed. After last night the prospect was suddenly more thrilling than threatening. Scattered remnants came to her then, of a warm hand and a silken touch, of the press of thigh and a puff of breath at her neck, and the press of lips...

She must have been dreaming again.

She pulled on the robe she'd left lying on the end of the bed just as the chimes of a clock on a mantelpiece rang out, drawing her eye. Ten in the morning! Even allowing for the two-hour time difference with London, she hadn't slept in so late for months. No wonder Andreas wasn't here. He'd probably gone to work hours ago. And no wonder she was so hungry, it was hours since they'd eaten on the plane. She was halfway to the bathroom when it caught her eye, a patch of blue through the whisper-thin gauzy curtains billowing in the soft breeze, so blue that she was compelled to draw the curtain and investigate.

What she saw took her breath away. There was a terrace outside the window, whitewashed and dazzling in the morning sun, and then the earth must have fallen away beneath them, for a long way below shimmered a sea of the brightest blue she'd ever seen, a sea that stretched before another island that rose, tall and long and dusted with white buildings. And to the left sat another islet, low and wide and dark.

So this was Santorini? No wonder Kurt had raved about it to her. Even if he had never visited, even if he'd never intended bringing her here, maybe for once he hadn't been lying. It was breathtakingly beautiful.

And now she had four weeks to enjoy it, to share it with Andreas…

'You're up, then.'

She turned with a start to see him standing in the doorway. He looked as fresh as the morning, his hair damp at the ends where it curled over his collar, a white shirt and fitted trousers making the most of his lean shape.

And suddenly she wasn't sure what to be the more embarrassed about, finding herself staring hungrily at the delicious V of olive skin where his shirt was unbuttoned, or the knowledge that without intimacy they'd slept together and would do again, tonight. Damn it if her nipples hadn't already tightened under the robe in anticipation, her pulse sending blood to all the places that shouldn't even know he existed, but seemed to anyway. It was only sleep with him they had to look forward to, but that seemed to make no difference; she tingled all over.

'I thought you'd gone to work.'

'There were some things I had to attend to.' He stopped in front of her and curled a hand under her hair, skimming her neck with his fingertips and drawing her closer, his eyes on her mouth. She sensed he was going to kiss her and she made no move to shift away, her eyelids fluttering closed on a sigh. Why should she when his touch felt so good, and when he'd agreed to her terms? Sex might be out but a kiss was definitely within the bounds of conditions she'd set. She could deal with that. Surely this was the best of all worlds?

'Good. You didn't jump,' he said, abruptly letting her go before their lips had even connected.

She blinked, swaying momentarily until she regained her bearings. 'I what?'

'We seem to be curing you of your habit of jumping every time I touch you. This is a good start. Perhaps now you will be more convincing.'

'Oh, of course.' She studied her toes, while she pushed her hair back behind her ears, feeling a total fool for thinking he wanted to kiss her, a total fool for being so eager. 'That is good.'

He was already turning to go when he turned back. 'Breakfast is being served on the terrace if you're hungry.'

She nodded, looking to his eyes for a hint, hoping to find a trace of the warmth and comfort she'd felt last night in her sleep, but there was nothing there and she knew what she'd felt had been a dream.

'I'll be along as soon as I'm dressed.'

There was nothing to feel disappointed about, she told herself as she took a shower in the luxurious marble bathroom, the spray from the shower more like a downpour, raining down sense on an otherwise wayward brain. What was her problem? She had a job to do for four weeks and then she would return home, a millionaire. Tenderness didn't come into it.

She stepped out onto the sun-washed terrace and any remaining sense of disappointment evaporated in the wonder of the place he'd brought her to. What she'd glimpsed through the bedroom window had been magical. But outside on the terrace the view was simply breathtaking.

She could see from one end of this island to the other, the sweeping curve of dark cliffs topped with whitewashed villages that clung to the very edge of the cliff like icing spilling over the sides of a cake.

Andreas sat at the table already but, despite her growling stomach, she was too excited right now to sit and eat. How could she even think about eating when there was so much to devour with her eyes?

A breeze toyed with the ends of her hair as she stood at the balustrade, the air pure and clean as she gazed out across the sapphire-blue waters. The light was wonderful, more like the bright sunlight of home rather than the grey misty blanket that so often shrouded London, defining everything with sharp detail, so that even islands far beyond this ring of cliffs could be clearly seen.

Either side of her, the town of Fira spread across the clifftop, a jumble of closely packed buildings, some adorned with splashes of colourful bougainvillea and punctuated by stairways and narrow paths that somehow combined harmoniously to create a picture of charm, while far below two sleek cruise ships sat anchored. For a second memories of Kurt once more invaded her thoughts, but only for a moment. She was no day visitor here; she was living here for a month.

'What do you think?'

Andreas appeared at her side, his arm looping casually around her shoulders. *Appearances*, she told herself, willing away the jag in her heart rate, *he's merely keeping up appearances for the maid busy filling up coffee cups.* But it didn't matter so much any more, not when she was being treated to a place of such amazing beauty that the man-made seemed not to detract from but to complement the natural.

'It's the most beautiful place I've ever seen. I don't know how you can bear to leave it.'

He smiled as if pleased with her reaction. 'It is always good to come home. Come.' He drew her further around the terrace, pointing out the various islands. 'This is the main island, known as Thera. The island across the water is called Therassia, and the tiny one between is known as Aspronisi.'

'What about that one?' She pointed to the low dark isle she'd noticed earlier.

'That is Nea Kameni, the volcano.'

Her head swung around. 'Volcano!'

He laughed, a rich deep sound that in normal circumstances would allay her fears. But these were hardly normal circumstances. He expected her to live on the edge of a volcano? 'Like I was telling you last night, this ring of islands and these cliffs are the remains of the caldera after an eruption thousands of years ago. The empty chamber filled with sea water causing a massive explosion into which the volcano collapsed. This ring of islands is all that's left.'

Despite the warming rays of the sun, Cleo shivered. The island cliffs formed a crater that was enormous. That something so beautiful could be created from something so devastating beggared belief. 'But it's safe now, isn't it?'

'Oh, yes, the volcano hasn't erupted for some decades.'

Cleo wrapped her arms around her midriff. 'You mean it's still active?'

Andreas shrugged, a wry smile on his face. 'The volcano is rebuilding itself. Sometimes the island rumbles with the reconstruction, and sometimes she makes herself known in more obvious ways and lets off a little steam, but for the most part the earth is quiet. You are no doubt much safer here than on the streets of London.'

She breathed out. 'Maybe you're right, but Kangaroo Crossing is looking better by the minute. We lack the views of course, there's nothing but red dust and Spinifex bushes as far as the eye can see, but at least it comes with no nasty surprises.'

'You mean you don't have poisonous spiders or snakes? What part of Australia is this?' And she had the grace to blush.

'Come,' Andreas said, 'let's eat, and then I must return to work. There is a pool on the lower terrace where you can swim or you can explore the town on foot. Do you think you will be able to amuse yourself during the day?'

'I'm sure I will,' said Cleo, surprised by his apparent interest in her, but her attention snagged as she sat before the breakfast table laden with what looked more like a feast. There were bowls of creamy yoghurt drizzled with honey and platters of pastries and rolls along with a selection of cheeses and fruit from which to choose.

'Good,' he said, 'and then tonight I will show you the sunset and you will see it's not so bad to live on a cliff top overlooking a volcano.'

'I'll take your word for that,' she said, ridiculously pleased with herself when she caught his answering smile.

Refreshing was the word, he decided as he headed towards the suite of offices housed within the mansion. There was an innocence about her, a lack of sophistication that was charming.

Did she really fear for her safety here on Santorini when she came from a country with a reputation for its dangerous wildlife? It was laughable.

'Andreas, you're back at last.' Petra perched herself on the edge of his desk, crossed her legs and smiled, flashing two rows of perfect white teeth between blood-red lips. 'Your mother called.'

He didn't miss the show of leg revealed by the split in the skirt, a skirt he'd never seen before. Was it his imagination or was Petra putting up a fight for his attention, first with her skin-tight clothes display last night, and now a skirt that was split to her thigh? 'Did she leave a message?'

'She said she'd like you to visit, said she hasn't seen you for ages. I said you'd call her back later.'

Andreas wondered what else she might have said. 'Was there anything else?'

Petra looked miffed, the coffee she'd brought them both forgotten. Coffee together in his office around this time of day had been almost a daily ritual, where they would discuss whatever business had arisen or opportunities that might be in the offing. To him, there'd been nothing more in it than one colleague talking to another. Clearly Petra had read things differently.

'No, nothing.' She eased herself off his desk, straightening her skirt with her hands, the motion accentuating her cleavage. So different from Cleo's ingenuous innocence that he almost felt sorry for her. Cleo didn't have to play games to draw attention to herself. He'd noticed her attributes even before the makeover experts had woven their magic. Hers was a natural beauty, fragile, buried under a lifetime of feeling not good enough.

Cleo was more than good enough. Having her in his bed last night and trying not to touch her had been sheer torture. Only when he had been sure she'd drifted off, he'd allowed himself to gather her against him and breathe in the subtle scent of her skin and hair. Without even realising, she'd spooned her body next to his and it had taken every shred of self-control he owned to leave her sleeping when every part of him had been screamingly awake.

'Although,' Petra continued so abruptly that he looked up, surprised to see her still there, 'I guess I should remind you about the Kalistos ball tonight. You'll be taking Cleo, I imagine. Otherwise you and I could travel together…'

'Of course, I'm taking Cleo,' he barked as he sent her on her way. He suppressed a groan as he leaned back in his chair. What was wrong with him? It was clearly marked on his diary, but at breakfast he'd forgotten all about the ball and was thinking in terms of sunsets with Cleo instead. He knew what he'd rather do. But with Kalistos still to give his decision on Andreas' latest proposal to tie their businesses together, a proposal that could benefit both companies to the tune of millions of Euros, there was no way he couldn't show up. As for taking Cleo, she was starting to relax with him, but ideally he'd like another day or two before he could be sure she'd be completely convincing on his arm.

Another day or two he didn't have.

Cleo had never been more nervous in her life. She'd wondered why Mme Bernadette had insisted on her taking the numerous gowns and had half suspected she'd been merely feathering her own nest—a Greek island sojourn surely wouldn't require ball gowns?—and yet here she was, dressed in the pale gold halter-neck gown, her hair piled high on her head with coils trailing around her face courtesy of the hairdresser Andreas had sent to their suite, curtailing her sightseeing plans for today.

Andreas hadn't helped relax her when he'd taken one look at her and whistled low through his teeth, sending her pulse and her senses skittering. And he certainly wasn't helping relax her now as they drove down the windy switchback road to the port.

'Constantine Kalistos is not only one of the major business and political leaders on the island, but also owns the largest charter boat operation in Greece,' he told her, in a tone that suggested she should be taking notes. 'He's considering a business proposal I put to him and he's the main reason we're here tonight. He's the perfect host but, at the same time, he's a man you don't want to offend.'

Cleo battled to absorb the information, growing more nervous by the second as the car pulled closer to a wharf lit with coloured lanterns, music spilling from the massive yacht moored alongside, couples dripping with jewellery and designer fashions emerging from the limousines and sports cars lined up before them.

Help. She'd never been on a boat bigger than a canoe and she'd never been to any function more glamorous than the Kangaroo Crossing Bachelor and Spinster Ball, where Akubras were just as likely sighted as bow ties. She swallowed. There were no Akubras here.

Andreas followed her from the car, his hand collecting hers, and she'd never been more grateful to have him alongside. She was so nervous she was sure she was going to wobble straight off her gold kidskin spike-heeled sandals, especially as she stumbled with the gentle movement of the gangplank under her feet.

'Relax,' Andreas whispered, setting her coiling hair dancing around her ear. 'And smile. You'll be fine.' And then he was tugging her forward, onto the brightly lit boat with the even more brightly lit people, and they were greeting Andreas and giving her openly curious glances and she wondered how a girl from Kangaroo Crossing got to be here, in a softly swaying yacht filled with Santorini's who's who with clearly the most handsome man on the island. One look around at the glittering attendees was enough to confirm that.

'Are you okay?' Andreas asked softly, breaking off a greeting to someone, and she looked up into his dark eyes, confused. 'I thought you wanted something,' he added. 'You squeezed my arm.' And she smiled and nodded, not even having realised she'd done it. 'I'm fine,' she told him, wishing for nothing more than for the butterflies in her stomach to settle down.

Something passed between them then, some spark of approval or warmth, she didn't know what to call it, but she felt it in his glance all the way down to her lacquered toenails, and she knew from his answering smile that he'd felt it too. So what if the only thing that bound them was a business contract? Would it be so wrong to like the man into the deal?

Someone slipped a glass of champagne into her hand as the boat slipped from port and Cleo felt the first uneasy twinge as the vessel rocked sideways before pulling away. Slowly it built up speed in preparation for its circuit of the islands and Cleo prayed that they'd soon find calm water as the butterflies turned to moths. Somersaulting moths. She forced a smile to her lips as Andreas introduced her to more and more people, all of whom seemed oblivious to the motion, and all the while shuffling on her stiletto heels in search of the ever-elusive balance as the boat sliced through the gentle swell.

She abandoned the barely touched glass of champagne, exchanging it for water, which still failed to settle her stomach. The fresh air on deck didn't help, not when all she could notice was the line of lights atop the cliffs moving up and down and the passenger catamaran skipping away from them on the seas. When perspiration started beading at her forehead, she knew she was in trouble.

'Andreas,' she said, one hand on her stomach as they moved between groups on the deck. 'I don't feel—'

'Andreas! There you are.'

Cleo stepped back, wondering if she could just slip away as Andreas was swept into a man's embrace, his back slapped by one beefy hand. It was no mean feat given the man barely came up to Andreas' shoulders, his black jacket widest around his ample stomach, and his features creased and heavy with age and excess.

'Constantine,' Andreas said, 'it is always a great pleasure. Allow me to introduce Cleo Taylor, all the way from Australia.'

'Ah,' said the beaming Greek, his eyes sizing her up and taking her hand gallantly. 'Then it is in fact my pleasure.' He held out a hand and gestured around him. 'Tell me, what do you think of my little runaround?'

It was hitting the ferry's wake that did it. Her stomach felt as if it had speared into the sky only to be slammed down again and she knew it was too late. If she opened her mouth, she was lost. She pushed her glass into Andreas' free hand, shoved a path between the two men and bolted for the bathroom.

CHAPTER NINE

WHAT had he been thinking? Cleo was hopeless. A blow-up doll would have made a more convincing mistress. And the look Constantine had given him when they'd been offloaded back on shore had spoken volumes. Andreas wasn't holding out for good news in that department any time soon. The 'I told you so' look Petra had thrown his way as they'd disembarked hadn't helped.

The car slowly wound its way up the cliff-face road, the lights of Con's yacht heading once more for the sea, the music and laughter drifting upwards on the breeze, rubbing salt into his wounds, while alongside him Cleo sat hunched and looking despondently out of her window.

Damn it, was it too much to ask to get *something* for his million dollars?

Carrying her shoes in one hand, Cleo made straight for the bathroom where she spent at least five times the recommended daily time with her toothbrush and at least that again holding a cold towel to her red and swollen eyes. Andreas had thank-fully kept silent all the way home, although she'd known that simmering silence would erupt at some stage, especially after the pleasure boat had had to make a special trip back to the wharf to drop them off.

So be it. She knew she was already a disappointment to him. And now she'd probably blown a million-Euro business deal. But she'd warned him she wasn't the right woman for the job. Maybe now he might listen. Maybe now he would let her go. If he didn't throw her out first.

She sniffed, close to tears again. Did it matter? Either way, she was going.

He was sitting on the bed, flinging off first one shoe and then the other when she emerged. Following them with his silk socks. Without following her progress across the room, he spoke. 'Why didn't you tell me you get seasick?'

She stopped, just short of pulling open the wardrobe door. So the volcano was about to erupt? She was surprised he'd kept quiet this long. 'Maybe I didn't know.'

This time he did look up, disbelief plain on his features. 'How could anyone not know?'

'I've never been on a boat before. There's not a big call for boats where I come from.'

He answered with nothing more than a grunt. 'It could have been worse,' she offered, trying to sound light but having to bite down on her lip to counter the prick of tears.

'Do you think? Do you really think it could have been worse?'

'Sure. I could have thrown up all over the both of you.'

'You might just as well have, for all the good taking you tonight is going to do me.'

She closed her eyes and swayed against the door, liquid spilling from her eyes, and the sound of his clothes hitting the floor piece by piece like a series of exclamation marks. 'I know. I'm sorry.' She took a deep breath and reached in, hauling out her pack from the depths of the wardrobe. 'It won't happen again. There's no way it will happen again.'

Andreas seemed to come from nowhere, his arms forcing

her around even as she clung onto the pack. 'What the hell are you doing?'

She couldn't bring herself to look at his face. But it was no compensation that her eyes were met by the wall of his naked chest, a naked chest she'd never see the likes of again after tonight. 'I can't do this, Andreas,' she said as her mind set about imprinting every square centimetre of his perfect skinscape on her memory while he slipped the pack from her hands. 'I'm going home.'

'You can't go. We have a contract!'

'I can't do this. I'm sorry, I'm hopeless in this role, and you know it.'

'No! That's not true.' He didn't know where the words came from. Hadn't he thought the very same thing himself tonight? But he had no answer for that mystery. All he knew was that he couldn't let her go, couldn't let her walk out of his life. Not like this. Not when he knew the sunshine of her smile. Not when he knew he was the one who had taken it away from her.

She tried to shrug away, even as his thumbs stroked her collarbone. 'You don't have to try to be nice to me. I know you're angry and you have a right to be. I told you I wasn't the right person for this job. I'm a cleaner. A cleaner who jumps every time you touch her. A cleaner who's just discovered she gets seasick. Not exactly an asset to you.'

'Not every time.'

She blinked up at him, frowning. 'What?'

'You don't jump every time. You're not jumping now. And I'm touching you. And I'd like to go on touching you.'

Her blue eyes widened. 'Andreas?'

And he answered her question the only way he knew how. With a kiss that he hoped would tell her he wanted her to stay. That he didn't want her to leave. He drew her closer against him, until the silk of her golden gown pressed warm and slippery and seductive against his skin. He managed to prise his lips away from hers long enough to say the words. 'I want to make love to you, Cleo.'

She was gasping for breath, and no doubt searching for reason. 'The contract...' she uttered.

'This is nothing to do with the contract. This is between you and me. Make love with me, Cleo.'

Did he mean that? Her thought processes were blurred, her senses packed to overload. What he could do to her skin with the touch of one thumbnail. What he could do to her breasts with just the brush of one fingertip. What he could do with one whispered request...

'Make love with me.'

He wasn't playing fair. Sex as a by-product of their arrangement—it should be clinical and dispassionate, surely. And then she could be rational and sensible in her rebuttal. But this assault was like a drug, winding logic into sensual knots, feeding into those parts of her that longed for more of what Andreas could provide.

His hands slid down her arms, captured her breasts and forced the air from her lungs. *'Make love with me.'* And the only answer she could find was to lift her hands behind her neck and unclip her halter top, so that the fabric slid down over the hands that now supported her breasts.

He growled then, and swept her into his arms, carrying her like a prize and laying her down on the bed, peeling down the silk until her breasts lay exposed to his gaze. She watched him watching her, her hands around his neck, his dark eyes heavy with longing, and never had she wanted anything more.

And then she felt nothing beyond the ecstasy of his hot mouth on her breast, his tongue hungrily circling her nipple.

'Andreas,' she implored, not knowing why or what she wanted. He growled a laughing response and she almost cried out in despair when he withdrew and cold air replaced where he'd been, only for his mouth to claim the other. His hands scooped her sides, moulding to her flesh, drinking it in as his lips drew her breast deeper into the furnace of his mouth.

Somewhere in some vague recess of her mind, she was aware of his hand at her back, and the downward buzz of a zipper, but it was the sensation of the silken gown sliding down her body that took precedence and the feel of his hot mouth at her belly.

Some time, she couldn't remember when, she'd wrapped her arms around his neck and tangled her fingers in his hair. It was thick and silky, the waves curling around her fingers possessively.

And then there was nothing between them but underwear, nothing that could disguise his need or hide her want.

Oh, God!

The panic welled up even as his hand scooped down her body, from shoulder, over breast, to stomach, to *there*, where she forgot about panic and ached instead with something that felt like desperation. His fingers slipped under the lace, scooping low, driving her crazy with his feather-light touch.

And then so gently, so tenderly he parted her and her back arched from the bed. She could feel what he could, her slickness, the moisture that let his fingertips glide against her tender flesh like satin over silk, while his thumb circled a tight bud of nerves that combined agony with ecstasy, the pressure building and building until they screamed for release.

His lips found her nipple and it was Cleo who screamed, Cleo whose world fractured and split apart in a blinding explosion of colour and sensation that left her shattered and gasping in his hands.

She was more responsive than he'd imagined and now he wanted her more than ever! He dispensed with his underwear and reached for protection in almost the same movement. The scrap of lace hit the floor in the next as he kissed his way up her still-shuddering body, positioning himself over her. He'd known he would enjoy her body. She was lush and curvy and her breasts filled his hands better than he could have hoped.

His erection bucked, eager now, and more than ready. Still, he took a moment to lap at one rose-coloured nipple, to nuzzle at her neck before brushing the hair from her turned-away face and pressing his lips to her cheek, only to taste salt.

He took her chin in his hand and pulled it around to face him. Tracks stained her cheeks, moisture clung to the lashes of her closed eyelids and her lips were firmly pressed together. 'You're crying? Did I hurt you?'

Reluctantly her blue eyes opened to him. Awash with tears, they looked the colour of the sea as she slowly shook her head, swiping at her eyes with one hand. 'I'm sorry,' she sniffed, 'but that's never happened to me before. I didn't know…'

Never happened? Confusion clouded his mind for a moment, clearing just as quickly as a wave of fury rolled over him. He sat up. 'You are a virgin!' *Vlaka!* He was such a fool. He left the bed and strode across to a wardrobe, plucking out a robe that he lashed around himself, giving the tie a savage tug. No wonder she had been so coy, so sensitive to his touch. No wonder she had been so bad an actress! She had been touched by nobody!

He rounded on the bed, to where the girl now sat huddled over her knees, scrabbling for her golden gown in an effort to cover her nakedness. A virgin! That was the last thing he needed. 'You told me you had slept with men before! You told me you were not a virgin. What the hell are you doing here?'

She dropped her head onto her knees as a fresh flood of tears spilled from his eyes, only magnifying his fury.

'What kind of woman are you? Were you so hungry for money that you would risk that which is most precious to you?'

'No,' she cried, raising her tear-stained face up at him, 'because I'd already thrown that away for nothing!'

She sniffed again and swiped the back of one hand across her cheeks, swinging her legs over the side of the bed and standing, the gown bunched ineffectually around her. 'I'm not a virgin, if that makes you feel any better. So you don't have to worry about deflowering me. Somebody else got there first.'

He supposed he should have been relieved. He watched her flight for the bathroom while he stood there wondering why all of a sudden that thought was somehow so very unappealing.

'You made out like you'd had sex plenty of times.'

She didn't even turn around. 'So sue me.'

'But you've never even had an orgasm.'

This time she did, glaring over her shoulder at him. 'I don't recall seeing that condition in the fine print.'

He consumed the distance between them in a handful of purposeful strides, catching her by the arm just short of the bathroom door and swinging her around to face him.

'So why not? How many times have you had sex? How many men?'

She looked down at his hand on her arm, before turning her face slowly up to his. The tracks of her tears had messed up whatever had been left of her make-up. There were dark smudges under her blue eyes and her hair was still tangled and messy from thrashing her head around when she'd climaxed. *When she'd climaxed for the very first time.*

He'd given her that. Despite the tears and smudges and tangled hair he saw only that. He felt the thrum of blood return, the heaviness building once again in his groin.

'How many?'

'One.'

And he felt himself frown. 'One man?'

Her eyes looked sad and pained at the same time, before she blinked and turned her head away and he knew.

'Why didn't you tell me?'

She flinched and tried to pull away and he couldn't blame her. He'd growled out the words so harshly that even to his own ears his question had sounded more like an accusation. But damn it, she was supposed to be pretending to be his mistress. 'You should have told me, instead of making out you'd had sex plenty of times.'

Her head snapped around, her blue eyes blazing. 'You think it's easy to admit to someone you barely know that you've had sex only once and it was so lousy anyway you really wish you hadn't bothered? Especially when sex isn't part of the deal.' She gave an exaggerated shrug to accompany a wide-eyed look of innocence. 'And you so understanding. Heck, why didn't I tell you?'

He wanted to shake her. He wanted to tell her she'd been wrong ever thinking she could pull this off, that she should have admitted the truth when he'd first put his proposition to her, and maybe he would do both of those things, but first of all there was a raw pain in her liquid eyes that made him want to tear somebody else limb from limb first.

'Who was he?'

'It doesn't matter. He was just some guy. It was just for a laugh.'

But her eyes told him differently.

He cupped her neck in one hand and drew her head to his shoulder. For a moment she stayed stiff but the strumming of his fingers on her skin soon soothed away her resistance. 'But it was no good. At least, not for you.'

She gave what he suspected was meant to be a laugh, but came out more like a hiccup. 'It was awful. It hurt and it was over in no time but I thought…'

He drew her closer into a hug. What kind of man was so uncaring of an innocent? 'You thought what?'

She shrugged and tried to lift her head. 'It doesn't matter.' Her voice was flat and lifeless but her body was warm and pliant against his, as if she'd forgotten to be afraid. His fingers stroked her neck, tracing the bones of her spine up into her hair and then down again.

Her scent surrounded him, the smell of her hair, the remnants of her fragrance and the warm scent of her earlier arousal. She had come apart in his arms. His and nobody else's and the knowledge made him hard. She was almost a virgin and she needed to know it could be better. He kissed her hair and breathed deep.

'He was a fool. He did not deserve the gift he'd been given.'

She raised her face and blinked up at him. 'I thought you would be mad with me. *Were* mad with me. And you'd have every right. I'm sorry. I know I should never have agreed to do this.'

He listened to her words and nodded on a sigh. 'You're right. You clearly do not have the experience necessary for the job.' And he felt her stiffen in his arms and try to pull away.

'But perhaps that is something we could remedy together.'

It felt as if her heart had skipped a beat. Or maybe it had just stopped altogether. But no, she was still standing and there was her heartbeat, pounding louder than ever in her ears.

She looked up at him, afraid she'd misconstrued what he meant, afraid in case she hadn't.

Afraid.

And he took her face in his hands and pressed his lips to hers.

'I promise you your second time will be better.'

She was in his arms in the next moment, bundled still with the golden dress tangled around her and feeling strangely disjointed and other-worldly.

'Andreas,' she whispered as he placed her like a treasured prize in the centre of the bed. 'What if I can't? I mean—' She felt the heat flood to her face. 'You're so…big.'

And he smiled as he unwrapped her from the coverlet, uncovering her bit by bit until she lay naked on the bed before him. 'I will not hurt you,' he said, and his dark eyes held a promise as intense as their desire so that even when he untied his own robe and revealed the full extent of his arousal she believed him.

Time became irrelevant in the minutes following. Colours blurred and merged with her feelings into a sensual overload. And nothing mattered but the sensations Andreas conjured up inside her as he worked his brand of slow magic upon her body.

No part of her escaped his attention. Nowhere was ignored by his clever fingers or his heated mouth or the hot flick of his tongue.

Until she was burning with a need that she'd never known. Burning for completion.

'Did he do this to you?' Andreas asked as he parted her thighs and dipped his head lower. And she tossed her head from side to side, the sensations inside her robbing her of the power of speech.

'Did he make you feel this way?' He wanted to know as he pressed his hot mouth to her very core, almost tipping her over the edge.

'Did he make you call his name?' he demanded.

Her cry was torn from her, his name on her tongue as he sent her once again over the edge. 'Did he?' he demanded, raining hot kisses on her eyes and on her mouth. Hot kisses that tasted of him and of her.

'No' she breathed when finally she could talk once more, her head still spinning, her body humming. 'No.'

'Then he was not a man. He gave you nothing and so what he took from you was nothing.'

She shuddered under him, though whether from the intensity of his message or from the obsidian gaze meeting hers, she couldn't tell. Nor could she think as she felt the nudge of him against her.

She gasped and felt a moment of panic but his eyes stayed her.

'You are ready,' he told her. 'Trust me.'

Strangely she did. And this time there was no stab of pain, no discomfort. This time she felt her muscles slowly stretching as he eased his way inside, until he filled her completely, all the time his dark eyes not leaving hers.

He kissed her then, a slow, deep kiss that spoke of possession as he started to move inside her. She gasped into his mouth as he slowly withdrew. She gasped again when he returned, awakening nerve endings she'd never known she possessed, inviting their participation in this sensual dance.

Every part of her felt alive. Every part of her awake to his slow seduction, welcoming him as he increased the pace and the rhythm. And still his eyes didn't leave her face.

She clung to him, inside and out, feeling it building again, that relentless ever-increasing tension as he took her higher and still higher with each deep thrust until there was nowhere left to climb, nowhere left to go.

And then her world exploded, shattering into tiny fragments as he pushed her over the edge. And this time she wasn't alone. This time he came with her.

* * *

Clearly the man had been a fool. Andreas lay there listening to the sound of her deep even breathing as the moonlight spilled through the long window and over her creamy skin, giving it a pearl-like sheen. He'd always made a point of not bedding virgins. He didn't want to build false hopes. He didn't want attachments based on first times. He didn't want attachments full stop.

So whoever had clumsily relieved Cleo of her virginity had handed him a gift. She was unbelievably responsive, her delight in an unfamiliar act refreshing and light years away from that of the women he normally associated with, who tended to go mechanically through the motions with a brisk, businesslike efficiency. Not that there was anything wrong with that; it was no different from the way he himself operated. But now that he had been handed this prize, it would be refreshing to spend a few weeks having sex with someone who wasn't quite so practised, someone for whom the art of love-making would be more of a novelty.

Far from being the disaster he'd been contemplating earlier tonight, his four-week plan had been inspired, now that she'd clearly dispensed with that no-sex clause. A few weeks with Cleo in his bed would suit him perfectly and then she'd depart back to wherever she'd come from and meanwhile Petra would have well and truly got the message.

He sighed, congratulating himself as he relaxed back into the bed, the scent of a woman's hair on his pillow, the scent of their love-making in his bed.

A few easy-to-take weeks with Cleo, and life would be back to normal.

CHAPTER TEN

ANDREAS started work early the next day, hoping to work out a way of getting Constantine back on side, but he wasn't returning calls and with growing frustration Andreas picked up a file from his desk, flipped it open and found documents he'd been waiting on since before his trip to London. Good. He glanced over them once and frowned when he couldn't remember a thing he'd just read. Took a second look and still nothing stuck. He closed the file, pushing it away as he leaned back in his chair, spinning it around to face the view of the caldera from his office.

What was Cleo doing today? He'd left her snug in bed, the scent of their recent love-making perfuming the air. Had she decided on a late breakfast and a swim? Or had she decided to explore the streets of Fira on her own after he'd curtailed her exploration yesterday? She didn't speak Greek. Santorini's tourist venues catered for tourists of course, but still…

'Where are you going?'

'I'll be back,' he told Petra as he strode past. 'Later.'

An hour later he *was* back, his mood foul because he'd missed her, still no call back from Con and still the damned papers made no sense. He opened another file. Signed some papers awaiting his signature, relegated some more marked for his attention to the out-tray, read and reread another batch of files before he decided his heart wasn't in it and he pushed his chair back with a rush.

Where was she? He'd told the staff to let him know the moment she returned, and he'd heard nothing. Surely they couldn't have forgotten his instructions.

Maybe they had. By four o'clock he'd had enough of waiting and guessing. How much time did one woman need for shopping? Fira wasn't *that* big a town.

He found her in the suite preparing to take a shower, already in her robe, and he knew he'd been right to suspect she was up to something because not one shopping bag littered the room. 'Where the hell have you been?'

She turned, startled, her cheeks reddening. 'You told me I could go out.'

And he had. He exhaled, trying to rid himself of hours of frustration in one single breath. 'You were gone a long time. You clearly weren't shopping. What were you doing?'

Her face brightened again, warily at first, gaining enthusiasm as she spoke. 'Fira is amazing! The paths and the houses and even the gates. Did you realise how wonderful the doorways are here? They beckon you with a glimpse of paradise, a snatch of view, like some wicked temptation, and opening to stairs you don't even know are there and that lead to terraces hidden below. It's incredible. I've never seen anything like it.'

She was like a powerhouse, so lit up with the joy of her discoveries that her joy fed into him. He should be used to the everyday sights that surrounded him but she made them all fresh and new and now he wished he'd been there to see it through her eyes and feel the joy of her discovery with her.

'And there are donkeys with ribbons and beaded headbands that carry people all the way up and down to the port…'

For a moment her blue eyes misted and lost a little of their joy. She shook her head. 'I walked. I felt a bit sorry for them. But then,' she said breathlessly, her eyes lighting up again as if she'd discovered the meaning of life itself, 'then I found the Archaeological Museum.'

'You what?' He smothered a snort of disbelief, but it was only just. Nobody he'd ever brought to Santorini had bothered to look it up. Not one of his former women had ever been interested, preferring to shop for the gold jewellery the island was renowned for or designer trinkets to take home. 'Why did you go there?'

'I was curious about Santorini, and it was amazing! I couldn't believe the history of this place. There was an entire city buried under ash. A whole city buried, just like Pompeii, but thousands of years earlier and they'd found pots and urns and the most incredible artworks.' She held out her hands and sighed, her blue eyes bright with discovery, her cheeks alive with colour and all he knew was that he wanted that enthusiasm and joy wrapped around him. He wanted her. *Now*.

He saw the change in her eyes as she realised, saw the movement in her chest as she hauled down air and felt the air crackle between them as if it were alive. 'Andreas?' And then she was in his arms as they tumbled together onto the bed.

Last night's tenderness was history. They came together in a heated rush, Cleo grappling with his shirt buttons and his belt while he plundered her mouth with his kisses and drove her to the edge with the hot sweep of his hands before plunging into her depths. It was brutal and savage and fast but they both wanted it that way, needed it to be that way, the all-consuming fire of their need driving them on. Her cries melded with his as he drove into her one final time, sending them both spinning and weightless and once more into the crater.

Panting and slick with sweat, he cursed himself for his lack of control. That was no way to take a woman with so little experience. 'Are you all right?'

She blinked her blue eyes up at him, eyes that were still dizzy and lacking focus. 'Wow.'

'Was I too fast? Did I hurt you?'

'Oh, no. Just, wow.'

Strangely, in a place he didn't even know he had, he felt a surge of pride. Still inside her, not caring that he was still half dressed because he didn't want to be apart, he cradled her face in his hands and kissed her softly. 'What was that for?' she breathed.

'Just because.' He traced a hand down her throat and up the incline to one perfect breast. 'Did you see the women, how they were portrayed in the wall paintings?' She gasped as his fingers circled her nipples, her flesh firming, responding to his touch. He growled in appreciation. So responsive and yet she'd just come. And in turn, so was he. He felt the change in direction in his blood. Felt the heat return. 'Did you see how they were dressed?'

She blushed the delightful way she did. 'Did the women really go bare-breasted? I wasn't sure.'

He arched over her and flicked her nipple with his tongue. 'They did. The Minoans celebrated life and nature and all things beautiful. And these…' he dipped his head to her other breast '…are beautiful. You would have been a goddess in those times,' he said, feeling himself swell once again, feeling the need to take her once more. 'A fair-headed goddess from across the seas.'

This time the rhythm was slower, more languid and controlled and he watched the storm once more build inside her, her arms woven around his neck, her legs anchored at his back. He watched her face as she neared the summit, he watched her azure eyes widen as the waves of pleasure lifted her higher and ever higher and then he watched her features freeze into that mask of ecstasy as her muscles clamped down around him and took him with her.

It seemed like for ever until he could breathe normally again. Slowly, gently, he withdrew and found reason to curse himself all over again.

Vlaka! Like some hot-under-the-collar schoolboy he'd forgotten to use protection. What the hell had he been thinking? But he hadn't been thinking, not beyond being inside her and sharing that glorious enthusiasm that had streamed out of her like sunshine.

'Cleo, are you safe?'

The words made no sense in the context of their love-making. She was safe. She felt safe being with Andreas. Until a cold wave of realisation washed over her. They hadn't used protection!

'Oh. I…' When was her last period? Was it three weeks, or only two? 'I don't know. I can work it out, though.'

'So work it out,' he said gruffly as he tore off what was left of his clothes and headed for the shower.

She curled up behind him on the bed. 'You make out like it's my fault.'

He took a deep breath. In a way it was. He'd never lost control like that before. Never been so obsessed with being inside a woman that he'd forgotten something as basic—as necessary—as protection. Who else's fault was it?

His.

He looked over his shoulder to where she now sat, huddled on the bed, her robe drawn back tightly around her like a shield. 'You're right.' He forced the words through his teeth. 'I'm sorry. But sorry isn't much good if you become pregnant.'

Pregnant? Oh, God. She'd been so blown away by Andreas' love-making that she hadn't stopped to think of the consequences. Pregnant. No wonder he was so angry. It couldn't happen, could it? Surely life wouldn't be that unfair when she was going home in just a few weeks.

Although knowing her luck…

She swallowed. She'd be going home pregnant and unmarried. A loser. Again.

Or would she?

The bright side, she thought, knowing she was probably being irresponsible to even think this way. The bright side was she'd be going home with Andreas' baby. Would it matter that she was pregnant if she had something of Andreas to keep for ever? Was it wrong to think that way? At least the money she was going home with would ensure that their baby would want for nothing.

And the chances were, nothing would happen, and she would go home alone.

She jacked up her chin. 'We'll deal with that *if* it happens. But I don't have stars in my eyes, Andreas. I know I have a use-by date. I'm not looking for more.'

He nodded and told her she was welcome to join him before stepping into the bathroom. He didn't expect she would now, he thought as he turned on the powerful jet of spray and adjusted the temperature, the familiar smell of salt from the mineral-rich water thick in the steamy atmosphere. Which was a shame. He would enjoy her body slick with soap and water. Another time.

He could see he'd hurt her and that bothered him. Not that he'd hurt her, but that he even cared. Especially when her words should have given him comfort. She didn't want any more from him. That was good, wasn't it?

He lifted his face up into the stream of water and soaped his body. He'd make it up to her. Petra could hold the fort for a few days. He'd show Cleo his Santorini, the world that he loved, seeing as she was interested in more than just the usual souvenir shops.

After all, if they only had a month, they might as well enjoy it.

The next few days passed in a blur for Cleo. Andreas surprised her by wanting to tour the island with her and he was a consummate tour guide. He took her to the town of Oia at the very tip of the island and let her explore the narrow laneways and discover the blue-domed churches and the elegant remnants of Venetian occupation and the windmills that clung to the sides of the cliff.

And then he delighted her by taking her to the mountain of Mesa Vouno where hand in hand they climbed the path to the ruins of Ancient Thera, the remnants of an ancient Greek and later Roman city. With the wind whipping in her hair she discovered more of that fascination for the ancient that she'd found while touring the museum. People had lived here, thousands of years ago. They had left their mark on the earth in the walls and the columns still standing and in the engravings on the rocks, of eagles and dolphins and strong-featured men.

Andreas could be one of them, she thought, chiselled and strong-jawed and handsome beyond belief. He caught her watching him, the wind in his hair so that it looked alive. 'What are you thinking?'

And she smiled and celebrated a brand-new discovery: that a girl with no education and no career wasn't necessarily doomed to clean rooms all her life, that she'd found something she could be passionate about. 'I'm going to go home,' she announced, on the top of a mountain overlooking the entire island, 'and study. I'm going to find a course where I can learn about the people who lived here and left these marks on the rocks. I want to know more.' And she spun around laughing.

And he laughed too, because her mood was infectious, even though he suspected she'd go home and the memories would fade and she'd forget all about a bunch of old rocks on the top of a mountain somewhere halfway across the world.

They stopped for lunch at a *kafenio* in a nearby village on the way back and enjoyed simple fare of the freshest vegetables and seafood cooked superbly and that tasted better than anything she'd ever eaten before, and they walked it off again along a black sandy beach.

And wherever they went, it was to a backdrop of azure seas and sky, black volcanic rock and whitewashed buildings that all melded with incredible beauty.

'You are so lucky,' she sighed later that night as together they watched another fiery sun sink into the ocean, the sky a painter's dream of scorching red and gold. They hadn't missed a sunset since that aborted ball and she knew that she would never get sick of the sight.

She turned to see if he'd heard and caught him watching her, the intensity of his eyes sending vibrations down her spine that converged on her heart and made it lurch. 'The sunset. You're not watching.'

And he smiled. 'I'm watching it reflected in your expression. I never knew how beautiful our sunset was until this moment.' He curved a hand around her neck, drawing her closer into a kiss. 'How long do we have left?' he murmured, his lips in her hair, his breath tickling her ear.

She trembled against him. She knew exactly what he was asking. She'd been counting off the days and nights since she'd arrived, at first with enthusiasm, and lately with a sense of dread. 'Um, two weeks and four days.'

And he pulled her closer until their bodies were aligned, length to length. 'Then let's not waste a minute of it.'

* * *

Half an hour in the mornings was all he needed these days to clear his desk of anything needing his attention. He was sick of looking at files that meant nothing, sick of worrying about unreturned calls and he'd discovered the joy of delegation and the freedom it brought. Half an hour was enough to clear his desk and his day for Cleo. So it was lucky she chose then to call.

'Sofia.' He grimaced, remembering he was supposed to call his mother back days ago. 'I was just about to call you.'

'We need to talk,' she said. 'It's been too long.'

It had been. And he had things he needed to tell her, things he'd meant to tell her when he'd returned from London. 'Aren't we talking now?'

'Come to Athens,' she said. 'I need to see my son. I have news I can't tell you over the phone.'

Ice slid down his spine. 'What's wrong?'

There was a moment's hesitation and he sensed her wavering, almost able to see his mother holding onto the edge of the table for support. 'Come to Athens.'

There would no doubt be a breeze later, she'd learned enough about the weather since she'd been here to know that it would whip up over the clifftops around midday, but for now the waters of the caldera showed barely a ripple under the perfect spring sun, and the waters of the infinity pool stretching out before Cleo showed even less. In the distance she could hear the odd group of tourists passing by, exclaiming over the perfect photo opportunity—there seemed to be one around every corner on Santorini—but the pool deck was private and tucked away from the main tourist trails and their voices and snatched words drifted away and all was quiet again. She was breathless from the slow laps she'd done but that was good. She had a pile of books on Santorini, its history and archaeological treasures to read, and that was good too. She needed to keep busy, given Andreas wouldn't be back until at least tomorrow.

She clamped down on the stab of disappointment that accompanied that thought. Soon enough she wouldn't see him at all. Surely she could live with his absence for a couple of days?

But after the bliss of their last few days and nights together, the news that Andreas had taken the helicopter to Athens and would be away overnight had been a major disappointment. She liked being with him. She liked his company and his conversation and she'd surprised herself by loving being in his bed. Then she'd received the message he would be another night at least.

Two days to fill. Two nights alone in his bed, with the smell of him on his pillow and the empty space alongside her where he should be.

How quickly she'd become accustomed to his touch. And how quickly she'd abandoned the concept of pretending to be his mistress.

Every night they made love. As far as she was concerned, she didn't have to pretend. To all intents and purposes, she was his mistress, in every sense of the word.

She put down the book she couldn't concentrate on and dived back into the pool. She needed to do more laps. The more tired she was, the less she would notice the empty space beside her in bed and the better she would sleep. And the better she slept, the less she would miss his magic touch.

Strange, how she could think his touch so magic after just a few nights. But for the first time in her life, she had felt like a woman. Andreas had done that, unleashing sensations within her that she'd never imagined were there, sensations that yearned to be released again.

Lap after lap she drove herself until, weak limbed and

gasping, she staggered from the pool and collapsed into a lounger. She closed her eyes and tried to blank her mind, but it was still pictures of Andreas she saw, pictures of what they might do together on his return. She'd already decided it was time to be more proactive, to take matters into her own hands.

She could hardly wait to surprise him.

'*Kalimera*. I hope I'm not disturbing you.'

Cleo came to with a start. With Andreas away she'd assumed Petra would be busy in charge of the office. She hadn't expected her to turn up poolside wearing the black-scrap-of-nothing bikini with tie-around skirt that, given its brevity, did nothing to protect her modesty and everything to accentuate her endless legs.

'*Kalimera*,' Cleo replied with almost the extent of her Greek, instantly on edge. Her own bikini was a Moontide original that Mme Bernadette had insisted she take, swirls of blue and green that accentuated her eyes and complemented her skin now that it was starting to take on the tan she'd lost while in England. She knew she looked good in it, but compared to the tall, slender Petra she felt awkward and lumpy. And definitely too exposed. 'I didn't expect to see you,' she said, reaching for a towel to cover her on the pretext of drying her knotted hair. Anything to protect her from the other woman's laser-sharp scrutiny. 'I thought you'd be flat out in the office with Andreas away.'

Petra unhitched the tiny skirt and let it flutter to the lounger alongside, an action clearly designed to draw attention to her legs. It worked. Cleo instantly felt short and squat. 'It is very busy, of course, but I was feeling a little queasy this morning and thought a swim would refresh me before the afternoon's appointments.' She put an impeccably manicured hand to her waist.

Cleo followed the movement and wished she hadn't. Did the woman not have a bulge anywhere? 'You're not well?'

The woman gave a shrug and checked her hair. 'We had a reception with lunch yesterday. Most likely just something that disagreed with me.' She walked lithely to the water's edge, descending the stairs into the pool's liquid depths as regally as a Miss Universe contestant, where she breast-stroked two lengths of the pool without a splash, emerging from the water with her hair as sleek and perfect as when she'd gone in.

'Ah, that's wonderfully refreshing,' she said as she lowered herself to the lounger. 'And finding you here is even better. We haven't had much of a chance to get to know one another, have we? Andreas selfishly keeps you all to himself.'

'I guess not.'

'I love your swimsuit,' Petra said, patting herself dry with a towel. 'Those colours are wonderful on you.'

Cleo blinked. The words sounded sincere enough, and she wondered if she'd misjudged the woman. All she'd had to go by was one car trip from the airport and she'd been tired. Maybe she'd imagined the snippiness. 'Thank you. Yours looks gorgeous too.'

Petra smiled and nodded her thanks. 'You're Australian, aren't you?'

Cleo relaxed a little. At least here was a safe topic. 'That's right. From a little outback town called Kangaroo Crossing. It's dry and dusty and nothing at all like here.'

'I've always wanted to go to Australia. Tell me about it.'

Cleo obliged. It was good to talk of home, of a place that was so much a different world from this one that it could have been on another planet, of a place of endless drought and strug-gling families and mobs of kangaroos jumping across paddocks of red dust. And the more she spoke of home, and the more the other woman smiled and laughed, the more she relaxed. It was good to talk to another woman. She'd missed that in London.

'Now I simply must go and visit your homeland. But Andreas said you met in London. What were you doing so far from home?'

Cleo shook her head. 'You really don't want to know. You'd think me a total fool if I told you.'

'Oh, no, never.' She reached one long-nailed hand over to Cleo's and patted it. 'It's all right. You can tell me. I'll understand, I promise.'

And then, because it had been so long since Cleo had been able to pour her heart out to anyone, it all came out in a rush, how she'd found Kurt through an Internet chat room and how he'd seduced her with his promises of romance and travel and how she'd fallen for it, hook, line and sinker. She didn't tell her about his making love to her, of relieving her of her virginity and then casting her aside. She'd had no choice but to tell Andreas, but that part was nobody else's business.

'So you were stuck in London? You poor thing. But surely you had a return ticket?'

She shook her head. 'I'd only enough money for one way. I never thought I'd need to head home so soon. Except my nanna had lent me the return fare just before I boarded the bus to the city, just in case the worst happened. Only I didn't have a bank account so Kurt said he'd look after it for me…'

'And he took your money? What kind of man was he?' She patted her arm again. 'You are much better off without him and here in Santorini.'

'I know.' She took a deep breath. It felt surprisingly good to get that all off her chest. All the emotions and guilt and self-flagellation that had plagued her every day since he'd dumped her felt as if they were sloughing away, as if she'd confessed her sins and all would be right with the world.

'And how fortunate for you to meet Andreas after all that had happened to you. You must feel very lucky.'

'I do,' Cleo agreed, sure Petra hadn't meant that to sound as it had.

'So how are you enjoying Santorini, then?' she asked, changing tack. 'This is your first time here?'

Cleo relaxed again, certain she'd been reading too much into the other woman's tone. Santorini was another topic she could easily and honestly enthuse about. 'It's so beautiful! You're so lucky living here, being surrounded by all this—' her arm swept around in an arc '—every day. The sights and atmosphere, even the history is amazing.'

'I'm so glad you're enjoying it. We're very proud of our island home. We want visitors to be happy here.'

'I'm very happy. The sunsets are amazing.'

'Honeymooners come here just to experience Santorini's sunset. It's supposed to be very romantic. What do you think?'

Cleo suddenly felt too tied in knots to answer. It was romantic, or it would be, if you were here with the right person. But Andreas wasn't the right person, was he? They'd just been forced together by circumstances and soon she would leave. Although the way he'd looked at her the other night on the terrace... 'I guess it could be, if you were here with the right person.'

'Oh, I'm so sorry. I'm making you uncomfortable.'

'It's okay. It's not like I'm here for the romance exactly.'

The other woman's eyebrows arched approvingly. 'No? Well, I guess in your place that's the best way to think about it. Andreas has quite a reputation for moving on. And now I must get back to work. Thank you so much for talking with me. I feel like we're going to be good friends while you're here.'

'Are you feeling any better?' she asked as Petra retied the tiny skirt around her hips.

'Oh, I'm feeling *much* better, thank you.'

Cleo watched her slip on her gold sandals and wander away, wondering why it should be that she was suddenly feeling so much worse.

'It's just a lump, Andreas. There's no need to go on about it.' Sofia Xenides stiffened her spine and sat her slim body higher on the chaise longue, her ankles crossed demurely beneath her, her coffee balanced on her knees. Andreas knew the posture, recognised it as his mother closing the subject down again.

To hell with that.

'You should have told me.'

'You were busy. In London apparently. And then with who knows what?'

He bristled. 'You could have called me on my cell phone.'

'And told you what? That I had a lump? And what could you have done besides worry?'

'I would have made you see a doctor.'

'Which is exactly what I did do. And tomorrow I will get the results of the biopsy and we will know. There was no point worrying you unnecessarily before, but I am glad you will be with me tomorrow. And now we have more important things to discuss. When were you planning on telling me what exactly you were doing in London?'

Andreas sighed. 'You know, then?'

'Petra tells me you found Darius. Is that true?'

'I found him. He'd gambled the last of the money away, all he had left was a seedy hotel filled with mould and rising damp. He was ripe for a low-interest loan in order to fund his gambling habit.'

'So you found him, and you exacted the revenge you have been looking for all these years. I imagine you ruined him in the process.'

'It is no more than he did to us!'

'Andreas,' she sighed, 'it is so long ago. Perhaps now you can put the past behind you?'

'How can you say that? I will never put the past behind me. Don't you remember what he did to us, what it was like back then? He destroyed Father and he walked away and left us with nothing. *Nothing!*'

She shut her eyes, as if the mention of her late husband was still painful, but a breath later she was still firm. 'And it has driven you all these years, my son. Now that you have achieved the goal you have aimed for all your life, what are you going to do with the rest of your life?'

Andreas stared blankly out of the window and shrugged, the question unnerving him. Hadn't he been feeling an unfamiliar lack of motivation lately, avoiding the office because suddenly it was all too uninspiring? Below the terrace lay the rolling expanse of Athens city, apartment blocks jostling with anti-quities in the sprawling city. No, he was just temporarily dis-tracted with Cleo, that was all. Soon she would be gone and he would refocus on his work again. 'I will go on with my business,' he said, resolutely. 'Already the Xenides name is synonymous with the most prestigious accommodation on offer across all of Europe. I will make it even bigger, even better.'

She gave another sigh, except this one sounded less indul-gent, more impatient. 'Maybe there is another goal you might pursue now.'

'What do you mean?'

'Perhaps it is time you thought about family.'

'I have never neglected you!' Even though he felt a stab of guilt that he'd never returned her call as he'd intended.

'Did I say you had? But the time for looking backwards is past. It is time to look to the future, and to a family of your own.'

He sighed. If this was about getting married again... And then something he'd never seen coming hit him like a brick. 'You want grandchildren.'

'I am a Greek mother.' She shrugged. 'Of course, I want grandchildren. Maybe now you have satisfied this lifelong quest for vengeance, you might find the time to provide me with some, while I can still appreciate them.'

'Mother—'

She held up one hand to silence him. 'I am not being melodramatic. It is not just that I have had this scare and I must face the prospect of the results not going the way I would prefer, but you are not getting any younger, Andreas, and neither am I. I do not want to be too old or too sick to appreciate my grandchildren when they eventually come.'

'Stop talking this way! I'm not about to let you die.'

'I have no intention of dying! At least not before you bestow upon me the grandchildren I crave. I am not blind. You have quite a reputation with the women, I believe. After all this experience, do you not know what kind of woman would suit you for a wife?'

It was ridiculous to feel like blushing at something his mother said, and he wouldn't, but still her veiled reference to his many lovers made him so uncomfortable he couldn't bring himself to answer. Besides, could he in all honesty answer? The women he had through his bed had one resounding attribute, but it hardly made them wife material.

'Petra said you have a woman staying with you.'

He almost growled. Petra had always been like family,

they'd practically grown up together, but there were times he resented the closeness and the fact Petra knew his mother so well. This was one of those times.

'It's none of Petra's business. Or yours, for that matter.'

'Tsh, tsh. Who else can ask if I can't? Petra said she's an Australian woman. Quite pretty, in her own way.'

She was more than pretty, he wanted to argue, until another thought blew all thoughts of argument out of the water.

And she could be pregnant.

They'd had unprotected sex. Twice. Right now she could be carrying his seed.

A baby. His mother could have the grandchild she yearned for. And as for him? *He would have Cleo.*

Strange, how that thought didn't send his blood into a tailspin.

But marriage? Was that what he wanted? He took a deep breath. But his mother would expect it, and, besides, there was no way he could not marry the mother of his child. Especially not now.

Granted, they'd shared but a few short days, less than two weeks, but those days had been good. The nights even better. Surely there could be worse outcomes?

'Petra said—'

He snapped away from possibilities and turned back to the present. 'Petra talks too much!'

'Andreas, she only wants the best for you, just as I do. In fact, I once wondered if—'

It was like a bad soap opera. Or a train wreck where you couldn't look away. He had to keep going till the bitter end. 'Go on.'

'Well, you and Petra have lived together for a long time now.'

'We share a building, not a bed!' And the mood his mother was in, he wasn't about to confess that they had. *Once.*

'And,' she continued, without missing a beat, 'you have so much in common.'

'She works for me. Of course, we have a lot in common.'

'Anyway,' Sofia said with a resigned shrug of her shoulders before she turned her attention to pick at an invisible speck of nothingness alongside her on the sofa, 'sometimes we don't realise what's right there in front of us, right under our noses. Not until it's gone.'

His teeth ground together. 'I'm not marrying Petra.'

She smiled up at him, blinking innocently as if his outburst had come from nowhere. 'Whoever said you would? I just wondered, that's all. And there's nothing wrong with a mother wondering, is there, Andreas? Much better to consider the options than to let the grass grow beneath your feet.'

The grass was feeling comfortable enough where he was standing right now. Or it had been, until his mother had laced its green depths with barbs that tore at the soles of his feet and pricked at his conscience.

'About this appointment tomorrow to see your doctor…'

'I get the point, Andreas. But enough about doctors too. Would you like some more coffee?'

CHAPTER ELEVEN

CLEO was in the pool resting her elbows on the edge, one of her glossy history books perched in front of her. Hungrily Andreas' eyes devoured her, from the streaked hair bundled in a clip behind her head, her bare shoulders and back, and her legs making lazy movements in the water. She looked browner than he remembered, her skin more golden. Clearly the weather here suited her better than that dingy hotel in London where her skin was never so much as kissed by the sun.

And an idea, vague and fuzzy inside him, found dimension and merit. She could be pregnant with his child, even now. And even though the news for his mother had been good, the tests had come back negative, that still didn't change the fact that his mother yearned for grandchildren.

Sofia was right. She wasn't getting any younger, although he'd never thought of his mother as a number with a finite span. And he'd never thought of his own age and the possibilities of family. Because he'd thought of nothing beyond the one thing that had driven his life for more than a decade.

Retribution.

And now he'd achieved it all, he'd built himself up from nothing until he could exact the revenge he'd been planning for twelve long years, and yet somehow he didn't get the same buzz from the achievement any more. He didn't even care any more if Constantine turned his proposal down flat, and that had never happened before. But the prospect that the grandchild his mother hungered for could already be in the making caused a new and unfamiliar buzz.

Fate? He shook his head. You made your own opportunities in this life, he knew. He'd lived by that mantra for years. He believed in it. It had been what had kept him focused, until he'd found Darius and pulled what was left of him down.

He'd made this opportunity. And like any other, he'd make the most of it.

He padded noiselessly to the side of the pool. He doubted she would hear him anyway, even if he had made a noise. The books she'd bought on Santorini and its ancient civilisations seemed to have her completely in their thrall. Maybe it wasn't just talk, maybe she really was interested in more than a superficial picture of the island. Or maybe she was just killing time until his return.

Option B, he much preferred.

She turned a page, the angle of her head shifting, still totally oblivious to his presence.

She wouldn't be for long.

He dived into the water and crossed the pool, taking her by the waist as he erupted like a sea god from the water.

'Hey!' She turned, her fright turning to delight when she saw who her assailant was. 'Oh, you're back.'

Her legs were cool where they tangled with his, her shoulders deliciously warm from the sun and her lips so slick with gloss he wanted to find out if they were as slippery as they looked. 'Did you miss me?' he asked, his hands caressing curves they had sorely missed.

'Not really,' she lied, unable to keep the smile from her face or the tingling from her skin. 'I was kind of busy here, catching up on my reading. You know how it is.'

'Liar!' he said. 'Believe me, I know how it is—' before pulling her into a deep kiss that had them both spinning together into the depths. They came up gasping but Andreas wasn't finished with her yet. Already he'd untied her bikini top, one hand at her breasts while the other pushed at her bikini bottoms.

'Andreas…'

'Do you realise how long I've dreamed about having you in water?'

'Andreas…' She clung to him. She had no option but to cling as he brought her flesh alive and made her blood sing. His hands pushed inside her bikini, rounded her buttocks and delved deeper.

'I've missed you,' he growled, burying his face at her throat, his words so heavy with want it made her head spin. 'And I want you, so badly.'

'I… I got my period.'

He lifted his head slowly and gazed at her, his vision blurred by a rush of blood. Bad blood. 'I see.'

'But that's good news, isn't it? I thought you'd be pleased. Now there are no complications. That's what you wanted.'

He let her go and turned towards the edge of the pool, powering himself up with his hands to step from the pool like an athlete. He pulled a towel from a nearby stack and buried his face in it. 'Yes, it's good news. Of course.' Only it didn't feel like good news. It felt as though all the shifts he'd made, all the changes he'd made in his thinking were for nothing, and he was left stranded. He didn't like the feeling.

He could have done with the odd complication. It would have suited his purposes well.

So much for making opportunity happen.

Petra brought them both coffee as he checked his files the next day. Or she brought him one. Her nose twitched as she deposited the cup on his desk. 'You're not having one?' he queried, surprised she wasn't joining in with this long-time ritual.

Her nose twitched again. 'I seem to be off coffee. Don't know what it is. Probably just that time of the month.'

Andreas blanked out. He was over that time of the month, big time, and he certainly didn't want to hear about Petra's. He was irritable, he was short-tempered, and the sooner he got Cleo back where he wanted her, the better for all concerned. And maybe he'd even forget to use protection all over again. Only she'd probably be gone before she was fertile…

Damn.

Mind you, he could always change the contract terms… His mood brightened considerably. That was definitely one option worth pursuing.

'Poor Cleo,' Petra said, sifting through mail as she perched herself on the edge of his desk in her usual way, 'what a dreadful thing to happen, being cheated of her money like that.' She slapped a couple of papers down in front of him. 'Though I guess she brought it on herself to a large extent.'

His ears twitched at the mention of Cleo's name. He'd almost forgotten Petra was there again, already working out how best to tackle the subject of an extension to their terms. 'Brought what on herself?'

She shrugged. 'She must have told you. She went to London to meet this guy she'd hooked up with on the Internet and he ripped off the money for her return fare and left her with nothing. Awful. Mind you, you'd have to be pretty stupid to fall for something like that.'

Andreas sat back in his chair, letting the silence fall between them like an anvil. He knew for a moment that his scowl would say everything he needed to while he untangled the threads of his anger in his mind.

'Are you saying Cleo's stupid?'

'No! I mean… Well—' she shrugged and screwed up her nose, like she was making some kind of concession '—maybe just a bit naïve.'

'Or are you saying that my father was stupid?'

'Andreas! It's hardly the same thing.'

'Isn't it? My father trusted someone and lost everything to him. Cleo trusted someone and suffered the same fate. Tell me how it's different.'

He stood up and peeled his jacket from the back of his chair, shoving first one arm and then the other into it. 'You deal with the mail, Petra. I've got more important things to do.'

'Andreas, I didn't mean anything, honest.'

No? He was sick of the niggling, sick of Petra's snippy put-downs of Cleo with just a look or a snide remark. He'd been wrong to think she would take a not-so-subtle hint. Maybe it was time for a more direct approach. 'It's not going to happen, Petra, so don't think it is.'

She looked innocent enough, but he knew there was a computer inside that was as sophisticated as it was devious. 'You and me. That night was a mistake. It won't happen again.'

He found Cleo sitting out on the terrace overlooking the caldera and reading another of her books. In spite of the still-smouldering anger that simmered inside him, he smiled. In a lemon-coloured sundress that made the most of her newly acquired tan, she looked both innocent and intent at the same time.

She looked around, almost as if she'd been able to feel his eyes on her, and she smiled that heart-warming smile as her azure eyes lit up with enthusiasm. 'Back already? You'll never guess what I just read.'

Her enthusiasm was infectious. So infectious he didn't want her to leave in however many days they had left. It was to his advantage she was in a good mood. It would be easier to convince her to stay. 'Tell me,' he said, pulling up a chair alongside.

'Well, when the volcano erupted going back three thousand years or so ago, it wiped out not just the cities on the island itself, but some think it brought down the entire prehistoric Minoan civilisation with it.'

'It's possible,' he acknowledged with a nod. 'Nobody knows for certain, but it could explain why the Minoans were such prosperous sea traders one minute and wiped from the face of the earth the next.'

Her azure eyes sparkled like the waters of the caldera itself. 'But this is the really exciting bit. Some say that the eruption and the fallout are the origins of the legend of Atlantis. A world that sank beneath the sea— and this is where it all happened! Do you believe it? Do you think Santorini is actually what's left of Atlantis?'

His cell phone interrupted them and he pulled it out, took one look at the caller ID and switched it off. Petra could wait.

'I think it's highly possible,' he conceded, repocketing his phone.

She sighed, hugging the book to her chest, and looked over to where the volcano, now silent, spread dark and low in the midst of the waters. 'I believe it. I did a Google search and found a Classics course in Sydney.'

'Cleo…'

'I'm going to enrol in it as soon as I get home. I'll be able to afford to live there now, thanks to you.'

'About going home.'

She turned her head, the spark gone from her eyes. 'Do you want me to leave earlier? I… I don't mind, if that's what you want.'

And he almost laughed at the idea. He shook his head. 'No. I don't want you to go earlier.'

'Then, what is it?'

He took a second to frame his thoughts. 'What's waiting for you at home? I mean, you've never talked about your family. Are they close?'

She gave a curious smile, her eyes perplexed. 'Well, not really. My mum's great, but the twins, my two half-brothers, keep her pretty busy and she's got a baby coming apparently.' She screwed up her nose. 'And then there's my step-dad, of course.'

'What's he like?'

She shrugged. 'He's okay, a bit rough around the edges maybe, but a lot of blokes are like that out there, but Mum loves him and he's good to her.'

'And to you?'

Excess baggage. The words were indelibly inscribed on her psyche. She sucked in a breath. 'We moved out there when Mum got the job as his housekeeper. I think he always saw me as a bit of an add-on, always hoping I'd make something of myself and move out. He'll be relieved I'll finally be off his hands.'

'Is that why you took off for the UK?'

She put the book she'd been holding up on the table and rubbed her arms. 'What's going on?'

'What do you mean?'

'Why all the questions? You've never bothered about all this personal stuff before.'

'Maybe we had something else to keep us busy then.' And even under her tan she managed to blush the way she did that made him warm all over. 'And maybe I'm just interested.'

She looked up at him warily through lowered lashes, as if she still didn't quite believe him. 'Okay. I guess wanting to prove myself was part of the reason I left. The job opportunities at home were non-existent and I kind of fell into cleaning, like

Mum had.' Her hands knotted in her lap, her grip so tight it sent the ends of her fingers alternately red then white. 'I thought meeting Kurt was the opportunity of a lifetime and the chance to escape. I was so desperate to make a success of myself, I made every mistake in the book. I was such a fool.' She fell silent on a sigh, moisture sheening her eyes.

He reached over and untangled the damp knot of her hands, taking one of them between his own, lifting it, and pressing his lips to its back. 'It's no crime to trust someone.'

She blinked up at him, trying to clear her vision. Why did he have to be so kind? It had been easier when she'd thought him completely ruthless, easier when she remembered the way he'd taken over the hotel, issuing orders like a general in battle.

But lately he'd been beyond kind. The way he'd abandoned his work to escort her around the island, the way he'd watched sunset after sunset with her because she didn't want to miss a single one because she wanted to store them all up and remember when she went home, and the way he'd woken her softly just this morning with a kiss and brought her to climax with his clever fingers and his hot mouth.

And now he was listening to her as if what she said mattered. As if he cared for her as much as she was beginning to care for him.

She gulped down a breath.

Oh, no, don't go there! Don't imagine it for a minute. Because once before she'd thought someone cared for her. Once before she'd fallen for him because of it. Look where that had got her.

No, she'd made a deal. Under the terms of their contract, she would leave here in little more than two weeks and they'd never see each other again.

She turned her eyes away from the thumb now stroking her hand, his long, tapered fingers and neat nails, up, and up to his face, knowing he was waiting for some kind of response, something to show that she'd put what had happened in the past behind her. But it wasn't what had happened in the past that was bothering her. It was what lay ahead that scared her most of all.

Two weeks of sharing Andreas' bed and pretending to be his mistress, *being his mistress.*

Two weeks of guarding her fragile heart.

And two weeks to work on not falling in love with Andreas Xenides.

She dragged in oxygen to steel her resolve. She'd learned from her mistake with Kurt. It wouldn't happen to her again. She wouldn't let it. She couldn't afford to let it.

'Thank you,' she managed at last, trying to keep things as impersonal as possible. 'I appreciate it.'

'How much?'

It had taken her ages to form a response. She wasn't ready for his. 'Pardon?'

'How much do you appreciate it?'

She shook her head, still uncertain. 'What do you mean?'

'Would you consider an extension to our contract?'

'No.' This time it was her rapid-fire response that took him by surprise. He jerked back, as if she'd fired a shot from a gun. 'I mean, I'm not sure that's possible, with this course, and everything I've got planned.' She plucked at a crease in her dress, her mind in turmoil. Leaving after another two weeks would likely be hell. How would she calmly walk away if she stayed longer?

'I'll double what I'm paying you. Two million Australian dollars.'

'It's not about the money!' And it wasn't. Just lately the thought of being paid for what she was experiencing here on Santorini sat uneasily on her. If he'd been a bully and as ruthless as he'd first seemed, she might have felt as if she deserved it for putting up with him, but he wasn't like that. He was kind and generous and he seemed as if he cared.

'But you like it here. You like being with me.'

She pushed herself out of her chair, striding to the balustrade, her hands grasping at its reassuring solidity. The season was warming up. Three cruise ships lay at anchor today, lighters zipping through the spring mist between them and the port with their cargo of today's photo-hungry tourists.

It's no crime to trust someone.

His words came back to her. Andreas was right. It was no crime to trust someone. Once. But it was a fool who let themselves be burned a second time.

How could she tell him she was scared? He was a businessman. He dealt in contracts and clauses and certainties. Those he understood. Those he lived by. And that would have to be her angle.

She sensed when he joined her at the terrace edge, on the very lip of the ancient crater where the fresh salty wind met the sky. Her skin prickled, her blood fizzed and her flesh became alive with want.

'You *do* enjoy my company, don't you?'

There was no point answering his question. The truth would get her nowhere. 'We have two weeks left, Andreas. Maybe we should just make the most of them.'

A noise alerted him, something other than the cry of seabirds or the distant buzz of conversation and exclamation as tourists wended their way through the narrow paths and came upon another magnificent photo opportunity. He swung his head around and saw her standing there, in the doorway leading to the terrace. *Gamoto.* How much had she heard?

'Petra, what can I do for you?'

'*Kalimera*, Cleo,' she started. 'I'm sorry to interrupt, but, Andreas, your phone was switched off and I had to talk to you.'

'Can't it wait?' He didn't care if he sounded rude. The last thing he needed was Petra spying on them. Already she'd somehow wormed more information out of Cleo than he had wanted her to, and if she'd been here while he'd been talking about the contract…

'I am sorry. But you must excuse me. I'm not feeling very well, Andreas. I wanted to let you know I really think I'm not much good in the office today. I'm hoping it's all right with you to go to my apartment and lie down.'

Damned time of the month again, he supposed, though why all of a sudden she had to fall victim to the curse, he didn't know.

'Are you still feeling unwell?' Cleo asked, moving away from him to take Petra by the arm. 'Can I get you anything?'

'I really don't want to interrupt you,' Petra protested, and then with a smile, 'but that would be so sweet. I am feeling a little dizzy.'

And Andreas watched in bemusement and not a little frustration as the woman he had brought here to deflect the attentions of another was now giving that woman all of hers.

'Come straight back,' he called out to her. 'I want to take you shopping.' And she waved her hand to him, acknowledging she'd heard, even as she shepherded Petra into the building. It wasn't really a lie, he thought as he paced the length of the terrace waiting for her, watching the last of the morning mist burn off the deep blue waters of the flooded crater. She wasn't big on shopping, preferring to explore the churches and villages than the flash boutiques and jewellery stores, but there was something he wanted to buy her, something special he knew would remind her of the intense blue of the sun and sea of Santorini and would at the same time be the perfect complement to her eyes.

And something that might even help persuade her to stay.

Why she was so vehement about leaving, he didn't understand. She loved it here, she loved all of it, even coming to terms with the fact the islands were part of a volcanic system that had been changing over thousands of years and would keep on changing.

But he was determined to make her change her mind and he was confident he could do it. Everyone had their price. A million dollars had got her here.

He didn't care how much it took to keep her.

An hour later, Andreas excused himself to make a phone call and Cleo happily agreed to wait, a rack of blue-beaded key rings catching her attention. It was probably time she thought about buying a few souvenirs to take home. The last two weeks had gone in a flash. The next couple of weeks would probably fly past even quicker.

She dodged out of the way of a group of tourists taking up the width of the street. The streets of Fira were busy today, the day tourists growing in number by the minute, making the narrow lanes and streets even more crowded. If she'd known, she might have stayed at home.

Home.

Now there was a notion. Since when had the mansion she was temporarily occupying ever been her home?

A silver donkey key ring caught her eye, strung on blue cotton with blue beads that looked like eyes. She selected two. Her half-brothers would both love one. She found another, with spinning letter beads that spelt out SANTORINI with more of the eye beads and a beautiful blue stone at the base. Her mother, she decided instantly, slipping it from the rack.

Now she just needed something for her step father. She looked over the racks and decided that with the blue beads there was nothing 'blokey' enough, so her gaze widened, her eyes scanning the contents of the store for that perfect easy-to-pack memento.

And that was when she saw him.

CHAPTER TWELVE

HE WAS checking out the postcards, his face and chest puffier than Cleo remembered, or maybe that was just because they were both pink from the sun, and his arm looped around the shoulders of a girl who looked as stringy as her hair.

He was here.

The key rings slipped from her fingers, clattering to the floor.

'I'm sorry to leave you so long.' She registered Andreas' voice, clung onto the sound like a lifeline even as he bent down to pick up the items she'd dropped. 'Cleo, what's wrong? You look ill.'

'That's him,' she croaked through a throat clamped as tight as every muscle and organ in her body. 'That's Kurt.'

Kurt chose that moment to widen his own search, scanning the shop for opportunities. He looked around, the skin between his eyes creasing into a frown when he saw Andreas scowling at him, a frown that became confused when he looked at the woman alongside the stranger, until the moment he recognised her and his expression became one of abject terror. He tugged, already half outside the shop himself, at the girl next to him who was busy trying on sunglasses. Kurt didn't care, the need to escape clearly paramount, as he dragged his protesting girlfriend out with him, the unpurchased sunglasses still covering her eyes.

'Stay here,' Andreas said, barking out orders to the proprietor in Greek in the same breath before he took off after Kurt. A moment later a woman brought Cleo a chair, insisting she sit down, clucking over her like a mother hen as she pressed a bottle of spring water into her hands. Cleo didn't argue. She was still punch-drunk from seeing Kurt.

So he'd come to Santorini. All that talk of the Greek Islands hadn't been for nothing. But who was the girl? Someone he'd picked up on the Internet who did make the grade? She didn't want to feel hard done by, she had had a complete wardrobe and cosmetic makeover, but surely even before all that she'd been a cut above her?

God, was she that much of a loser that she couldn't even hang onto a man like Kurt?

The woman returned to her side, pressing a small plastic Santorini shopping bag into her hands. The key rings of course, she thought as she felt the beads inside. Andreas must have passed them on to her. She reached for her purse but the woman waved her away. 'No charge,' she said, smiling, bowling Cleo over with more of the warmth and hospitality she'd found everywhere on the island, so that her eyes threatened to spill over with it.

It seemed to take for ever but it was probably only fifteen minutes and Andreas was back. She stood to greet him. 'How are you feeling now?' he asked, collecting her inside his arm.

'Better, thanks. What happened to Kurt?'

'I'll tell you once we're alone.' And she understood why. There was a crowd gathered around the store now, sensing the excitement, wanting to find out what was happening and be part of the action, a crowd that seemed suddenly fascinated in blue-beaded key rings and postcards and bookmarks featuring church domes and cats.

She turned to the beaming proprietor, who was busy exchanging Euros for trinkets, but not too busy to be able to do two things at once. *'Efharisto poli,'* she said, in her slowly improving Greek, repeating it in English in case she'd made a complete hash of the words. 'Thank you, so much,' and the woman beamed and nodded and replied with a torrent of words Cleo was at a loss to understand. 'What did she say?' she asked as soon as they'd re-entered the busy street and he'd steered her towards the mansion.

Andreas didn't look at her, his gaze fixed somewhere ahead, his jaw tight. 'She said we would have beautiful children.'

'Oh. How…quaint.'

Andreas didn't answer. He was too busy wanting to believe it.

'I believe this is yours.' Staff had brought coffee and pastries to a table on the mansion terrace overlooking the caldera that Cleo knew should be listed as one of the wonders of the world, when Andreas handed her the envelope.

She eyed it suspiciously. 'What is it?'

He pressed the envelope into her hands. 'Take a look.'

She opened the flap and peered inside. A stack of notes sat plump and fat inside. She frowned. 'What is this?'

'I had a chat to your former friend.'

'You mean Kurt? You're kidding! You got Nanna's money back. I don't believe it!'

'It seemed he was only too happy to refund you the money he'd borrowed from you in order to escape a charge of shop lifting, plus a bonus for the inconvenience he caused you along the way.'

'Shoplifting?'

'The sunglasses. His girlfriend didn't have time to put them back on the rack. It ended up being a handy levering device.

It seems he didn't want to hang around on Santorini and explain it to the police when his cruise ship was sailing tonight.'

It really didn't matter how or why, it didn't matter that soon Cleo would have more than enough money to repay her many times over, the simple fact was it was her grandmother's money she was getting back, the money she had entrusted to Kurt and haplessly thrown away in the same instant. And getting it back was as if she hadn't lost it at all. 'Thank you,' she said, throwing her arms around his neck. 'I love you so much.'

It wasn't so much hearing her own words. It was feeling his hands still at her sides that alerted her. She slid down his body, appalled at the gaffe she'd just made. 'That's just a figure of speech in Australia. A kind of thank you. Because I really appreciate what you've done.'

'I understand,' he said, but still putting her away from him as he was suddenly craving distance. 'I need to drop by the office, check everything is all right, given Petra is sick. Will you be okay?'

She nodded stoically, thinking that if Andreas had wanted her to stay longer before, he'd no doubt now want her gone tomorrow. 'Of course. I'll see you later.'

And then Andreas was gone and Cleo was left alone, in the sun and breeze and clear blue sky. There were clouds gathering in the distance, she noted absently, thinking that maybe they were in for a storm, while at the same time wishing that one day she would learn not to be so impetuous and admit things she didn't really feel.

Because she hadn't really loved Kurt. She could see that now. She was in love with the idea of being in love and being loved and she'd wanted it to work. So desperately that she'd thought that once they'd had sex, she should tell him that she loved him.

And she didn't really love Andreas either. Not really. He was

just kind and she was just grateful and it was crazy to think,
that just because he had behaved better to her than Kurt, this
gratefulness she felt for him was somehow love.

Liar.

An inner voice brought her to task. She didn't want to stay
because she knew what would happen. Not that she was at risk
of falling in love with him, but because she would be at risk
of loving him more.

Because she already loved him.

The wind whipped stronger around her, the cruise ships
below straining at their chains. Kurt was down there, she
realised, on board one of those ships and soon to sail once more
out of her life.

But Kurt was nothing to her now. As Andreas had said, that
first night they'd made love—*had sex*—Kurt had given her
nothing.

It was Andreas who had given her everything. It was
Andreas who had opened her heart.

It was Andreas she loved.

Andreas reread the fax with increasing frustration. There was
a problem with the paperwork on the takeover of Darius' hotel.
The bank needed more signatures. His. Or the papers could not
be processed and the transaction could not proceed and Darius
would retain ownership by default.

He would have to go to London.

It would take no time. A day. Two at the most. Cleo could
come with him.

'I love you so much.'

Her words came back to him in stark relief. Sure, she'd
tried to explain it away, to get him to accept it was some kind
of Australian equivalent for thank you. But he wasn't buying that.

There was no way he could take her. As much as he wanted her and hungered for her, as much as he'd wished she'd been already incubating his child—maybe it was better that she didn't come with him.

Maybe, he thought with a tinge of reluctance, maybe it was even better that he sent her home early. He'd never wanted to get involved with virgins and with good reason.

Cleo had been the closest he'd got to having a virgin and maybe this experience had proven him right. Virgins and almost virgins. They were looking for someone to love, looking for someone special to make this huge physical leap they were taking into something emotional. Even if there was nothing there.

Except that his mother wanted a grandchild.

Cleo would be beautiful pregnant, her body rounded and blooming, her belly swelling with his seed, but she didn't want to stay and now he wasn't sure she should.

Maybe his trip away would do them both good, and put things into perspective, a perspective he was admittedly having trouble with himself. And then it would all make sense when he came back.

The idea appealed. Logic appealed.

Although, strangely, leaving her again didn't.

She'd blown it. Whatever sense of camaraderie had been building between them, she'd blown it with a few thoughtless and ill-timed words. He'd told her he was leaving in one breath and he was gone in the next, with barely a backward glance and even less warmth. She hadn't even rated a peck on the cheek.

It hurt, his physical withdrawal from her. It hurt more than the fact he would be gone for a day or two, because eventually he would return to Santorini, but things would be different between them.

At least it would be easier for her now to leave. Now there was no way he would want her to stay.

Restless and unable to settle into her books, she wandered into the town, to a small travel agent she'd seen tucked away alongside a heaving souvlaki shop. There was no reason why she shouldn't make enquiries about flights to Australia, the two weeks she had left would soon pass, but still she felt guilty, as if she were going behind Andreas' back. Which was ridiculous, she told herself as she forced herself to enter the narrow shop-front. It was not as if he didn't know she was going to leave. Not as if he didn't know when. What harm would it do to ask?

Then she saw it on the cover of one of the faded and tatty brochures that lined the walls, a picture of Ayers Rock amid a sea of red dust, and a wave of homesickness crashed over her. That was her world, a dusty, hot land where it never seemed to rain. That was where she belonged, not this island paradise, with its to-die-for-views and romantic sunsets and a man who would never really be hers.

A little over two weeks and she could be home.

Maybe it would be wise to make a booking now.

She found Petra in their suite, rifling through the drawers on Andreas' side of the bed. 'What are you doing here?'

'Ha!' the woman said, clearly not feeling guilty in the least as she turned, holding up a fistful of papers. 'There was nothing in the office but I knew I'd find it here.'

'What is it?' she asked, while fear uncurled in her stomach like a viper, hungry and hissing. 'What have you got?' But Cleo knew what it was. Andreas' copy of the contract. Their contract. And she remembered being out on the terrace and discussing an extension and them turning to see Petra watching them. Listening. She swallowed as the woman's greedy eyes drank in the details. 'That's none of your business.' She marched across the room and tried to snatch it from Petra's hands, but Petra whipped it away, staring at Cleo with such a look of triumph that Cleo was momentarily afraid.

'One million dollars! He's paying you one million dollars to sleep with him?'

'No, he's not! Give that back!'

'What does that make you? Some kind of high-priced whore?' Her eyes raked her as effectively as a blast of burning-hot Kangaroo Crossing dust. 'More like an overpriced one.'

'It's not like that. I didn't have to sleep with him.'

'No? But you are, aren't you? I've seen the way you look at him. I know what you're doing. How is that not selling yourself? How is that not whoring?'

'Get out! It's nothing to do with you.'

'Isn't it? I wondered where Andreas had dredged you up from, acting more like some frightened schoolgirl than one of his women. I knew something was up the minute you stepped from the plane. It was all a charade, all for my benefit.'

'What are you talking about? Why should it be for your benefit?'

'Because Andreas was my lover, until you showed up!'

Cleo reeled, feeling blind-sided. 'What?'

'And he didn't know how to tell me it was over. So he employed you—' she gave a theatrical toss of her head '—to be his whore.'

'Andreas wouldn't do that.' But even as she put voice to the words, the doubts she'd had from the start doubled and redoubled in her mind. Why had he needed someone to act as his mistress? To deflect gold-diggers generally, or one woman in particular? She couldn't believe it. Didn't want to believe it.

'But why couldn't he just tell you? Why go to so much trouble?'

'To totally humiliate me, why else?'

The other woman glared at her, as if she belonged here in this place and Cleo didn't, and a wave of revulsion rolled over her. Had Petra occupied this bed in this room before her arrival? Had Petra spent the nights lacing her long legs around Andreas' back as he drove himself deep into her? She closed her eyes, trying to block the pictures out.

No wonder the woman didn't like her. She'd been right from the start: Petra's edgy friendship had been laced with hidden meaning and snide digs.

But whatever his tactics and however repugnant they might be, Andreas had clearly made up his mind. It gave Cleo a much-needed foothold in the argument. 'So Andreas didn't want you, then.' It was her turn to smile. 'And you just can't take no for an answer.'

'You bitch! Do you really think he wants you, a woman who is so stupid she falls for someone over the Internet and loses everything? Do you really think he would prefer your type than someone who can talk business with him and understands his needs?'

Even while Cleo berated herself for revealing so much to this woman—too much—she was so grateful she hadn't revealed absolutely everything. And at least she had the advantage of knowing Andreas wanted her, at least for now. 'Clearly,' she countered, 'you ceased being one of his needs some time ago! Did you overhear while you were eavesdropping on the terrace that he'd asked me to stay longer? Tell me then, who is it he needs—you, who are so loyal to your boss that you skulk around in his bedroom looking for dirt, or me, who he would happily part with another million dollars to have stay?'

And Petra pulled out her trump card. She collapsed on the bed and burst into tears, the contract slipping from her fingers onto the coverlet. Cleo reached down and snatched it up, although the damage had already been done, the cat well and truly let out of the bag. But as for what to do next? Comfort the hysterical woman after the things she'd said and the names she'd called her? Not likely.

'Do you want me to call a doctor?'

Petra sniffed and shook her head, for once her perfect hair unravelling at her nape like the woman herself. 'There's no point. I know what's wrong with me.' She snatched a tissue from the holder on the bedside table and blew her nose.

Maybe she really was heartbroken, thought Cleo. Maybe she'd really loved Andreas and thought he'd loved her back and she couldn't bear the thought of someone else having him.

'I guess it wasn't easy seeing me here.' She wasn't hoping for conciliation. She still hadn't sorted out how she felt about being used by Andreas to ward off his previous lover.

Petra responded with a snort. 'You could say that.'

'It's always hard when the person we want doesn't want us.' Hell, she'd been there herself. 'But sometimes it's for the best. Sometimes they're not the right choice for us after all.'

The woman looked sideways at her, her eyes red-rimmed and swollen. 'So now you're giving me advice. How sweet. Perhaps you might give me advice on another matter?'

Okay, so she probably wasn't the best person to be comforting this particular woman. But at least she was trying. 'I'll do my best.'

'Do you think I should have an abortion?'

CHAPTER THIRTEEN

LIGHTS swam behind her eyes, blood crashed in her ears and Cleo felt the urge to run. Run as fast and as far as she could. Run till her lungs burst and her legs collapsed under her. Run till she hurt so much she couldn't feel any more pain.

'You're pregnant, then.' It all made sense, Petra's morning queasiness by the pool, her dizziness this morning and her mood swings and tears.

'How clever you are. And have you similarly worked out whose child it would be?'

And Cleo's fantasy world crashed down around her. Andreas' child. His baby.

'It's not a crime to trust someone.'

Maybe not. But it should have been a crime to make the same mistake, over and over and over, like a broken record. *The bright side, Nanna, where's the bright side?*

You have a booking to go home in two weeks, a voice in her head told her. *Change it.*

And Cleo knew that was what she had to do. She had to leave, and now, while Andreas was away. Staying was pointless. She didn't want anything to do with him any more, a man who could treat women as he had, pitting one against the other like queens battling it out on some chessboard.

Besides, there was Petra to consider, and a baby. Andreas' baby.

She put a hand to her own stomach. For a few days there, the possibility had existed that it could have been hers. That she too could have been pregnant.

Thank God it had never happened! What a mess that would have been.

'He doesn't know, then?'

'Not yet. I only just found out myself.'

'I think you should tell him as soon as he comes back. I'm sure… I'm sure he'll do the right thing.'

Petra nodded, still looking at the floor. 'I know he will. His mother desperately wants grandchildren. At least she will be delighted.'

Oh, God. More words she didn't need to hear. More words that rocked the foundations of her soul. Andreas had forgotten to use protection with her that time. Surely not intentionally? And yet he'd seemed almost annoyed when he'd learned she wasn't pregnant. He'd offered her more money to stay—to give him more time to get her pregnant? It didn't bear thinking about. She didn't want to know the answer.

'I'm leaving,' Cleo told the woman still hunched and bowed on the bed. 'I'll pack my things and be gone this afternoon.' It was still early in the day. She was sure she could get some kind of link to Athens, be it by plane or ferry. She'd get out now, before Andreas returned and threw her out because there was no point continuing with their charade. She'd get out now while she still held some shred of pride intact.

Petra sighed and sent her a watery smile. 'That's probably for the best.'

Halfway to London, Andreas was growing restless, still searching for the answer to a question that had been plaguing him for hours. Why had she told him she'd loved him? Why would she do that?

She'd turned down a million-dollar offer to stay. Turned him down flat, talking about returning home as if she couldn't wait to be out of there.

And then he'd given her an envelope full of Kurt's money and she'd told him that she loved him. It made no sense, no sense at all.

He toyed with the plate of dips and antipasto, took a sip of his cold *Mythos* beer and watched the landscape beneath his window slowly roll by. What did she want by saying such a thing?

He sighed and pushed back into his seat, smiling about how excited she'd been when she'd told him what she'd learned about the legend of Atlantis. Why did she want to go home so badly to study when all she wanted was all around her here? She couldn't study in a more perfect place. No, she had to stay, there was no question.

But she wouldn't take his money. What else could he offer? *Family.*

The idea was so simple! If she were part of his family she would stay. And she could bear him the children his mother so desperately wanted. He wasn't interested in looking for a wife. He couldn't even think about it with Cleo occupying his bed and his thoughts. And she had said that she loved him. It was perfect.

He took a celebratory swig of his beer and sighed. He'd marry her. Hadn't he come to terms with that very idea when he'd thought she could be pregnant? So what was to stop him marrying her when she was not? She would be pregnant soon enough then.

It was all settled.

He picked up the phone that connected him with the pilot. 'Change of plans. We're going back to Santorini.'

There was no argument, no question from the flight deck. They were turning around. So he wouldn't make it to London to sign those papers, but did he really care about Darius anyway? He'd put the fear of God into him. Wasn't that enough? He could do what he damned well liked with the hotel; one more wasn't going to make any difference to the Xenides portfolio. And the kicker would be that Darius would still have to pay him back the loan.

He put his hands behind his head and leaned back into the soft upholstery. It was perfect.

'Three weeks, Mother, that's right. Are you busy that weekend?'

'Too busy for my son's wedding? Tsh. Of course not.' Even here, standing at the window to his office overlooking the caldera, he could hear the tremor of excitement running through her voice, could imagine that five minutes after this conversation the entire who's who of Athens would know about the upcoming nuptials. 'Although I have to admit to being a little surprised.'

'Really?' Not half as surprised, he'd bet, as he had been when he'd returned home to find Cleo gone and a teary Petra apologising, not making any sense. Petra and tears. He'd never expected to see the day.

He'd been about to head straight back to the plane and follow Cleo when Petra had dropped the bombshell that she was pregnant. He wouldn't wish the news she'd given him on his worst enemy. It wasn't the world he'd imagined so perfect, with Cleo sitting on the terrace, her belly swelling, ripe with their child. But it was a child. *His child.* And there was no way he could walk away. 'Why's that?'

'Well, you seemed so sure when you were last here that you weren't planning on marrying Petra.'

'It was something you said,' he said, clutching at the excuse.

'Something about not realising what was right there under your nose.'

'Oh.' There was a short silence and for a moment he thought the line had dropped out. 'I guess I did say that.'

Strange, Andreas thought, as one of his staff slipped a note to him. He'd imagined his mother would be delighted with that little snippet. He could see her even now telling all her friends at bridge that she'd played matchmaker.

'Anyway, I'll send over the helicopter for you a few days in advance.'

'That would be lovely. I'll enjoy coming over to help with everything. And, Andreas?'

'Yes?'

'It all seems such a rush. I know I put some pressure on you and, while that's a mother's prerogative, I'd hate to think you were rushing into something you might regret later. Are you sure you're making the right decision?'

His head collapsed back, his hand going to his brow. It was the right decision, wasn't it? Morally. Ethically. For the sake of his child. He was doing the right thing. The note in his hand fluttered against his brow. He looked at it, trying to focus, trying to make sense of the words it contained in the context of the query he'd sent to the clinic.

We are unable to provide information on our patients but can advise that we have no patient by the name of Petra Demitriou.

And it was signed by the very doctor Petra had claimed had confirmed her pregnancy.

No wonder she hadn't wanted him to accompany her!

'Andreas? Are you still there? I asked if there was any chance you were making a mistake.'

He was, but his teeth were grinding together and it took a force of will to prise them apart. *Thank God he hadn't told his mother why it was all such a rush!* 'Very possibly, Mother. I'll have to call you back.'

'Possibly? What do you mean?'

'I'll call you back.'

Right now he had something more important on his mind.

He found her in his suite, supervising the removal and packing of Cleo's clothes. 'What the hell are you doing?'

'Andreas! I didn't hear you coming.'

'Who asked you to take Cleo's clothes away?' He gestured to the staff, clearing the room with a click of his fingers.

'Andreas, Cleo's gone. I thought I should make room for my things, seeing as I'll be moving in soon.'

He swallowed back on a surge of revulsion. He hadn't been able to stomach the thought of Petra back in his bed when he could still smell Cleo's scent on his sheets, the smell of her hair on his pillow. Although Petra had made it clear she'd like to resume sexual relations ten minutes after she'd dropped the double-barrelled blast that Cleo had gone and that she was carrying his child.

And now she was planning on moving in. It was all he could do to keep a tenuous hold on the contents of his stomach.

'When's your next appointment with the clinic?' he asked disingenuously. 'I'd like to come too.'

She smiled and closed the wardrobe doors, he guessed so he couldn't see how empty they now were. Empty of Cleo. As empty as he now felt. 'There's no need for that. It's just routine. Tests. You know.'

'No, I don't know. And neither, it seems, does Dr Varvounis.'

'Wha…? What do you mean?'

'You're not registered at the clinic. He's never heard of you. You haven't been, have you?'

'You probably have the wrong clinic—'

'I think I have the wrong fiancée.'

'What's that supposed to mean? I'm the one who's having your baby!'

'Are you? Or is it as fabricated as your affection for me? You made it up, didn't you? Made the whole story up in one final desperate attempt to get rid of Cleo and get your talons into me. And it nearly worked. Well, no more. The wedding is off. And you are no longer in my employ. I want you out of here.' He turned on his heel and strode out of the room and suddenly she was there, tugging at his arm.

'But I love you, Andreas! We can make a baby just like your mother yearns for, I know we can.'

Fury flared inside him. 'What did you say? Did she tell you that? Is that how you came up with this plan to trap me? I'm sorry, Petra. Maybe I wasn't clear enough before. I don't want you. I never really did. I want Cleo.'

'She wasn't good enough for you. She was young and naïve and stupid.'

'I love her!'

And her eyes went wide. 'You couldn't. You can't. Andreas, please, listen to me—'

'Get out, Petra. I never want to see you again.'

And then she was gone and he was alone. Alone to the realisation that had shocked him as much as it had Petra.

He loved Cleo.

And he was going to get her back.

CHAPTER FOURTEEN

SO MUCH for autumn. Cleo wiped the sweat from her brow as she lugged the vacuum cleaner along the balcony of the Kangaroo Crossing Hotel, the last pub, the sign boasted, this side of the Black Stump.

It might be April but a last hoorah from summer had the sun shining down like a blowtorch, turning the already parched earth to yet more red dust. As if they needed more. A convoy of four-wheel drives roared down the main street, turning the air red and rich with diesel fumes.

Welcome to the outback, she thought as she tackled the sticky doors of yet another balcony room.

Inside was thankfully cooler, the thick stone walls protecting the rooms from the worst of the heat, but still she managed to work up a sweat as she cleaned the last of the rooms.

She'd been lucky to score this job. Her mum had had to give up work as her pregnancy was now quite advanced and she was happily awaiting the arrival of her baby. Cleo couldn't help but be excited for her, not only because she'd been able to take over the cleaning job from her. She could even supplement her income by pulling beers in the bar at night.

And the best thing was the job came with its own accommodation. True, it was in the basement, but it was nothing like the poky closet she'd endured in London. This was a real room with a real bed, and so much the cooler for being underground.

She'd save up now she was home and when she had enough she'd enrol in that Classics course in Sydney. She'd discovered she could do it by correspondence and hopefully she'd be able to start next semester. She could hardly wait. The books from Santorini she'd brought home were so well read they were dog eared and slipping from their covers.

She looked around and gave a small sigh of satisfaction as she straightened the last kink out of the queen bed's coverlet and stopped to smell the roses she'd salvaged from the twisted climbers covering the beer garden. A VIP had booked for tonight, the manager had proudly advised, the room had to be perfect. And it was. Dubbed the honeymoon suite because it boasted its own bath and loo, it was the grandest room the hotel had to offer. She smiled. Some honeymoon suite. Nothing at all like the suites she'd shared with Andreas in London and Santorini. But then, this was Kangaroo Crossing, and if she was ever going to have a honeymoon herself this was the best she could hope for.

Not that that was likely. Since coming home, she'd sworn off men for good. Clearly she had no idea how to fall in love with the right one. She hauled the vacuum cleaner and her gear back out into the hot still air, allowing herself just a second to remember what it had been like in those first few giddy days and nights she'd shared with Andreas on Santorini, when there'd been times she'd actually believed he'd cared about her, those perfect days before she'd discovered she was being used as some sort of shield between him and Petra, the woman who was carrying his child, the woman he was probably already married to.

The vacuum cleaner thumping almost reassuringly against her shin brought her back to reality. Her time with Andreas had been nothing more than a fantasy. This was her life now. This was her world, a world that had shrunk in the last two weeks to one big wide dusty stretch of highway lined with low timber-board buildings.

Another car was making its way through the town, a trail of red dust behind it, a car impossibly shiny and as low slung and inappropriate for the outback roads as you could imagine. She stopped to watch for a moment, expecting it to keep right on going, only to see it slow to a halt, pulling up alongside the hotel in the shade of an ancient gum tree. Could this be their VIP, then? Kangaroo Creek didn't get many of those. She put down the machine and rested her arms on the timber balustrade to watch. And then the driver stepped out and the air was punched from her lungs.

Andreas.

Dressed in light-coloured chinos, a white shirt unbuttoned halfway down his chest and a gold watch glinting against his olive-skinned wrist, he looked cool and urbane. And then she thought of what he'd done to her, of his hot mouth and his clever tongue, and the very concept of cool and urbane tripped into overload.

Dry-mouthed, she clung to the railing now, knowing that if she didn't her legs would never hold her up. Why was he here? What could he possibly want?

Unless it was to show off his new wife…

The honeymoon suite. A VIP. It all made sense. But why bring her here? Surely Andreas wouldn't stoop that low?

But he was alone, and as she watched he tugged a single leather holdall from the boot. She should go before he saw her. She should disappear back to the basement and hide.

And then he looked up, and their eyes jagged, and her heart flipped over. *Please*, she thought, *please, I want to hate you for what you did. I want to be angry about how you used me. I want to forget. Please don't make me remember…*

But just one look at him was enough to know that she still hungered for him, and then he pulled the sunglasses from his face and she knew that he wanted her too.

Oh, God, why was he here? What could it mean? And why did she have to look such a bloody mess? She pushed back from the railing, preparing to flee, when he raised a hand and spoke.

'*Kalimera, Cleo,*' he said, in that gorgeous accent that always made her insides quiver. It was probably the first time the greeting had ever been uttered in Kangaroo Crossing. And probably the last, if she had anything to do with it.

'What the hell are you doing here?'

'I love Australian women,' he shouted from below. 'They always speak what's on their mind.'

There was a murmur of agreement from below, no doubt from the blokes lining the verandah watching the occasional car go by, but she was already intent on her reply. 'Have you known that many to know?' And instantly she wished she'd fled when she'd had the chance because it seemed as if half the pub's contents had suddenly spilled out onto the verandah below to watch the proceedings.

'Only one,' he admitted. 'But that was more than enough.'

A ripple of laughter drifted up from the crowd. They'd all seen the car, they'd all seen the man that had stepped from it like some Greek god dripping with money and influence. She didn't have to see their glances to know what they were all thinking. That anyone would be mad to turn this man away. But they didn't know what he'd done. They didn't know he had a woman back home pregnant with his child.

'Go to hell, Andreas!' Damn him. She battled the vacuum cleaner down the outside stairs, thankfully in the opposite direction from where he was standing, and headed inside for the basement stairs, her mind too confused to deal with whatever was going on, her heart too filled with hurt to assist.

She was too slow. He met her in the lobby, where the entrance hall met the stairs going down to the basement. 'Cleo.'

'How ironic,' she said, her feet riveted to the ground, 'that we should meet like this again. Have you plans for taking over the Kangaroo Crossing Hotel, then? Should I start looking for another job?'

'I didn't come for the hotel.'

'No?' She clutched the rounded stairway newel like a safe haven. If she hung onto that, surely her legs would keep working. Although maybe she should be more worried about her heart. Right now it felt so big it was a wonder it didn't spill right out of her mouth. 'Then what are you doing here?'

'I came here to see you.'

There was no way her legs were going to get her down those stairs, not with the way he was looking at her now.

'And what if I don't want to see you?'

The noise from the bar next door was almost overwhelming as the customers spilt back into the cool interior, one topic of conversation and conjecture clearly discernible amongst the shouts and laughter.

'We need to talk. Not here. Somewhere private. Have dinner with me tonight and I'll explain.'

'Mr Xenides, I presume?'

Daphne Cooper, the manager's wife, primped her hair and giggled like a schoolgirl as she spun the register around to face him. 'If you'd just sign here, please. And if you need somewhere private,' she continued with a wink in Cleo's direction, 'I can serve dinner for two in the honeymoon suite?'

'I would appreciate that very much,' she heard him say before Daphne's answering giggle, and Cleo took advantage of the interruption to flee.

She slammed her door, grabbed her bathroom gear and escaped to there before he would have a chance to follow her.

Why was Andreas here? Why now, when he hadn't bothered to contact her in all the days since she'd fled Santorini and she'd made a start at a new life and forgetting…?

Who was she trying to kid? she asked herself, when she stepped under the shower. She would never forget those perfect few days and nights in paradise.

There was a card under her door when she returned.

Join me for dinner, it simply said, with a time and a room number. The honeymoon suite. What a joke. For a moment she was tempted to send a note back, telling him what he could well and truly do with his kind invitation, before sense got the better of her.

Why shouldn't she listen to what he had to say, the excuses he had to offer? Why shouldn't she hear him out? And then she could tell him exactly what she thought of him and tell him to get the hell out of her life once and for all.

She refused to hang around the hotel wondering what he was doing all afternoon, so instead she hitched a ride out to the homestead to see her mum, thinking that helping her with the washing or just sorting out the twins would distract her for a few hours. Nanna was there too, full of baby stories that made her laugh and made her almost forget the queasy feeling inside. She didn't tell them about Andreas. She didn't want to hear Nanna's take on the bright side. Because there wasn't one. Not this time. There couldn't be, except that soon he would be gone.

Her stepfather, Jack, wandered in for afternoon tea around four, his khaki work clothes dusty, his hair plastered to his scalp where his hat had been stuck all day. 'G'day all,' he said as he plonked his big frame down on a chair, and as Cleo's mum fussed with getting more tea and cutting slabs of cake. 'Bit of a commotion down at the pub. This mate of yours, Cleo, what's he doin' here?'

Her mother and nanna swivelled their heads simultaneously, their voices in chorus. 'What mate?'

'This rich bloke, from Greece, they reckon. Come to see our Cleo.'

Her head swung around to look at Jack. *'Our Cleo'?* Where had that come from?

But everyone else was apparently more interested in the rich bloke. Questions fired at her from all sides. They'd known it had all gone wrong with Kurt, but this job she'd had in Santorini she'd said precious little about. What was her former boss suddenly doing here? And why?

She fended them off the best she could. After all, she didn't know the answers herself. But she promised she'd let them know. First thing tomorrow when she came out on her day off. By then he'd be no doubt long gone and might cease to be a topic of conversation.

Her stepfather offered to run her back into town, another surprise. But the biggest surprise was when he pulled up outside the hotel. She was halfway out the door when a big beefy hand landed on her arm. She jumped and swung her head around. Her stepfather's face looked pained, preferring to study the steering wheel than look at her. 'Cleo, one thing. Close the door, love.' He suddenly nodded towards the line of men sitting outside on the verandah, sipping their beers. 'There's a pack of vultures out there waiting for any hint of gossip to brighten up their sad lives.'

She pulled her leg back in and closed the door and he resumed his scrutiny of the steering wheel, crossing both his wrists at the top.

'I know we've never been close. I know I've never made you feel welcome. And I should have. Because you're family. I was glad when you came back. Your mum was beside herself with worry and…' He sighed. 'Well, it was just good to know you were home, safe and sound. And I just want you to know that if this bloke tries to take advantage of you, or tries to hurt you, I'll wipe the bloody floor with him myself.' He swung his head around. 'Understood?'

She'd never known Jack to make such a long speech. She'd never known him to more than grunt in acknowledgement, and here he was, letting her know he'd defend her. As part of his family.

She flung her arms around his beefy neck and hugged him. 'Thank you.' And then, because she was as embarrassed as he was, and close to tears, she flung open the door and was gone before either of them could say goodbye.

She dressed carefully, or as carefully as she could given her now limited wardrobe. A wraparound skirt and vest top with mid-height sandals were the best she could do, although she could still use the make-up she'd been given in London to make the most of her eyes. She wasn't interested in seducing him, she told herself as she applied mascara. She just wanted him to see that she was surviving, and surviving well.

And then she was ready. She took one last look at herself, took a gulp of air and headed upstairs.

He was waiting for her knock, opening the door and standing there, all Greek god and potent male, so potent that the words almost dried in her throat and would have, but that there were questions she needed answers to. 'What are you doing here, Andreas? What is it that you want?'

He looked at her hungrily, as if she were the meal. 'Dinner is served,' he said, fuelling the feeling, and despite the desperate logical waves from her brain that told her to cling to her anger, to hold onto her hatred of what he'd done, her body hummed with his proximity as she let him usher her inside.

The door closed with a snick behind her, the table laden with dishes awaiting. The steaming dishes could have smelt good, the cooking here was renowned as the best country cooking could offer, but right now her senses were full of the scent of him, and nothing incited her appetite more. Oh, no. She had to get out of here. She couldn't do this!

She turned suddenly, 'Andreas, I—', and was surprised to find him so close behind her that they almost collided. He reached out and steadied her with his hands at her shoulders, warm and strong, and the feeling was so intoxicating, so real after the memories she'd been hanging onto, that she forgot what it was she wanted to say. She felt the tremor move within him then as he exhaled, as if she wasn't the only one fighting their demons. But that was crazy. What demons could possibly plague Andreas?

Unless he felt guilty about seeing a woman while his child grew within another.

'Come,' he said at last. 'Sit.' And so she did, watching him pour them both wine, knowing she dared not touch it for fear of losing her resolve. 'How are you?'

'Andreas. Can we please cut to the chase? What are you doing here?'

He took a deep breath, and placed an envelope before her plate. 'You left without this.'

With trembling hands she picked up the envelope and pulled the paper from inside. A cheque. For five hundred thousand pounds. 'You left without your money.'

She stared at the cheque feeling sick. So that was what this was about. Mr Businessman handling the money aspect, ensuring all the i's were dotted, all the t's crossed. Of course. Strange, though, when he could have just posted it. Although then she would never have had the opportunity to do this…

She slipped it back in the envelope and pressed the flap down with her thumb, her eyes not leaving his. His mouth was halfway to a smile, as if he was expecting her to pocket it, which in turn made her smile. And then, over a snowy china plate, she ripped the envelope in half, and tore those two pieces into half again, over and over, until the tiny fragments fluttered to her plate. And then she stood. 'I don't want your money. So if that's all?'

He was on his feet, blocking her exit, 'What the hell is wrong with you? We had a deal. The money's yours. You earned it.'

'No. I didn't. I left before the contract term expired. Besides which, even if I had stayed, I wouldn't want your money anyway. I don't want anything of yours, don't you understand that?'

His features looked strained, the flesh across his cheekbones drawn tight. Clearly a man unused to not getting his own way. 'I pay my debts, Cleo. We had a contract and I—'

She wanted to scream, suddenly grateful for the foresight Daphne had had to organise dinner for them here in a private room as opposed the dining room, where this discussion would have provided gossip for the next decade at least. 'I will not take your money! You will not reduce those days I spent with you, making me feel like some overpriced whore!'

It was Andreas' turn to stand. 'I never thought of you like that!'

'No? But Petra did. She found the contract in your suite and made it clear that's what I was. Remember Petra,' she charged, 'the mother of your child?'

'You don't have to remind me about Petra,' he said, his teeth clenched. 'Petra was the woman who took you away from me.'

How could he be so blind? How could he avoid the truth that had sent her away? The truth that meant he shouldn't be here with her now or ever, whatever the reason. 'She never took me away from you. You did that all by yourself, when you got her pregnant and used me as some kind of human shield. How do you think that made me feel? Knowing that all the time I was in your bed, your previous lover was already carrying your child!'

'She was never my lover and she was never carrying my child!'

Cleo felt the wind knocked out of her sails. 'She what? But she was pregnant. She told me… And she said you were paying me to humiliate her…'

His hand raked through his hair; the other rubbed his neck. 'We had sex. Once. It was a mistake and I told her. But she knew my mother wanted grandchildren, and that she'd had a cancer scare and was worried I'd never get around to it. She admitted as much to Petra, who decided she'd have to bring out the big guns if she was going to get rid of you and clear the way for her. She faked the pregnancy to trap me.'

'But she was sick, dizzy…'

'All of it put on. All of it designed to make everyone believe it was true.'

It was too much to take in. Too much to accept. And there was still so much that didn't make sense.

And yet hadn't Petra said the very same thing—that Andreas' mother wanted grandchildren? And hadn't Cleo remembered his unexpected response when she'd informed him her period had arrived?

She swallowed. 'Is that why you're back here? Because you need a child and you think I'll provide it for you?'

'What? Cleo, what are you saying?'

'You wanted me to be pregnant, didn't you? You seemed strangely disappointed that I wasn't. That was right after visiting your mother, wasn't it? She told you then that she wanted grandchildren.'

He took a step closer, knowing the bridge between them was much longer and way more fragile than he'd realised. 'Cleo—'

'And then you asked me to stay longer, offered to pay me more. Why do that if you weren't going to try and get me pregnant?'

'It wasn't like that.' Except he knew that it was. Hadn't that been his exact plan? Keep her longer, get her with child. *Make his mother happy.*

'And then you discover Petra was faking it and you turn up on my doorstep.'

'No! I'll admit—' He spun away, troubling his hair again with his fingers, raking his scalp with his nails until he flung himself back, his arms slashing through the air. 'Yes, I'll admit I was hoping, that it seemed like an easy option. I'll admit that I wanted you to stay because I thought you might fall pregnant. But that's not why I'm here now. I didn't come for a child, Cleo, I came for you.'

Her chin kicked up, her blue eyes liquid and shimmering in the rays from the sun setting outside the window. 'And you expect me to believe that?'

'Cleo, I know I don't deserve your trust. I know I'm the last person to deserve that. But on that flight to London when I'd left you behind, I learned something. That I wanted you. That I wanted to marry you. And so I turned the plane around and came home.'

Her face was paler now, her fingers clawed around the back of her chair. 'Isn't it the same thing? Why decide to marry me, unless it was to keep me around longer and increase your chances of having a child?'

His features were tight, his jaw line growing even tighter before he conceded in a nod. 'Okay, that's what crossed my mind—initially—and no, I'm not proud of it. And then I got home and learned you'd already left and was about to follow you and bring you back, except there was Petra saying she was pregnant and I knew I had no choice but to let you go.'

He held out his long-fingered hands in supplication. 'Do you have any idea how that feels? To bow to responsibility when it feels wrong and when your heart wants something different, even if it doesn't understand why?'

She swallowed again and he followed the movement in her throat and down to where she crossed her arms under the breasts he'd missed so much, but not just because of their perfection, he'd learned, but because of the woman he missed more.

'So tell me, Mr Businessman, what is it that your heart wants?'

He took a deep breath. 'You once said you loved me.'

'A figure of speech—'

'So you said. I promise you, at the risk of thoroughly humiliating myself here, my declaration won't be.' He watched her perfect blue eyes, saw the questions, the suspicion and maybe, maybe, just a flicker of hope to mirror his own. 'I love you,' he told her. 'I don't know when it happened, or how, or why it took me so long to realise that that was the reason I couldn't let you go, that you had to stay. And you will probably never forgive me for the way I treated you and for being so blind for so long, but I pray you will, because I love you, Cleo, and I had to come and ask you, beg you if necessary, if you would do me the honour of becoming my wife.'

Time stood still. There was the odd shout from the verandah downstairs, the odd drift of laughter through the French doors and outwardly her world hadn't changed. But inside it was as if someone had taken the pieces of her world and rearranged them and everything was suddenly new and unfamiliar.

'Cleo, for God's sake, say something.'

And she blinked to find Andreas still there, not a dream, not some wild imaginings of a woman who'd been too long in the sun.

'Me? You love me?' Cleo, the high-school dropout. Cleo, the cleaner, who would never amount to anything. A bubble of hope burst from her heart. 'You want to marry me?'

And she must have looked so shaky that he snatched her in his arms and held her so close that she could feel his heart thudding powerfully in his chest, but still she couldn't quite trust him. 'And babies, then. I guess you want babies.'

And he stilled for a moment and held her away from him with his big broad hands until he could see her face. 'Right now, all I want is you. I love you, Cleo. And if a child never happens, so be it, my mother will have to deal with it. Because it's you that I want, nothing more. '

Her eyes swam with tears, happy tears, as she looked up into his perfect face. 'I guess you've got me, then, Andreas.'

His dark eyes still looked uncertain. 'Is that a yes?'

And she flung her arms around his neck and held him tight. 'Yes!' she cried. 'Because I love you, Andreas, I love you so much!'

And he kissed her and swung her into his arms and carried her, the meal laid out for them forgotten, to the soft embrace of the queen-sized bed.

Later, much later, when the passion of their reunion had temporarily abated, they stirred. 'There's something else I brought you,' he whispered, nuzzling her cheek, before disappearing for a moment to withdraw a small package from his jacket. He didn't hand the box to her; instead he snapped on her bedside light before holding the pendant up before her. She loved it immediately, the geometric Greek pattern in gold surrounding a circle of amazing blue gemstone that looked as if it were on fire.

'I bought this in Fira,' he said as he clipped the chain around her neck, 'but I never had a chance to give it to you. But I think it signifies everything about us. For this,' he said, tracing one finger around the gold border where it lay on her chest, 'is the Greek, while the core, the inner beauty is an Australian opal, that shows, like your eyes, every colour of the sea and sky.'

'It's so beautiful,' she said, lifting and cradling the pendant in her hands so she could study its colour and depth.

'It's you and me,' he said. 'The Greek and the Australian, together.'

And they kissed and held each other tight.

'There's one thing I still don't understand,' she murmured a little while later as she nestled against him.

'What is it?'

'You said you turned the plane around. Didn't you go to London? I thought you had to go or you could lose the hotel deal.'

His fingers stilled momentarily in her hair, and she nestled closer, allowing her own hand to explore the perfection of his chest, the feel of his satin skin, the wiry dusting of dark hair that coiled around her fingers, the nub of a masculine nipple. 'It was important, as you say. But suddenly the hotel didn't seem to matter any more. And neither did getting even with Darius—or Demetrius, as you knew him.'

'What happened to the deal, then?'

He shrugged. 'Last I heard, he was back in charge. Probably still losing money hand over fist to his turf accountant.'

It was her fingers' turn to still. 'You let the deal fall through? I thought you hated him so much.'

He sighed. 'I did. Once.'

Troubled now, she let her fingers resume their exploration,

down his chest and circling his navel with her fingertips. 'But why? What did he do to deserve that?'

'Does it matter?'

'I need to know the kind of man I'm marrying. I need to understand. You seemed so ruthless then, so driven.' She shivered and he tucked her in closer, his thumb stroking the nipple of one goose-bumped breast and flicking her thermostat to simmer.

'A long time ago he was my father's partner. They'd built a strong business together and everything seemed to be going well. But he'd asked my mother to marry him once, a long time before my father had married her. It seems he'd never forgiven him for that. Or her. So he bided his time watching the business grow and waiting for the perfect opportunity, when the business was cashed up and ready to make a major investment. He took the lot and left us with nothing. My father died barely a year later, a broken man, and I swore on his grave that I would one day get even.'

'Oh.' He'd tensed with his words, and her fingers worked to massage the pain away, stroking his flat belly and following the trail of hairs that arrowed downwards where she encountered him, thick and pulsing once more into life. 'I understand now,' she said, and she did. 'I can see why you needed to get even.'

He flipped over her then, so suddenly that she didn't see it coming. 'It's history,' he said as he buried his face in her neck and settled between her legs. 'And it doesn't matter any more. My mother tried to make me see that, but it was you who made me understand.'

She shook her head as his hot tongue circled her nipples, first one and then the other, his breath like a heated caress where his tongue didn't touch. 'How?'

But she did see the foil packet he had ready in his hand. She shook her head. 'I want you, this time,' she whispered. 'It's you I want to feel inside me, your flesh against mine.' And he cast it aside and kissed her, hot and desperate and soul deep.

She gasped into his mouth as he entered her in one tight, fluid stroke, gasped again when he started to move inside her, the delicious friction of his increasing rhythm sending tremors through every part of her. 'For too long,' he muttered through teeth clenched tight, 'I was looking to the past. But in you…' He stilled for a moment, poised at the brink as he looked down at her, caressing her face with the pads of his thumbs. 'In you, I found something different. In you I found my future. I love you, Cleo.'

And he lunged into her again, his cry rent from him like a cry of freedom, as together they spilled into their future.

EPILOGUE

HER mother was hanging out sheets on the line, her nanna sitting in the shade of the ancient peppercorn tree, when Andreas' car pulled up alongside the homestead late the next morning. Cleo had warned them they were coming but still her mother turned and stared, while the twins bowled around a corner of the house, shooting each other up with guns they'd improvised from sticks and rubber bands and skidding to a halt when they saw the red sports car Andreas was unfolding himself from. 'Wow,' they said in unison. 'Is that your car?'

Andreas turned on his million-wattage smile as he pulled off his sunglasses and shook his head. 'Sadly no, it is a hire car,' and the boys' faces dropped. 'But I have one much better than this back on Santorini,' and they wowed again and positively drooled as they circled the car like a couple of sharks.

'I'll give you a ride a little later,' he said. 'That is, if you like.' Their eyes lit up on their combined, 'Awesome!' Cleo laughed and wondered how he could read children so well when he'd had so little to do with them. Maybe he'd make a pretty good father, she figured, if his reaction to her half-brothers was any indication. Maybe having his babies wouldn't be such a hardship.

Making them, she already knew, would be nothing but sheer pleasure.

Her cheeks colouring into a blush she suspected she shouldn't be brandishing when she was about to introduce the man she loved to her family, she slipped her hand in his and led him to where her mother stood, her eyes as wide as her expanding stomach, while Nanna's watched on keen and interested. 'Mum, Nanna, I'd like you to meet Andreas Xenides, the man I love, and the man I intend to marry.'

'That is,' Andreas added, turning on his dazzling smile again and bowing as he took first her mother's and then her nanna's hand in greeting, 'if you permit me your daughter's hand in marriage.'

'Oh, my,' her mother said, the concerned look she'd had on her face when they'd driven up transforming into her own wide smile. 'Jack!' she called as the screen door slammed and her husband emerged from the house. 'Jack, come and meet Andreas. Cleo's getting married!'

Jack didn't rush. He took his own sweet time, Cleo thought, as he let his laid-back stride carry him closer, his beefy arms swinging loosely by his sides and his eyes narrowed by the sun and still drinking in the scene, missing nothing. He pulled up a metre shy and the two men faced each other off, the Greek billionaire in the white shirt, with money clearly at his fingertips, and Jack in his moleskins, his sandy hair for once not flattened by his hat, and who clearly felt that out here, even being the dirt-poor farmer he was, he was king.

He nodded, extending a wary hand. 'Mr Xenides, Jack Carter.'

'Call me Andreas, Mr Carter.'

He nodded. 'Andreas, it is. And just plain Jack is fine with me. I hear you made quite a ruckus in town with your fancy car. And now, I hear, you want to marry Cleo.'

Beside her Andreas smiled. 'That's about the size of it, if you'll allow me to, that is.'

And Jack turned to Cleo. 'And is this what you want, lovey?'

Cleo beamed at the endearment. 'It's everything I want, but only on one condition.'

Her stepfather's face turned dark and he looked ready to take Andreas on, in case he took issue. 'And what's that?'

'That you walk me down the aisle and give me away.'

And she could have sworn her sun-hardened stepfather melted right there before her eyes.

'Well,' said her mum with a tear in her eyes, wiping her hands on her apron and looking for something to fill in the stunned-mullet silence from her husband, 'you will both be staying for lunch? I've got a lamb roast on.'

And they did stay, and afterwards Andreas rang his mother while his new family were busy with dessert, knowing it was morning now in Athens. 'I have a surprise for you,' he told her.

'You're marrying the Australian woman after all?'

And he did a double take. 'You knew?'

She laughed. 'Didn't I tell you? Sometimes you don't know what's right there under your nose until it's gone.'

Andreas laughed then too. 'You did,' he told her, wondering if somehow she hadn't known all along but still not understanding how.

Then after dessert he took the twins for a spin in the car, after which they put their own two and two together.

'You're leaving again?' they asked Cleo, almost simultaneously, sounding disappointed that with Andreas gone they might be deprived of an occasional ride in a sports car.

And their nanna nodded wisely, as always. 'But look at the bright side, boys, you'll be able to visit Cleo and Andreas on Santorini and have a ride in his sports car there. Isn't that right, Andreas?' And Andreas nodded and Cleo laughed and knew

right then and there she could stop looking for her own bright
side, because she'd found it.

Love.

There was no brighter side.

FRIDAY NIGHT MISTRESS

Jan
COLLEY

Jan Colley lives in Christchurch, New Zealand, with Les and a couple of cats. She has travelled extensively, is jack of all trades and master of none and still doesn't know what she wants to be when she grows up—as long as it's a writer. She loves rugby, family and friends, writing, sunshine, talking about writing and cats, although not necessarily in that order. E-mail her at vagabond232@yahoo.com or check out her website at www.jancolley.com.

Thanks for all the stories, Dad!
And thanks to Stephen Bray, our friendly family
lawyer, who let me pester him about courtroom
legalese and only charged me a chocolate fish.
And to Maureen Coffey of Havelock Sea Charters
who answered my questions about chartering a boat
in the Marlborough Sounds of New Zealand.

One

"All rise."

Spectators and participants in the Wellington High Court rose as one. Day one of the defamation case brought by Randall Thorne, founder of Thorne Financial Enterprises, against Syrius Lake had begun.

Seated behind his father in the front row of the gallery, Nick Thorne frowned as his younger brother slipped into the empty seat beside him. "You're late," Nick muttered without heat. Adam was always late, even while on holiday.

The judge bustled in and motioned for everyone to take their seats.

"Would you look at that?" Adam whispered, nudging

Nick. "Little Jordan Lake, all grown up and pretty as a picture."

Nick tilted his head and flicked a glance to his right. He'd noticed her earlier, surprised at how demure she looked with her hair tied back, wearing a white blouse and a knee-length black skirt. Everyone here would be more used to seeing her in the tabloids, partying it up with some rock star or other, her golden hair flowing and plenty of long, smooth leg on display. She was every inch the heiress, daughter of one of the richest and most flamboyant men in New Zealand.

Adam leaned in close. "I'm surprised you've never considered hooking up with her. An alliance with the Lake princess would be one way to bury this stupid hatchet that's been the bane of our lives forever."

"She's more your type than mine," Nick murmured, settling back in his seat as his father turned his head and sent him a disapproving look.

It was true. Jordan and Adam were rebels, whereas Nick was duty-driven and responsible. The brothers could almost pass as twins with their olive coloring, dark hair and brows and their father's tall, broad frame. But Adam, with his designer stubble, flashy suits and bad boy demeanor, was far removed from the quieter, more conservative Nick.

"True," Adam whispered, rubbing his chin thoughtfully, "but I live in London."

The infamous feud between Randall Thorne and Syrius Lake had tainted their whole lives, especially their late mother's, a former close friend of Syrius's wife, Elanor. Nick felt a pang of compassion for the woman sitting at the end of the row in the aisle to his right. Elanor had spent thirty years in a wheelchair because of Nick's father, all the more galling because she and his mother were once national ballroom dancing competitors and partners in their own dance studio.

"You can't help your looks, big brother," Adam went on, "but you're still not a bad catch. CEO of the biggest privately-owned finance company in New Zealand..."

"Not yet," Nick said tersely.

"Soon." His brother waved a nonchalant hand toward Jordan Lake. "Cultivate something with her. It's a dirty job, but somebody's gotta do it."

Their father turned again, this time with a stern look at Adam.

The respective counsels droned on. Nick shifted impatiently. He'd felt duty-bound to stand by his father today on the first day of the trial, but there was no way he could afford to be here all day, every day for the next week or however long the trial lasted. That would fall to Adam, who'd come home for a few weeks' holiday and to support his father through the trial.

To his right, Nick caught a flash of tanned leg as Jordan shifted. His eyes lingered on her black pump-clad foot as it bounced up and down. Was she as bored and impatient as he was? Hell, she had nowhere else to be. She didn't work, unless you counted the pursuit of a good time work.

The hair on the back of his neck prickled and Nick looked up. The heiress was watching him, her mouth slanted in a cool smirk. Then she tilted her head toward her mother and whispered in her ear.

Adam cast him an amused glance, seeing the direction of his gaze. "You know you want to," he murmured.

Nick gave his brother a wry smile. It was great having him around. Nick missed him, even though their father constantly played them off against each other, unheeding of Adam's wish to have nothing to do with the family business.

Randall raised them with an abiding fascination for money, but Adam preferred to be at the cutting edge while Nick liked to have his finger on the pulse, maintaining and building strength. Adam departed four years ago to live his dream as a trader in London's stock exchange.

At the break, his father and lawyer seemed supremely confident, Randall declaring none too softly that he intended to annihilate Syrius Lake, whatever it took. With a sinking heart, Nick realized that if it wasn't this case, it would be something else. Without his mother's tempering influence, Randall would stop at nothing to get his revenge—and that directly impacted on Nick's future. He intended to be named successor of Thorne Financial Enterprises when his father retired in a few weeks. *If* his father retired...

Adam's words played over in his mind. Could he honestly consider cultivating something with Jordan Lake? Putting an end to the bitterness their fathers had supped on for three decades? The more he thought about it, the more he agreed with Adam. His eyes followed the swing of her ponytail as she walked ahead of him back into the courtroom and a smile tugged at the corners of his mouth. Jordan Lake would be the ultimate takeover.

Days later, Nick stirred as the mattress shifted and the woman next to him rose and walked into the bathroom. Sated, a little sleepy from the late nights he'd been keeping since his brother hit town, he wondered idly if he'd drifted off.

In a few short weeks, Adam would be gone, back to the high-velocity stock exchange world he ruled. Privately, Nick worried how long his brother could handle the pressure. He might be flavor of the month now, lauded by all and making an absolute fortune. But that was the thing about the share market. There was a never-ending supply of hungry young sharks circling, just waiting until someone made a mistake. Adam had been one of them not so long ago.

Nick stretched and plumped up his pillows, resting one arm behind his head. The bathroom door opened and a tall, slender blonde walked into the room. She moved to the dresser mirror, her arms raised as she fiddled with her long, tawny hair. Nick's eyes feasted on the long line of her spine, the curvaceous swell of her hips, and her skin, which had a luster to it even with the heavy drapes drawn against the afternoon sun. He liked how at ease she seemed about her nudity.

"Got time for a drink or are you rushing off?" he asked, aware that his question would surprise her. They didn't make a habit of small talk after their lovemaking sessions.

She flicked him a curious look in the mirror and con-

tinued twisting her hair expertly into a knot that looked
at once messy but sophisticated.

"Let me guess." Nick clicked his tongue. "Cocktails.
The Zeus Bar."

Again, he felt the wash of cool blue in her glance as
she turned. "A little early for me." She bent and plucked
something from the floor.

Clothing would be scattered all over, he thought. It
was always like that. The moment they were inside the
room, there was no decorum, no neatly undressing and
folding and hanging. Sometimes they were lucky to get
out of here without ripped garments.

Today she'd worn a short fuchsia shift dress, with a
strap over one shoulder tied in a big extravagant bow.
Easy to get in—and out—of, and entirely suitable for
cocktails in any of the bars she was frequently photographed at, although never with him.

Despite her accessible outfit, it had still seemed to
take an age to get his hands on her today. Time moved
like a slow-motion movie clip when he entered this
suite at the five-star hotel every Friday. Each image
burned into his brain: the silkiness and fragrance of her
creamy skin, the tumble of her hair as he tugged it into
disarray, her sighs as he bared her to his hungry mouth
and hands. As if she, too, had pictured this moment,
his kisses and touch, the way he tore at her clothing.
As if she, too, had longed for it every day between.
Each set of images stayed with him, replayed over and
over in his mind throughout the week until he could
have her again.

Once a week for four months, and Nick knew nothing personal about her, except for what she brought to his bed.

"I saw you on TV last night," he commented as she untwisted her panties from her dress. "A short, puffy black skirt." He paused. "And a tall puffy pale man."

The woman daintily stepped into her underwear. "Not me. I stayed home last night."

Nick's mouth went dry at the little shimmy her hips did to facilitate the placement of her underwear. "I'd know those legs anywhere," he countered mildly. "I could sculpt them."

She blinked, shaking out her dress. Probably wondering what on earth did it have to do with him, he thought.

"I do have a short black puffy skirt, and—" a breathy huff of amusement burst from her lips "—a tall puffy man or two, but it wasn't last night."

She raised her arms fluidly and the dress floated down like a pink cloud, veiling her body.

Nick gazed at her, desire curling its claws into him again. Even after two tumultuous orgasms in less than two hours, he wanted her again, quite savagely. "Where do you go, Jordan Lake, when you leave my bed?"

Jordan had managed to lower her brows and close her gaping mouth by the time the dress passed over her head. She wasn't bothered that he didn't believe her about last night—she owed him no explanations. It often happened that on a slow news day, the press or TV used file pictures of her on a night out. It had been a couple of weeks since she had worn that skirt.

What surprised her was that he'd asked. They had been meeting here every Friday for four months and Nick Thorne never once expressed an interest in her activities outside of this suite.

She turned her back, arching a brow at him in the mirror. "Jealous, Nick?" she asked, deliberately imparting an edge of sarcasm.

She recalled blushing the color of this dress after their very first time together. She'd lain in bed, covers drawn up to her chin, waiting for him to return from the bathroom. What next? she'd wondered. Would they talk? Cuddle?

But Nick made it painfully obvious that this was merely a sexual arrangement. He had quickly dressed, commanded her to be here the same time next week, pressed her hand to his mouth and was out of there in five minutes flat. No backward glance, no promise to call. Nothing.

Jordan had been shocked, a little hurt and felt foolish. He thought she knew the game but she wasn't nearly as sexually experienced as the media portrayed her to be. Of her four previous lovers, two of those were fairly serious relationships. It was just that her taste in men ran to playboys, pro athletes and musicians. But her wild days were definitely behind her by the time she met Nick.

Holding his gaze, she carefully tied the bow on her shoulder and then reached behind her to tug at the zipper of her dress.

Nick threw back the covers and in a second, stood behind her, his knuckles pressing purposefully into every nub of her spine as he worked the zipper slowly up.

He took her breath away, even after all this time. His shoulders seemed an aircraft wing-span across compared to her narrow frame. He was a full head taller than her, his short, dark hair a little disheveled. In the dimly-lit room, he looked almost Latin with his thick dark brows, dusky skin and full, sensuous lips.

Lips that brushed her ear, generating a flutter of excitement deep in her belly.

Bad sign. She should definitely go. Her mother was expecting her for dinner, anyway.

But then his eyes locked on to hers in the reflection and he bent his head to nuzzle at the top of her shoulder. "No hurry, is there?"

Jordan leaned her head back to nestle in his throat, watching him with half-closed eyes. Behind her, his hand continued its slow progress, now in between her shoulder blades, each centimeter a wand of heat that caused her back to arch. She sent a silent apology to her mother for her anticipated lateness.

Nick Thorne was irresistible to her. It had been that way since the first clash of their eyes in an elevator in this very hotel. She was leaving an aunt's eightieth birthday afternoon tea party. Nick was leaving a banking conference. A chance meeting so powerful, she couldn't believe they'd even made it out of the elevator without her skin blistering. The intense attraction led to an indecently quick drink at the bar and an even more indecent mutual decision to take a room, there and then. The thrill of it all was intensified by how forbidden it was because of the hatred between their fathers for the last thirty years.

The zipper was fully up but Nick's green-gold gaze was not that of someone who wanted her dressed. He caressed the back of her neck close to her hairline, an exquisite touch that made her breath catch. The heat of him behind her, naked and masculine, bathed her skin. He slowly moved his hand to the bow on her shoulder, watching her as if challenging her to stop him. The ribbon had as much resistance as her mind, and the front panel of the dress collapsed in front but was supported by the zipper at back. Not supported enough for the weight of her breasts, which spilled out, taut and aroused.

"Now look what I've done," Nick murmured in her ear. "And I was only trying to get to know you better."

Jordan swallowed and raised her hands, cupping her breasts. "You know me," she said breathlessly, playing the game. "You know these."

"Yes, I know these." His big hands relieved hers of their burden, kneading and squeezing just the way she liked. Jordan welcomed the onslaught of sensations that had become familiar yet never failed to render her boneless. Even as she wondered vaguely why the sudden interest, it was beyond her to resist his touch. She swirled in a hazy pool of delight at his breath on her neck, his hands on her flesh, the hot, hard wall of him pressed up against her back.

He used his hands unhurriedly, feathering down her sides to her buttocks, pausing to caress them in a circular motion that made her shiver.

"I know these…" he murmured as his hands slid over the sensitive backs of her thighs, down to her knees and up again, the fabric of the dress slipping and sliding over her smooth skin, higher and higher until it was bunched around her hips.

Her breath came in shallow gasps now as he held her captive in front of him. She ought to feel wanton and ashamed, watching them in the mirror, observing her total submission to his hands, his mouth as he nibbled and licked her neck and the top of her shoulder. This was, after all, what everyone expected of her. A spoiled, rich, man-eating socialite who spent her entire life in the pursuit of pleasure.

She was on her way to perdition and pleased about it, she thought, feeling the scrape of her panties down her legs. When Nick Thorne touched her, she felt beautiful and proud that he wanted her. He was a man of substance, successful and wealthy in his own right, not some flighty playboy. Their relationship may be based on the most primitive of urges, but his desire for her, the passion he evoked from her, made her feel his equal. Love didn't come into it, but Friday afternoons were the best thing in Jordan's life and she wouldn't give them up.

She brought her fingertips down to the dresser to steady herself, just as his thigh wedged between her trembling legs, nudging them apart. His breath skittered up the length of her back, making every downy hair stand to quivering attention. Anticipation backed up in her throat.

"I know this," he insisted, his fingers lightly probing while she moaned softly, her eyes closing to contain the most sublime pleasure.

He shifted closer. A red-hot streak of sensation ripped through her and she realized it wasn't his fingers probing and gliding now, sliding in between her legs. The weight of him leaning over her back forced her forward and she pressed her palms down on the dresser, bracing herself.

"Open your eyes, Jordan," he instructed, sliding one arm around her waist.

Her head lolled heavily back and hit his chest. She pried her eyes open and found his, fierce and compelling, staring back at her through the mirror.

"Does it bother you," he asked roughly, "this secret of ours? This thing between us?"

Jordan was past reason. She wanted much more of "this thing" between them, and she wanted it now. She stared at him, pushing back into his body, squeezing her thighs together to trap him.

With an effort almost too much to bear, she forced her mouth to open, to speak. "I know the score, Nick," she told him tightly. "I'm playing the game."

Sex.

Simple. Sensational. Secret.

It was what she wanted. What she lived for. Her Friday afternoon delight.

TWO

"It's all right for you," the stooped man with the trembling hands told her belligerently. "You get paid to sit around all day. I had to take the morning off work and now it looks like I won't get seen at all."

"I'm sorry, Mr. Hansen. It's been very busy this morning." Jordan tried to warm him up with a sympathetic smile but the man sighed loudly and stomped back to his seat in the crowded waiting room.

She exhaled slowly. Not even lunchtime and already a tension headache throbbed dully in her temples.

It was her turn on the voluntary roster to work two full days in Reception at the Elpis Free Clinic, and just occasionally, uncharitable though it was, she found it a little overwhelming dealing with unwell people. Thinking she was unobserved, she dropped her head down onto her arms for a second.

Behind her, Reverend Russ Parsons put his hand on her shoulder and she jerked up.

"You should have told him that no one gets paid around here. Not the doctors, cleaners, admin staff or our beautiful receptionist."

Jordan laughed ruefully. "Some receptionist! Some days I just don't seem to have the knack with people."

"You'll never get it right all of the time, but what's important is that you try so hard." He took some leaflets from the counter in front of them and handed them to her. "Why don't you give him some info on our natural healing classes?"

She took them, silently berating herself for not thinking of it.

In addition to the free clinic, the Elpis Foundation she'd set up a year ago helped Russ's parish to identify at-risk families who were stretched financially. They also provided a raft of self-help courses. Jordan was incredibly proud of the strides they'd made in a short time, but her lack of work experience spoke volumes about how she had chosen to spend her time up until recently.

"Are we still on for the Working Bee this weekend?" Russ had turned to go but stopped at the door.

Jordan nodded enthusiastically. She had recently purchased an old backpackers hostel in the beautiful Marlborough Sounds at the top of the South Island. The hostel had gone out of business years ago and was rundown and neglected, but with the volunteers from Russ's parish, she hoped to develop it into a retreat for the families in the program who never got to have a holiday. "How many are coming? I'll book the ferry tickets."

"Ten. Is Friday afternoon all right? I'll have to get the late ferry back on Saturday for services on Sunday."

Friday afternoon? Jordan's heart lurched. She shook her head and lowered her eyes, feeling the onset of an embarrassed blush. "Sorry. You guys could go but I won't be able to until Saturday morning." Philanthropy was one thing; denying herself Nick Thorne's body quite another—especially on her birthday. "My parents are putting on a thing for my birthday."

A "thing" by her father's standards would probably cost the annual wage of four or five of the people in the waiting room combined. This year, her twenty-sixth, she had prevailed upon Syrius not to go too over-the-top. "You're welcome to come," she added lamely, hoping Russ would decline. Her father didn't approve of the way she spent her time and money and she was afraid his infamous lack of tact would offend the gentle reverend.

Syrius Lake was a man of unfashionable and inflexible opinions, especially to do with women. They were to be protected and indulged but not to be taken seriously in the workforce. "I didn't work my fingers to the bone so that my princess would have to," he was fond of saying.

That made her cringe these days but Jordan had made

the most of her privileged upbringing for a long time—
way too long—before coming to the realization that
being a princess was a fairly boring existence.

"Speaking of invitations," Russ said as she rounded
the reception counter, leaflets in hand and Mr. Hansen
in her sights, "this charity ball and auction you're organizing...shouldn't we be promoting it? It's only a
couple of weeks away."

Jordan paused, aware that this project departed
somewhat from the more conventional fund-raising activities of the church, but the Elpis Foundation, though
closely affiliated, was not a religious organization. "It's
not that sort of auction, Russ. It's more of—" she
searched for the right word. If there was one thing
Jordan Lake knew, it was rich people and parties "—an
event. It's invite only and no press."

She knew how to put on a classy yet original
function, and she'd managed this one on the cheap. She
would pay the orchestra herself but the ballroom was
gratis, courtesy of her mother's old dancing contacts.
Friends in a local venue management company had
agreed to take care of the lighting and decorating for
nothing. She had plenty of "volunteers" as wait staff
since she'd promised an amazing after-party. The champagne hadn't been confirmed yet but the *coup-de-
gras*—the catering—was coming together nicely. A
truckload of fish and chips would be delivered on the
night to astound the ballgown-and-tuxedo-wearing
guests, courtesy of an old beau whose family owned a
chain of fast-food restaurant outlets. Jordan was noto-

rious enough to be able to pull off such a cheeky gesture. "It's all in hand," she assured Russ. "At this stage we have about a hundred people coming, but I have a bit more time."

Russ pursed his lips. "I'm sure if we advertise, we can do better than that."

"Russ, that's a hundred extremely wealthy people, the movers and shakers of the country. Trust me, the really rich want discretion with their philanthropy."

He smiled wryly. "Is that why you're so reluctant to put your name on all the good work you do?"

Jordan shot him a warning look. "No one takes me seriously. The kind of publicity people associate with me is not the kind of publicity I want for the Elpis Foundation. That was the condition of me setting it up. It's better that way, believe me."

Famous for being famous… She walked into the waiting room, determined to make Mr. Hansen like her. Forever the focus of the newspapers and TV cameras but for all the wrong reasons, even though she had toned it down over the last year. Reporters didn't care a jot if most of what they wrote was wrong. Philanthropy was a serious business and she needed to protect the Elpis Foundation. It was her one redeeming feature.

On Friday morning, Jordan passed Nick in the corridor of the High Court. He paused as they drew level, looking straight ahead. Since court was in session, there were few people around.

"See you at three?" he asked in a low voice.

Her pulse skittered as it always did when she looked at him. His presence in the courtroom for most of this week had underlined her desire for him and the forbidden thrill she got from knowing that he wanted her.

But they had to take care. It wasn't just the stress her father was under. Nick was different. Somehow, she wanted to keep him to herself.

She hadn't expected the amount of public interest there was in the case—every day she ran the gauntlet of photographers and reporters, all of whom seemed more interested in what she was wearing and how her love life was than the actual semantics of the trial.

"Nick, there are so many reporters," she whispered back. "Don't you think we should cool it, just till this trial is over?"

He turned his head and met her eyes and Jordan's heartbeat went wild. If eyes were the windows to hell, then Nick was on fire—for her. Right now, this moment.

Her knees turned to water.

Nick nudged her toward the stairwell a few steps away. She kept her head down, aware that if anyone looked at her face, they'd know exactly what she was thinking—that she wanted his hands, his mouth on her. Preferably both and *now* would be good.

He pushed through the door, her hot on his heels, then turned and crowded her against the wall, his arms resting on the wall above her head. The rest of his body did not touch her at all.

The sweep of his eyes over her face, down her body

and back again, was a tangible caress. Thankful for the support of the wall at her back, Jordan pressed into it, squirming with a restless heat.

His face was close—not close enough, but close.

"You want to 'cool it?'" Nick demanded in a hot whisper.

"I don't *want* to," she whispered back. "Your reputation as a steady, conservative banker will suffer a lot more than mine if we're caught."

"It's driving me mad, seeing you in there," he growled. "So close, not able to touch."

She reeled with the need to touch him, and with her own panic. Nick had never done anything so reckless before. "Oh, Nick, this is dangerous."

"I haven't touched you," he murmured, his eyes burning. "Yet."

He knew, as Jordan did, that if he touched her, she'd offer no resistance, despite the fear of discovery.

"Someone is going to walk through that door any minute," she cautioned him.

His eyes tracked a heated path, lingering on her lips, then in slow, hot increments down her body. "All part of the fun, isn't it?"

Their eyes met. Clearly, steady and conservative Nick Thorne was as hooked on the danger of the situation as she was.

She shifted again, craving his touch, knowing she shouldn't. It was torture being this close, seeing him this excited, yet denying her.

His hand landed in her hair, then moved around to

cup her chin. Despite her alarm, her lips parted in anticipation.

Nick stared down, his thumb moving softly over her cheek. "You are seriously beautiful."

Her eyes flew wide. That was new, too. Nick preferred a more earthy flavor to his compliments, more show, don't tell. The daily exposure in the courtroom must be having an effect on him as well.

Meantime, his gaze moved down to her mouth, stayed, heated. His thumb circled down and laid on her bottom lip. His face bent, inched closer. He was, quite simply, driving her mad. Who cared if anyone saw? She clamped her lips around his thumb, drawing it slowly into her mouth. Nick's eyes widened, and then some more when she swirled her tongue around the tip. Two could play at that, she thought triumphantly, watching the torture darken his eyes.

But then he slid his thumb slowly out of her mouth. "Cool it? I don't think so. I'll see you at three o clock."

He stepped back and Jordan ducked smartly out from under him. She looked back as she passed through the heavy door. He still leaned on the wall, his head raised, looking after her.

The cooler air of the corridor was a welcome relief. Away from Nick's potent presence, she pressed her hand on her stomach, aflutter with nerves. Even if he was willing to take the risk, she couldn't embarrass her father while he was under so much stress.

Still, her mind and body hummed with anticipation. Instinctively, she knew that their afternoon rendezvous would have more bite to it than usual.

* * *

Spending every morning in court was impacting his work, so Nick sighed when the intercom buzzed and his personal assistant's voice informed him that his brother was here. The door opened and Adam appeared, looking relaxed in jeans and a leather jacket. He turned side-on to Nick's desk and approximated a smooth golf swing. "It's a beautiful day, big brother. What say you play hooky for the afternoon and we hit the golf course for a quick nine?"

Nick shook his head. In little under an hour, he would be at the hotel, relieving a certain heiress of her clothes. And for that reward, he didn't care if he had to work all weekend to catch up. "I have an appointment."

Adam frowned and flopped down in a chair facing Nick. "Cancel it."

"If I get this backlog cleared tonight, I might be free tomorrow," Nick said with a pointed look at the stack of papers in front of him.

Jasmine, his personal assistant, appeared at the door. "Would you like coffee?"

Adam spun around in his chair. "I would, thank you, Jas*mina*."

The beautiful brunette blushed and turned away.

Nick frowned. Adam had a hide like a rhino. No way could he have missed Nick's "I'm busy" hint. And the last thing he needed was his Casanova brother upsetting his workplace. "Stop flirting with my personal assistant."

Adam turned back to him. "Why? Something going on with you two?"

"Adam, she works for me."

"So? If she worked for me, I'd add to her job description."

Nick sighed and made a show of checking his watch.

"I thought you should know," Adam began, "Dad's been ear-bashing me over lunch again about staying on and giving you a hand."

The real reason for his visit… "I don't need a hand," Nick said in a long-suffering tone.

"I know that, Nick. You have more than earned your place at the helm of this ship. I have no intention of muscling in on your territory."

Nick's jaw tightened. "There's the rub. It isn't my territory, is it?"

It was Randall Thorne's greatest wish that both sons run his empire after he retired. No matter how often Adam resisted, his father never stopped trying to lure him back from London. The disbursement of their mother's will last year had shocked the brothers and delighted their father. Instead of a sizeable chunk of the company shares going to Nick, as everyone expected, he got baubles and a beach house and Adam got the shares. Whether his mother intended it or not, she had handed his father a lofty weapon to pit brother against brother. To delay, yet again, announcing his retirement and naming Nick as his successor.

"Dad was nearly resigned to the fact that you didn't want it," Nick said moodily. "But now—he'll do anything to have both of us on board."

"The will stated that I can't sell my shares to you, but

I can vote with you, Nick. Tell me how you want to play it. And remember, the old man can't put off retiring forever—he's seventy next month."

"Since Mom died, there is no reining him in." Nick scowled at the newspaper on his desk. "Her past friend-ship with Elanor Lake was the only thing that stopped him from going after Syrius years ago. He's using the court case as another tactic to postpone announcing his retirement." He reached out and turned the paper toward Adam. A good portion of the front page covered the court case—and Jordan Lake's wardrobe. "If it's not one thing, it's another." His mother's illness and subsequent death, Adam's presence or absence—his father threw excuse after excuse into the pot to put off the inevitable.

Adam nodded thoughtfully. "I'm pretty sure he's got something else up his sleeve to get at Syrius. He was being very cagey at lunch, always a sign that he's plotting something."

Nick tugged on his earlobe, a wry grin on his face. "I've tried telling him that once he's retired, he can spend twenty-three hours a day going after Syrius Lake if he wants to, but he's adamant he wants to bury him before he retires."

Nick wasn't alone in thinking his father would win the defamation case, but had a nasty feeling that the small victory wouldn't appease him for long.

Adam cast an interested eye over the newspaper. There was a footnote to the court case: Jordan Lake's birthday bash tonight, organized by her father. The paper called it an "ostentatious display of wealth." He tapped the paper idly. "I told you. The best way to stop this stupid feud is to get Jordan Lake to fall for you. That man cannot, it seems, deny his little girl anything."

Before Nick could respond, Jasmine entered with a tray. She set it down on Nick's desk and lifted the coffeepot. Adam leaned in closer than he had to, Nick noticed, and held up a cup, smiling into her face. "How long have you worked for my brother, Jasmine? Must be nearly five years."

Jasmine blushed to the roots of her severely pulled back auburn hair. "Yes, I—ah—think so. Nick?" She raised her eyes to him.

Nick nodded, mildly surprised by her discomfort. He'd known English-born Jasmine for years. Her composure was legendary. "Have I told you, Jasmine, that my younger brother is nothing but a flirt and not to be taken seriously?"

He noticed the slight tremble in her hand as she poured the coffee, and how resolutely she kept her eyes on the task at hand and nowhere near Adam's face. Could his calm, efficient, very proper personal assistant have a thing for Adam?

Adam raised the full cup and saluted her. "Why don't you give all this up and come work for me? London's where it's at."

Jasmine kept her eyes averted and poured Nick's coffee, apologizing when she slopped a little in the saucer.

"Thanks," Nick said drily as she finished and left the room.

He glanced at his brother and warned, "Don't even think about it. She is much too good for you."

Adam turned his palms up innocently, then glanced toward the door. "You work too hard if you haven't noticed how very lovely she is, in a quiet sort of way."

"I don't want you messing with her," Nick told him shortly. "Good staff are hard to find, and you're leaving soon." His brother's trail of broken hearts stretched a million miles.

Adam shook his head, amused. "You're too good, Nicky. You wouldn't dream of tupping your personal assistant, just as you wouldn't dream of going after Jordan Lake and risking Dad's wrath. Mom was right, you need to live a little."

That was a low and quite unnecessary dig. His brother referred to the letter Melanie Thorne had left with her lawyer to give to Nick at the will reading. "You're a good son, Nick, strong, ambitious and loyal." Christ, he sounded like a golden retriever! "But it's time you learned to live. Want something you shouldn't. Take something you have no right to. Fight the good fight and have some fun."

He didn't know what the hell his mother was on about, but she was right in that he always did the expected thing.

After Adam had gone, Nick got up and opened his office safe. Inside were three jewelry boxes, his bequest from his mother, gifts from his father over the years. There was a blue diamond cluster ring, a necklace with a centerpiece of a four carat blue diamond and a pair of blue diamond earrings.

Nick had the relevant documents from the IGI, the

world's largest gem certification and appraisal institute. He knew the worth of the stones. He also knew that his mother would expect him to present these priceless gifts to his bride one day. And Nick always did what was expected of him, didn't he?

He glanced at the newspaper on his desk. She wouldn't expect him to give blue diamonds to Jordan Lake, he was sure of that. Neither would his brother, and his father would probably disown him if he found out.

Nick closed the ring box and returned it to the safe, wondering what Jordan herself would think if her Friday lover gave her diamonds. He lost himself for a long moment, imagining the incredulity in her blue eyes.

He closed the necklace box, berating himself for even considering changing the dynamic of a relationship—a good relationship—based on sex.

His hand reached toward the box containing the earrings, and at that point, he fully intended closing it and replacing it in the safe with the others. But something made him pause and lift the box toward the light above. Would she wear them? She might if she recognized that the jewel's electric blue were very similar to her own eyes, especially when she was helpless with lust—like earlier in the stairwell.

He closed the box and put it in his pocket. Nick was going to do something irresponsible for once. Not for her or for anyone else. Just for himself.

Three

Later that day, as the first mad rush of desire ebbed away, Nick rolled out of bed and picked up his suit jacket from the floor. "I have something for you."

Jordan lay in the middle of the big bed with the sheet pulled up around her middle, a sharp contrast between the pristine white sheet and her lightly-tanned body. The slight flush on her skin was fading, her breathing more steady than a minute ago. She lifted her chin, watching him curiously.

"But first…" Nick grabbed the edge of the sheet and tugged it away, leaving her naked.

She maneuvered herself into a sitting position and crossed her long legs at the ankles, but made no effort to clutch at the sheet or cover herself. He liked that she was totally without guile or vanity in this room. It occurred to him that he also felt comfortable standing, walking around in front of her naked. Had he ever felt this level of ease with a casual girlfriend before?

Unable to recall, he offered her the jewelry box.

Jordan hesitated before taking it, her eyes on his face. "A birthday gift?" Her voice was low and puzzled.

Nick perched on the edge of the bed. "If you like."

She dragged her eyes off his face and opened the box. Her mouth moved in surprise, a soundless question. She tilted the box this way and that and finally spoke, still looking at the earrings. "Nick, a man gives me diamonds. What am I supposed to think about that?"

He shrugged. "Don't think about it at all."

She looked up at him, a crease of perplexity between her eyes that he'd never seen before. He silently cursed himself for confusing her. What was he thinking, messing with the natural order of things? "Don't read anything into it," he said a little roughly. "I believe I thought more of my own pleasure than yours."

The little frown deepened, as if she couldn't make sense of it.

Damn Adam and his crazy notions. Nick exhaled loudly and leaned toward her. He picked up one of the precious, glinting jewels, brushed her hair behind her ears and went about fitting it. "They matched your eyes. I wanted to see you naked, wearing only these. That's it."

That wasn't it. Hadn't he done it because he was sick of being labeled the good son, the one who never rocked the boat?

Her face cleared, as if she'd solved a riddle. "They're a gift for your mistress."

Nick's lip curled in distaste. He hated that word. "I don't think of you as my mistress. Neither of us is married. We're free to indulge ourselves."

She gazed at him solemnly. Nick picked up the other earring, pried the butterfly clip off and indicated that she turn her head.

She obeyed. "What *do* you think of me as then?"

"If we have to put a label on it, I'd call you my luxury," he said as he pushed the other earring through the piercing in her lobe. He secured the post and drew back, looking at her face.

"Your luxury." She nodded and her smile was without reproach. "I'll save them just for this room. They'll be our secret."

Nick sat back, admiring his handiwork, thinking she did indeed look spellbindingly luxurious. Her golden hair, a mass of loose curls today, cascaded over her shoulders like the caps of a choppy sea captured and molded in gold. Yesterday, in court she'd worn it straight and smooth.

And then her words hit him, or more, her tone. Had he imagined a slightly sarcastic edge to her voice?

Nick dropped his hands to his bare knees. "I'm not ashamed." Not of her. Maybe of himself for confusing her. "Hell, Jordan! They're yours. Do what you want with them. Sell them, if it pleases you."

Hurt showed in the little press of her lips and the way she suddenly looked away from him. "I don't need any *more* money from a Thorne," she said quietly.

Nick had made a real pig's ear of this. An off-the-cuff gesture and he'd ended up bringing the past into this room. He should have remembered that whatever this madness was between them, the past would always be a barrier.

Thirty years ago, Nick's father was driving the two couples home from a night out when a tragic accident nearly claimed the life of Syrius Lake's pregnant wife. The injuries she had suffered put her in a wheelchair for life and killed her unborn son, but five years later she endured a difficult pregnancy and gave birth to Jordan. Lake never forgave Randall Thorne and when his financial situation worsened because of high medical costs, he demanded assistance. Randall signed over a huge valuable block of real estate in Wellington's CBD, with the understanding that when Syrius was able, he would repay the loan. But on the day of Jordan's birth, the bitter ex-friend transferred the property to his daughter's name.

Prevailed upon by guilt and his own wife, Randall Thorne let it ride, but it rankled. Both men went on to become business icons in New Zealand's capital city and the bad blood simmered away, helped along by repeated sniping from both camps.

So technically, Jordan was rich on Thorne money, but Nick didn't care about that. It wasn't her fault or his. It just was.

He put his index finger under her chin and turned her face to look at him. "I'm sorry. I didn't intend to hurt you…"

Her smile, when it came, was more rueful than hurt.

"You haven't." She lifted her hands and touched her new adornments. "I'll wear them with pride."

Nick's instincts were right on the nail about how perfectly the blue diamonds matched her eye color. They gazed at each other, gratitude and regret gradually giving way to an acute awareness of where they were, what they were to each other. The urgency escalated, the air between them smoldered with its hot breath.

They moved toward each other in a rush, their hands reaching greedily. She was fine, they were fine, nothing had changed. He'd done the right thing, giving her blue diamonds that twinkled and trembled with desire and anticipation when he pushed her down on the bed, ravaging her mouth. That warmed with sultry promise as he drew her arms up over her head and moved into position. That exploded with blue sparks when he filled her, an inexorable upward motion into infinite pleasure...and crackled with the fury of reaching for, overtaking, plunging into blissful release.

He'd done the right thing giving her the earrings and who cared if was for her or for him? They'd both enjoy them.

But somehow, he left the hotel feeling he'd missed an opportunity of some kind, or they both had. If Jordan Lake was his luxury, could he pay the price?

Jordan was late for her own birthday party. She rushed up the stairs of the up-market club, apologizing loudly, knowing her parents expected her half an hour ago.

She needn't have worried. Everything was under

control and most of the guests hadn't arrived yet. The champagne was chilled and delicious, the lighting perfect, security on the door. Of the expected one hundred and fifty guests, twenty or so would be friends of hers, the rest would be her parents' friends, business colleagues, local celebrities in the arts, politics and sports and a smattering of reporters and photographers. Jordan would pose with all the usual suspects, regulars of the It crowd. And then she would go home alone, as she had for most of the last year. Even her father would yawn at her lifestyle these days—except for her Friday afternoons.

She bent to kiss her mother, knowing this was the last real kiss she'd get all night. As she drew back, her mother's hands firmed on her cheeks for a few seconds, holding her. Elanor Lake frowned at the earrings. "They're lovely, darling. Where did you get them?"

She hadn't been able to resist wearing them no matter how often she told herself to lock them away. But, oh, they were so beautiful, and Nick hadn't said not to wear them. He hadn't even stipulated that she wasn't to tell who gave them to her.

Vanity won. The earrings were perfect with the pale yellow dress she wore, lending it a hint of boldness.

Jordan straightened and flicked her hand in the air. "Just one of my many admirers."

Her mother gave her a measured look. "Which admirer is giving you blue diamonds?"

Her father snorted. "Anything less than diamonds, then he isn't worth his salt, princess," he declared.

One by one, the beautiful people arrived and she laughed and kissed air so many times, her lips were bruised. But often, she touched the earrings and her thoughts turned to the confusing man who'd given them to her.

The extravagant gift had blown her away. Up to now, Nick was the only man she'd met who'd been completely straight about what he wanted from her—her body. There were no expectations past that, on either side. Their weekly meetings in the luxury Presidential Suite were all about an extraordinary attraction and nothing else.

She couldn't put her finger on when things had started to feel different, but it was recent. He'd changed. Suddenly he was asking questions, taking risks, talking to her. He'd watched her today as if trying to divine her thoughts. Hurt her a little by admitting he'd thought more of his own pleasure in giving her the gift. Then again, that admission spoke volumes for a man who was so spare with words: he saw something beautiful; he thought of her.

But it hurt her more when he reminded her of the origins of her trust fund, and the reason they could never have more than they had right now.

Her oldest friend, Julie, dragged her onto the dance floor and she happily acquiesced. But her mind strayed often to Nick. Jordan looked around at the glitzy lights and gay smiles, wondering if he'd like this sort of place? Would her friends like him, and vice versa? Was he a dancer? When it came down to it, she knew so little about him, just that they fit together perfectly in the bedroom.

"Oh, my God! Look-it!" Julie pointed through the throng to a tall, handsome man leaning on the bar, looking their way. "Isn't that…?"

Jordan looked over and her heart did a weird slide. "John West," she said in dismay.

Jordan's first heartbreak. She'd been in her first year at high school, he in his last. His interest in her caused a ripple of excitement through all her friends; someone of his stature expressing interest in a first year was unheard of.

Alas, the romance floundered quickly.

"Let's see if we can pick who he's here with," her friend said.

Jordan wondered if it was the same girlfriend he'd dumped her for two days after he'd first crooked his brow at her, commanding her to parade around the school quadrant with him like his queen.

She shrugged and turned away. Although it was a minor blip on her heartstrings that she hadn't thought of in years, the one thing that stuck was the crushing realization that despite her money and social standing, she wasn't smart enough, pretty enough, interesting enough to hold his attention, not even for a week! Her father's shameless indulgence reminded her that the world saw her as a bubble-headed trophy with only her wealth to offer. She knew better. She was different now, more than that.

Nick Thorne was the real deal—respected, smart, ambitious and successful. Whatever he called it, she was his mistress. She'd live up to his expectations in that regard, but she'd do her best to protect her heart.

* * *

On Monday, the court clerk announced the lunch break to sighs of relief. The morning had dragged. Nick looked forward to getting back to his office, if only for a break from the steel thread of sexual tension that came with sitting ten feet away from the object of his desire, and the knowledge that it would be four torturous days before he could have her again.

Suddenly the wiry figure of Syrius Lake bounded across the aisle. His face was an interesting shade of plum. He sidestepped Randall's counsel and stood defiantly in front of the complainant's bench.

"Randall Thorne," he rumbled, his deep voice belying his rather slight frame. "Keep your pup away from my daughter."

Nick's heart stopped and he involuntarily flicked a glance at Jordan. She had jumped to her feet, and stood with one leg in front of the other, ready for flight, the line of her body taut with tension. Her eyes were huge but they were on her father, not him.

Randall rose, towering over Syrius, the table in between them. Nick rose, too, and brushed past Adam to stand by his father's side.

"Nick's got too much sense…" Randall began.

"Not him." Syrius pointed a long, bony finger at Adam, still seated in the row behind.

Adam! Nick turned his head slowly, and in those few seconds, everything inside him went cold, and his throat closed as if gripped by a vise.

His brother raised his brows in studied nonchalance

and shrugged. "I hooked up with a couple of lovelies at a bar, tagged along to a party. How was I supposed to know it was Jordan's birthday bash?"

Through the ice-cold rage bathing his belly, Nick barely noted that Adam directed his explanation—and a quizzical look—at him, rather than Syrius.

All around people had stopped, enthralled by the drama. And then his father gave the crowd what they wanted.

"If he's a pup," he suggested, "perhaps she's a bitch in heat."

Nick tore his eyes off his brother's and glanced at Jordan's white, shocked face. He gripped his father's arm firmly. "You'll apologize for that."

"The hell I will!" Randall blustered.

The two Lake women reached Syrius. Elanor spoke in urgent whispers while Jordan grasped the sleeve of her father's suit, tugging at it ineffectually.

Randall lifted his arm in a half hearted attempt to remove it from Nick's grip.

Nick only gripped harder. "*Now*, Dad."

Accepting defeat, Randall launched a scathing glance at his enemy, cleared his throat and nodded vaguely in Jordan's direction. "I beg your pardon, Jordan." Turning back to Syrius, he raised his chin, "When I've finished mopping the floor with you here, Lake, I'm going to start all over again. I wouldn't let your lawyer take a holiday anytime soon if I were you."

"Bring it on, Thorne," Syrius snarled. He shot one last look of loathing that encompassed all three Thornes, then he stomped off with his counsel in tow, making no effort to assist Jordan with her mother's wheelchair.

Mortified, Nick couldn't look at Jordan, but as she pushed her mother's chair past him, Elanor met his eyes and gave him a distant but not unfriendly nod. Despite the ridiculous circumstances, Nick found himself admiring her for her fortitude and grace when she had more reason to hate his family than anyone. He watched until they disappeared out of the courtroom, then turned back to find his father glaring down at Adam.

"Well? What have you got to say for yourself?"

Nick's jealousy returned full force, crushing his chest and throat again. The thought of his playboy brother anywhere near Jordan incensed him. "Did you—" *touch, dance, kiss* "—speak to her at the party?" He could barely get the words past his clenched teeth.

Adam's glance was sharp as a tack. "Nick, I didn't get a toe in the door before Syrius was bleating at security to have me removed. Why?"

Intense relief laced Nick's exhalation. He unclenched his palms and they were damp. Ignoring Adam's question, he turned abruptly and reached for his jacket. The act of putting it on, gathering up his phone and briefcase, gave him a few seconds to think about that relief. *Okay, we've ascertained that I'm not fond of the thought of anyone else's hands on her. Fine. We can work this out.*

Now composed, he gave his father a stern look. "I have to get back to the office, but try and behave yourself this afternoon." He frowned at Randall. "Insult Syrius all you like, but leave his family out of it."

He strode away, allowing himself a small smile when he heard his father say to Adam, "Why can't you be more like your brother?"

Four

Nick pressed the doorbell, glowering at the peephole when he heard her ask who it was. "It's Nick. Open up, Jordan."

He still waited half a minute, tapping his thigh impatiently, until she opened the door. She peeked around the corner of the door, one hand covering her lower face. Her hesitation became immediately clear; a pale green chalky substance covered most of her face. Her hair was loose but held back from her face by a headband. She wore silky light blue pajamas, a less than welcoming expression, and her feet were bare.

That didn't mean she was off the hook. "Are you ill?"

"No." Frowning, she looked over his shoulder into

the empty corridor of her apartment building and then stepped back.

"Expecting someone?" he asked, giving her a thorough inspection.

"Do I look like I'm expecting someone?" She lifted her hand from her face and gestured him forward impatiently. "Come in before someone sees you."

Nick stepped inside and then turned and waited while she closed the door.

Jordan leaned her back against the door her skin flushing pink beneath the green facial mask. "How did you get up here?"

He shrugged. "Someone was coming up, I followed."

"Nick, you shouldn't be here."

His temper bridled. He'd been on a slow burn for about twenty-four hours now. He'd had a huge row with his father last night after confirming his plans to hire a P.I. to investigate one of Syrius's directors for corruption. It became more and more obvious that the old man had no intention of retiring any time soon, not while Syrius Lake was around to take potshots at.

Reading the papers today had turned the heat up. Nick's frustration had about hit boiling. "We had an arrangement."

"I sent you a text."

Nick swore under his breath. A text that said nothing. *Sorry, something's come up.*

He would have accepted her canceling their regular appointment if she hadn't been photographed eating a late Friday afternoon lunch with Jason Cook, the most worthless playboy on the planet. An ex-pro rugby player who destroyed hotel rooms, threw things at bartenders and went through money like water. And who'd reportedly had a steamy romance with Jordan a year ago.

His father's next potential campaign against Syrius made Nick's decision to ally himself with her all the more attractive, but the lady herself seemed comfortable with the status quo. Somehow he had to persuade her that she wanted more, knock her off balance enough to start thinking of him in a different light.

Hence the unannounced visit. It didn't hurt that the thought of Cook's hands on her infuriated him. He reached out, hooking his finger into the V of her pajama top, and pulled her into him. "You and Jason in the newspaper this morning… You want him, Jordan?"

As her unresisting body bumped against his, the impact caused the top button to slip through the hole. The material gaped as she inhaled in surprise. The creamy swell of a luscious, unfettered breast taunted him.

How many men did she share her body with? The question had tormented him for hours. How many men savored that perfect mouth, nuzzled her impossibly soft and fragrant skin.

Under his glare, her eyes sparked with annoyance and her pink cheeks burned through the green streaks. She laid her hands flat against his chest and braced against him. "I didn't realize that giving me a gift branded me as your exclusive property."

"It doesn't, but your Friday afternoons are mine, not bloody Jason Cook's."

"Jason is only a friend these days. Not—" she lifted her chin defiantly "—that it's any of your business."

"Some friend. I thought you were satisfied with our arrangement."

"I was." Her eyes flickered away and back. "I am. But I think we're being watched."

Nick raised his brows, waiting.

Sighing, she clasped the edges of her pajama top closed and pushed past him, padding down the short hallway through a stylish kitchen and to a side table in the lounge. Nick followed, his eyes closely monitoring the sensual slide of blue silk-clad hips.

Jordan picked up an envelope from the table and turned to him. "These came yesterday."

Nick took the envelope and pulled out two enlarged photographs of Jordan entering and leaving their Friday hotel, wearing a little black dress with a wide belt. He remembered it because the belt had an unusual clasp and his eager fingers had wasted at least three seconds fumbling with the damn thing. The photo was dated last Friday, their last meeting. "You're always being watched and photographed." He handed the photos back. "What of it?"

"These were couriered to me here, yesterday morning. No note. No sender details."

Nick pursed his lips. "And that was enough to send you rushing into Jason Cook's arms."

She gazed at him steadily. "Why do you suppose we went to the Backbencher's Bar, Nick?"

"Probably the only place in town he hasn't been thrown out of."

"Because it's the press's watering hole, where most of them spend their Friday afternoons. I did it to throw whoever might be watching us off the scent."

Nick processed her tone and earnest expression and battled down the jealousy bubbling in his blood. Considering the publicity surrounding the court case, she would have known her presence at that bar, especially with a man of Jason Cook's reputation, would end up in the next day's papers.

Not to make him jealous. Not to patch things up with a past lover. The relief surprised Nick with its intensity. He had to remember his purpose here tonight—keep her guessing, spike her interest. His very real jealousy was an added bonus.

Jordan shifted under his gaze as if uncomfortably aware that her face was covered in green goop. "Get yourself a drink," she told him, pointing at the small bar in the corner of the room. "I'll go and clean up."

Nick's eyes stayed with her until she turned into the first door down the hall. Her bedroom, he presumed, relieved to be left alone momentarily. It gave him a chance to explore, try to get a handle on her.

He moved fully into the lounge, his eyes busy.

Her apartment was modern, minimalist, but surprisingly homely and welcoming. One of the two black leather sofas was scattered with papers. There were more papers on the coffee table and a mug of something in the middle with steam coming off it. The expansive drapes were drawn but he'd bet there was an amazing view of the city and harbor beyond from her thirteenth story apartment. The walls were bare except in the dining nook where two large, striking sketches faced each other above her elegant dining table. One depicted a 1920s couple sitting at a table, the woman looking coyly away as the man held her arm by the wrist and above the elbow, kissing his way up her arm. The other was a couple dancing, maybe the tango, he decided.

The bar had everything he could want but Nick wasn't in the mood for alcohol. He walked to the sofa, sweeping the papers into a pile and setting them on the coffee table.

There was a property listing on top, torn from a real estate magazine. It depicted an old villa in the Marlborough Sounds at the top of the South Island. Not the sort of place Jordan would be interested in, surely. The lady could afford to buy the entire South Island. She was luxury all the way. What use would she have for a broken-down old villa?

Then again, what did he know of her likes and dislikes outside of the bedroom?

While waiting for her return, he glanced at the next item on the pile and saw a newsletter headed The Elpis Foundation. He only took note because the author was Reverend Russ Parsons, an old family friend.

Before he could read the contents, Jordan returned, her face clean and her hair released from the headband. Nick nearly smiled when he saw she'd changed. A cream sweater and soft black pants were probably safer than the lovely but flimsy pajamas. She obviously didn't trust him to keep his hands to himself.

Jordan perched on the arm of the couch, her hands restless. Her feet were still bare, toenails pearly-pink and gleaming. Nick swallowed the remnants of his unwarranted anger and jealousy, thinking that this was how she looked alone in the evenings. Freshly bathed, by the clean scent of her. Her hair brushed out and gleaming. Skin scrubbed and glowing.

She fidgeted under his scrutiny, her mouth a little sullen.

"Nice apartment," he commented pleasantly.

She glanced at his empty hands. "Did you not want a drink?"

He wasn't bothered but then again, he liked the idea of her waiting on him. It would also serve to prolong his visit, break the ice, open the way for him to try out a little charm.

"A Scotch would be good."

She hadn't expected him to say yes, he knew by the little twist of her mouth. He settled back while she prepared his drink with a kind of polite displeasure. No smile when she handed it to him, either.

Nick reached for the mug on the coffee table. The liquid inside was cooling by the pinched look of the surface. He handed it to her, thinking how improbable this was. Jordan Lake home alone on a Saturday night with only a face mask and mug of chocolate for company.

She took the mug. An awkward silence descended.

"Looking to invest in some property?" he asked, picking up the leaflet. It would be a good investment. Marlborough Sounds boasted some of the most desirable real estate in the country.

"I already bought it."

Nick looked up in surprise. "Can't see you in the DIY store, somehow."

Her mouth twitched but the smile didn't reach her eyes. "You'd be surprised."

He leaned back, spreading his arm along the back of the couch. Their eyes met and held for long seconds and that old familiar awareness arced between them. She was so naturally beautiful, larger than life beautiful, even with little or no makeup on. Nick's chest swelled when her eyes widened and then hazed over with her own recognition of the incredible desire between them. She felt it, too, he exulted, this pull that gripped his throat and stole his breath. Every time was like their first meeting in a sterile elevator. An unquenchable desire that hit him like a bullet between the eyes.

Just like now.

Jordan broke the spell and looked down into her drink. "You're—different," she said. "What's changed?"

She shifted one foot to rest on top of the other, her restlessness showing insecurities he didn't know she had.

Nick faced her fully. "I want you, Jordan," he answered truthfully. "That hasn't changed."

She looked up under her lashes. "And you can have me. On Fridays. At the hotel."

It didn't surprise him that she'd picked up on his recent change of behavior toward her. In their brief conversations to date, she'd shown a perceptive intuitiveness, eroding his assumptions that she was nothing more than a spoiled heiress who liked making an exhibition of herself.

Damn his brother for putting the thought in his head. Damn his mother for the will and her belief that he was the perennial dutiful son, and his father, too, for being such a vindictive, intransigent bastard. But for their interference, Nick would be perfectly happy with the prior arrangement. The thrill of a forbidden pleasure. A once-weekly event that, while momentous at the time, belonged in a compartment of his brain that had no bearing on how he lived his life or the decisions he made.

"Perhaps it's seeing you in court every day," he suggested. It was as good a lie as any, he supposed.

She nodded. Her feet were still playing with each other, he noticed. "By the way, I'm sorry about my father's behavior the other day."

Jordan shrugged, drawing his attention to her front, his interest quickening when he saw she wasn't wearing a bra under the soft wool.

"They're as bad as each other," she responded.

"What would Syrius do if he found out about us?" Nick probed.

She rolled her eyes. "I don't even want to think about it."

Nick knew that was his major stumbling block. He had to get her so interested, so wound up in him that she'd forget about her father's wrath.

"And yours?" she inquired politely.

He sipped his drink, wondering how truthful to be. Lies had a way of tripping you up, so it was best to keep things simple. "He wouldn't like it," he said slowly, "but it's not up to him, is it?"

Jordan sighed and looked away. "Maybe we should…"

Nick's whole being jolted in rebellion. He knew what she was going to say. Stop? No way! He was already on edge after only a week's abstinence. It was torture sitting in that courtroom day after day, watching her every move out of the corner of his eyes. Her mile-long legs crossing and uncrossing, the drift of her expensive scent, an occasional hot-blooded glance in his direction. Nick was at the end of his tether. He shook his head adamantly. "I'm not ready to give it up just yet."

Jordan pursed her lips. "And the photos?"

Nick had had enough. The desire he felt for her was too close to the surface. Besides, it wouldn't hurt to allow her to see that she affected him. Intensity so often created the same interest in the recipient.

He stood abruptly, looming over her. She raised her head just as his hands dived her hair, lifting her face to his. "You think I want this? Need this?"

Her eyes were wide with surprise. She gasped in a quick breath.

"You're like a drug to me," he gritted, glowering down. "An addiction. Every Friday, I leave that hotel and think, yes. This time, I've got her out of my system. This time…"

Despite this being about knocking her off-kilter, his own body was primed like a detonator. He exhaled, fighting for control, searching for the innate good manners and responsible behavior that had shaped his life. He was a businessman, dammit, not one of her playboys.

He gentled his hands, stroking her hair. Soothed by the silky soft strands running through his fingers. "But then I change my mind, start thinking about next Friday."

He caressed her cheek and her eyelids fluttered as he knew they would.

"It's just sex, Nick," she whispered, turning her face to press a kiss in his palm, that one small act softening her cavalier words.

In her hurry to wash, she'd missed a tiny patch of green by her earlobe and he rubbed his finger over it, his own excitement rocketing when her lips parted involuntarily on a sigh.

"Yes it is," he murmured. He stroked one finger down her throat, felt her pulse leap. She ghosted a fraction closer while keeping her backside in contact with the arm of the sofa. Her head fell back even more in invitation and he bent to nuzzle the fragrant skin under her earlobe. Soft and smooth, her skin was still slightly damp from being freshly washed. Whatever she'd used in her face mask smelled good enough to eat, to taste, again and again.

She strained up, her face turned to his. Darned if he could remember what they were talking about when her mouth bumped against his cheek. It was too much of a temptation, even though he was pretty sure he'd started the body contact not intending to kiss her, only to tease a little. To make the point that she wanted him as much as he wanted her.

Just before his lips met hers, he touched his index finger to the corner of her mouth and frowned down into eyes that smoldered with electric blue desire. "I won't give it up just yet."

Her expression softened. Dipping his head, he took her mouth, filled her mouth, sank in welcome relief. His desire flowed from him into her and back again in a heady rush. She moaned low in her throat, trying to rise, pressing up into him. Happy to help, he slid one arm down her back and brought her hard up against him. The kiss deepened, she opened for him, hungry, appealing for more, her tongue eagerly seeking his.

With one arm supporting her back, he slid the other hand under the sweater, needing the silky slide of her skin. Always when he touched her, some part of his mind registered the softness of her skin. Never had he felt such soft skin; his fingers rejoiced in it. He palmed her torso; she felt hot, so hot. She swayed, her hands clutching at the backs of his arms. Nick slid his hand up, climbing the taut slope of her breast. He heard her breath catch, felt his, when she twisted and pushed her nipple, tight and hard, into his palm. He held her like this, almost horizontal, one arm supporting her back, the other playing with her breasts, exulting in the response he knew he could elicit in her.

But then she sucked in air and shrank away, her mouth stilling under his. When she opened her eyes he could see the battle she waged, need versus denial. Self-denial.

Jordan swallowed audibly. "Not here."

"Are you sure, Jordan?" He ran his thumb over her nipple again, loving it's proud texture.

Jordan closed her eyes and her mouth fell open on a

gush of air. "You can't…" She arched her back to press against his hand once more.

Nick bent his head and sucked at the pebbled peak through her sweater, hearing her whimper. He doubled his efforts when he felt her knee nudge in between his legs, stop, and rub again.

"I can," he whispered, raising his head. Still supporting her, he took his hand from under her sweater and placed it between her thighs.

She tensed and squeezed, her body stiffening.

Nick cupped her, feeling her damp heat. "We both know I can."

He took her mouth again, recognized her capitulation in the way she strained against him, the insistent push of her knee into his aching groin. He'd held this woman in his arms, practiced his seduction on her enough times to know she was fast reaching the point of no return.

To know he was, too.

But even as her arms came around his neck, as she sagged back onto the arm of the couch, her weight dragging him down with her, his brain kicked into a higher gear, sending messages he didn't want to hear right now. He tensed, listening to her breath come in gasps, feeling her fingers tugging at his shirt buttons.

Yes, he could take her right now, right here. He'd proved it. But that made it just another coupling that underlined the shallowness of this affair. He needed her to believe he felt more for her than just a quickie once a week, to wonder if he had real feelings for her. If that was his goal, he had to stop.

Now.

Groaning, Nick pulled back, tearing his mouth away. She stilled, clutching a handful of shirt and confusion and desire smoking up her eyes. He pulled her upright and removed his hand from between her legs. "You're right." His thought processes might be on target but his hands were unsteady and awkward as he tugged the hem of her top down. "Not here. Not now."

Jordan sank back onto the arm of the sofa, her breathing still labored. As she fussed with her clothes and hair, a deep blush crawled up her throat and face.

Nick sighed. He hadn't meant to embarrass her. "I didn't come here tonight to take you to bed."

Her eyes slid over him briefly, then she leaned forward and rested her elbows on her knees, studying her feet. Her hair gleamed, a sparkling curtain in the dim light. Nick reached out and stroked it, feeling ridiculously tender.

"Come out for a drink with me." He tugged on a long lock of silky hair. "Who cares what anyone thinks?"

She shook her head, not looking at him. "I can't go out for a drink with you."

"Because of our fathers? How long are we going to let two old men dictate our lives?"

"It's just not worth the hassle, Nick." For a moment there, he almost thought she sounded sad.

"I think it is," he argued, surprised at how stubborn he felt.

"Let's just stick to Fridays for now." She reached out and covered his hand with hers, looking at him beseechingly.

If she didn't care a little, wasn't secure in the knowledge that he cared a little, she wouldn't have looked at him like that.

Mission accomplished. At least, he'd given her something to think about. He couldn't afford to push too hard or force her to choose between family loyalty or him until he was assured of success.

His breath returned, along with the blood to the rest of his body. He checked his buttons—often an occupational hazard with Jordan's impatient fingers. "Next Friday?"

Jordan rose to show him out. "Shouldn't we at least change the time or place?"

She was obviously still wary about the photos she'd received but Nick wasn't worried. "It's just some eagle-eyed reporter sniffing around. If he'd meant business, there would be a photo of me leaving the hotel, too, or a blackmail note."

Besides, he paid the hotel handsomely for their discretion. Why improve the odds of discovery by going somewhere else? "Make it earlier, then. Two p.m."

Five

To heck with chocolate! Jordan took her mug into the kitchen and tipped the cold contents down the sink, then poured herself a glass of pinot noir. Frustration, confusion—she paced the floor restlessly, going over every minute of the last half hour.

The whole episode was an embarrassment, starting with him catching her in a stupid avocado, cucumber and milk-powder face mask—oh, very elegant! Her humiliation was complete once he touched her, kissed her. He'd said *she* was like a drug, but he'd lit her up so quickly.

Thank goodness he'd had the sense to stop. Nick Thorne was already commanding way too much of her mind lately. Not that she'd ever tell him, but she thought about him plenty outside the hotel room. Several times a week at least, and always with a shiver of erotic anticipation. And when she did, suddenly the days of the week until Friday were an interminable bore.

The last thing she needed was the memory of him here in her lounge, naked, making love to her.

She flicked through the TV channels in an attempt to banish that enticing vision. Although—Jordan turned off the TV—thinking about sex with him was safer than thinking about anything else with him. Confident she could hold him enthralled in the bedroom for a while longer, she determinedly crushed the hope that, someday, Nick might see her as more. Starting a relationship with sex gave her no room to maneuver. He would never take her seriously—no one did. Even her father, her biggest fan, considered her an ornament. Despite her best efforts to change her lifestyle and prove everyone wrong, it really was easier to accept the cynicism and get on with the job. But she had the right to protect her heart along the way.

Even so, she hugged the memory of his jealous face tightly to her all night long.

On Tuesday, she was nearly involved in an accident when a car pulled out behind her into the path of an oncoming car. Jordan thought little of it until she noticed the same gray car behind her ten minutes later. It followed her to the supermarket and then to her parents house. Bemused, she drove around the block a couple of times. The car followed. Jordan pulled up and opened her door. The gray car slowed and then sped up and turned the corner. As it streaked past, she saw a bullet-shaped dark head in dark glasses atop a pair of burly shoulders.

She tried to shrug it off. Like Nick said, probably just a nosy photographer.

But the strange feeling stayed with her. The next day, as she waited for the lift in her building, a giant of a man stepped out. He wore a black suit and dark glasses. His head was close-shaven. She couldn't see his eyes but something about his expression, the look he gave her, made her shiver. He turned as she passed him and did not take his eyes off her until the doors closed.

The hairs rose on the back of her neck at the intensity of the look he gave her. Even once inside her apartment, she couldn't shake the feeling. She drew the drapes, poured herself a soda, started on dinner, all the while berating her vivid imagination.

She was being silly. Was it the photos, or her fear that if she and Nick were found out, she'd have to give him up?

She'd always felt perfectly safe here. There was no designated doorman manning the entrance, although there was a building supervisor. The residents used a swipe card to get in, which, as Nick had proved with his unannounced visit on the weekend, wasn't foolproof.

On her way to the court next morning, she asked the building super if he'd noticed a big man in the building yesterday.

"Big man, suit, dark glasses?" Robert said, and she nodded, her stomach doing a weird slide.

"Not in the building but there was a bloke across the street for most of yesterday, either sitting in his car or leaning against it. Seemed like he was watching the building. I thought it might be a cop."

"What kind of car?"

"Mercedes. Silver."

Jordan had no idea what type of car had followed her yesterday but the difference between gray and silver was open to interpretation.

Grow up in a fishbowl and you get suspicious.

But later, she thought she spied the same car following her home. Quickly pulling into a space on the street, she went into the nearest coffee bar and ordered a drink. Sure enough, a couple of minutes later, the big man in the glasses entered. He ordered from the counter and sat down by the door, facing her. She stared over the rim of her cup, her heart thudding, watching as he opened the newspaper he'd brought with him and raised it to conceal his face.

Despite herself, she smiled, looking for peepholes in the paper. What did he want? Feeling like a regular Nancy Drew, Jordan decided to have it out with him. Anything was better than wondering and at least there were people around.

Draining her cup, she stood and marched over to his table, flicking the newspaper smartly. "Is this it?" she demanded in a loud voice. "The rag you work for?"

The paper lowered and the man stared up at her, ridiculously still wearing his dark glasses. "Sorry?"

"I want to know who you work for," Jordan repeated.

The man picked up the cup in his dinner-plate-size hands and sipped before lowering it again. "I'm just hanging, reading the paper," he said.

Jordan frowned. Why wouldn't he tell her? It would come out anyway. "Do you deny you have been following me all over town, watching my building, every move I make?"

The woman at the next table stared intently with that gleam of sly recognition Jordan was only too familiar with.

The big man leered at her, leaving her in no doubt that he was enjoying the altercation. "I have no idea what you're talking about, Miss Lake," he said insolently.

Jordan sighed. She was getting nowhere, except making a spectacle of herself. At least the guy knew he was rumbled and when his story—whatever it was—hit the headlines, she'd have her father roast the editor.

She shook her head in disgust. "Just leave me alone," she muttered and stalked out the door.

He must be a reporter, she reasoned as she got into the car. The only other possibility was an investigator and why would someone want to investigate her?

Nick's thunderous face when he'd turned up at her apartment entered her mind. Jealousy, unwarranted as it turned out, but what if he hadn't believed her about Jason?

Jordan laughed out loud at the thought he would go to any trouble to keep an eye on her. Ridiculous! They each had their own lives and there was no tie between them. Sparked by the delivery of the photos, her imagination had spiraled into paranoia, just another example of her attention-seeking personality.

Nothing further happened that week and by Friday, she'd forgotten it and arrived at the hotel at the new time of two p.m., very much looking forward to seeing him.

Usually Nick checked in and waited for her in the

room. She headed for the elevators but happened to glance at Reception where two men stood with their backs to her. A thrill of excitement jetted through her when she recognized one as Nick. Jordan hesitated by a tall potted plant and decided to wait until he'd gone up, just in case she was recognized.

She thrummed with anticipation. Maybe he was right about their increased exposure to each other in court. She'd felt his eyes on her several times today, like a hot caress, making her tingle, building her excitement.

As she watched, Nick turned away from the reception clerk and spoke to the man beside him. A big man, with shaven head, a prizefighter's body and dark glasses.

Jordan froze. It was him—coffee bar man! She was sure of it.

She barely noticed as Nick walked on toward the elevators. Her eyes remained glued to the man, who just stared after Nick until he disappeared behind the elevator doors.

She moved right behind the plant now, shaking her head to clear it. Stay calm…she needed to think this through. The sequence of events was only seconds and she went over each one in slow motion. Nick reaching for the keycard, talking to the smiling receptionist, turning away from the counter, pausing to talk to the big man beside him. And then walking to the lift.

The man now had his back to her and Jordan took the opportunity to escape. She drove home in a daze and let herself into her apartment. And then she began to tremble.

Could it be true? Was Nick behind a sinister campaign to unsettle her? Was he having her followed because he thought she was sleeping with Jason? She sat there for nearly an hour but peace of mind eluded her. When her phone rang, she answered it with a sense of ominous fatalism, remembering his face on Saturday night, the hard tone of his voice that she'd never heard before. *"You want him, Jordan?"*

But it was her mother to say Syrius had suffered a heart attack and was being rushed to hospital. Jordan ran, forgetting all about Nick Thorne. Just as she reversed out of her space, she noticed Robert, the building supervisor, waving out to her. Next thing, there was a huge bang and sickening crunch, so loud, she thought there had been an explosion.

Her heart racing in fear and shock, she checked the rearview mirror to see a gray car at the back of hers, its front passenger door crumpled. A gray car—it filtered through the funk in her mind and she looked wildly about for Robert. Her panic eased slightly when she saw him crossing the car park toward her. She pushed open her door, her veins flooded with adrenalin.

And just as she did, Nick Thorne alighted hurriedly from his dented car. His gray Mercedes.

She froze, her mouth dropping open, keyed so tight, she thought she might scream.

"Are you all right?" In two steps, he was beside her, his face full of concern.

"Just *what* do you think you're doing?" she demanded, curling her hands into fists by her side.

"Are you all right, Miss Lake?" Robert approached, his eyes wide.

She ignored him and stared at Nick's face, catching the tension that rolled off him in waves.

"Why don't you look where you're going?" he demanded. "You could have been hurt…"

"You hemmed me in on purpose," she fumed. "Why are you following me?"

"I came to see where you were. I waited for nearly an hour."

"You had your stooge to keep you company. Get this—" she flicked her hand disdainfully toward his car, "—out of my way. I'm in a hurry." Turning, she stalked back to her car and yanked the door open.

"Oh, no, you don't!" Nick skirted around the car and grabbed her arm.

Vaguely she heard Robert offer a protest but all she could see was Nick's furious tight-lipped face.

"I'm not hanging around waiting for you, Jordan. That's the second time you've stood me up. You'd better have a damned good reason."

She tugged her arm from his grasp, desperate to get away and be with her father. "You're following me, stalking me," she said loudly for Robert's benefit. "And I want it to stop."

She slid into her car but he barred her door from closing. "What are you talking about?"

"Keep away from me, Nick!" Her demand was almost a yell. She glanced at the doorman. "I have a witness and he'll back me up. You're stalking me and I want you to leave me alone."

She gave a mighty pull on the door but he held it firm. "Request granted, and gladly." His eyes glittered like the ice in his voice. "You have much too high an opinion of yourself, Jordan Lake."

With that, he slammed her door and swiftly made his way to his car, flinging a sour look at Robert, who backed off quickly. Then he gunned the engine and sped from the car park, leaving only the tinkle and crunch of glass.

The aftershocks hit Jordan in a series of hot waves. She laid her forehead on the steering wheel, trembling with emotion. Incredibly, her anger had vanished along with Nick, and although he hadn't denied following her, the confusion in his face confused her. But she didn't have time to worry about that now. She had to get to the hospital.

Robert tapped on her window. "Your taillight's broken, Miss Lake. It'll need seeing to."

She grimaced. "Later. Robert, was that the car you saw outside the building this week, the one with the big man in dark glasses?"

Robert shook his head. "No, ma'am. It was a Mercedes, but silver, not gray."

Six

At eight-thirty on Monday morning, Nick exited his office elevator to find his brother sitting on his assistant's desk. His black mood darkened even more. "What do you want at this time of the morning?"

Noting Jasmine's flushed and suddenly busy demeanor, it occurred to him that maybe Adam wasn't here to see him at all. Scowling, he strode on into his office.

He'd spent the whole weekend stewing about the fight with Jordan—not that he had any idea what it was all about. One minute he was eagerly anticipating their lovemaking after a week's abstinence. The next, spun into a rage when she didn't turn up. Her accusations in the car park outside her building floored him and he could still hear the anger in her voice when she demanded he stay away from her.

Well, she'd got her wish. He flung his briefcase onto the desk, glad he was finished with it. Now, at least, he wouldn't have to lie about being booked up every Friday afternoon.

He hadn't even taken off his jacket when he heard Jasmine's startled "Wait!" and looked up to see the subject of his thoughts stalking in through his door. She marched straight in and flung the newspaper in her hand onto his desk.

Nick froze, his jacket half on, eyes leaping eagerly to her face. Jasmine appeared behind Jordan. "Nick, I'm sorry."

"Excuse us, please."

Jordan stood tall, her cheeks pink, eyes blazing. "What the hell are you playing at?"

With effort, Nick tore his eyes off her face and glanced down at the "Stepping Out" page of the local daily, picturing Jordan leaving the hotel. A brief caption read "Jordan Lake takes a break from the court case between her father and Randall Thorne looking glam as always in her little black dress." It was the same photo as the one that had been sent to her home. So it was a newshound after all.

But what did that have to do with him? He looked up into her face. "What am I supposed to have done now?"

"Don't give me that," she fumed. "Having me followed, watched—badly, I may say. Your goon didn't even care that I caught him."

Nick stared at her, uncomprehending.

She huffed out an agitated sigh. "The same gorilla I saw you with on Friday?"

Shaking his head, Nick finished removing his jacket and draped it over the back of his chair. "Gorilla?"

"At the hotel reception."

He eyed her while unbuttoning his cuffs and rolling his sleeves up. He'd never seen her angry before last Friday. Two minutes ago, he hadn't cared if he'd never seen or spoken to her again. Now, treacherously, his whole being warmed at the sight of her, sparks spitting from her eyes, her haughty chin raised high and mouth plump with a sullen moue. Nick was dangerously close to enjoying himself. "Jordan, what possible reason would I have to follow you?"

"I want it to stop, Nick." She leaned forward and rapped on the newspaper. "Now even my mother is asking questions, thanks to this."

She thought *he'd* sent the photo to the papers? Completely bamboozled—and worryingly exhilarated with it—he bit back a smile. The clouds that had darkened his weekend vanished in her presence, but he was astute enough to discern that if he smiled, she would probably deck him.

So he looked her straight in the eye. "Why don't you sit down and tell me about it," he suggested, doing his best not to sound patronizing. "I'll order some coffee and we'll..."

"I don't want coffee," she blurted, "and I don't want

to talk. I just want you to leave me alone." She stabbed the air between them with her index finger.

Nick started, filled with concern. There was something very wrong here. She was close to tears, more upset than he'd realized. Glistening eyes, the tremble in her voice… "Jordan…" He stepped around the desk but she whirled and made for the door.

He saw red. She couldn't just leave without giving him the chance to defend himself. He strode after her, his fingers grabbing her arm as she yanked the doorknob. "Don't you walk away from…"

"Keep away from me!" She lifted her arm to shake him. The door flew open and there was Adam, standing close, blatantly eavesdropping. Several heartbeats went by while both of them glared at him. At least he had the grace to step to the side and look contrite.

With a little huff of disgust in Adam's direction, Jordan turned her head to Nick. "In fact, keep your whole family away from mine."

Randall Thorne chose that moment to walk out of his office, stopping dead when he saw Jordan.

Jordan's eyes narrowed, all trace of her heated passionate plea lost in cool disdain. "You'll be pleased to know," she addressed the room in general, "that you won't be required in court this morning. The case has been adjourned."

Nick shot a warning look in Randall's direction in case the old man smart-mouthed her again.

"My father had a heart attack on Friday," Jordan continued. "He had an angioplasty and is still in the hospital."

Nick exhaled and took a step toward her. "Jordan…"

"Don't you dare say you're sorry," she snapped and gave each of the men in turn a bitter, recriminatory look. "Just keep away from us."

She stalked to the elevator, pressed the button and left.

No one spoke for a long moment, all eyes on the elevator. Even Jasmine looked stunned. Nick turned and walked stiffly to his desk, trying to assimilate what just happened. She thought he was stalking her, trying to blackmail her? And her father—sympathy welled up. God in heaven, what more damage could his family inflict on hers?

Adam and his father walked in. "What was *she* doing here?" Randall Thorne demanded.

Nick gave him a narrow glance. "Her father? What do you think?"

Adam cleared his throat and sat. Nick decided not to look at him, guessing his brother had heard a little more than he was entitled to.

He sat and rubbed his face briskly. "Christ, a heart attack." He felt somehow responsible and he could see on Randall's face that he felt the same. "This has got to stop, Dad."

"What did I…?"

"This bickering and fighting between you and Syrius. I don't care if you never shake hands and make up, but no more, do you understand?"

"He started this…"

"No, you started the latest outbreak by taking that award off him. He just carried it on."

"I've been insulted and slandered for years by that man. I've been the soul of patience and tolerance because your mother begged me..."

Nick raised his hand sharply and his father's voice trailed off. Come to think of it, he was just in the mood for a family conference. His blood was pumping—frustration, indignation at Jordan's wild accusations and shock about her father. And, if he was honest, the zing he got every time he looked at her...

It was time he got a few things sorted out around here. "Dad, I want you to announce your retirement at the birthday party."

His father looked up in astonishment. "Next month!"

"You'll be seventy. It's time to go."

"I'm in good health—" Randall harrumphed "—and things aren't settled yet." He cast a sideways look at Adam.

Both brothers raised their brows at their father.

"Adam hasn't decided—"

"Yes, I have, Dad," Adam cut in quickly. "And I've told you repeatedly."

"You're not on the plane yet, my boy," his father rumbled. "I want both my boys here."

"It's not going to happen," Adam stated.

Nick studied his hands. At thirty-four, the managing director of this place in all but name, he was tired of being fed crumbs and kept hanging. Of his father constantly playing him off against his brother. Nick had to show he was strong and worthy of the position. Randall valued strength above all else.

"Let's have this out right now," Nick said, leaning

back in his seat. "Face it, Dad. Adam is not coming back to Thorne's."

His father's eyes bored into him. "He would if you needed him, if you asked him."

Nick inclined his head. "Maybe. But I don't and I won't."

A sly light leapt in Randall's pale green eyes. "You jealous of your brother, Nick?"

Nick clasped his hands together, a small smile tugging at his lips. "Not at all." He flicked a glance at Adam who had the same thoughtful expression he'd worn since walking in here. "He knows that. But if you keep pushing, you'll lose him to London for good."

Nick hoped not. Adam had always said he'd settle in New Zealand eventually but for now, the lure of the world financial markets was too strong.

His father turned to Adam.

"Nick has it in one," Adam said, preempting the next salvo. "I'm doing what I want to do."

Randall's thick silvery brows knitted together. "This company is my legacy to you both…"

Nick sighed. He'd heard it all before, many times. "Are you unhappy with my performance?" he demanded, leaning forward intently.

His father blinked. "Of course not. You're doing a fine job."

"Then step aside," Nick said quietly. "Give me the recognition I deserve for running this place in all but name for the last five years."

Randall got heavily to his feet. "And do I interfere?

No! Why can't you be happy with that until Adam comes to his senses, dammit?"

Nick eyed him steadily. "Would you be?"

He knew the answer to that. Randall was a pioneer of his time. The empire he'd started was now one of the top three financial lending companies in the country, with a triple-A international credit rating and branches in all the main centers. Randall Thorne had never played second fiddle in his life.

"Not even to fulfill your mother's last wishes?" Randall had turned to glare at Adam's dark head.

Oh, he was good, Nick thought with a grudging admiration. He'd used every excuse in the book over the last couple of years. The truth was, he liked to keep an edge. Didn't want anyone getting too comfortable, too secure in their positions. Randall liked nothing better than having everyone scurrying around currying favor, vying to please him.

The old man left the office with a heavy step.

Adam stirred only when the door had closed behind him. "Good performance," he said quietly. "You weren't bad, either."

Nick leaned back, exhaling. "Am I being unreasonable?"

"Not at all. It's not like he does anything around here anymore."

"And I don't have a problem with him dropping in as often as he likes. But this is my domain now, and he's encouraged me every step of the way. He can damn well follow through."

Adam nodded. "You'll get there. But," he stood and moved to the window, "you have options, Nick."

Nick joined his brother at the window, glancing at him curiously. They were very alike, same height and coloring, although Nick was broader. He took after his father in physicality while Adam had a touch more of Melanie, slightly finer of bone, sharper facial features and fuller lips. Nick used to call him a pretty boy when they were young. He absently rubbed his nose, remembering some epic fights. Pretty Boy could pack an impressive punch, even if he was smaller.

"Maybe I'm tiring of the traveling, the women, the excitement—or it's tiring of me." Adam grinned. "I'm setting up an entrepreneurial start-up company. Savvy people with big ideas apply for funding and mentorship, but it's not just another angel investment company. I'm thinking big—global—and with some big names behind me."

"You've been watching too much reality TV," Nick said drily, but it was an interesting notion and one he'd like to hear more about. "Who are your investors?"

Adam named several captains of industry and IT. "I have my eye on a couple of big names, investors who will bring expertise and notoriety, not just money. If all goes to plan, I'll be ready to roll in the new year. But I could use a good man here. New Zealand is ripe for this type of opportunity." Adam turned to him with a glint in his eye. "It's not that different to what you do here, except that most of your clients are retirees and farmers." He approximated a yawn. "Be in on the ground floor, new innovative ideas, the future of the country."

Nick smiled, welcoming an old memory. "Remember when Dad used to bring us here on Saturday mornings before rugby? I'd watch him, listen to him talking to clients, working them. For all he's a bit rough around the edges, he knew how to treat people."

"So do you." Adam shoved his hands in his pockets. "You're just more refined."

Nick returned to his desk and sat. "Thanks, Adam. I appreciate the offer, but like you, I'm doing what I want to do."

Adam nodded. "I know. I'm just saying, you have options." He started for the door, then turned back. "Are you going to tell me what is going on between you and the Lake girl?"

Nick involuntarily glanced at the photo in the paper. His assault on Jordan's affections had hit a temporary snag with her father's heart attack. She wasn't likely to view his advances with a friendly eye while Syrius was in any danger of leaving this mortal coil.

But it was still the best option open to him, especially in light of his father's intransigence. And she was more than just a roll in the high thread-count linen of a five-star hotel. Nick hadn't even started showing her how much more.

But she would be the first to know. Meeting his brother's curious gaze, he smiled. "Nothing," he said firmly. "Nothing at all."

"Yeah, right," Adam muttered skeptically and sauntered to the door. "See you later, big brother."

Seven

"This beautiful Marlborough Sounds property for three million dollars, going once."

Nick scanned the crowd for the flash of blue silk that would give her away. He'd caught glimpses only, which probably meant she was avoiding him. It was nearly the end of the evening and he had only just arrived in time for the big item being auctioned tonight. He'd planned it that way.

"Three million dollars going twice."

A few faces close to him turned and nodded, their expressions curious and friendly. This was a media-free event, in as much as a hundred or so of New Zealand's high society could be secret. The organizer had wanted it that way. If Reverend Parsons hadn't filled him in on

Jordan's full involvement in the charitable Elpis Foundation, he'd be pretty miffed at throwing away a king's ransom just to impress a woman.

"Sold to the highest bidder."

Strangely, Nick felt little emotion for the huge outlay. No doubt his conscience would prick him tomorrow, especially when Adam or his father found out, but it was his own money he was using.

The auctioneer appeared and led him to a discreet table upfront, but to the side of the sumptuous ballroom to allow the dancing to resume. A couple of acquaintances patted his shoulder or winked as they passed but he invited no further conversation. His goal was to see Jordan.

"Please sit, Mr. Thorne," the auctioneer invited. "Can I get you some champagne?"

"No, thank you. Could you fetch Jordan Lake for me, please?"

The older man's face leaped with surprise and anticipation, but he immediately bowed his head. "Certainly. Feel free to look over the sale documents."

For the last three days, Jordan had refused to return his calls and after her performance in the car park, he was reluctant to go to her address. This morning, a wealthy client let slip that she was attending a charity auction for the Elpis Foundation. Nick recalled seeing the name in Jordan's apartment and that Russ Parsons was involved.

While he waited, he flipped through the pages of the Purchase agreement and assorted documents. Even with the real estate photographer's skill, the property looked shabby. The ad said the lodge was built at the turn of the century and still retained its "old-world charm"—another way of saying dilapidated. For one brief second, he wondered what the heck he was thinking.

But then he smelled her perfume, heard the swish of silk and the uncertainty of her voice when she spoke his name.

Nick got to his feet and stared at her for so long that the auctioneer who'd accompanied her backed off quickly. Jordan sat down stiffly.

She looked absolutely incredible. If he could recapture this moment in his mind forever and a day, he would recall every detail: the shade of her dress that matched her eyes—and the blue diamonds at her ears, he thought with a stab of triumph. Her glorious golden hair piled high with ringlets coiled around her face. The exact shade of pale pink lipstick as that which graced her fingernails, and her toenails, if he remembered correctly. The dress was a dramatic sheath of crisp silk, strapless, with a split bodice that emphasized her bust and cinched in her waistline. She was every inch the princess.

"You look lovely, Jordan," he said simply.

"Thank you. I'm—surprised to see you."

"Didn't Russ tell you? I asked him for an invitation, since mine obviously got lost in the mail."

"I didn't realize you knew him," Jordan said, smoothly ignoring his dig.

"My mother has always attended his church. He was a regular visitor to my parents' house during her illness."

Russ couldn't have been more enthusiastic with his endorsement of Jordan's many virtues. Tonight's glittering shindig she'd organized on the smell of an oily rag, begging favors all over town. Nick learned that she'd set up the Elpis Foundation with her own money a year ago. He heard all about her volunteer work at a free medical clinic and numerous other projects she had initiated.

And about her refusal to have her name associated with any of it. That interested him most of all.

He realized he was still gazing at her face when she shifted and cleared her throat.

"If you'd like to sign the contract…" she said with a pointed look at the papers on the table.

Nick sat down, giving her a smile that didn't quite reach his eyes. "Just as soon as you have the last dance with me."

She shook her head, confirming that she didn't trust him an inch—or was she worried about being seen with him? He observed that no one was paying them any attention. The orchestra was two minutes into the feisty *Die Fledermaus* and they were mostly obscured by the throng of dancers moving around the floor.

He faced her and leaned forward. "Come on, Jordan, do all your stalkers throw away a couple of mil just to impress you?"

She gave him a guarded look. "Some of my father's closest friends are here."

"I've just topped your sales for the evening. He'll understand."

"He's not well," she retorted. "And anyway, this isn't the last dance."

"Good, then you have a few minutes to explain why you think I've been stalking you."

Jordan sighed, staring moodily into the dance crowd. "You know why. The silver car. The big burly man with dark glasses, watching my building and following me everywhere." She picked up the pen, turning it over in her hands. "He gave me the creeps, staring at me all the time."

Nick decided not to point out that any red-blooded male in the world would have to be blind not to stare at Jordan Lake, especially tonight. "For someone who's made a career out of spicing up the gossip pages, you seem a little tense about some old photographer."

Her brows knitted in irritation. "It wasn't a photographer. I confronted him when he followed me into a coffee shop and he denied it—why would a newsman do that if his paper is about to run a story?"

Nick shrugged, skeptical. "What made you think I had anything to do with it?"

Jordan hesitated. "I—I remembered how you looked when you came around that night, when you thought I'd been with Jason."

"How I looked?"

She flushed prettily. "Angry. Jealous."

Nick leaned back in his seat. "And I don't have the right to be jealous, do I?" He knew he didn't. He'd given nothing of himself to this relationship, such as it was.

She looked down at the pen in her hands.

"I swear to you, Jordan, I had nothing to do with anyone following you. I was as invested as you were to keeping our meetings under wraps, especially with the court case going on. What possible reason…?"

Jordan took a deep breath. "Okay, I might have been

prepared to admit I was wrong about your involvement. And five minutes before I hit you in the car park…"

"Rammed me," he injected drily.

"You hemmed me in," she retorted. "I'd just been told of my father's heart attack. But it was seeing you with the man in the hotel that really spooked me."

"Back up. You went to the hotel on Friday?" He cast his mind back to Friday, a roaring of anticipation in his ears, fading with each passing minute, then an hour. The black rage of frustration that had him speeding over to her apartment building to have it out with her.

"Of course." She sounded surprised he would even doubt that. "I wouldn't let you down without calling."

He shook his head, confused. "I wasn't with anyone at the hotel."

The arch of one perfectly sculpted brow confirmed her skepticism. "I'd just walked into the lobby when I saw you talking to a man. You were both standing at Reception."

Nick started to deny it but her raised hand stopped him. "It was the same man, Nick. I got a great look at him in the coffee bar."

"I just picked up the key card…" Nick began, and then a memory kicked his indignation into touch.

"You were talking to him," Jordan insisted, "and then you walked to the elevators and he just stayed there, staring at you."

Nick remembered an insignificant detail. "Someone asked me the time." His mind had been so full of Jordan, he'd barely noticed the man who stood at the reception desk while he checked in. He hadn't given it another thought but in hindsight, it was a strange request considering the hotel wall behind reception had about a dozen clocks, all displaying time zones from around the world. "That was it. I told him the time and walked away."

Maybe this was something to be uneasy about after all. "Are you sure it was the same man, Jordan?"

"Yes."

"Perhaps you should call the police," he told her. "It's probably nothing, just a photographer hoping for a story, but just to be on the safe side…" He didn't want to spook her but she'd described quite a catalog of incidents. Some of it could be imagination, some less likely.

"The photo in Monday's paper was the last straw," she said gravely. "I thought you were playing some sick game."

"So you stormed into my office." No wonder she was rattled, and with her father's heart attack coming on top… He leaned forward again, resting his arms on the table. "Jordan, do you believe I had nothing to do with any of that?"

Jordan gazed at him for a long moment. She wouldn't describe herself as a great judge of character but she could see only concern and sincerity in his face— exactly what she wanted most to see. The past few days, she'd been miserable, hoping against hope there might be an alternative explanation.

His eyes reassured, soothed, seemed to see deeper into her than anyone had before. She nodded. "Yes. I'm sorry. It was just a weird couple of days."

The master of ceremonies announced that Strauss's *Wine, Women and Song* was the last dance of the evening. Nick stood and extended his hand. She rose, looking around nervously, but when he enfolded her hand in his and gave a reassuring squeeze, her reservations about her father finding out seemed trite. The man had made an enormous boost to the fund-raising coffers tonight. It would be surly to refuse him a dance.

She wanted to trust him. She'd trusted him with her body for months, and now her fears seemed silly. That aside, he was still the son of her sick father's oldest enemy. And she was afraid of risking her heart to someone who would tire of her soon enough.

They joined the other dancers on the floor and as the first notes rang out with military drama, the men bowed low to their partners. There was a lengthy introduction but at least this waltz was one of the shorter selections tonight. Jordan stood stiffly, waiting for the waltz steps to start and Nick moved close and put one big warm hand on her back.

And then she forgot everything, lost in the music she loved, the million double-quick turns and jaunty steps that he seemed to know as well as she. Jordan was a student of waltz for many years and liked to think she had inherited some of her mother's grace and ability. Nick moved well, full of confidence and purpose. Like he did everything, she thought wryly. But of course, his mother had been an outstanding dancer and teacher, too.

The music swirled, lifting her spirits, and she followed his commanding lead in perfect synchronicity, thrilled to find such a capable partner. Nothing beat the rapture of a fast Viennese waltz when two capable participants clicked on the floor.

Well, almost nothing…Nick rarely took his eyes from hers and she could see he, too, enjoyed the self-imposed discipline of being this close and yet perfectly proper. The teasing brush of his thighs, the masculine pressure of his hand at her lower back, the flat of his palm upon which her fingers rested, it all merged into a dance of restraint. How she knew was a mystery but she sensed how much he wanted to pull her close, mold her body to his. His hand wanted to close around her fingers, his other, to stroke up her back. That he managed to convey all this without a word was testament to their undeniable physical connection.

She sighed and tore her eyes from his. If the last week had shown her anything, it was that she'd become too vulnerable where he was concerned. It seemed Nick could elicit all sorts of wants and needs that she had no idea she was missing.

"Whoops, did I miss a step?"

He'd misinterpreted her sigh. She shook her head. "You dance well," she told him as the dance concluded and everyone ringed the floor and clapped the orchestra.

"My mother was determined that Adam and I could hold our own on the dance floor." He put a hand under her elbow and led her back to the table, his eyes suddenly troubled. "I'm sorry. It can't have been easy with your mother in a wheelchair."

Jordan was touched that he'd remembered, that he

cared enough, felt bad enough on his father's behalf, to mention it. "She supervised. We often watched videos together of her and your mother, the competitions."

"They were quite something," Nick agreed, pulling out her chair. But Jordan remained standing, somehow feeling she had more power that way.

How charming he could be. How strange that in nearly half a year's acquaintance, she was only just finding that out now. Not that he'd ever treated her with anything but respect, but what was his game now? What did he want from her?

The more she saw of this new Nick, the more she was being drawn in, but it couldn't be. Not now, not ever. He would find her out, find her wanting if he dug beneath the surface. And by then, she would be hopelessly in love.

And her father was ill, seriously ill. She couldn't add to that. She raised her chin. "Thank you, Nick." Picking up the pen, she held it out to him.

Nick glanced at it and then back to her face. "Am I being dismissed?"

"I have things to see to." She had to be strong, had to resist him.

He took the pen but made no attempt to use it. "You do believe that I had nothing to do with any of that last week?"

She held his gaze. "Yes. I believe you." Silently, she implored him to sign the paper. Leave while she still had a hope of saying no.

Nick's eyes bored into her, glinting with comprehension and disappointment. "This isn't over, Jordan. I want more."

Maintaining eye contact and a casual tone when every cell in her body clamored to know how much more wasn't easy. "It was fun, but it's over."

He didn't move one facial muscle but his flinty expression warned her it wasn't over, not yet. "That's it? One dance for three million dollars?"

It was like a slap with a cold fish. Charming when things were going his way, but ultimately, out for what he could get. She summoned an icy look of her own. "Why, no. You get this lovely property in a beautiful part of the country. It's an excellent investment."

The corner of his mouth lifted but his eyes were cool. "There is a condition of sale. I want you to show me the property."

Her eyes widened. "An auction is unconditional..."

"You want it sold or not?"

Damn, damn, she'd made a huge tactical error, shot her bullets too soon. "Nick, you can't go back on your word. This is for charity."

He scowled. "Are you willing to risk a bird in the hand?" He turned his head, gesturing at the queue of people lining up for their coats, the catering staff clearing empty tables, the orchestra packing up. "The evening is over. I'm your only buyer—*potential* buyer."

Her heart sank. How could she refuse with three million dollars at stake? How could she ever explain the collapse of the deal to Russ? They were counting on this money. "Why are you doing this?"

He picked up the contract and folded it. "I'm waiting."

He had manipulated her with cold, calculating

finesse. That was bad enough but how would she handle going off into the middle of nowhere alone with him?

Was it him or herself she didn't trust?

She had no choice. "If you think we're just going to pick up where we left off…" she muttered furiously. "Your three million bought this—" her fingers flicked the folded contract in his hand "—not me!"

He raised his hands. "That's your choice. Nothing will happen that you don't want."

That was cold comfort. They both knew she was incapable of resisting him once he started touching her.

"Be at Aotea Marina at eight a.m. on Saturday."

Great. She'd have to spend the three-hour ferry trip pretending she didn't know him—not that she would be talking to him. "The ferries don't leave from Aotea Marina," she said testily.

"Aotea Marina. Eight a.m sharp," Nick said firmly and tucked the contract into his jacket pocket.

Eight

"Something wrong?" Nick asked from the wheel of the Liberte 1V luxury cruiser.

Jordan closed her cell phone, frowning. They were an hour out from Wellington and her phone had just died in the middle of a text. She normally got reception most of the way across the Strait on the big public ferries.

She looked up into his questioning gaze. "One of the girls in our Outreach program has gone missing. Russ wants us to keep an eye out for her."

Letitia was fourteen. She came from a large family who'd hit hard times. They were loving and kind people who qualified for the support the church and the Elpis Foundation offered—and they gave much.

But two nights ago after a fight with her parents over

a cell phone—Letitia wanted one and they couldn't afford it—she'd left home and hadn't been heard from since.

Nick grunted. "Probably just hanging with her friends."

Jordan hoped so. In fact she could remember running away to friends to cool off herself at fourteen. But there was little comparison between the places she'd hung out and the options open to a young girl alone on the streets of Wellington.

"She came out here a couple of weeks ago. We had a Working Bee."

"At the lodge?"

Jordan broke off a little of the fluffy croissant on the plate in front of her. Nick had promised her a decent lunch on the floating palace, but for now, she was making do with coffee and still-warm croissants. "We've had a couple. Mostly picking up rubbish around the place and pulling up old carpet. Letitia had a ball and hasn't stopped talking about it, according to her parents."

"And Russ thinks she might have come back?"

Jordan sipped her coffee. "I don't see how. She has no money for the ferry, or the water taxi from Picton."

Talk of the Working Bee reminded her... "Do you mind if I bring back some stuff that we left last time? Some tools and food we were keeping for the next Working Bee. I'll bring it back today and get it out of your way."

He nodded briefly, but if he'd noticed the reference to coming back today, he didn't say anything.

Jordan had arrived at Aotea Square as instructed at eight sharp. Nick helped her aboard and then immersed himself in skippering the cruiser out of the harbor and into Cook Strait, that turbulent stretch of water linking the North and South Islands of New Zealand. He estimated the trip to their destination to be under four hours, plenty of time to make it back today.

And that was the only option, as far as Jordan was concerned. She was still miffed at his strong-arm tactics to get her here but she would play along—for now.

"Why were you holding Working Bees there when you intended to auction it off?"

"I hadn't intended to sell it at that stage. I'd planned to develop a retreat for families who never seem to have enough money to take a holiday." She felt her cheeks color. The idea seemed to have merit at the time she'd purchased the lodge, but in the cold light of day... "It was a pipe dream." She lifted her shoulders carelessly.

"Why?"

Jordan glanced at him. Nick looked like he was born on a boat. He wore tan chinos, moccasins without socks and a casual white shirt that he'd left untucked. A world removed from his suits and crisp business shirts. The breeze ruffled his dark hair, spinning it with dark gold tips. With the backdrop of the sparkling sea, his hands strong and capable on the wheel, he was master of his destiny.

And she'd do well to stop admiring his physical attributes and remember that she was here under duress. "I hadn't thought it through. Needy people don't want a holiday, they want tangible support, support they can see in their wallets and on their table. I meant well, but..." Jordan had no idea, really. How could she with her upbringing?

Nick frowned. "Doesn't sound like such a bad idea to me. Is it only the well-heeled who deserve holidays?"

"No, of course not." She lapsed into silence, feeling foolish.

"Why did you change your mind?"

"The big boy toys were a bit light."

He raised his brows.

"The auction," she qualified. "We expected a few more high-value items to put up for the charity auction. When they didn't eventuate, I thought the property might provide a draw card and fetch a good price for the coffers."

"Did you get what you hoped for?"

More time with you? The thought popped into her brain with the speed of light. That was how it had turned out but Jordan knew that wasn't what she needed. She merely nodded.

"Why all the secrecy, Jordan? Most women in your position can't wait to let the world know about the good works they do."

She knew that, but she'd also had a lifetime of people looking down on her because she was rich. "It's better that way. No one takes me seriously but this—the Foundation—is a serious business. The minute people realize that I'm involved, a lot of the support would dry up." She looked at him candidly. "For example, did you see an amusing headline about me three weeks ago? The Penny-Pinching Million-Hair-ess!"

Nick nodded. "Something to do with buying up shampoo on special."

"A woman took a picture of me with half a dozen

bottles of cut-price hair products in the supermarket. Neither she nor the rag she gave the photo to bothered to find out that I'd bought them for one of Russ's jumble sales. I often do things like that, but maybe I should cover myself in sackcloth and ashes."

"That would be a crime," he quipped, but there was genuine sympathy in his face.

She turned away from it. "I brought it on myself, the way I behaved—used to. People don't want to see me as anything other than a rich bitch."

"You're being too hard on yourself," Nick commented. "It's a lot more than most people are doing."

He was right, she supposed. Pity it had taken her so long to get a conscience.

"Tell me about Elpis. It means hope, doesn't it? Something to do with Pandora's box?"

"Technically, it was a jar," Jordan murmured, surprised at his interest. "A curse given by Zeus to punish mankind. It was entrusted to Pandora and when she opened it, all the good spirits were lost to mankind, except for hope." She shrugged self-consciously. "Something like that, anyway." Russ's interest in Greek mythology had inspired the name.

"And you set up the Foundation, financed the lot?"

Jordan nodded. There were no prizes for guessing what was going through his mind, that it was Thorne commercial real estate her trust fund was built on. Paid for by his father, so ultimately him. "Yes, it was from the trust fund that came from your father's land. But I think you know that."

"Do you think I'm after reclaiming that money, Jordan?" His tone was casual, his long considering look anything but.

She searched his face for hidden meaning, liking his directness. "No."

"Do you feel guilty about it? Is that why you give it away?"

That had occurred to her before. She had plenty of money apart from this particular trust fund. What had spurred her into suddenly developing a philanthropic streak a year ago, when this fund matured? "Do *you* think I'm guilty?"

It took a while but when it came, his smile was warm and melted her insides. "Guilty of being too good and too hard on yourself, maybe."

Too good? She wondered if anyone, especially her father, would see it that way if her torrid affair with Nick Thorne was discovered. "I'm no angel. I just have too much time on my hands."

"Did you never have any plans or ambitions of your own?" he asked.

Jordan liked art, which played right into her indulgent father's hands. A hobby rather than a career choice. "Daddy didn't exactly imbue me with a good work ethic." The sad thing was that Jordan had let him get away with that for so long. Taking his handouts, indulging in every pleasure, pleasing herself.

"Surely he could have set you up in one of his businesses somewhere."

She laughed out loud. "He doesn't believe in women

working. How he gets away without sexual discrimination charges for the lack of female employees—especially in the corporate sector—is beyond me." She glanced at him sideways. "And you are the very last person I should have shared that with."

Nick gave her another of his long, assessing looks. "I'm on your side, Jordan."

Her heart sank because something in her knew he spoke the truth. Suddenly his words at the ball the other night—I want more—took on ominous meaning. This wasn't just about sex or resuming their previous relationship. Somehow, for whatever reason, Nick Thorne wanted something more from her. And that was going to cause her heart all sorts of problems.

Jordan stayed silent, pretending he hadn't said that.

"You never wanted to get away, strike out on your own?"

"I'd miss Mom too much." That was a little twist on the truth. Syrius was a social animal whereas Elanor preferred home life. It was common knowledge he'd had a mistress for several years, but his wife and daughter always came first. The fact was, her mother would be more alone than ever if Jordan left Wellington.

It was a beautiful day with none of the bad weather and big seas that Cook Strait was famous for. Jordan asked Nick how long he'd had the big boat. He told her this was a charter.

"I had something similar but sold it three years ago. I never seem to find the time these days."

"Will you take over from your father when he

retires?" She knew her father and Randall Thorne were similar in age. Her mother made noises about Syrius retiring but Jordan privately thought they'd haul him out of his office in a body bag. That he had no son to take over from him was a source of great sorrow for her father, and something he constantly alluded to as proof of Randall Thorne's sins.

"That's what I'm working on."

She wondered why he sounded so grim, but he didn't elaborate.

After awhile, Jordan explored the plush vessel, surprised at the level of luxury on board. The stateroom was lavishly furnished, the kitchen nearly as good as hers at home, the bathrooms and hot tub inviting. To her surprise, she found two big cabins, both with beautifully decked out queen-size beds.

Jordan fully intended to ensure they got back to Wellington today but it was comforting to know she had a choice.

They weighed anchor in an inlet at the very tip of the Marlborough Sounds with the lovely name of Curious Cove. True to his word, Nick provided a fantastic picnic of chewy focaccia bread, tedaggio cheese, cold meats and crayfish. For dessert, there was a warm blackberry tart. There was wine, too, but Jordan declined, feeling she needed a clear head about her with Nick around, especially when he wasn't drinking.

After lunch, they made their way through the beautiful bays leading to the famous Queen Charlotte Sound, and finally they arrived at the jetty that led to the lodge.

"Don't expect too much," Jordan warned as she packed away the food while he prepared to tie up the boat. "No one has lived here since it went out of business seven years ago. The owner died, someone in the family contested the will and it's been tied up in an estate wrangle till I bought it two months ago."

The jetty was quaint but serviceable, but Nick's smile faded fast when confronted with the deteriorating facade of the house. Weatherboards missing or rotting away, crying out for a lick of paint, broken windows...

She quickly drew him away from the spot where the veranda sagged alarmingly, handing him the keys before he bolted.

"How often have you been here?" he asked dazedly.

"Three or four times, twice with the Working Bee." There was a tense moment when she wondered if he'd actually rip up the contract before setting a foot over the threshold. The old house was in terrible condition, but there were some lovely features inside and the setting made up for it.

They spent the first hour on the upper level and discovered the three bathrooms needed serious remodeling and plumbing. The seven bedrooms were dated but dry and she noted a little more enthusiasm from Nick when he saw the views they had to offer. From every window, hills toasted by the sun gave way to slopes of dense dark green forest, rising out of the network of sparkling waterways.

Then it was downstairs to the three living areas. There was a huge room that could almost have been a ballroom, complete with some lovely leadlight windows, all of which seemed to be intact. A smaller room with a conservatory boasted wonderful water views. Finally, the large open dining room with built-in rimu wood benches and tables, leading into the kitchen. The wallpaper was peeling, the paint on the kitchen cupboards too, but it was big and bright and airy.

Jordan moved into the kitchen, hoping their efforts last trip had eliminated the rodent problem. The large sports bag she'd left on the kitchen bench last time was open, a box of teabags sitting beside it with some of the contents spilling out onto the bench.

Funny, she could swear she'd packed everything away before leaving.

"I've seen something like this before," Nick called from the dining room.

Jordan looked up to see him gazing at the large bold mural on the wall.

She zipped up the bag, wondering which of the kids had nicked her large Tupperware container filled with biscuits.

"Something similar, anyway," Nick said, peering closely at the mural. "No signature."

Jordan felt no need to volunteer the fact that she was the artist. Drawing was just a hobby, not something she took seriously. She had been rained in on her second trip here, alone without the group. Sketching seemed a great way to pass the time, although she fully expected the wall to be painted over sometime soon.

Nick turned around. "This was in your apartment. Not this exact one," he gestured at the mural "but something similar. Same tone, a couple dancing." His face suddenly cleared. "*You* did this."

Jordan hoisted the bag. "Uh-huh." She wondered where to look for the other tools and paraphernalia the Working Bee had left.

"These are good," Nick enthused. "Do you sell them?"

"No. It's just a hobby." Jordan frowned at the sight of the old black kettle sitting on the bench. She thought she'd emptied it and set it on the gas cooker. She reached out to touch the kettle.

"How do you expect anyone to take you seriously if you don't yourself?"

Jordan didn't answer him because she was distracted by the warmth of the kettle. She spread her fingers on the belly of the vessel, frowning. "It's hot," she said, more to herself than him.

Nick came over to lean on the bench. "It's sitting in direct sunlight."

Right, and it shouldn't be. There were matches on the bench by the gas cooker. "I wonder...I could swear I packed everything in that bag before we left last time and zipped it up. And there's a big box of biscuits missing."

Nick shrugged, his interest waning. He wandered over to the huge open pantry, his nose wrinkling in distaste.

Jordan nearly smiled. Rodent droppings, perhaps, or a corpse in one of the many mousetraps she'd set.

There were no cups in the sink. If there was an intruder, they were house proud. "I'm thinking of Letitia, the missing girl."

"More likely to be a hunter or tramper. This is on the Queen Charlotte Track, isn't it?"

The Queen Charlotte Track was one of New Zealand's most popular tourist destinations, a seventy kilometer walk through lush subtropical native bush, showcasing the tranquil and stunning scenery of the Marlborough Sounds. Many thousands took to the track all year around.

"The door was locked," Jordan pointed out, unconvinced. The house seemed secure downstairs, but perhaps someone could access one of the broken windows upstairs from the crumbling exterior fire escape. She tried to call Russ to see if the girl had returned home but there was still no cell phone reception, even on Nick's phone.

"Atmospheric conditions." He shrugged.

They decided to explore the grounds. After all, that's what they were there for. But now they had an additional purpose: looking for Letitia.

They wandered the expansive and overgrown grounds for the next few hours. Nick wasn't much of a gardener but even he could see that under the neglect, this was a pearl of a property. There were treasures everywhere. Human faces carved into punga fern trunks, hammocks entwined with ivy, perishing between their supports, stone seats set in the most glorious positions to catch the late sun over the web of waterways and forested cliffs.

Jordan spotted a plastic wrapper; the brand of biscuits that were supposed to be in the Tupperware container in the kitchen. "It could have been there for ages," Nick cautioned, not wanting to get her hopes up.

"Our Working Bee went through here with forks and bags, picking up all the rubbish."

Perched on the hill behind the lodge was an old rickety chicken coop, the straw molding and smelly. And there was the empty Tupperware container, sitting in the corner.

"It *must* be Letitia."

Although Nick was skeptical, he accompanied her, clambering around the steep slopes and thick scrub high above the house, calling the girl's name.

No one answered their calls. Finally, Jordan looked at her watch and gasped with dismay. "Are we going to get home before dark?" He'd told her it was a condition of the charter that the boat be moored after dark.

"If you really think she's around here somewhere, then we'd best stay and have another look in the morning," Nick said casually as they started down the hill. "Besides, I hired the boat for two days."

Jordan stopped abruptly and turned her head. "Two days?"

Nick gazed at her unrepentant. Surely she didn't think this was just about sex, did she? His plan was to get her to himself for a while, away from the hotel room and the constant worry of discovery. He wanted to see if they clicked outside of the bedroom as well as they did in.

Anyway, this wasn't his fault. If she hadn't been adamant her runaway was here, they could have started for home two hours ago.

Jordan turned fully to face him, something close to

a pout on her lovely mouth. "And if I have plans for the evening?"

"Then he's going to be disappointed," he said evenly, absorbing the jolt he always got when she looked at him face on and close. The shape of her brows provided a perfect frame for those gorgeous almond-shaped blue eyes. Her luscious mouth with the prominent bow in the center just begged to be kissed. Beauty was in the eye of the beholder, he knew, and for Nick, he could never tire of looking at her face.

His body, too, rarely escaped the knowledge without a reaction of some kind. His mouth dried, his stomach muscles tensed. Every nerve ending sent an "I want" message to his brain.

"I didn't bring anything with me," she said curtly. "Clothes. Toothbrush."

"There are spare toiletries on board. As for clothes…" His gaze swept over her white top and long white shorts and sneakers. It was too late for them, streaked with dirt and plant matter. His own weren't much better. "I think there are robes in the bathrooms," he said innocently. Clothes were optional for what he had in mind…

Her eyes narrowed as if she read the path of his thoughts. "Well, that's worked out nicely for you, hasn't it?"

She was right, it had all worked out perfectly. The missing girl situation was an unexpected stroke of luck.

Still, he didn't want her sulking all night. "We'd have finished exploring the gardens two hours ago—plenty of time to make it home before dark—if we weren't looking for your friend," he reminded her. "Jordan, you have options. There's enough food and wine for dinner, I think. And there are two cabins on board, as I'm sure you noticed."

Nick wanted this chance for her to get to know him. It would take a major leap of trust for her to consider a public relationship with him while her father was ill. But if she thought he was really into her…Randall and Syrius had to be persuaded that further offenses would hurt their children.

As he watched her struggle with the desire to keep a cool distance between them, Nick knew he was getting under her skin. She could dictate the time frame and boundaries—to a point—but he would use the irresistible sexual connection between them to achieve his goal.

Nine

They searched the house once more, then locked up and walked back down the jetty to the boat. Jordan rubbed her arms briskly. "I hate to think about her all alone out here."

"If she's here, she'll know we're looking for her," Nick reassured her. They'd yelled themselves hoarse. "She'll come down to the boat when she gets cold or hungry."

Together they prepared a salad and the leftovers of their lunch. Nick had brought pre-baked rolls which they warmed up in the small oven in the galley. He opened the wine, his eyes following Jordan as she moved around setting utensils and crockery on the table, lighting candles. He wanted her more with each passing second, but tonight was going to be her call all the way.

The meal was simple, enhanced by the wine and the candles she'd lit. The reheated blackberry tart tasted even better than at lunch. They got through it all with an easy rapport, the wine mellowing her initial reticence.

"This is a novel experience," he commented as they finished. "Sitting across a table from you, eating and talking."

"We did that at lunchtime," she reminded him.

Nick pushed his dessert plate aside. "Will your father be in court on Monday?"

"If the doctor is happy." Jordan paused then rolled her eyes resignedly. "I spoke to him yesterday and he was looking forward to it."

"You know he's going to lose, don't you?" He wasn't being confrontational. There was little doubt about it.

Jordan nodded. "We've all told him but he's too stubborn to accept it."

"What's he like?"

She smiled fondly. "Impossible. Everything is black or white with him. He has an opinion on everything and I don't think he has ever been persuaded to change it, even in the face of irrefutable evidence."

"And you're crazy about him." Nick wondered if one day her eyes would mist with emotion for him.

"There's being crazy about him and there's driving me crazy."

Their eyes and smiles met and tangled but curiously, every time they did, Jordan would take a sip of wine. Her nervousness was unexpected.

She sat across from him in a decidedly grubby top,

her ponytail slipping and a twig in her hair. Used to seeing her light up the tabloids in designer clothing that flattered her magnificent body—or alternatively, naked on Fridays—Nick warmed at the sight of her. The sparkle in her eyes could be put down to the wine or candlelight, but he hoped he may have contributed there in some small way.

Operation Jordan was under way. "It must have been unreal growing up in that mansion as an only child." The Lake mansion in Kelburn was infamous for its grandeur.

Jordan relaxed back into her seat. "I think there was a friend roster. I don't recall being lonely at all."

"Spoiled rotten," Nick grinned. "The biggest and best birthday parties…" The ostentatious celebrations were legendary in Wellington society.

"They were insane! Clowns, animals, costumes, so much cake and sweet stuff that we'd all get hyper…the tantrums when it was all over!" She gave a mock shudder. "My poor mother. I'd make myself physically sick with the excitement of it all!"

Jordan picked up her glass again. He was going to have to carry her to bed at this rate.

He stood, picked up the bottle and topped her glass off, smiling at her. While he was there, he pulled gently at the twig tangled in her hair, handed it to her and then went back to his seat.

"It's interesting," he said as he sat. "You have the whole world at your beck and call and yet you hide behind some foundation, too scared to show yourself.

You don't want anyone to know that you have values and talent."

"I know I have those," she said, lifting her shoulders in a careless shrug, "but it's the money that makes the difference, that differentiates me from anyone else."

Nick laughed. "I must be wearing rose-colored glasses then because from werc I sit, I see something else entirely."

Jordan didn't respond, toying with the twig he'd handed her.

But Nick was interested. She seemed to have everything a young woman could want. What was she afraid of? "Gorgeous," he began, smiling again when she frowned, "Talented as I can attest to, having seen some of your art…"

"Drawings," she interjected.

"Art," Nick went on, heedless. "Proactive—you're doing something that makes a difference to a lot of people."

"Lots of people do that…" She snapped the twig in half and laid it on the table, looking at it as if it personally offended her.

"Probably, but they don't hide it. Did I mention creative? That ball the other night was a work of art, if I'm any judge of things."

"You think putting on a party makes you an artist?" she asked innocently, but sarcasm laced her tone.

"Don't knock it. People go to college to learn that stuff. The skills required get you a diploma. You just get on with it and make it happen."

"Because of my money." She insisted, nodding vigorously. "Do you honestly think I would have put together that ball without my father's influence and contacts?"

She sat back as if she'd won the argument.

"The difference, Jordan, between you and most rich people is that you use your money, you do something useful with it."

"Oh, I've frittered away a lifetime of money, believe me."

"I believe you," he said, grining, "but take some credit for making up for it now."

"What was your childhood like?" she asked, twisting the stem of her glass, moving the focus from her.

"Pretty normal. School. Rugby. Sailing. A few family holidays."

"Were you close?"

Nick had no complaints about his upbringing. "Adam and I were—are—I suppose. Mom and Dad—we got on all right. They weren't very demonstrative and they were always so busy with their respective careers. Dad liked to pit me and Adam against each other all the time. Everything was always a competition." He rolled his eyes. "Still is, far as Dad's concerned."

"Who won?"

"It was about sixty-forty. I was bigger but preferred negotiation. Adam liked to pretend he was David to my Goliath."

Her smile faded as she gazed into his eyes over the candlelight. Nick nearly groaned aloud. She was killing him here, so damn beautiful, so desirable. The sexual chemistry between them was a palpable pull, one he wasn't used to tamping down. That was the main disadvantage of starting as they had started—having to exercise self-control.

But he had to, just for a while longer. Until she accepted that what they shared was worth the fire and brimstone their fathers would rain down on them.

The moment lay between them like a suffocating cloud of fizz-edged awareness, stretching for long seconds.

Finally she looked away, frowning. "I was trying to imagine you as a boy."

Yeah, right, Nick thought. She was wondering why he hadn't moved, leaped across the table, pushing and demanding as he usually did when she looked as him with naked desire in her eyes.

Your move, baby.

The silence lengthened as they stared at each other, rocking gently in the swell of the waves lapping the jetty.

What was the deal? Jordan wondered. Didn't he want her anymore?

Nick's smile was strained at the edges, his eyes feverish with want. She recognized that because she saw it every Friday when he opened the hotel door to her.

Yet he sat there, one hand spread on his thigh as he lounged in his seat, the other on the table. Looking at ease and yet ready to pounce.

Why wasn't he pouncing? He always made the moves. In the time it took for them tonight to prepare dinner, eat and then have a nice little chat, they would normally have made love two or three times.

Was it a test of some kind? Jordan shifted in her chair, a meter away from a man bristling with sexual tension and yet concealing it—not even that. Accepting it.

What was his game?

She stood abruptly, needing some space. "Do you mind if I take a shower?"

He moved his head from side to side, his eyes hooded.

Jordan made her way to the small bathroom off the second cabin. True to his word, there were unopened toiletries, toothbrushes in their wrappers and a stack of soft white towels on the vanity. She turned the shower on and scrutinized her grubby clothes. After clambering around a dusty house and up cliff and vale, the white lacy top was a shambles and the cutoffs weren't much better. She stripped and took the top and her panties into the steaming shower with her; the cutoffs wouldn't dry before morning.

The hot blast of water was bliss after a long day. She'd drunk too fast. Nervous. He made her nervous because he was different. Holding back, even though every look told her he wanted her. The only conclusion she could make was that he wanted her to make the moves. But why?

She turned and let the water pummel her back while squeezing shower soap through her clothing. It was all so confusing. At the ball, she'd told him it was over. Now she wished they could return to sex on Fridays, where they both knew where they stood. Two unattached people sharing an amazing attraction.

That reminded her of what he'd said at the ball. *"I want more."*

She turned off the shower and grabbed a towel. Did she want more? Of course she wanted more. The idea grew and grew until it pushed everything else out of her head. More with Nick than Friday afternoons. Dating Nick. Making love with him in her apartment, his house. Talking about their day. Making plans.

She had drunk too much to be thinking along these lines. The prudent thing to do in the circumstances was to poke her head back into the saloon, wish him good-night and go to bed—alone—in the second cabin.

She rubbed the steamed mirror with a corner of the towel. Looking at herself, her naked body, reminded her of when he'd made love to her in front of the mirror at the hotel. She could see him behind her, his dark hands on her white breasts, his face above hers, eyes holding hers fiercely, compelling her to watch…unmentionable pleasure coiling through her body as he moved inside her, came with her.

Jordan flushed bright red. God, she was hot for him. He was addictive. She craved him. And trying to deny the craving, she began to justify herself. It was she who'd said they weren't going to pick up where they left off. Her rules, she could break them. Going meekly off to bed alone was going along with him, changing the direction of what was a great sexual relationship.

The best solution was to go out there and seduce him. Remind him that they were about sex. Remind him how good they were at it. Keep things on the only level she was prepared to contemplate. Because she didn't want to risk her heart, which she feared was already attached.

She dried herself, brushed her teeth and her hair, and hung her panties and top over the towel rail to dry. Then she went out to seduce Nick Thorne before he turned her head with his charm and his patience and his tests.

Jordan walked out into the stateroom wearing only a towel. He lifted his head and watched her approach, his eyes gleaming. She tried to pretend this was the Presidential Suite at the hotel on a Friday afternoon. She'd done this a dozen times…

He'd cleared the table and now sat on the sofa, holding his glass. "Shall I find you a robe?"

Jordan shook her head, confusion welling up again. Why wouldn't he just stand and take charge? Tear the towel off, put his hands on her…

"Would you like coffee?" His voice was so soft that she strained to hear him.

"Maybe later," she said huskily, moving closer. Her bare legs were just inches from where his stretched out in front of him.

"You want me, Nick?"

He moistened his lips. "You've never asked me that before."

"I've never had to."

He laid his head back on the back of the couch, watching her inscrutably. Never had she known him to exhibit so much restraint. Admirable restraint, considering the impressive bulge at the apex of his trousers.

Goose bumps rose on her arms and she shivered, the tension coiling up her insides.

"Remember our first time?" he asked suddenly, his

voice low and hard. "You trembled then, too, just like now. Were you nervous?"

She exhaled in a rush. "Just like now."

She hadn't meant to admit that.

She took a tentative step closer.

"Why?"

There was nothing in his upturned face she could read, no clue as to what he was thinking. "Because I was overwhelmed."

The back of her neck—her whole back prickled like freezer burn.

"And now?"

"Because I don't know what you want anymore." Jordan hadn't intended to say that either. But she couldn't think with his impenetrable eyes boring into her.

"I told you the other night," Nick said quietly. "I. Want. More."

Someone had switched scripts. She suddenly felt all at sea again—she nearly snorted but it wasn't funny. Desperate to regain the lead—wasn't that what he wanted?— she slipped her fingers between the folds of the towel, under the knot, peeling the sides back a little, slowly revealing what was underneath. "You can have everything."

Nick smiled then, as if to himself. "Oh, I intend to."

It sounded like a threat.

Firmly pushing her worries aside, she stepped inside his legs and sank down onto her knees before him. That got a result. Quickening breath, eyes widening and alert. The column of his throat bobbed in a hard swallow. *Got your attention now,* she thought.

She reached out and spread her hand on his groin, soaking up the heat that radiated out. The answering surge of welcome under her palm made her smile and she pressed down gently. "You want this?"

His chin dropped down to his chest. Nick always liked to watch.

"You know what I want."

She bent to her task, brushing off the niggling unease about his unaccustomed passivity, the way he answered her every question with a variation of "I want more." His arms were still, hands on his thighs, when usually he moved, directed, arranged her to his satisfaction.

Thankfully as she unzipped him, her natural instincts took over. Jordan was enthralled, turned on beyond belief. She didn't need to ask again. She knew by the fire in his eyes. The way the veins on his hands stood out, even though they appeared to be relaxed. The muscles in his upper thighs tightened with each swirl of her tongue around his swollen flesh.

She knew exactly what he wanted when she felt his hands in her hair, firmly holding her in place while he moved under her.

But then someone changed the script again. His hands tightened in her hair and he lifted her head and pulled her up over him.

Nick had never stopped her before.

It cost him. The strain on his face, a single bead of sweat crawling down his temple, told of the cost. He framed her face with his hands and kissed her, deeper and deeper, and it was somehow more intimate than her ministrations a minute ago. She felt heavy, dragged down by desire.

They kissed and kissed, cupping each other's faces, learning the shapes of their cheekbones and skulls, fingers lacing through hair. There seemed to be no urgency and neither of them closed their eyes. To Jordan, the sight of him was just so good.

His hands slid inside the still-knotted towel, stroked slowly down her body, massaging gently while they kissed. Lying on top of him, feeling him hard and wanting underneath her, she drowned in pleasure.

Maybe she'd begun by seducing him, showing him how sexy he made her feel, teasing him until he begged. But he was involved now, involving her completely, taking her under. She needed skin and squirmed to get her arms down, trying to get to his buttons. There was too much between them. She fumbled and tugged and got his shirt undone so at least she could feel his warm skin on her front, the hairs on his chest causing fantastic friction on her breasts.

Under her towel, he stroked and stroked, his hands questing and probing. She lay across him, lifting her hips. His fingers played her like music, inside and out, and she flowed into orgasm with blinding ignorance, not even realizing she was close. Her hands fisted, her knuckles pressing into his chest and for the first time since she'd walked out from the bathroom, she broke eye contact and sank into deep and shuddering satisfaction.

Soon, he slid out from under her, sitting her up, pulling her forward—this was more like it, she thought, taking charge, directing operations. All thought fled when he knelt in front of her and made love to her with his mouth.

Too sensitive to bear, she had nowhere to hide. Her hands plunged into his hair. She arched her back, fighting for breath that refused to come and then roller-coasted over her with a low keening sound that went on and on.

When it was over, she attempted to relax her stiff fingers from his hair, but it wasn't easy. "Yes," she said and her voice sounded a million miles away. The boat rocked gently on its mooring. "This. This is what I want."

Nick sat back and pulled his shirt over his head. Sated yet burning for more, she watched him strip and take care of protection. Then he pushed her down on the couch, moving purposefully over her and looked into her eyes.

"No," he said, matter-of-factly. "It's not all you want." He nuzzled her lips before raising his head again, his gaze triumphant.

She felt his tip nudge her, realized he was right.

"You just don't know it yet," he said in a voice that told her with certainty that the lesson was about to begin.

Her eyes flew wide as his hands moved up her forearms, pushing her arms above her head, lacing their fingers together.

She was tired of wondering and wanting. She just wanted him inside her. "Nick…"

He obliged. The blistering invasion, slow and strong, deep and relentless, filled her so utterly it forced the air from her lungs. He stilled, tense as a board, his hands pressing hers down into the sofa, forcing her to look at him. They gazed at each other for long seconds while he pulsed inside her, and Jordan understood. Never again could she not take this seriously. Never again could she think it was just sex.

Not just sex. Sex of the mind and body and soul. As he moved, slowly withdrawing and then sliding home again, imprisoning her eyes, she forgot everything but the wonderful warm rush of emotion that accompanied this act, this time.

Countless Fridays, countless orgasms, but never a bond so deep before. It shone from his eyes, so strong she turned her head but he wouldn't let her. It pumped through his body till she felt it in her womb and in the pulse beating through his fingers as they gripped hers. *I want more,* his eyes said as he moved, each deep thrust shattering her fears. "More," she answered him, exhilaration bursting through when he smiled down, warming her heart.

Drunk on it, she wrapped her legs around his waist as he plunged with consuming intent. The pace and intensity got crazy, the flashpoint poised, hissing, and then boiled over in a rush. He choked out her name once as she moaned her satisfaction. And she knew nothing could ever be desired again. The rush slowly ebbed. The thud of their calming breath and the occasional sound of small waves lapping the hull was all she could hear.

Still looking into her eyes, Nick slid his arms around her and held her, for the first time ever.

Ten

Jordan awoke slowly, in her customary manner. It took a few seconds to realize she wasn't alone, quite a few more to replay the night's events in her mind and think about how she felt, waking next to Nick.

They'd enjoyed many sexual adventures in the past, but last night easily qualified as the best night of her life. It was almost like a real date, spending the day together, making dinner together, talking. And then, the most emotionally-charged lovemaking she'd ever experienced. How could she even think of holding anything back? He wouldn't let her.

Nick stirred behind her with a contented growl. Jordan sighed, her erotic memories scattering. Moving an inch at a time, she began to edge toward the side of the bed but hadn't gotten far when his warm arm clamped around her middle.

"Morning," he mumbled.

Jordan mumbled a similar response.

"Where do you think you're going?" He shifted closer, his big warm body enfolding her back like a heated cloak.

She half-turned, craning her neck to see him. "Bathroom. I need to clean my teeth."

Nick lifted up on one elbow, blinking owlishly.

She squeezed her eyes shut. "You're not allowed to look at me until I've got my face on."

He tapped her on the nose until she looked at him. "I've seen you with the green goop, remember?"

Oh, God, how could she forget?

"You, Jordan Lake," he said gallantly, "don't need makeup to look beautiful."

She smiled into his eyes, thinking she could get used to waking up next to a sleepy, unshaven, tousled man whispering sweet nothings in her ear. But within seconds, his gaze sharpened and flared with heat. He shifted his body, imprisoning her under him and she felt his arousal, thick and hot against her thigh. The messages to her brain had nothing to do with vanity now.

How long before this wanes? she wondered, running her hands over his long, broad back and thickly-muscled arms? With one look, like the flick of a switch, he turned her on instantly. Her body responded, quickening, moistening. Would the time come soon when they could look at each other and resist succumbing to the most urgent and primitive desire?

Nick's hand slid under the small of her back, lifting and angling her hips, then bent and sipped at the corners of her mouth. She kissed back and decided to enjoy it while it lasted. "While we can both still walk," she murmured against his chin. He pulled back an inch, his eyes questioning. In response, she hugged him tighter, welcoming his advance, his slow, slick invasion. Welcoming him home.

An hour later, she was in the galley making coffee when she heard strange noises outside. Peeking out the porthole window, she saw her runaway sitting on the wooden jetty, hugging her knees to her chest and sniffing loudly.

"Letitia!" Jordan rushed out and sank down beside her. The poor girl sobbed with relief, nearly hysterical with nerves and cold. She wore scruffy dungarees, sneakers with no socks and only a thin hoodie.

Nick responded to her calls and they helped the teen aboard and wrapped her up in a duvet. It may have been late spring, but the sun hadn't made it over the valley yet and the air was crisp and cool. Nick set about making breakfast while Jordan sat with the girl, rubbing her frozen hands between hers.

Letitia had sneaked under the tarpaulin of a utility as it boarded the inter-island ferry in Wellington. She then walked from Picton to Anakiwa and linked up with the Queen Charlotte Track to get here, which had taken "at least a whole day." She'd eaten the biscuits and made cups of black tea from the provisions the Working Bee left in the old lodge kitchen. But the cold was her enemy.

"There was nothing to sleep in, not even any old curtains."

The Working Bee had disposed of all the moldy old drapes that had hung in the lodge for decades.

When Nick and Jordan docked, the girl hid, determined not to be discovered, but another night alone in the cold had changed her mind.

"Why didn't you answer our calls? You must have heard us." It occurred to Jordan that while she and Nick were making love here on the boat last night, this poor girl was frozen and alone. "You should have come to the jetty and called me."

Letitia wolfed down eggs and toast like she hadn't eaten in a week. Then Jordan tucked her up in the bed in the second cabin. "Poor kid," she said to Nick as they prepared to set off back to Wellington. "She just wants some attention. She's the youngest of six. Her older brothers are in and out of jail and her sister has leukemia. Her parents spend all their time either at the hospital or bailing the boys out. No one has time for Letitia."

Jordan couldn't comprehend that, coming from a one-child family, the apple of her parents' eye. She resolved to keep a much closer eye on the girl from now on.

"Told you so," Nick said lightly.

"What?"

"Sounds to me like that family needs a decent holiday, spend some quality time with their kids…somewhere nice and remote with fishing and tramping…"

Jordan felt her face color in pleased embarrassment.

He liked her idea after all. That meant a lot, even though it was no longer hers to develop.

They made good time on another amazingly calm day. After a couple of hours, Letitia appeared and helped Jordan cobble together enough leftovers to make some sandwiches. Then they sat out of the sun in the state-room, leaving Nick on deck. Since neither had gotten much sleep the night before, it wasn't long before they stretched out on the sofas and their chatting dwindled to sleepy sighs.

Jordan awoke an hour later and the city of Wellington sprawled on the horizon. Letitia was on deck, steering the powerful boat, supervised by Nick. Jordan smiled at the nice picture the two of them made. It was kind of Nick to spend time connecting with the troubled teen.

"Letitia is going to talk to Russ about letting me join the Outreach team," Nick told her, as if it was something he'd always wanted to do. Jordan grinned, thinking if only he knew what he was getting himself into.

"Nick knows some people at the Marina," Letitia enthused, "and he's going to speak to them about teaching us water sports."

"I believe I said water safety," Nick cut in, reaching across her to nudge the wheel slightly.

Jordan had never seen him so relaxed and at ease. His teeth gleamed in his tanned face and his eyes shone when they looked at her. He was so breathtakingly handsome. She imagined drawing a frame around him, depicting with fine detail everything a man should look like, should be.

As she watched him smile and tease, and the young girl's shining face as she bantered with her new hero, something warm and heady washed over Jordan, through her. The cautionary walls she'd erected to protect herself melted and seeped away. Her heart began to beat, slow and strong, so strong she could feel it in her fingertips. A giddy feeling made her wobble on her seat and grab the side.

She loved him. It was as clear and shining and joyful as Christmas. She loved him and wanted him, and all the problems that would entail were as far away as the shoreline. Still there, still beckoning, but with a lower level of importance.

Nick said something to her and she was so distracted with her newfound knowledge, she had to ask him to repeat it. He reached out and ruffled her hair and she felt his hand there for long seconds after he'd taken it away, caressing, caring, branding her as his.

Once ashore, they reunited Letitia with her grateful parents and then Nick drove Jordan home. Her stomach growled as they entered her apartment, reminding her that the meager sandwich she'd had at lunch was many hours ago. "Would you like to stay for…"

"I thought you'd never ask," Nick growled, pushing her up against the wall in the passageway. Her bag hit the deck, her clothes were roughly pushed aside. He ravaged her mouth and she soared so high, so quickly as he took her against the wall. They didn't even make the bedroom.

Nick stayed the night, waking her early to make love once more before he had to go to the office. Jordan linked her arms around his neck as he kissed her goodbye. "Aren't you forgetting something?"

He smiled and leaned forward to sear her with another kiss.

"The sales agreement?" she laughed.

"Ah." He nodded. "I'll have my lawyer witness it."

"What are you going to do with it?" Jordan asked, leaning back on her pillows, looking like Aphrodite.

"I haven't decided yet," he told her. "Maybe I'll turn it into an exclusive art gallery and exhibit some starving but brilliant artist who's got a bunch of insecurities about her work."

Her eyes shone with amusement.

"And people will come from miles around," he continued, enjoying himself, "and she'll be famous the world over."

Jordan chuckled. "Except that no one will ever know because the gallery is so exclusive, no one can find it."

"Which will add greatly to her fame, in turn, making her forever grateful to me."

Nick found he liked this, waking with someone, sex, chatter and banter before getting on with the day. The prospect of making it a permanent arrangement entered his mind. It was a win-win, as far as he was concerned. He enjoyed her company, and the sex was beyond incredible.

"Did you get around to having plans drawn up for the refurbishment?"

"As a matter of fact, I did," she said, her eyes shining.

"Give me a look at them sometime."

Jordan kissed him fervently and asked if she'd see him Friday.

Nick groaned. "Friday is eons away. I have to go to Sydney on Wednesday for a meeting, but I'll be back late Thursday." He lifted a strand of her hair, ran it slowly through his fingers. "You'll be in court today, right?"

Jordan inhaled, her expression becoming cautious. "Nick…"

He knew what she was going to say: Don't let anyone know that they were together. Not that they'd articulated anything yet… "Don't worry," he reassured her, bending for one last taste of her lips. "We'll talk about it later."

He drove to his apartment, struggling to keep the smile off his face, an alien concept to his facial muscles, he was sure. This was a watershed weekend, one which had gone exactly to plan. She was crazy about him, he saw it in her face every time she looked at him. And that was just fine by Nick. Things were moving along smoothly and he was enjoying the ride.

He showered, changed and headed in to the office, looking forward to seeing her in court in an hour or so. He wondered if anyone would guess they'd spent the weekend together, if something would show in the way he looked at her.

"I'll be back after lunch—probably," Nick told Jasmine as he left for court. Adam and Randall had gone on ahead after the court clerk had called to confirm that Syrius was fit to attend.

Leaving the office building, he noticed an eye-catching pale blue limousine parked outside. He noticed it because he'd seen it before somewhere. The driver leaned against the car but straightened when he saw him and tapped on the back window, then gestured for Nick to approach. He did so, frowning.

The back window slid down. "Hello Nick," Elanor Lake said pleasantly. "May I have a few minutes of your time?"

After a moment's hesitation, Nick got into the limo and sat opposite her, his mind racing.

Jordan definitely got her looks from her mother. Soft golden hair clouded around Elanor's face. Her skin was creamy and smooth, her clothes elegant. She regarded him in a friendly, frank manner. The driver remained outside and Elanor pressed the window control closed.

"What can I do for you, Mrs. Lake?"

"It's Elanor," she said. "And I want you to stop seeing my daughter."

He saw from her demeanor that there was no point denying it. "I would gladly do almost anything you asked of me," he said sincerely, a slight inflection on the word you; his father's guilt ran deep. "But not that."

Her facial muscles tightened and she studied him at length. "This has gone further than I thought," she said finally.

Nick wondered if it was she monitoring her daughter's movements.

"I've always liked you, Nick. I've watched you grow, followed your career. You're well known for being straight. Responsible."

He inclined his head. Her approval of him could be

helpful in the bun fight that would ensue when Syrius found out.

Elanor sat back clasping her hands in her lap. "My husband has heart disease. It's quite serious. If he finds out about this—affair—it will possibly kill him. If it doesn't kill him straight off, then he will take a gun and shoot you."

Nick pretended to give it due consideration, allowing three heartbeats to go by. "I'll take my chances, but thank you for the warning."

"You're not listening. I believe you are an honorable man. Your mother was my best friend for many years. We resumed our friendship in secret a couple of years before she died."

Nick remembered then that's where he'd seen the limo. At the cemetery on the day of his mother's funeral. The windows were tinted and he couldn't identify the occupant. The car left before the end of the interment.

"Your mother was incredibly proud of you. She said you were honest and fair-minded. Very strong without the headstrong traits of your brother. She said you could always be relied upon to do exactly the right thing."

It seemed to Nick she enunciated every syllable with great care—*do exactly the right thing*. He continued watching her steadily, waiting for her to get to the point. His family owed her a hearing.

"Nick, I've watched my husband struggle over the years to try to modify his personality, and fail to do so. I've watched him have affairs and that's all right because I can't give him what he needs, and he always comes home to me. He treats me with the utmost care and allows me my dignity by being discreet. He loves me." Elanor leaned forward, watching his face intently. "But that love pales in comparison to what he feels for his daughter. Syrius loves Jordan more than his own life."

Nick grappled with some residual familial guilt that had unfairly passed down from his father. He and Jordan should never have started...it was self-indulgent and irresponsible. But it was too late now. "Elanor, I am sorry for what my father did to you. He is sorry for what he did to you. But it's unfair to expect Jordan and me to take the rap for past mistakes."

Her eyes were bright with sharp emotion. "I lost everything in that accident. My unborn son, only three weeks from birth. The use of my legs when my greatest passion—and my career—was dancing."

Nick flinched and swallowed to clear the ball of sympathy that had closed his throat.

Elanor saw it and her mouth thinned. "Syrius will never accept this relationship, do you understand?" She raised her hand, pointing at him. "Your father took his son. He would die rather than let a Thorne have his daughter."

Nick felt the blood drain from his face. He wanted to look away but a twisted respect forced him to keep eye contact.

Elanor wasn't finished. "I will lose everything. Again. Jordan will never be able to look at you without seeing the tragedy of what will confront her beloved father, who will be either dead or in prison. Your own father will probably cut you off."

He could only stare at her. For the first time, he began to truly understand the magnitude of the battle ahead.

"And all for a sordid turn between the sheets once a week. Something you could get from anyone."

Nick inhaled. He wasn't having that. "I care for her. I believe she cares for me." He knew she did.

A ghost of a smile softened her lips for a second. "Jordan falls in and out of love every other week."

He wouldn't dignify that with a response.

Now her eyes implored him. "I beg you, Nick, on your mother's love for me, do the right thing."

He knew his facial expression hadn't changed, outwardly resolute, but it was a different story inside. Emotions that he wasn't accustomed to slammed him, one after the other. Pity for the woman in front of him. Injustice that he and Jordan should pay the price for their fathers' sins. And anger that Elanor obviously had no intention of broaching the subject with her daughter. That meant it was up to him. If he agreed to her demands, if he agreed to finish it, he was the bad guy.

He couldn't give her what she wanted. Not yet, not without a fight. Hadn't his mother been on the mark? Want something you shouldn't. Take something you have no right to. He raised his chin. "I'll talk to Jordan. *We'll* decide."

He reached for the door handle but she laid her hand flat on his arm. When he looked back, the respectful demeanor of a minute ago had lapsed into ominous regret.

"Then you leave me no choice but to take this information to your father."

Nick settled back in the seat, rallying for another blow. Randall would hate it, there was no doubt about that. He needed to prepare the ground first.

"Nick," Elanor said quietly, "you've worked hard to get where you are, yet still your father stalls about naming you as his successor." She paused, building the tension. "You being involved with the daughter of his most bitter enemy would be a big strike against you, wouldn't it? He'd wonder about your loyalty."

Nick said nothing but silently agreed. Loyalty was a favorite catch phrase of Randall's.

"One strike against you in this situation is bad enough. Two might just tip the balance."

Nick frowned. What did she mean? A fatalistic sense of foreboding stabbed him at the sympathy in Elanor Lake's eyes.

"What's the other?"

"You're not his natural son, Nick," she said quietly. "You're not even legally adopted."

Eleven

Nick drove straight home after leaving Elanor's car and took his birth certificate from the safe. His mind soared with relief. She was lying. It was a bare-faced lie by a bitter woman intent on having her own way. Obviously Syrius didn't hold all the vindictive cards in his family.

But still, something inside him continued to niggle. He drove to his parents' house and asked the housekeeper where the family photos were stored. It was a standing family joke that if it moved, his mother photographed it. Nick spent hours poring through boxes and albums, searching out familial similarities. Nothing conclusive came of it. He was bigger, broader than his brother. His facial features were thicker than either of his parents, while Adam bore a striking resemblance to his mother. Coloring and eyes were similar enough to all members of the family to reassure him.

His scant relief receded when he opened a pack marked Pregnancy and flicked through tens of snaps of his mother during pregnancy but they were all dated 1979. Adam's year of birth, not his. Feverishly, Nick went through the rest of the box but was unable to find one picture of his mother pregnant in 1975.

He drove back to the office, told Jasmine he was not to be disturbed and sat there for the rest of the day, building up a good head of steam.

Had they treated him differently? He racked his brain for childhood memories. Nick was the eldest, mature beyond his years so he got lumbered with most of the chores and was expected to keep an eye on his younger brother. Elder kids always thought their younger siblings were spoiled and he was no exception. But one thing about Adam, he followed Nick around everywhere, "helping" him, he'd say.

The bond was real between the brothers, but he wondered about his parents. They weren't the hands-on parents of modern times because they'd always put career first. Randall worked tirelessly building up his financial business while Melanie ran her dance studio six days a week. Public—or even private—displays of affection were rare.

He checked his watch for the umpteenth time. This rated as the longest day of his life. No matter how often he cautioned himself not to jump to conclusions, something told him Elanor had spoken the truth. Recent events backed it up. His mother leaving the share package to Adam, her *natural born son*. His father wanting Adam, his *natural born son*, to run the company.

The moment Randall returned from the court, Nick marched into his office, threw the birth certificate on his desk and demanded the truth. Randall insisted on knowing who he'd been talking to; when Nick told him, he blanched and did not deny it. And Nick faced the fact that up until now, his whole life had been a sham.

Two years after their marriage, the Thornes were told that they could never have children. Coming on the heels of the accident and Syrius's decree that banned Melanie from seeing his wife, Nick's mother fell into a state of deep depression. Randall, acutely aware of his business reputation, ensconced her in a luxury villa in one of Sydney's beach suburbs and commuted between Wellington and Sydney every other week.

Deeply depressed and lonely, his wife befriended a pregnant and unmarried housemaid. The next thing Randall knew, they had arranged an illegal adoption. Much money passed hands. Melanie even procured a forged birth certificate naming the Thornes as parents. Nearly a year after she'd left, Melanie returned to New Zealand with Nick in her arms. The couple maintained that he was their own miracle child. Four years later, against all odds, Melanie became pregnant with Adam.

"Did you know about this?" Nick asked Adam, who'd unwittingly walked into the tense confrontation.

"God's truth, I didn't," Adam assured him. "But it doesn't make a scrap of difference. You're my brother, Nick."

"Nor to me," his father said shakily. "Blood or not, you're my son."

"I want details," Nick declared. "Names, dates..."

"What's the point, Nick? We raised you as a Thorne, loved you from day one. Why rake it all up again?"

"Afraid you'll go to prison for fraud, not to mention buying a baby?" Nick looked at him scathingly, then immediately felt wretched. He softened his tone. "I'm going to Sydney tonight rather than Wednesday. I don't know when I'll be back. I need the address of the villa, her name, her lover—my father's—name, the dates she worked there..."

He wondered if his birth parents had ever contacted the Thornes again. Had they ever wanted to see him, or was it all about the money? Nick wondered what he was worth. "I see now why you want Adam to run the company, not me."

He heard Adam's sharp, indrawn breath, but his eyes were on his father's pale face.

"That's not true," Randall's voice implored him. "Not just Adam, not just you. Both of you."

Nick saw a world of fear in Randall's eyes. How long had he worried over this day?

Even so, he couldn't bring himself to say "Dad." Not yet.

"Nick, my feelings remain the same in regard to the company—and you." Adam lounged in his chair, seemingly relaxed but his expression was bleak, his face as pale as his father's.

Nick stood abruptly, knowing he had to get home and pack for the flight he'd booked earlier. "I'll be leaving for the airport in about two hours. Call me with those details."

"I'll come with you," Adam said quickly, rising.

Nick stopped and turned to face his brother.

Not his brother. Not even his legal adoptive brother… "This is something you can't help me with…"

"But…" Adam looked as stunned as Nick felt and it hit him a vicious blow. They were close, always had been. They even looked like each other. God's little joke… All these years, they'd believed in that blood bond, enjoyed each other's company, missed each other when they were apart. Would this revelation dent or change their relationship? How could it not?

Nick reached out and patted Adam awkwardly on the arm. "Thanks anyway, but I'd prefer to do this on my own."

Jordan left the courtroom on Monday, disconcerted about Nick's absence. When he didn't show up for the rest of the week, she began to worry. Which days had he said he'd be away? She'd been half asleep when he'd kissed her goodbye.

Calling his office was out and he didn't answer his cell phone. Not wanting to be labeled a nag, she decided against leaving a message but her unease grew with each passing day.

When he stood her up at the hotel on Friday, her

miserable confusion gave way to anger. Was he just playing with her? Surely she wasn't alone in thinking they'd forged new ground last weekend in the Sounds.

Heedless of being recognized, she inquired about the booking. "I'm sorry, the booking we have for Room 812 was cancelled on Monday," the receptionist said and looked at her with such pity that Jordan hurried out without another word, feeling quite ill.

Come to think of it, she'd felt unwell yesterday, too, but passed it off as nerves. A fleeting thought that she might be pregnant crossed her mind but she dismissed that. Nick always used protection, even though she was on the pill.

That day, she felt entitled to leave a message on his voicemail and his house phone, which also went unanswered. And even though she felt nauseous and lonely, she forced herself to go out that night to a film premiere with two friends. They bumped into Jason Cook and went clubbing. When Nick didn't call over the rest of the weekend, even after she'd left several more messages, she went out both nights and made sure she was photographed.

The trial entered its expected last week, but still Nick didn't show and her phone remained silent. Oh, why had she allowed herself to hope, to believe that she was enough for him? She would have been happy, she *was* happy knowing it was just sex, until he made her fall in love with him.

Forget him! She called Jason and a few of the party hounds she used to spend time with. It was easy to slip right back into party mode, like the Jordan of old. Club openings, premieres, she attended every glitzy occasion she could think of to court the press. Even the tummy bug that lingered didn't stop her, although she was unable to stomach alcohol. Nick Thorne had blown it, she thought angrily. No one rejected Jordan Lake! She intended to make him so jealous he'd come crawling and then, she'd kick him aside like a dog.

Only he didn't come crawling. Jordan played at being the life of the party because she dreaded going to bed. The only way she could contain the pain slicing her up inside was to curl into a ball, rocking and hugging herself hard enough to bruise her flesh. In this bed, he had made love to her, had kissed her goodbye for the last time. Unshed tears dogged her day and night, making her eyes and throat ache. What was so wrong with her that he didn't want her anymore?

One night in a crowded club, someone tapped her on the shoulder and she turned to find Adam Thorne smiling down at her.

"Are you going to have me thrown out of here as well?" he asked jovially.

Jordan responded to his friendly manner like a lifeline. They'd never had an official introduction so they remedied that now. Her friends raised their brows and whispered about how hot he was. Adam was considered one of the most eligible bachelors in the city. But she could see little of Nick in his face. There was no magic there.

She longed to ask about him but knew the hurt was

too close. Her heart may just break and bleed all over the floor. No one must see how empty and sad and hurt she was.

Adam stood behind her chair, bending his head to hear over the music. They chatted for some time about the case and their impossible fathers. "You know, I told Nick the best way to end this stupid feud is to hook up with you."

The knife in her heart twisted painfully but she managed to keep some semblance of a smile, she hoped. "Really? When?"

"When the trial started." Adam sent a huge smile of welcome to a pretty woman who'd just entered the club. Jordan recognized her as Nick's secretary.

"Nick wants to run Thorne's," Adam said distractedly. "He can't do that while the old man is around, and the old man is so busy chasing your old man around a courtroom, he won't retire."

"And what did Nick say?" she asked faintly, chewing on the straw of her drink.

Adam straightened, still looking at the woman. "Oh, Nick's way too clever to take my advice. It was nice meeting you at last, Jordan Lake. See you in court." He paused and winked at her. "I've always wanted to say that."

Jordan sat for at least a minute with the same stupid, dazed smile on her mouth, trying to make sense of it. He had a plan? A sick dread blanketed down over the misery of unrequited love in her heart.

Was it right from the start? she thought dazedly—no, Adam had said the start of the trial. That was about the time things changed between them. He'd started bringing gifts and acting jealous.

She tried to breathe but the ache inside constricted her chest. Dear God, he'd planned it all along. He didn't want her. This wasn't about them. It was a cold, calculated plan to get her to fall in love with him and realize his ambitions.

The reality twisted the knife some more, causing bile to rush to her throat. She rushed to the bathroom where she was violently sick. Someone helped her out of the club and into a cab. And the tabloids faithfully reported her incapacity the next day.

"You're certainly burning the candle at both ends, dear," her mother commented. "What on earth were you drinking?"

"I hadn't had anything," Jordan said defensively. Her mother had a knack of drawing her secrets to the fore. Her broken heart was one secret she wouldn't discuss, not with her mother or anyone else. She couldn't bear the humiliation. "I have a bug, that's all."

By day, she sat in court, staring stiffly ahead, acutely aware of the empty space across the aisle. After her fifth consecutive night out, she was exhausted and low as she could ever remember feeling. The lack of sleep and this interminable tummy bug had her head spinning, so on Wednesday night, she bought a home pregnancy test. It was just a precaution. She was ninety-nine percent certain she wasn't pregnant; surely she'd feel something—a bond, a connection—instead of just miserable and confused and god-awful sick.

The digital display on the stick flashed *Pregnant.*
No, no, no. This couldn't be happening.

When was her last period? Things had been so up in
the air lately. Working bees, nosy newspapers, charity
balls. Nick. Taking a deep breath, churning up with
nerves, she took the second stick from the box.

She was late to court on Thursday. Her heels seemed
inordinately loud on the wooden floor as she entered.
Heads turned in the gallery and the judge gave her a
baleful look. "Sorry," she whispered loudly.

And then she saw. He turned his head and looked
straight at her, his expression cold. Scathing.

Jordan sat shakily, absorbing the rush of elation that
always came with seeing his face. The emptiness inside
her began to fill…but then his icy expression filtered
through her joy.

Her stomach churned. What gave him the right to
look at her like that? It was she who should feel ag-
grieved. He'd used and discarded her without so much
as a word.

You have to tell him.

"Not yet," she whispered. Her mother turned and
looked at her, eyes full of concern. Jordan could only
shake her head mutely.

Not yet. Home pregnancy tests were not foolproof.
She would say nothing until she had seen a doctor.
Which doctor? She couldn't rely on the discretion of the
Elpis Clinic doctors—they were all volunteers.

He'd think she'd trapped him. Worse, he'd question

whether he was the father. So many morbid thoughts surged through her brain, even as common sense told her Nick was a decent, responsible man. He'd do the right thing by her.

It was the longest morning of her life. She made it until lunchtime, then bolted for the bathroom, throwing up for the third time that week.

When she came out, Nick was about to descend the steps outside, alone. Jordan felt like death but she couldn't cope with the misery any longer. Forcing herself to stop shaking, she filled her heart with steely determination.

He'd shoved his hands in his pockets and his head was bowed. For a brief moment, as she approached, she thought he looked unhappy. But then all the tortured hours of the last week or so swamped her. He'd made her feel a failure as a woman, a lover, a friend. She wasn't about to let him off scot free. She strode up behind him, grasping his arm firmly. "I want to talk to you."

As he swung around to face her, just for a second, she saw something so uplifting, so eager in his face, as if he was glad to see her. But then the shutters came down like the night. His cold, closed expression slayed her.

This wasn't the man she knew—*thought* she knew. This was someone else entirely. She almost quailed before him and if she hadn't just lost her breakfast, that would have been a real possibility.

Nick glanced around quickly. "This isn't the time or…"

"Well, if you'd returned my calls…" Jordan felt like she was swimming in treacle. But then he grasped her arm and pulled her around the side of the building, out of sight of the trickle of people emerging from the court.

"I'm surprised you could drag yourself out of bed this morning—whose bed was it today? Do you even remember?"

Oh, that was a slap in the face. Okay, she had played the party girl this week but that was down to him.

She pried her arm out of his grasp. "What *is* it with you?" she demanded. "All over me one minute, then nothing?" Her voice rose high and shrill and she sucked in a furious breath. She didn't know him. His tight, hard face mocked her. A nasty, bilious taste rose from her chest, burning her throat.

She swayed, fear flooding her. Fear that she'd throw up right here. Fear that the next words said would be their final words ever. "I thought we had—" her voice cracked and broke "—something special."

His expression did not change. She hadn't reached him, only given him another chance to kick her. A hard little knot of anger formed. That was a mistake she wouldn't make again.

"Looks like you've been enjoying a lot of something special with a lot of men," he muttered, not looking at her as if the sight of her made him sick. "How's *Jason?*"

"Jason's just fine," she retorted. Apart from a dose of frustration, since she'd spurned his advances all week. Nick had no reason to be jealous.

"How many men, Jordan?" he asked in a deadly low voice. "How many does it take to satisfy you?"

This was too much. She had done nothing wrong!

She was the one who'd been wronged. "You have no right to ask me that," she told him angrily. "Not when it was all a lie. You used me. It was all about the job, wasn't it? Getting a promotion?"

Nick flinched and she saw she'd hit the mark. She wanted to howl with rage. "You wanted the feud finished and thought being with me would do it. All you had to do was lay on the charm and you knew I'd take it seriously, poor, gullible fool I am."

He recovered fast. "Let me tell you something, no one takes you seriously, Jordan Lake. You're just a spoiled little rich girl who dabbles in charity work with about as much feeling as you dabble in men."

Jordan saw red, buckets of it. Her gut churned with injustice. The hurt and anger rolled through her with impetus. She straightened her spine and fixed him with as imperious a look as she could muster. "Well, you better start taking me seriously, since I'm carrying your baby!"

Nick jerked back as if she'd slapped him. The blood drained from his face so quickly, a tangible dragging that left him lightheaded. He thought he heard his stomach gurgle.

Pregnant? His whole world crashed around him. On top of the week he'd just endured, this was too much. He stared at her face, her deathly pale face. Pregnant? His lips moved soundlessly, shaping the word.

"You can't be," he managed in a strangled whisper. "I always protected you."

He had. Who knew about Jason Cook? "You're on the Pill."

She stared back, eyes wide open and shocked, her lips firmly pressed together.

Nick took a step back, fighting for control. So many revelations, so many life-altering shocks, one on top of the other. But this...this was the last thing he expected.

Jordan was never far from his mind over the ten days he'd been away but between business, meeting his mother and trying to ascertain his father's whereabouts, he couldn't bring himself to call her. He was picking through an emotional minefield. With Elanor's demands that he finish it still ringing in his ears, his pedigree—or lack of—added another dimension, another burden to bear. These were things best said in person, not over the phone.

But he didn't expect to have to read about her in the newspapers and woman's magazines. Headlines leapt out at him, everywhere he went, at his mother's house, walking past bookstores in Sydney's business district, the plane on the way home. A quick trip to the Internet got him hundreds of hits on Jordan Lake's antics since he'd been away. Everyone seemed very excited about her reconciliation with Jason Cook, although apparently she wasn't limiting herself and had been seen with others. Being snapped drunk and sick with alcohol poisoning just capped it all off perfectly. She was weak, he realized, weak and self-indulgent. Not what he needed right now.

As far as Nick was concerned, Elanor Lake had done him a huge favor.

Now she stood in front of him, pale and weary from her hectic social life, telling him she was pregnant. To him?

Glancing around quickly—the ramifications if this little tidbit got out did not bear thinking about—he swung back to her, glowering.

"I want the truth right now," he gritted. "Are you pregnant—by me—or not?"

A sheen of perspiration glowed on her upper lip, lips that had drained of color. Her normally vibrant skin looked thin as tissue, but Nick clamped down on a spurt of unwelcome worry. Get the truth—and the proof— and decide what to do about it then.

She blinked quickly, opened her mouth. God help him, she looked as shocked as he felt. Even her anger would be better than this frozen-in-the-headlights look. "Well, you can't blame me for asking," he said roughly.

Her trembling mouth firmed. "You stood me up, you bastard. Not so much as a phone call. Just how long did you expect me to sit around waiting?"

The bleak wind of betrayal went through him, spreading its poison. "Poor little Jordan," he said wearily, feeling like he'd gone ten rounds with Mike Tyson. "You've just got to be the center of attention, haven't you?"

She backed off, swallowing, her eyes sliding all the way to his shoes. Her head was down, and for the first time, he noticed that her hair, her beautiful golden hair, looked lank and lifeless. A hank of it fell forward over her face. And then she looked up at him, and he reeled at the disappointment in her eyes.

"You're just like everyone else, aren't you?" Her voice held an element of surprise.

Nick wanted to rage, to put his hands on her and shake the disappointment out of her. But somehow he couldn't do anything other than glower down at this woman, this addiction he had, this spoiled, self-indulgent woman who'd filled a hole inside of him that he hadn't even known was there.

Pregnant! How ironic. Someone had gotten pregnant thirty-four years ago, but had decided money was more important than raising a child. Illegitimate, disenfranchised—he wasn't even adopted.

"Nick!" Adam called from the top of the steps. "The judge is coming back."

The verdict was expected today. Jordan hadn't even glanced up when Adam had spoken. Nick exhaled loudly. "I can't deal with this right now."

She raised her head slowly, met his eyes. He didn't want to read what was in hers.

"You don't have to *deal* with anything," she said curtly, then spun on her heel and walked away.

Nick's head rolled back and he looked skyward, feeling the anger ebb away. Now he just ached with wretched need and disappointment. She was like a drug to him, and despite everything, the withdrawal symptoms were powerful. But a drug was a drug. It pulled you down and sucked you dry. You had to kick it to survive.

Twelve

The judge gave his decision, awarding damages of five hundred thousand dollars to Randall Thorne. Everyone agreed it was a predictable outcome. Nick declined the celebratory drinks mooted and returned to the office, aware of Randall staring sadly after him.

He let Jasmine go early and poured himself a Scotch, trying to obliterate the memory of Jordan's face, twisted with anger and fear and—disappointment. In him.

Nick hated disappointing anybody. But Jordan—Jordan with the big blue eyes that reached in and touched him, connected with him on some level that no one else ever had. No matter how many times he told himself it was just an overpowering sexual attraction, he knew deep down it was real.

Having his baby…

Nick had decided weeks ago to go after her, forge a future with her to force an end to their father's feud. But this…this was definitely not what he envisaged. Not when he was only just getting his head around being illegitimate himself.

Did he believe her? Yes. She might cheat, she might make the wrong choices sometimes—Nick scowled, wanting to smash Jason Cook's face—but if she said the baby was his, it was his. She was too good a person to let him take the rap for someone else.

The Scotch slid down his throat smoothly. He listened to the sounds of the office packing up, the noises of the city down below. It rarely happened that Nick searched for answers in the bottom of a bottle. The foundations of his life had been swept away, but he was who he was. He would do the right thing by Jordan.

After all, that's what he'd wanted, eventually. Did it matter that the schedule had changed? Feud or no feud, his baby would not be born illegitimate, like him.

Randall knocked and poked his head around the door. "Son, we need to talk. There are things I should have said a long time ago."

Nick nodded toward the bottle and glasses. They hadn't spoken about their situation since his return from Australia. Now was as good a time as any.

"Nicky." His father brought his drink to the desk and sat, looking very ill at ease. Nick knew talking from the heart wasn't the old man's strong point; it never had been.

"If I've made you feel less important to me than

Adam, then I'm very sorry. It was unwittingly done. You mean just as much to me—did to your mother, too. I couldn't be more proud of you."

"I know that," Nick said gravely. "Which is why you'll cooperate when I get my lawyer to apply for a new birth certificate showing my birth parents' names." He watched Randall's cheeks hollow. "Did you know that I cannot be legally adopted in this country after the age of twenty?"

"I didn't know that."

"I doubt there will be consequences, after all this time," Nick continued, pursing his lips.

"I'll take the damn consequences," Randall interjected. "And while we're crossing the T's and dotting the i's, I'll make a new will naming you as an elected beneficiary, or whatever they want to call it."

Nick settled back in his chair.

"It's the least I can do," his father finished bleakly.

Nick studied the older man's face. It was time to press his case, once and for all. Perhaps he'd lose, perhaps he had underestimated Randall's feelings for him, but at least he'd go out trying. "It's taken me a while to figure out why you're reluctant to name me as managing director but I think I'm getting there."

His father started to interrupt but Nick stopped him. "You're afraid of being left alone. Mom's gone. Adam's in London. With this illegal adoption…hanging over your head all these years…so many years building a business that you want to live on after you're gone."

He sipped his Scotch, his gaze steady. "I may not be

your blood, Randall but I'm in this for the long haul. You've taught me—us—well. You need to have faith that you've done your job. Have I ever let you down?"

Randall shook his head at the quick question, subdued. "You never have."

"I won't leave you," Nick said firmly. "Nor will Adam. That's a promise. It's time you stopped worrying about this."

Randall was old school, brought up to keep his emotions carefully hidden. But Nick saw the love and support—for him—on his father's aged face and knew he was on the mark. "I may not be your blood, Randall," he repeated, "but I'm your best—no, I'm your *only*— option to take this place, keeping all your values and integrity intact, and grow it to pass on to my kids one day."

The old man's eyes gleamed and he suddenly found something very interesting in the bottom of his glass.

"And you'll be around to see it," Nick finished.

Randall sat for a minute, swallowing several times, his aged throat bobbing. Then he slowly got to his feet and came around to Nick's side of the desk. "Nick. Son." He extended his hand. Nick rose and they clasped hands. "I couldn't bear to lose you," his father mumbled, clapping him hard on the back in a semblance of an embrace.

Nick thought that might be the only time in his life his father had hugged him and he knew playing hardball and declaring his loyalty had been the right thing to do.

"Right, then," Randall huffed, drawing back, patting pockets, buttoning his jacket and generally doing a good impression of businesslike busyness. "You'd better start packing in here in preparation for your move to the corner office." He stepped back and raised his glass. "I'll announce it at the birthday party next week. Get yourself a new suit and bring a date."

Nick nodded. A date…since it was a day for revelations, he could do better than that, couldn't he? "Sit down, Dad. I have something else to say."

Jordan sat on the couch, leaning on Elanor's shoulder. "Do you think he'll be all right?"

Elanor nodded. "He'll appeal, just to be bloody-minded, but deep down he knew he'd lose. Even the lawyers warned him this was the likely outcome." She slipped her hand through her daughter's arm. "I'm more worried about you, rushing off like that."

Jordan heaved a heavy sigh. "I'm sorry. I just felt so ill." She hadn't been able to face going back into the courtroom after Nick's cold, hard put-down. His words his face—her throat closed and she was overwhelmed at last by the tears that had backed up for days, threatening to choke her.

She threw herself into her mother's lap and sobbed out the whole story, while Elanor stroked her hair and murmured comforting platitudes. Then, with typical pragmatism, she phoned her specialist and got Jordan an appointment immediately. "Home pregnancy kits aren't always accurate. We have to be sure."

Jordan washed her face and helped her mother into the car.

"Do you love him?" Elanor asked quietly.

That started a fresh round of crying. "With all my heart."

Mopping her face with tissues, she heard her mother sigh, and looked up. Elanor's yes were very troubled. "Oh, Jordan."

"I know. I'm spoiled and selfish, just like he said. He's the son of Dad's worst enemy, but did I let that stop me?" She shook her head miserably.

"Darling, it's not that. We can't always control these things." She took Jordan's hand. "I have a confession to make. I warned Nick off last week, insisted he stop seeing you."

Jordan's head jerked up. "How did you…?"

"I had you investigated," her mother said quietly.

Speechless, Jordan could only stare, wondering if she'd heard correctly.

"I'm sorry. Your social life until a few months ago was well documented. At least I had an idea of what was going on. But there has been no one for months, nearly a year. I just wanted to make sure you were all right. And when I found out who it was, I tried to scare him off."

"I can't believe you'd…" Jordan reeled with the revelation that her kind, sweet mother would go to these lengths. That sounded like something Syrius might do, but…another thought twisted through her over-loaded brain. "What—what did he say? Nick?"

Her mother bit her lip. "That he cared for you."

That should have elated her. It didn't. After the altercation earlier, it only intensified the ache.

"I didn't realize the extent of your feelings," Elanor

continued. "With the court case going on, your father would have exploded if he'd found out. But if I'd known how you felt about him, I would never have spoken to him…told him…" Her voice trailed off.

"Told him what?"

Her mother hesitated. "That's better coming from him. You need to talk to him."

"Except he doesn't want anything to do with me," Jordan said, sniffing. "Apart from your interference, I've spent the last week childishly trying to make him jealous. He thinks I'm sleeping with every man and his dog."

"I'm sure once he calms down and gets over the shock, he won't believe that."

The car turned into the consultant's car park. Jordan took out her compact and checked her face. "You sound almost hopeful." She grimaced at her red, swollen eyes and blotchy cheeks. If she was seen going into a private ob-gyn clinic looking like this, the press would have a field day. She tied her hair back hurriedly and slid her sunglasses on. "But the fact remains that Dad will never accept it."

"Let me deal with Syrius," her mother said grimly.

As they waited to be seen, Jordan tried to make sense of it all. If Nick had refused her mother's demands, what had happened between then and now, when he could barely look at her without disgust?

She had happened. Hurt by his silence, she had lived up to his expectations of her, as she so often did. What had he said? That she always had to be the center of attention.

The consultant took a blood test, which their on-site

lab rushed through. Less than two hours later, they returned to the car. Exhausted after the stress of the day—and of the last week or so—Jordan leaned back in the seat and turned her tear-streaked face to her mother. "Oh, Mom, it just hurts so much."

Elanor stroked Jordan's hair and wiped away her tears, her own eyes glistening.

"Can I stay with you tonight?" Jordan felt so helpless, so out of control. She needed the comfort of her old room, familiar surroundings, the arms and love and sympathy only a mother could provide.

"Of course you can," her mother murmured. "For as long as you like."

Nick tossed and turned all night, despite the whiskey sedative that should have ensured sleep. What was the matter with him? He'd achieved his goal. He would be named as the managing director of Thorne Enterprises the following week. He'd made peace with his father over his parentage and gotten to know his mother a little. Surely he had everything he wanted.

Except…the woman carrying his baby thought he wanted nothing to do with her. The pain in her eyes as he'd heaped insults and scorn upon her haunted him. He tried to justify his behavior by remembering the publicity of her partying up with her new/old lover. And she hadn't denied it—not that he'd given her much of a chance.

He should have called her; he knew that now. With her insecurities and mystifying low self-esteem, his lack of communication must have hurt. She wasn't responsible for what his personal life had served up to him. All she knew was that he'd stayed away.

The sunrise began to streak the sky with gold. Nick gave up on sleep, pulled on some track pants and sat on the step of his large, modern town house, cradling a mug of black coffee. Looking out over the easy-care garden, across the busy road that ran alongside the bay, he suddenly wondered if this house would be suitable for a child. Built on three levels, not fenced in—Lord, it was a death trap!

A baby. He allowed his mind to process the word, but found he couldn't assimilate it quite yet, couldn't conjure up a picture in his mind. But Jordan pregnant—now that was easier. She would make a beautiful mother-to-be. His mind wandered back to waking snuggled up behind her on the boat, and then he imagined his arms around her swelling middle, feeling the baby move, sharing the appointments, buying...whatever prospective parents bought in preparation for the event.

A ripple of exhilaration swept him from head to toe, and he threw his head back at the lightening sky. A baby. A chance to right the wrongs of the past. To stamp his identify on another human and show him or her that they were precious, wanted, loved.

Suddenly he could hardly wait to start sharing the experience. He had to wait, thought, since it was only five-thirty. He dragged on a T-shirt and some trainers and set off for a run along the stony beach, needing physical exertion to curb his growing elation at the thought of becoming a father.

And what of Jordan herself? He'd changed their intense and forbidden affair into another step on the ladder of his ambition. Technically, now that he had what he wanted, she was surplus to requirements. Pounding along the long stretch of beach, sweat dripping into his eyes, he asked himself the question: *if* he hadn't gone away and *if* she hadn't fallen pregnant and *if* she hadn't taken up with her former lover, would they have continued their affair, even after he'd been made managing director?

Yes. They would have. Other than their fathers' prejudices, he and Jordan were great together. The time, effort and resources she put into trying to make a difference suggested she would work hard to support his career and make their marriage and family succeed. He could help her grow in confidence and develop her foundation. Even now, as his lungs screamed, the incredible sexual pull that they shared had him wanting her more than his next breath. She was fun, kind and sexy. He felt comfortable with her and yet fiercely passionate about her.

And insanely jealous…. The storm clouds gathered in his mind as he turned for home, his steps accelerating. Nick would fight to the death to keep her. No one, neither Jason Cook nor her sanctimonious father, would keep him away from the woman he loved.

Nick rang the doorbell at the Lake mansion, filled with grim determination. Walking into the lion's den on the day after the verdict was not the most sensible thing he'd ever done, but he'd had no luck tracking Jordan at her apartment.

The Lake's housekeeper opened the door just as Elanor wheeled herself into the impressive entrance. "Thank you, Helen," she said, then dismissed the housekeeper, keeping her eyes on Nick. It may have been the early hour, but she looked strained, as if she hadn't slept.

Nick girded himself for battle. "Is she here?"

"She's upstairs. Nick…"

He hesitated, awash with relief. If she were here, her mother must know about the pregnancy. "What about Syrius? I'll need to talk to him."

"He left early to catch up now that the case is over."

Nick gave a brief nod and turned his eyes on the stairs. "Which room?"

"Second on the right. Nick…"

He paused, his jaw set with impatience.

Elanor sighed heavily, her face lined with sadness. "She's—fragile right now. Go easy on her."

Thirteen

Nick's eyes narrowed with concern. What was that supposed to mean? Morning sickness or something more sinister? He remembered her words in the car—Jordan falls in and out of love very other week. What if Elanor was trying to tell him that her daughter was in love with someone else or, worse, pregnant to someone else?

Elanor fidgeted under his gaze.

Nick needed to get those answers from Jordan herself, no one else. He knew her. She wouldn't lie about him being the father of the baby. He'd do whatever he had to, but he wasn't going to allow her to throw her life, her talent, her goodness away on a loser like Jason Cook.

He snapped off a brief nod and headed for the stairs.

As he reached the top, aware of Elanor's anxious eyes following his every step, a door opened and Jordan appeared in the hallway. They both stopped dead, staring. She wore a bright orange floral robe tied at the waist. She seemed to have lost weight. The robe clung to her as she stood, the sharp angle of her hip clearly showing through the flimsy fabric. Her hair was loose and brushed behind her ears.

She looked done in. Her eyes were pink and puffy, her lips paler than lilac. Nick stroke forward, filled with an irrational worry that she might fall if he didn't catch her, hold her up. "What is it? Arc you sick?"

Her eyes widened as he approached, and she opened her mouth, but nothing came out. He reached out and ran his hand down her arm, needing to touch her, to make sure she wouldn't disappear into thin air.

Jordan shrank away, a tiny shift back that sliced at him. "What do you want, Nick? If my father…"

He shook his head, stung by her disapproving tone. "I went to your place," he began curtly.

"And naturally you assumed I was with someone else." Her surprise had cooled into sullen weariness.

"Whatever happened in the past week," Nick ground out, "we have to put it behind us."

Jordan swallowed and looked away. He imagined it was guilt making her chew her bottom lip, but then reminded himself of his purpose. The baby came first. Whatever mistakes she'd made—they'd both made— they could work on forgiving each other after he had an assurance from her that they had a future together. "I'm not blaming you, but I won't let you throw your life away on that loser."

She blinked. "You won't let me...who?"

"Jason!" he snarled, his jealousy perilously close to the surface. "Your ex—and soon-to-be ex again."

She huffed out a weary breath, shaking her head slightly. "You really believe I've been sleeping around?"

Yes. No. Hell, all he wanted was her denial.

"Haven't you noticed," she said with exaggerated patience, "that the papers don't care about true or false? If I trip over, it's because I'm drunk or on drugs. If I say hello to someone on the street, I'm engaged."

"You said yesterday—you intimated..."

"Oh, Nick." She sighed. "Can't you recognize when a woman is in love with you?"

Nick stared at her, the wind knocked completely out of his sails. She loved him. There was no one else.

Jordan stood in front of him, rocking on her heels a little. But at least some of the color was returning to her cheeks. She was still the most beautiful woman he had ever seen. Relief and elation threatened to overwhelm him.

"I didn't deny your accusations," she continued, "because you hurt me so much. You just disappeared off the face of the earth. I didn't know what I'd done. And when you looked at me like that yesterday..." Her voice broke. "Why, Nick? Why did you brush me off like I was something on your shoe?"

Nick closed his eyes against the pain darkening hers. Unfamiliar emotions slammed him. Elation that she loved him, relief that she wanted no one else, guilt for putting that pain on her lovely face. Moving purely on instinct, he reached out and took both her hands in his. "Didn't your mother tell you what was going on?"

Her hands lay limply in his. "She told me she warned you off. And that she'd had me investigated." Her voice was listless, as if declaring her love had drained her of energy.

She really looked done in. Nick pointed his chin at the door behind her. "Can we sit down?"

Jordan led him into a large, feminine bedroom. The colors were peach and sage green. The windows over-looked the rhododendron garden that the Lake mansion was quite famous for. His eyes darted to the sports and dancing trophies lining one massive bookcase, and to a clutch of photos of her at a young age, wearing ballet costumes or a net-ball skirt or a school uniform. He wanted to inspect them more closely, but she had sunk down onto an unmade queen-sized bed. As he joined her, she grabbed a pillow, hugging it to her stomach.

"I was away," he began, wary of implicating her mother in this part of it.

"Sydney." She nodded.

"I found out I wasn't Randall's son, or my mother's. I was—purchased."

Nick still couldn't believe it himself. He knew Randall and Melanie loved him, as did Adam. As for his birth mother, he'd made a start, and was grateful she'd given him up to the best possible family.

But he needed to be with Jordan. He needed her love

to make him whole. She was home to him in a way he'd never felt before.

He felt the pressure of her hand on his shoulder, warming him, as welcome as the comfort, acceptance and empathy that showed in her eyes.

"I spent ten days in Australia, tracking my birth parents. I thought of you—often—but it was just so complicated. I didn't want to get into it on the phone."

"Did you find them?" she asked after a few seconds.

"My mother, yes. Not my father, though I've got some leads I'll probably check out."

"Did you like her?"

He nodded. "She's nice, has her own family. She'd like to keep in touch." At least he'd gotten one thing clear in his mind. "She may have given birth to me but Melanie was my mother."

Jordan's hand slid off his shoulder. He missed it immediately.

"How did Randall take all this?"

"I think he's been expecting it—dreading it—for years. It's probably a relief."

Jordan looked down at her feet, swallowing. "That's huge, Nick. I wish you would have told me."

He should have, he knew that now. Maybe he was afraid that with all the barriers to them being together, his illegitimacy might be the last straw. Jordan wasn't the only one capable of holding things back.

"Nick, I need to know if you planned this whole thing so you could get a promotion."

He'd wondered when she'd get around to this. "We

met, fell into bed, kept meeting. Jordan, I lived for our Fridays. When the case started, Adam made a lighthearted suggestion that a union between us might persuade our fathers to cool it, stop with the fighting and the legal battles. That comment fell on fertile ground because I was already halfway there. It wasn't exactly a hardship," he said earnestly, taking her hands in his. "We're good together. Everything that grew out of that was real."

Her thoughtful expression gave no clue as to whether she believed him.

"Anyway, it's a moot point now. Dad's going to announce it next week. You're looking at the new managing director of Thorne Enterprises."

She smiled faintly, "Congrats."

Nick hadn't expected much enthusiasm under the circumstances, but still, he squeezed her fingers and ducked his head to peer into her eyes quizzically. "Jordan, I'm so sorry about yesterday, and the lack of communication. I never meant to hurt you."

She looked down at their joined hands. "I can't remember ever feeling so—" her shoulders rose and fell "—low."

"Hormones, I suppose," he said, thinking of the pregnancy. "This puts everything in a new light. Jordan," he said, reaching out to smooth a rogue strand of hair behind her ears. "I want our baby to be born legitimate, not like me. I want us to make a good home for him or her, a great family home…why are you crying?"

Tears began to slide down her face, and his heart did an ominous slide in his chest.

"I should never have said anything," she blurted. "Not until I was sure, but I've been sick, and the home test was positive—twice—and you got me so riled…" She tugged her hands away from his and covered her face.

He sat there stupidly, wondering what she meant, helpless in the face of her distress.

"I'm not pregnant, Nick," she said sadly from behind her hands. "I never was."

Jordan couldn't look at him, but felt his eyes on her. The sadness pressed down, making her neck ache. "Mom took me to a specialist yesterday for a blood test, and it came back negative." A shuddering sigh caught her unawares and she pressed the pillow into her stomach. "I'm supposed to go back in a couple of days for anther test, but I probably won't bother since I got my period in the night."

"But you were sick."

She shrugged, still not looking at him. "Nerves. Stress. A bug…"

They sat there for a minute in silence. She didn't want to see his relief. In reality, she should be relieved herself, having no desire to raise a baby on her own. But all she felt was a dragging grief, as if someone close had died and nothing would ever be the same again.

Nick cleared his throat. "No baby," he said, as if he still couldn't believe it. She braved a look at his face. Incredibly, he looked dazed and terribly disappointed.

Disappointed? He was off the hook. "You must be relieved."

She immediately wished the words back when he swallowed and looked away. "Relieved?" His eyes tracked slowly around each wall of the big room, an excruciatingly slow inspection, before finally coming full circle to her face again. "I don't know," he said slowly. "It's amazing how quickly I got used to the idea, even embraced the idea, of having a baby with you."

That was unexpected, although finding out recently that he wasn't who he thought he was probably had something to do with it. While she mulled that over, Nick reached out and lifted her chin, his eyes full of concern.

"How do you feel about it?"

"Sad," she whispered. She'd already told him she loved him. She didn't have to hide anything now. "It was something of you, and the most worthwhile and important part of me." She shrugged again. "So I thought, for a few hours, anyway."

Nick slid his hands up her arms and around her back to draw her close. It was a relief to hide her face in his chest, to rest against all that clean warmth and solid support. She closed her eyes.

"There'll be other babies," Nick muttered into her hair. "It doesn't change how I feel about you."

She smiled gently, remembering. "Your luxury." But she knew she couldn't go back to what they were. Everything had changed. She wanted to be worth something now. "Our Fridays are in the past," she said firmly, as if to convince herself. Would she ever feel the same burning need for anyone else? Perhaps companionship and common goals might be a safer gamble next time.

"I agree." His arms tightened around her. "But I still want to marry you."

Jordan snuggled in close, mentally saying goodbye to their Friday afternoons. Nick's words took an age to filter into her woolly brain. Lack of sleep, of food, of anything resembling sunshine since their weekend away on the boat had withered her comprehension.

Had he just said he wanted to marry her?

She leaned back a little, squinting over the crisp collar and blue silk tie, past the strong, square chin and into his piercing eyes. Her heart gave a healthy kick.

No trace of amusement sullied Nick's serious contemplation of her. Instead, he reached down and curled his fingers around her hand, squeezing gently. "I love you, Jordan, and I still want to marry you, baby or not."

Her eyes filled, and a lump the size of Gibraltar invaded her throat. She shook her head impatiently. Why cry when she'd just heard the words she wanted to hear more than anything in the world? When she lay encircled in the arms of the man she loved more than anything in the world? When the sincerity and love shone from his eyes, soothing the hurt of the past few days, giving her hope for the future? "Really?" she asked, aware of how inadequate the question was. But her mind hadn't yet cleared for takeoff.

Nick laced their fingers together and raised her hand to his mouth. "Really," he murmured. "I *really* love you, Jordan."

She shivered—delayed reaction. She could listen to those words all day.

"It was inevitable," he continued, "once I got to know you, saw how hard you tried, how generous and giving you were. So sexy, you should be illegal." He kissed her knuckles one by one. "You accepted me, although I gave you little enough. And I hate that it took me so long, and all this upset, to realize how I feel."

A bit, fat tear escaped and slid slowly down her cheek. "Oh, Nick, I love you so much, it hurts."

"Perhaps this will ease your pain." He wrapped her up in his arms and bent his head to kiss her. At the first touch of his lips on hers, she tensed, waiting for the irresistible thrill that never failed to suck the breath from her lungs and sent her heart galloping. But this was a healing kiss, a kiss to say sorry, a tender, nourishing lifeline that she never wanted to let go of. She relaxed into contentment, trying to burrow closer, loving his clean, warm scent and the strength of his arms around her.

"There is still," he told her a minute later, when he'd stopped kissing her into next week, "the matter of how your father is going to take this."

She blinked slowly, still dazed by that kiss. "Mom likes you. She's an amazing woman, my mother." Jordan couldn't quite believe Elanor had spied on her. "I'm only starting to realize *how* amazing—and exactly who wears the pants around here." She smiled up into Nick's eyes, feeling quite light-headed with happiness. Her stomach rumbled. It could be hunger. "What about your father?"

"He'll do anything to stay in my good books at the moment," he said, planting a kiss on each corner of her mouth. "I told him I was crazy about the devil's daughter. He said bring the little hussy to his retirement party next week."

"Will you protect me?" Her smile faded into pensiveness. "Wouldn't it be great if they could be friends one day?"

"They started that way," Nick said, nibbling his way around her jawline to her earlobe. "You'd be surprised at the impact a grandkid or two might have. It's our duty to work on improving relations between the two most stubborn old goats in New Zealand." He leaned back, his hands sliding from around her back to rest at the tops of her arms, holding her up. "To that end, Jordan Lake, would you marry me in the not-too-distant future? Any Friday will do."

Jordan caged his face with both hands, unable to stop a huge smile stretching her mouth wide. "Friday works for me." She leaned in and they touched foreheads, and stayed like that, smiling at each other, basking in a love that was sure to survive.

"Me, too," Nick murmured. "As long as I can have you every day in between."

Epilogue

The retirement party stepped up a notch once the formalities were dispensed with. It took Nick an age to get to the bar since everyone wanted to congratulate the new managing director along the way. He looked about for Jordan, thinking he'd barely seen her since the speeches. Randall had taken her under his wing and seemed determined to introduce her to every one of his cronies. With her tucked closely into his side, the old man practically dwarfed her slender form, in her striking, siren-red cocktail dress. He paraded her about proudly, as if she were *his* escort for the evening.

"Scotch, rocks," Nick said to the barman, and helped himself to an hors d'oeuvre from the platter on the bar. Jasmine had done an amazing job of organizing the retirement-cum-birthday-cum-promotion party on such short notice. Stunning floral arrangements and clusters of cheery balloons lifted the small former ballroom at the top of the Thorne building into an elegant venue, far removed from its normal function as a conference facility. The food and drink were top-notch, and the two hundred guests seemed to be enjoying themselves. Nick reminded himself to give his trusted personal assistant a decent bonus for her efforts.

"Well, big brother, it's your night, and not before time." Adam appeared out of the throng of people and saluted him with his glass. Nick reciprocated, and the brothers leaned with their backs to the bar, surveying the party.

"They look cozy," Adam commented, indicating their father and Jordan. "When are you going to let the best-kept secret out of the bag?"

Nick and Jordan's public relationship had sent the press into a frenzy, coming on the heels of the court case. Their expected engagement even had punters at the betting agency jostling for odds. "Soon," Nick replied. "I didn't want to steal Dad's thunder tonight."

"I suppose I'll have to come home for the wedding."

The happy couple wanted to get married as soon as possible, but Elenor confirmed that, even though he technically wasn't talking to them, her husband would expect the biggest and most flamboyant wedding ever staged in Wellington. They were doing their bit for family relations. It just wasn't possible to organize such a huge event before Adam left for England.

"You'll be back in the next few months, anyway."

Nick turned to Adam, but his brother wasn't listening. He was watching something or someone in the crowd. Nick followed his gaze and, sure enough, it was his personal assistant who held Adam's rapt attention.

Nick sighed. His brother hadn't taken his eyes off Jasmine all afternoon. Jordan had even commented on it. Hell, if he honestly thought Adam would ever settle down and take a woman seriously, Nick would be delighted in his choice. But Jasmine was too nice a person, and too valuable an employee, to have her heart broken by her boss's careless brother.

He took Adam's arm and turned him slightly. "I'd like to introduce you to a couple of our new corporate executives, Sandra and Melanie." He indicated two extremely attractive women in their twenties, deep in conversation by the punch bowl.

Adam didn't even look over. Jasmine had retreated to the corner of the room and slid her jacket off the back of a chair.

"I think I'll hit the road," Adam said, and drained his glass.

Nick laid a hand on his brother's arm. "Adam, you'll be gone in a day or so. Don't start anything with her."

Adam turned his light brown eyes on him. "I can give a woman a good time without breaking her heart, you know."

Nick knew there was little use in arguing once Adam's mind was made up. He was devilishly stubborn. Nonchalance might be a better weapon. "I'm only trying to keep you from making a fool of yourself. A woman like Jasmine wouldn't even give you the time of day. You're just not her type."

His brother only smiled, and giving him a look that clearly said, "Wanna bet?" Then he hightailed it toward the exit after the departing Jasmine.

Nick smelled Jordan's perfume and turned his head as a vision in red walked up to him. "I think your brother has just broken the hearts of every single female here by leaving," she quipped.

Nick gave her a rueful smile. "I should know by now that saying 'no can do' is like a red rag to a bull where Adam's concerned."

Jordan raised her brows.

Nick put his arms around her waist and pulled her in close. "Never mind. I have much more important things to think about. Such as—" he nuzzled her ear "—when can we leave?"

"Where are we going?" Jordan picked up his glass and stuck her nose into it, inhaling.

"I have a private function to attend at a certain hotel." Nick bumped their lower bodies together suggestively.

Grimacing at the smell of his Scotch, Jordan raised her eyes to his innocently. "I thought we were giving up the hotel on Fridays."

"Now why would we want to do that?"

"Because it's environmentally unfriendly, all that cleaning and polishing and lighting and so on."

Nick looked down into her shining eyes and beautiful smile, and silently thanked the Lord for cantankerous old men.

"And anyway," Jordan continued, "I spend half the week at your place and you spend the rest at mine."

"We're not married yet," Nick told his secret fiancée, "and until we are, you're my Friday mistress."

* * * * *

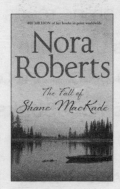